T0367486

Finding Joy

Finding Joy

Dona Buchheim

FINDING JOY

This is a work of fiction. All the characters, names, incidents, organizations, and dialogue in this novel are either the products of the author's imagination or are used fictitiously.

iUniverse books may be ordered through booksellers or by contacting:

iUniverse
1663 Liberty Drive
Bloomington, IN 47403
www.iuniverse.com
1-800-Authors (1-800-288-4677)

ISBN: 978-1-4917-7879-1 (sc)
ISBN: 978-1-4917-7878-4 (e)

Library of Congress Control Number: 2015916975

Print information available on the last page.

iUniverse rev. date: 11/16/2015

Chapter 1

Leah Anderly never imagined that she might at some point in her life hire a private investigator. Private investigators were the stuff of novels and television dramas. Yet here she was, standing in the second-floor hallway of a building on the north edge of downtown Chicago. She had seen an ad for the agency in the yellow pages, and because its owner/investigator, Nola Randolph, was a woman, she had decided to see if what she had in mind was crazy or worth pursuing. Now that she was in front of the door to the office, she was having second thoughts. Leah stood there for a good minute and had just about convinced herself to turn around and go back to work when a voice behind her asked, "May I help you? Did you want to speak to someone about investigative work?"

"Oh, I guess I was just trying to decide if I should go in or not. I've never done this before," replied Leah. *Now why in the world do I feel a need to explain myself to a perfect stranger?* she thought.

"I'm Nola Randolph, and I own this agency. Come in, and we can talk about whatever it is you have on your mind. I don't mean to put any pressure on you, but why not come in? I'll give you a cup of coffee, and we can chat."

Nola took out a set of keys, selected one, and opened the door. She snapped on the lights and held the door for Leah. In the small reception area a large window provided a view of the street. To the left of the window was a door leading into what appeared to be an office with a desk. Nola led the way in, and Leah observed a bank of filing cabinets that took up most of the wall space behind the desk. To the right were three chairs, side by side, no doubt where clients could sit. A low table beside the far chair held a scattering of magazines and a coffee cup.

"Come in," beckoned Nola. "I don't have anything but instant coffee right now, but if you prefer tea, I have that too. Sit down, and I'll get you what you want."

"Tea would be fine," replied Leah as she sat on one of the two chairs that flanked the desk.

Nola busied herself putting tea bags into two mugs, pouring water from a pitcher into each one, and putting them into the microwave. Then she pulled one of the other chairs away from Leah's and sat down facing her. Leah was surprised she didn't sit behind the desk. Didn't they always do that in the movies? It made her smile to realize she had made an assumption. *I'd better forget preconceived ideas,* thought Leah, *because I think Nola Randolph is quite different from what I anticipated.*

"I'm glad to see you smile. I hope I didn't scare you by being rather direct. Not everyone responds to that. So tell me: What brought you here?" asked Nola.

Leah twisted the handkerchief she had taken from her pocket, a nervous habit of hers. "Well, I've had some flashbacks, and I wanted to talk about them to see if you think I should look into what I think I may be remembering. It's a bit upsetting, or even more than that I suppose. Have you ever had any experience with something like this?" Leah looked expectantly at Nola.

"Oops, the tea is ready. Let me get it for us, and then we can discuss this subject. Do you take anything in your tea? I have the usual, all packaged and hermetically sealed," said Nola with a grin. Leah shook her head.

Nola retrieved the tea for them and said, "I've not had much experience with flashbacks but more with repressed memories, which I'm afraid I'm somewhat skeptical about, but there are instances where they are legitimate. Why don't you tell me what you remembered and in what context, and I'll try to help you sort it out, and we can go from there?"

"All right. My mother died three months ago from cancer. They tried radiation, and she was better for a week or so. They were hopeful, but two weeks before she died, they advised her to go into hospice. Instead, I took leave from work and cared for her at home. She preferred that, although she protested at first. We were rather close as mother and daughter. My father passed on about three years ago."

Leah shifted her position and continued, "On the day she died, my mother seemed to be hallucinating. I had to calm her with some medication the doctor had prescribed. Later that day she became agitated and called out, 'Lizzie, I'm so sorry. We shouldn't have done it. Forgive me, Lizzie.' I don't know anyone named Lizzie. I've looked for some mention of Lizzie or Elizabeth but have found nothing. Maybe this is just something she imagined. Do you think I should pursue this?"

"Interesting," replied Nola. "I get the impression you believe there might be more to this than you've been able to unearth. I'm wondering now what your flashbacks are about. You haven't mentioned them at all, so maybe we need to get those out in the open. Why don't you tell me about them?"

"I really don't know if there's any validity to these flashbacks, but perhaps I'm actually remembering something. The images are quite vivid. The first one I had happened before my mother died. We were having a conversation over tea, and she was talking about her childhood, something she seldom did. Suddenly I pictured a gray house with bright-red shutters and a big backyard with a sandbox and lilacs. I only figured out later they were lilacs, because in Chicago we've always lived in an apartment and seldom saw blooming shrubs in our neighborhood. I had to ask my mother again what she had said, because I was transported back, or transported somewhere at any rate, and had not heard her finish her tale about growing up in Minnesota." Leah paused in her narration.

"The next time it happened, I was visiting a friend on the South Side. She was the oldest in a family of four. Her younger sister, who was ten, had a lovely room with a canopy bed. It was done up beautifully in yellow and white, and when I saw it, I had a mental picture of another yellow-and-white canopy bed, this one with a dark-haired doll dressed in layers of purple ruffles lying on it. My friend had to shake me to get me out of the zone I was in. When I explained what had happened to me, she was skeptical. She thought I was overworked and just needed some time off. Maybe that's what it was. But it happened again a few weeks ago. I saw a boy with a red wagon. He was pulling it along the sidewalk in front of the house with the red shutters and was waving and calling to me. He called me Lizzie. At least I thought he was calling to me. I don't know what to think about all this. Could I have lived there early in my life? Is it possible that my mother knew this Lizzie and had some relationship with her?"

"I would say the fact that you had three flashbacks makes it seem more likely that you are actually remembering something from the past. Why don't you give me some basic information, and I'll get to work on checking it out. I need your parents' full names, where they were born, where they lived, and what kind of work they did. I'll also need your full given name and birth date and place, as well as information about relatives, with names and addresses. If you have any papers to corroborate any of this, as well as photos of family members, please include them as well. Okay, that's enough for a start. Let's see if we can trace Lizzie for you."

"What do I owe you for today's visit?" asked Leah.

"I bill by the hour. Here's my rate schedule. I charge only for work I actually do, not for just coming in and telling me what you're looking for, so today there's no charge. Does that work for you?"

Leah took the offered piece of paper from Nola and nodded. "Yes, it will be fine," Leah said. "I'll pull together the stuff you need and send it to you or bring it in as soon as I can."

4

Leah's head was throbbing, and she couldn't wait to get out into the fresh air. This was harder than she'd thought it would be, and right now she was having second thoughts about delving into something that didn't make sense and that might be unpleasant as well. What if her mother had been married to someone else? What if the boy from her flashback was a relative? Her brother? A cousin? What if her father wasn't her father? She shook off these ideas as she exited the building and headed to the taxi stand down the street. No taxi appeared in five minutes of waiting, so Leah began to walk back to her office. The stiff breeze out of the northwest helped clear her head, at least a little.

It was two fifteen when she arrived at her office building and took the elevator up to the fifth floor. As she was exiting the elevator, she almost ran into Jeremy Drexler, one of the other law clerks for the firm of Marsden, Willett, and Desmond. "Hey, Leah, where have you been?" he asked. "The boss has been looking for you. Better get in there quick. I think he needs the paperwork on the Quinlin case." Jeremy hurried into the elevator and waved to her as the door closed.

Leah picked up her pace down the hallway to her cubicle. As she passed the receptionist's desk, April Kramer called out, "Leah, Mr. Parkin wants to see you. He says to bring the Quinlin stuff when you go in." Leah nodded and kept going. Back at her desk she shed her jacket, smoothed her hair, and on her way out picked up the Quinlin file.

Alan Parkin was bent over his desk, jotting down something on a legal pad when Leah rapped on the half-open door. "Here's the Quinlin file you wanted. Sorry I was late getting back from lunch, but I had an appointment and couldn't get a cab, so I had to walk. Do you need anything else?"

"Yes, actually, I'd like you to brief me on this one. I've been working on two other cases that will probably go to court in the next couple of weeks, so I'm not up to snuff on the Quinlin matter. I know you were lead for the research, so tell me what I need to know before I meet with the others in about ..." He looked at his watch. "In less than fifteen minutes."

"I can give you a rundown, but I included a written summary on the first page, to save some time. It highlights all the facts we know, or at least those that the client provided. The conclusions at the end may change upon further research that's still ongoing, but I believe it won't be significant. That one page should pretty well lay it out for you." Leah watched as Alan Parkin read the one-page summary. Would that be enough, she wondered, or would she need to go into more detail?

"This is great. I appreciate having it condensed so succinctly. We won't be going into the fine details now, only trying to decide if we should proceed with the case and then who will get the assignment if we do. I hope it won't be me. I have enough on my plate right now. Thanks, Leah. Will you still be here at five thirty? I don't know how long my meeting will take, as we have several items of business to discuss," explained Alan. "I was hoping you might have dinner with me tonight, if you're not busy."

The invitation surprised Leah. She had been working with Alan since almost the first day he had moved down to the fifth floor. She didn't know how long he had been with the firm, but only a week or two after he'd begun working with her research team, Leah had been convinced he was one of the best, based on his knowledge and insight. She had occasionally been assigned additional prep work, and he had always been grateful for what she did. However, in all that time they had not had more than a few occasions to have a non-work-related conversation. Of course they had discussed case work in detail, and several times he had asked her opinion on strategy.

One evening in late August three clerks and several of the lawyers had gone out for drinks together, and she had sat next to Alan and had enjoyed learning about his educational background. She had been surprised but pleased to learn that they both had graduated from Northwestern. He was apparently three or four years older than she was if graduation dates meant anything. She wondered if she ought to pass on the invitation, but she found herself telling him that she would still be around at five thirty and that yes, dinner would be fine. She had to admit she liked Alan Parkin, and in addition, he was drop-dead gorgeous, as Mindy Brecklin had mentioned on more than one occasion. Mindy flirted with Alan whenever she was part of a research briefing.

Alan's response showed he was pleased that she had said yes. As he left to go to his meeting, Leah headed for the receptionist's desk, where she begged for a couple of aspirin to kill the pounding in her head. After a stop in the restroom, Leah returned to her cubicle, rested her head on her desk, and tried to clear her mind of the things she had revealed to Nola Randolph. There was work to finish before the end of the day, and she certainly hoped to vanquish the headache before her dinner date with Alan.

Leah raised her head, leaned back in her chair, and thought about Alan Parkin. She didn't know if she should read anything into his asking her out for a meal. A casual sort of friendship and a good working relationship between them had been the norm. She recalled his first day working with the team, when he had asked her to help him navigate his computer. Leah had been surprised but pleased he had asked for her help. The particular software the firm had recently installed was a bit daunting, and it had taken her time to figure out the ins and outs of everything. She had spent two evenings tutoring Alan after everyone had left for the day. He had ordered in Chinese both times. Did that make him predictable? They had spent the entire time concentrating on the software and had not engaged in much conversation, except he had asked her about her family when they'd taken the elevator together at the end of the last session. Since then, there had been no further calls for assistance. Perhaps this was nothing more than a need to discuss the Quinlin case.

Leah rubbed her forehead and realized her headache was not as severe as it had been. She also felt herself letting go of the stress the visit to the PI had engendered. Why was she stressed about it? She was only trying to figure out what those flashbacks meant.

The rest of the afternoon passed quickly, and Leah felt pleased that she was able to clear her desk of all but two cases she needed to review, neither of which were pressing. It was already a few minutes past five when she turned off her computer and made her way to the restroom to freshen up before Alan finished his meeting. She could hear voices as she passed the conference room where they were gathered, and it didn't sound as if they were discussing the Quinlin case or any other case at this point. She heard something about "the Illini" and "That damn coach needs to go." She smiled. Illinois football was an important part of the partners' and junior partners' lives. It didn't take her long to run a comb through her hair, freshen her lipstick, and return to her desk to wait for Alan. It was just past five forty-five when he appeared, apologizing for being late.

"Uncle Horace always has to end the meeting with a long discussion about what's wrong with Illinois football, and of course Jack Desmond and the rest of the lawyers enjoy getting into the conversation," he said. "Are you ready? I thought we might try the new restaurant down the block. I think it's called the Party Room. I heard the food is good, so if that's okay with you, we'll walk over there." He smiled at her.

"That's fine with me. I haven't been there, so it will be fun to try something new. I'll get my jacket and meet you at the elevator. It's rather cool out there today."

"See you at the elevator in five," called Alan as he disappeared around the corner of her cubicle and down the hall toward his office.

They soon discovered that the temperature had dropped considerably since morning or, in Leah's case, since lunch hour. Alan took Leah's arm, and they walked into the wind, fighting for their breath as they struggled against the gale blowing out of the northwest. Fortunately, the restaurant was only a block and a half away, and they were soon inside the warm and inviting waiting area of the Party Room.

The hostess was able to seat them immediately since it was only the two of them. As they were sitting down in their booth, a young woman seated across the aisle with three companions greeted Alan.

"Hello, Juneau," responded Alan. "Having a night out with friends I see."

"Yes I am. I haven't seen you for a while. I thought maybe you were out of town. Give me a holler when you get home tonight. Just knock on my door, okay?" Juneau said.

Alan nodded but didn't speak. He helped Leah with her jacket and then took off his own coat and hung them both on a hook next to their booth.

When they were comfortably seated, Alan leaned across the table. Before speaking, he looked over at the booth where the four woman were sitting. They seemed to be engaged in animated conversation. "That's Juneau Barkley. My Uncle Horace's wife was her aunt. You know Horace Marsden is my uncle, don't you?" Leah nodded. Alan went on, "Juneau has lived with them since she was twelve, when her parents were killed in an accident. After Estelle Marsden's death last April, Uncle Horace started trying to get me to take Juneau out. He asked me to escort her to a party, which I did early this summer, but all they did there was drink and make snide remarks about people they knew who weren't at the party. I couldn't wait to leave. So you see, I prefer to keep my distance."

"Sorry to hear you don't get along, especially since you live in the same house."

"I seldom run into her at the mansion. It's huge, and she lives in a different wing than I do. Thankfully I can avoid her most of the time, although weekends it gets more difficult. We're both expected to have Sunday brunch with Uncle Horace, but I try to schedule golf dates with clients or some of the other lawyers at the firm if I can. Have you met her by any chance?" asked Alan.

"No, I haven't, but I've seen her picture in the society column a time or two. She looks different now. I seem to remember she had very short hair, and now it's long, and I think the color might be different as well. So you both live in Mr. Marsden's house?"

"Yes, Uncle Horace is my mother's older brother. My parents are divorced, and Dad took care of me until I was fifteen. He died that year of an aggressive form of cancer, so I went to live with Uncle and finished high school in Evanston. Then I attended Northwestern, although Uncle Horace would have preferred the University of Illinois. During those years I was seldom around except on holidays."

Just then the waitress appeared, handed them menus, and asked what they wanted to drink. Leah asked for water, and Alan said he would have the same but added that perhaps they'd have coffee later. He looked inquiringly at Leah. "You do drink coffee, don't you? I seem to remember seeing a mug on your desk. Perhaps we could have coffee with dessert."

"No dessert for me," Leah said, blaming lack of exercise as the reason.

"I've been trying to cut down on sweets too," confided Alan. "I used to run in college and grad school, but it's not so easy now. I'm up before dawn and often leave work late, so that cuts into time for exercise. Where do you live, Leah?"

"I live in an apartment in Hyde Park, right near the bus line, so I can usually get to work in less than twenty minutes. The apartment is small, but it suits me, and I like the friendly confines of Hyde Park."

The waitress appeared to take their order, and when she left, Alan asked Leah if she had plans for the next day, explaining that he intended to drive to Champaign for the Illinois-Northwestern football game. "Would you go with me to the game?" asked. "We can cheer for the Purple and White amid a sea of orange."

"I'd like that. I've never been to Champaign, and it's been years since I attended a Wildcats game. I've heard tickets are hard to find, so how were you able to get them?"

"Uncle Horace has season tickets but is flying to California on Saturday, so he gave me four of the eight he has. I don't plan to invite anyone else though. I've not been down there for a game either, so it will be a first for both of us. I'm pleased you want to go. The game starts at eleven, so we should probably get going pretty early. I can pick you up at six thirty, and we can drive for a while and then stop for breakfast. Does that sound all right to you?"

"That sounds just fine." Leah dug in her purse and extracted a card, which she handed to Alan. "Here's my address and my phone number. When you get close to Hyde Park, give me a call. I'll come down and be waiting at the curb. Parking is hard to find because everyone is home over the weekend, so this way you won't have to drive around looking for a spot."

"I suppose that's a good idea, but Uncle Horace told me that when I have a date, I should always go to the door and escort her to the car." Alan grinned and continued, "But this makes more sense. I look forward to spending the day with you, Leah."

Just then their waiter appeared, carrying their food on a large tray. Everything looked and smelled great, and as soon as they began eating, it was clear that what they had ordered did not disappoint. "You ought to try this," Alan said, offering a small piece of his entrée to Leah. "Just take a bite. I'm sure you'll like it." Leah agreed it was delicious. She thought it was an unusual thing to do on a first date, yet somehow it pleased her.

The four women sitting across from Alan and Leah were getting ready to leave the restaurant, and Juneau Barkley stopped in front of them, leaned over, and whispered something in Alan's ear. Leah could have sworn he blushed, but the light was dim in the restaurant, so it was hard to be certain. Then she turned to Leah and said, "Be careful of this one. He's a heartbreaker." Then she headed down the aisle, hips swinging. She looked back once and winked at Leah, or perhaps it was intended for Alan.

Leah didn't know if she should say anything about Juneau's remark and decided not to. An awkward silence followed, and then Alan cleared his throat and said, "Juneau is a real pain in the-you-know-where. I've had to deal with her most of my life because the Marsdens, Barkleys, and Parkins have vacationed together as long as I can remember. We're all sort of related. Well, enough of family history."

It seemed a good idea to change the subject, but what to say? Finally she said, "I haven't worked at Marsden, Willett, and Desmond for very long, but it really seems to be a good place, and I enjoy my work there. I suppose you feel pretty comfortable by now. How many months have you been with the firm?"

"Actually, I've been with the firm for two years, but I was upstairs in Wills and Trusts, and they didn't let me out very often." Alan chuckled. "I've been working as a real lawyer now for four months … since I moved down to the fifth floor. And yes, I guess I do feel reasonably comfortable in that I know I can do the work, but I still don't know the whole staff, and frankly, I think some of them think my being related to Horace Marsden sets me apart. I don't want anyone to feel that way. Uncle Horace has been so good to me over the years, and I felt an obligation to come here to work when he asked me, but you might be surprised to learn that I considered becoming a public defender. Not much money there, Uncle said. In the end he was pretty persuasive. Besides, his house was my home base for nine years, so it would have been hard to say no to him."

"It's interesting that you wanted to be a public defender. I actually applied to work in that area but didn't find any openings, so I interviewed at Marsden, Willett, and Desmond. I really was fortunate to be hired because I've learned they don't take on many inexperienced people. I wanted to be a lawyer, but I ran out of money after my first year and a half of law school, and so I decided to become a pseudo-lawyer instead. That's what my friend Paula calls me."

The two sat for another twenty minutes, enjoying second and third cups of coffee and talking together on a wide range of topics, from Chicago to national politics to ideas for fixing the problems of the world. At ten thirty Alan suggested they ought to call it a night, since a six-thirty departure for Champaign would come all too soon. Because of the late hour, Alan insisted that Leah take a cab home, and he saw her safely into one, paying the driver for the fare. Leah waved from the backseat and watched him walk toward his train to Evanston.

Chapter 2

Leah was up by five the next morning. She showered and dried her hair and decided not to do anything else with it today. She would let it hang loose, as she did on most weekends, compared to during the workweek when she twisted it and pinned it tidily to the back of her head. The phone rang at fifteen minutes past six. *Ah, that must be my date,* Leah thought. She picked up the phone and said, "Hello."

"Good morning. Are you ready? I'm just turning off Lake Shore Drive, so I should be there in less than five minutes. I wanted to give you time to put on your purple and white, since I'm probably going to be there ahead of schedule. Of course, if you don't have purple and white, it's no big deal, but don't wear orange, okay?"

"I'm properly dressed and ready to go. See you out at the curb in five," replied Leah. She hurriedly pulled her jacket out of the closet, grabbed her purse, and started to leave the apartment, but before she had closed the door, she changed her mind and ran back into the kitchen. She put a tablecloth on the table, pushed the chairs in, and set a small vase of daisies on the table. "Just in case," she said to herself.

Alan was turning the corner down the block when Leah came out of her building. She waved, and he pulled over.

"Good timing," he said as she climbed into the front seat of the compact SUV. "It's going to be a beautiful day, and let's hope the roads aren't totally clogged with Northwestern fans

14

heading south. I think we actually have a chance of winning today. This team is four and one, which is better than usual. What do you think? Can we beat the Illini this year?" Alan asked, smiling at Leah.

"I have a good feeling about it and believe we can win. I just feel it in my bones," Leah said with conviction. As Alan pulled away from the curb, she couldn't help thinking that perhaps she and Alan could become good friends, or maybe more than good friends!

Travel was slow going on the toll road, but after they stopped for breakfast about thirty minutes down the road, the traffic cleared. They arrived in Champaign almost an hour and a half before game time. Alan said he really needed to get a purple cap, so he pulled into the parking lot of a mall, where he was sure he would find what he wanted. One of the stores had just what he was looking for, and he tried on several options before choosing one that Leah agreed suited him perfectly. It was a purple felt fedora-style hat with a white band.

"I was really thinking about a baseball cap, but this one just speaks to me," said Alan, looking at himself once again in the mirror. "Are you sure you like it?"

"It's definitely you," Leah said with a grin.

Alan grabbed another hat just like it and put it on Leah's head. "Hey, that fits you perfectly, and it really suits you. Why don't we get matching hats? My treat of course. I love it. Come take a look in the mirror."

Leah studied herself in the glass and smiled. She did like it, and the jaunty angle at which Alan had placed it on her head seemed to say, "I'm having fun!" And she was having fun. "I do like it, but I can pay for my own hat. Where do we find someone to take our money?"

"Not *our* money, Miss Anderly, *my* money. I said it would be my treat, and as I'm sort of your boss at work, I insist." Alan strode off toward the counter, where a salesperson was waiting on another customer. Leah followed, still trying to pay for her own hat. Alan merely raised them both above his head, out of reach, and when the salesclerk had finished with the customer she was helping, he laid them down and immediately pulled out his credit card. "Two purple hats to go," he said to the clerk.

She smiled and asked if they wouldn't rather have two nice orange ones in a similar style. She obviously had figured out from their purple-and-white attire that they were Northwestern fans. They assured her they had picked the right ones.

"That was fun, wasn't it?" asked Alan as they left the mall. "Now I think we're ready for the game with our proper attire. Shall we go?"

"I'm ready." Leah smiled. She couldn't remember the last time she had enjoyed a day like this, and it was only beginning. Maybe they would win today, which was something Northwestern had not done with any regularity, but this year things looked more promising.

Parking was not a problem, but they had a longish hike to get to the proper gate to enter the stadium. Leah was surprised to find they had some of the best seats in the house. Already sitting nearby were Jack Desmond and his wife and another couple Leah did not recognize. Alan and Leah sat down, and all around them the seats were filling up rapidly, mostly with Illini fans.

Alan greeted the Desmonds and then introduced Leah to Harriet Desmond and the other couple sitting with them. "Mrs. Desmond, this is Leah Anderly. She works at the firm as a paralegal." And to Leah he said, "This is George and Anne Mitchell. The Mitchells are long-time friends and neighbors of Uncle Horace, and I often see them bicycling on weekends."

Leah acknowledged the people she had just met. She was already acquainted with Jack Desmond, although not personally. She had worked only one case for him so far. Most of her work had been for the junior partners and just recently for Alan. Mrs. Desmond engaged Leah in conversation and seemed interested in knowing her life story. *Hmmm,* thought Leah, *she's checking me out to see if I'm good enough for someone like Alan, or maybe she's just trying to make polite conversation. No sense projecting my insecurities.*

The Northwestern band came on the field, and Alan and Leah stood to applaud. The Desmonds and the Mitchells were obviously Illinois fans, as they did not rise. In fact Mrs. Mitchell seemed a little annoyed. But Jack Desmond proceeded to tell her that it was live and let live and that Alan's parents and Alan himself were graduates of Northwestern. He pointed out that Alan's father had played basketball for the Wildcats. She smiled weakly and nodded to indicate she understood.

Leah and Alan were enjoying the band music when Juneau Barkley and the three friends from the restaurant the previous evening claimed the seats in front of them, but Juneau turned and sat down beside Alan. Grabbing Alan's arm and leaning in close, she said, "Look who's here. It's your date from last night. Aren't you going to introduce me? This must be serious. Last night for dinner and now the game. I'm jealous."

"Juneau, this is Leah Anderly. We work together at the law firm. Leah, this is Juneau Barkley. I'm sorry, but I don't know your friends' names."

Juneau didn't bother to introduce her companions and instead questioned Leah. "Where did you get your law degree, Miss Anderly? Northwestern I'm guessing." Juneau pronounced Leah's name as though intimating that she somehow already knew things about Leah that were suspect. "And where in God's name did you get those stupid hats?"

"I don't have a law degree. I'm a paralegal," Leah said, "and I work in research most of the time."

Juneau gasped, obviously trying to sound shocked. "What? Not a lawyer? I'm surprised." Then she smiled. "Oh dear, couldn't pass the bar, I suppose?"

Alan put his hand on Leah's arm and gave a little squeeze, as if telling her he knew what was going on but was allowing her to make her own response if she wanted. "No, I dropped out of law school because I couldn't afford the tuition." Leah had not wanted to share this information, but then, why should she be ashamed to tell the truth? She didn't say that her father had been ill or that they'd had to sell their larger apartment.

She wasn't ashamed, though perhaps disappointed, that she had been unable to complete her law degree.

Leah was glad Alan had not said anything and had let her handle Juneau. The little exchange had likely been uncomfortable for everyone. Jack Desmond, perhaps wishing to defuse the situation, said to Leah, "I think I've heard the name Anderly before, but I can't quite remember where. Was your father in banking perhaps? I seem to remember an Anderly over at First National many years ago … maybe your grandfather?"

"No, I'm not related to any Anderly in banking. My father was a janitorial mechanic. He kept things humming at Carson Pirie and Scott, but he died a few years ago," said Leah. She thought, *Why is pedigree so important to these people? My dad wasn't perfect, but he earned a good living for us. Isn't that enough?*

"We had an early breakfast, so Leah and I are going to get some food. Come on, Leah, let's go," said Alan, getting up from his seat and pulling Leah to her feet. They walked down the risers and headed off toward the booths that were hawking hot dogs, popcorn, and various other types of junk food for the hungry fans. He didn't say anything until they stopped in front of a stand selling tacos.

"I don't know if you'd like a taco or not, but I had to get out of there. I'm really sorry. I had no idea the Desmonds and Juneau and her friends would be here. I think I might have scalped some tickets and sat in the cheap seats if I'd known. I guess I should have realized they might be here. Juneau obviously has Uncle's other four tickets. I'm really sorry." Alan looked pleadingly at Leah.

"Don't worry about it. I've heard worse. I don't have a pedigree, but I've always felt one ought to be judged by character and perhaps achievement, not on birth circumstances over which no one has control. Oh, now I'm sorry. You're part of a very prestigious family. I didn't mean to say anything bad about you or them. I really am sorry," Leah said.

"Don't worry; I'm not in the least offended, and you're right. Character should be more important than family background. Let's put this to rest. I've got an idea. Let's go to a sports bar and watch the game there. We might have to keep a low profile since we're wearing Northwestern colors, but at least we won't have to endure the company of snobs."

"Oh no, we shouldn't leave. We can just sit there and enjoy the game, and if anything more is said, we can change the subject or at least refuse to be drawn in. I know you've been looking forward to the game, and so have I. Let's make the best of it. They are your friends after all, and the Desmonds might be offended if we leave. You have to work with him, and I might have to again at some point. It's not worth it to let this incident ruin the day. What do you think? Can we go back?"

"Sure, you're right. We'll get some food and go back. It's almost time for kickoff. We'll suck it up and sit there, and I won't tone down my enthusiasm for Northwestern. I hope we trounce them! Let's get some tacos and a couple of drinks and go back. I'm ready."

When they reached their seats, they saw that Juneau had moved over into the seat where Leah had been sitting, right next to Mrs. Desmond. Alan indicated that Leah should sit next to Juneau, and he sat next to her. Juneau, who had been in deep conversation with Harriet Desmond, turned to see Leah sitting down beside her and said, "I believe I have your seat. Why don't I move back to where I was sitting, and you can sit here?"

Alan, however, said he had tickets to four of the seats in the row and that she was welcome to sit where she was. In fact, he suggested to Leah that she move over one seat and everyone could put their coats on the seat next to Juneau. The day had warmed considerably, and the sun's penetrating rays had made most people shed their jackets.

Juneau's sour look told the story of what she thought about the new seating arrangement. At that point, the Illinois band began playing the national anthem, so they all stood and sang along with the rest of the crowd. Immediately after that, the Illini kicked off to the Wildcats. The game was under way.

Northwestern made three first downs in the opening minutes of the game. On the following series, the quarterback lofted a long pass almost to the twenty-yard line of the Illini, and a fleet-footed end caught it and took it into the end zone. The crowd of followers from Evanston erupted. Alan and Leah leapt to their feet, and while the band played, they linked arms and sang the school's anthem, something they had done as fans during their college days, although not with each other. At the end, they hugged and then sat down, smiles a mile wide on their faces. Leah glanced over at Juneau and saw the same sour expression still on her face. Or perhaps this was a new one. Whatever! Who cared?

At halftime Alan asked Leah if she wanted anything to eat or drink. She declined. Juneau, however, said she would like something and suggested that Alan accompany her to the snack bar area. "I'm sorry, Juneau, but I'm here with my date. It wouldn't be polite to leave her here alone." He smiled as he said this. "Anyway, I suspect you're quite capable of finding your way." He leaned back to let her pass, as did Leah. Her friends followed her out, and much to everyone's surprise, they did not return for the second half.

"Do you suppose Juneau was sick?" asked Harriet Desmond. "She appeared to be out of sorts, didn't you think?" She was looking at Leah as she spoke. Leah assured Mrs. Desmond she didn't think Juneau was ill but then confessed she didn't know her well enough to make that judgment.

Alan jumped in. "I think Juneau has an I problem." Of course the Desmonds didn't realize what he meant by the remark and inquired if he knew something they didn't about her eyesight. "No, not really, but she's had a problem with that before, so I was just thinking that might be what was bothering her. Too bad they left. The Illini are just about ready to score their first touchdown, and they'll probably miss seeing it."

The game ended with a Northwestern win—twenty-one to seventeen, a close contest, but a satisfying ending for Alan and Leah. They said their good-byes to the Desmonds and the

Mitchells, who left immediately. Alan and Leah, however, sat down and enjoyed the band music, even though it wasn't the Northwestern band. After twenty minutes, Alan suggested that the crowd had most likely dissipated sufficiently and that it was probably time to start back for Chicago.

In the parking area, a long lineup of cars was trying to turn onto the road leading to the highway. Police were directing traffic, and from the look of things, it could be a while before they would be signaled to move out. "I just wanted to say you were great today. I admire your willingness to risk another put-down from Juneau. I think even the Desmonds and the Mitchells may have been turned off by some of the things she said. And in case you didn't catch it, when I said Juneau had an I problem, I meant an ego problem. When her ego gets bruised, she gets pretty nasty."

"I caught that. I guess one should feel sorry for her. She doesn't seem to be a happy person," Leah said.

"You've figured that out. Many people don't. You know, you're a very perceptive person. I think that's one reason you do well in your job: you see a situation and are able to analyze it so easily. In case I haven't let you know before, I appreciate your work ethic and the way you do the assignments you're given. I'm glad to have had the opportunity to work with your team, but I'm especially glad to get to know you better." Then shifting the conversation, he asked, "Did you enjoy the game?"

"It was so much fun. This is the first time I've been to a game in Champaign, so thanks for inviting me and for breakfast and the taco lunch. And I love my hat." Leah smiled as she adjusted the fedora to a jaunty angle. "I owe you big time, so if you'd like, when we get back to Chicago, maybe you'd like to have a Coke and snacks at my place."

"I'd like that ... hey, our lane is moving." In a few minutes they were able to exit the parking area, and the traffic cleared. They were soon back on the highway to Chicago. Alan asked Leah is she had siblings or any extended family in the area?

"I have no family at all since my mother died. She was an only child, so I have no aunts and uncles. I never knew anything about my father's family. I think they came from up north somewhere, maybe Canada. Dad never talked about anybody, so I wonder if they were estranged, or maybe there wasn't anyone left in his immediate family. I grew up without relatives, which always seemed strange because my friends talked about their cousins and visiting grandparents, but it wasn't something we ever did. I know my mother's parents died in a tragic auto accident in Minnesota. I wish I had asked more questions, but now it's too late. I don't have brothers or sisters either, so I'm one of those only children."

"Well, I had two brothers. I still do, but they're much older than I am, and one lives in California and the other in Oregon. Because of our age difference we were never close. My mother lives in Oregon too, but she and my father divorced when I was six. I don't know what happened. I've asked Uncle Horace, but he says it's best to let sleeping dogs lie. Maybe one of these days I'll get him to talk about it. What can be the harm now? Dad's gone, and my mother isn't part of my life at all. I'd just like to know what happened."

They were quiet for several minutes, and then Leah said, "It seems like we both have unusual background stories. I've been trying to decide if I should tell you something, and I guess I want to. The other day when I was a little late getting back to the office, I had been to see a private investigator." Leah then related her meeting with Nola Randolph and Nola's instructions to put together as much information about her parents and herself as possible. She also told Alan about her flashbacks and what her mother had said on her deathbed. When she finished, she looked over at him. "Do you think I'm crazy to want to delve into this mystery? I wonder if I should just forget it. What difference will it make knowing what was going on in my mom's head or, for that matter, knowing who Lizzie is? What do you think? Should I go ahead with it or call the agency and say I've changed my mind?"

Alan looked over at Leah. He had never heard a story like that before, and he was intrigued by it. "I think you should go ahead with it. You wouldn't have gone there in the first place if it didn't mean something to you. Definitely follow through is my suggestion, but of course you're the one that needs to decide. There's always a chance that what you discover will not be something you want to hear. On the other hand, maybe it will be. You might discover aunts, uncles, and cousins you didn't know you had."

"I'm pretty sure I'll do it. I plan to spend tomorrow looking through my mother's papers. I should go through them anyway. I'll have to file her income tax return next year, so I need to see if there's anything there relating to financial matters. I probably should have looked at the stuff right after she died, but I had the car to sell and needed to get back to my job at the firm, so I put it off. But tomorrow is the day."

They arrived at Leah's apartment a little before five o'clock. The sun was dipping behind the tall apartment complex to the west, and the shadows stretched long in front of her building. They were fortunate to find a parking space less than a block away. Leah hoped she hadn't made a mistake inviting Alan to her place, but it was too late now. They took the elevator to the third floor and walked the few steps to Leah's apartment, which lay at the head of the stairwell. Leah inserted her key into the lock and led Alan inside.

The shadowed sunlight from the west came in through the living room windows. Leah thought everything looked all right, but of course Alan would be used to something much more elegant and spacious than her small five-room, one-bath apartment. He surprised her, however, by commenting on how homey it was as he took the liberty of sinking down onto the sofa. "Ah, it feels good to get out of the car. Thanks for inviting me up. It would be deadly back at Uncle Horace's place. There's no one around today at all, and I would have been rattling around in that mausoleum by myself. Uncle Horace would do well to hire you as his interior decorator. I love this room. It's inviting, and the furniture is actually comfortable. You should see the settee that passes for someplace to sit where I live."

"What would you like to drink?" asked Leah. "I have Coke, Diet Coke, Mountain Dew, and tea or coffee. Name your poison. Sorry I don't have any beer or alcohol."

"How about a Diet Coke, or bring me whatever you're having. I wouldn't mind tea. It's been a while since I've had tea, so let's have tea. No cream or sugar."

Leah headed to the kitchen, calling over her shoulder that she would be right back, but she discovered that Alan was right behind her. "I could bring the tea to the living room if you want to stay comfortable, or you can sit at the kitchen table while I get out something to go with the tea," she said.

Alan sat down at the table and watched attentively as she put water into an electric kettle, got out mugs, a teapot, and tea. She then opened a cupboard and pulled out a chocolate cake she had baked late the night before, just on the chance Alan might want to come up after the game.

The water was soon boiling, and Leah poured it into the teapot, put on the lid, and set it carefully on a trivet on the kitchen table. "Shall we sit here, or would you rather go into the living room? And there's chocolate cake in case you didn't notice. You do eat cake, don't you?"

"Only chocolate, so it's a good thing that's what you have. Actually, I like almost anything sweet, although as I said last night, I'm trying to cut down, but chocolate! Tell me it's all right," begged Alan, smiling. Leah agreed that it indeed was all right.

They carried their tea and cake into the living room where they could turn on the TV and watch the game wrap-up on ESPN. It would be sweet to relive the highlights of the win and revel in the victory for Northwestern. Leah went back to the kitchen and grabbed the vase of daisies and placed them on the coffee table. "A little decorative touch to help the digestion," she said.

After finishing the pot of tea and a slice of cake each, Alan and Leah talked nonstop. At eight o'clock they returned to the kitchen to fix sandwiches and get Diet Cokes, adding a bowl of potato chips and some carrots and celery. "Dinner is served," Leah said as they once again carried everything into the living room.

At ten Alan reluctantly said it was time for him to make his way back to Evanston. "Unfortunately, I have to be up early tomorrow to play golf with a couple of clients. But it's been a wonderful day, Leah. Thanks for saying yes to my invitation to the game, and thanks for the sumptuous spread. I really want to see you again. Can we go out to eat Wednesday night after work? Monday and Tuesday evenings I have meetings, but I'll definitely hold Wednesday open if you're available." Alan looked hopefully at Leah.

"Wednesday evening is free, and I'd love to go to dinner with you. I'll probably see you at work before then, and you can let me know the time. If it's a little later than five thirty, I can always find something to do in the office until you're ready to go." Leah hoped she didn't appear too eager for another date, but she had enjoyed Alan's company and their conversation and hoped the relationship might continue.

Leah unfastened the locks on the door and swung it open for Alan. He stopped right in the middle of the doorway, turned and put both his hands on her shoulders, and said, "Leah Anderly, you are one sweet girl. I want to get to know you much better. Good night now, and sleep well." Then he leaned in and kissed Leah. She watched him until he reached the elevator, where he turned, waved, and blew a kiss. Then he was inside the elevator and gone.

What a day, thought Leah. *What a glorious day!* She could hardly believe that she had now had two dates with Alan Parkin. He was someone she had admired from afar, but she'd never dreamed he could be interested in her. "Well, one day at a time," she said to herself, "one day at a time."

Chapter 3

After Alan's departure, Leah decided to start gathering material for Nola Randolph. A trip to the storage closet in the basement of the apartment building yielded a stack of old photo albums and scrapbooks, a metal file box of financial papers, and several more boxes that looked promising. It took two trips to drag everything to the elevator and ultimately into her apartment.

At first the search appeared a little bleak, but then she spotted a rather fat envelope at the bottom of one of the boxes. She undid the metal clasps and reached in to withdraw the material inside. There she found some small plasticized cards. She picked up the first one and discovered it was her father's driver's license from long ago. Leah grabbed a pen and notebook she had laid on the kitchen counter and wrote down the pertinent information. Name: Harold J. Anderly. Age: twenty-one. Address: Route 3, Elk Lake, Minnesota. Height: 5'11". Weight: 169 pounds. Eyes: brown. Hair: brown. Birth date: February 10, 1953.

It was hard for Leah to equate the description on the license with the father she remembered. The father she remembered had had greenish-brown eyes and salt-and-pepper hair, and he'd weighed at least forty or fifty pounds more than listed on his license. Obviously he had gained weight over the years. She laid the license aside and picked up another card from a hospital in Duluth that read, "Baby Girl Anderly. Seven pounds, four ounces, twenty inches long. Birth date: January 2, 1988.

Mother: Grace. Father: Harold Anderly." It was undoubtedly the card on her bassinet in the hospital, but she had never seen it before. Another large folded piece of paper was her parents' wedding license. They had been married by Justice of the Peace Duncan Forsyth in Duluth on April 5, 1980. Witnesses were Fay Carson and Gustav Schoemann. Leah wondered who they were. Relatives or friends? A postcard with a picture of Lake Michigan contained no message and had no stamp on it, just the date: April 6, 1980. From their honeymoon perhaps?

Leah shuffled quickly through the papers, most of which were typewritten. The top page had a newspaper clipping from August 15, 1983, attached to it:

> DULUTH, Minn. – Today in the courtroom of Judge Michael Dvorak, Harold J. Anderly, age 30, was found guilty of the crime of theft with the use of force. Anderly had been accused of robbing the State Bank of Duluth and threatening the teller with a gun. The teller, Gloria Burns, testified that the accused demanded that she put cash in a bag he handed to her. He was arrested less than two hours later. Anderly was observed disposing of the bag in an alley dumpster and then fleeing the scene. He was arrested at his home soon after, and the bag was turned over to the police by Philemon L. Tabor, who said he had seen the bag being disposed of and had brought it in. He also identified the defendant as the man who dropped the bank bag into the dumpster. Anderly was arrested but denied being in the bank or demanding money from the teller. Christopher Klaussen, vice president of the bank, testified that the stolen money had not been recovered. The reported amount was said to be in the neighborhood of $8,000.

> Anderly was sentenced to 15 years in the state penitentiary, sentence to begin at once. Information provided by Stephen Morrisey, clerk of the court.

Leah knew her father had been in prison, but she had been told her that it was for a very minor offense and that he should never have served time at all.

There was another clipping affixed to the back of the page:

Harold Anderly Set Free

> Harold J. Anderly was released from prison today after a witness at the trial, Philemon L. Tabor, recanted his testimony. At the trial Tabor testified that he'd observed Mr. Anderly run down the alley and dispose of a bank bag in the dumpster. Tabor also provided the police with a description of the getaway car that ultimately led to Anderly's arrest. In recanting his testimony, Tabor said he realized soon after the trial that he had made a mistake. He said he had not seen the suspected thief run from the bank and that he had found the bag when he happened to look into the dumpster, hoping to find something of value he could sell. He told the court he was a secondhand dealer and sold items he bought or found. A mistrial was declared, and the district attorney is not seeking a retrial for lack of evidence.

The next little card, stuck to the side of the box, was her mother's ID. It was issued in Chicago and gave her full name and address and her date of birth, July 10, 1958.

Leah set these pages aside and picked up a smaller envelope. Inside were a number of photographs, most of them black and white and obviously from years ago. One was a picture of a young girl in a white dress carrying a carnation in one hand and a diploma in the other hand. On the back it said, "Grace on her graduation." Another was a wedding photo of her parents. They were dressed in what was probably their best clothing, and her mother was carrying a small bouquet of flowers. The photo was a snapshot, so they probably had not had studio photos taken. Another showed the couple sitting in lawn chairs, a lake in the background. Two pictures showed what was obviously her mother's family, with "The McDermotts" penciled on the back of each. Another photo was of two young men, identified as Jesse and Hugh on the back. The final photo showed a rather good-sized house, with a front porch that stretched most of the way across, and at least fifteen people sitting and standing in various poses on the porch and on the steps. There was only a date, July 4, 1974, and place, Duluth, Minnesota, on the back.

Another envelope contained additional pictures. There was a small girl holding a ball. She was dressed in a one-piece outfit with ruffles around the waist and sleeves. On the back was written, "Leah, eighteen months." There were several more Leah pictures, none of which she had ever seen. There was one of her at three months, another at six months, and two different poses at what was most likely a second birthday, as there was a cake with two candles on the table in front of her. Two more pictures showed a Christmas tree with her standing next to it, a smile on her little face. The back read, "Leah, Jan. 2, age two." *My birthday,* thought Leah. *But why have I never seen these pictures?* She studied the photos of herself, trying to equate the pixie-faced child with pictures taken when she started school. She had obviously changed in those years between ages two and six.

The last picture in the envelope showed a young woman and a baby, identified on the back as Grace and Leah. Leah was quite sure the crabbed handwriting on the back was not her mother's and certainly not her father's either. The signature on his driver's license showed a bold stroke. Rather than clarifying anything for her, these pictures only presented more questions. She carefully gathered them up and put them back in the envelopes. Monday at noon she would deliver everything into Nola Randolph's hands. Meanwhile, she still had tomorrow to sort through the rest of the papers.

Leah took the photo album with her into her bedroom, laying it on her bedside table. She climbed into bed and reached for the album. The first few pages were pictures from a long-ago era. It had been ages since she had looked through the album, and she found it interesting that she had never questioned her mother about when the photos were taken or who the various unfamiliar faces were. She examined each photo carefully, but she recognized no one. Who were these people? On the last two pages she recognized several pictures of her mother at age seventeen or eighteen, dressed in the white dress from the graduation photo. Several more photos showed various young people at a picnic, and three pictures were of adults whose dour faces made Leah wonder who they were and why their photos had been taken.

Surely some of these people must be relatives, but why had her mother never mentioned them? Leah vaguely recalled being told that some of the people in the album were friends of her parents. Her father had said that his parents were dead and that his two brothers had left home to go west. He'd said he was not in touch with them at all. As she thought about it, her father had been vague about family and had told no stories of uncles, aunts, or cousins with whom he had spent time growing up.

It was close to midnight and Leah had not finished her quest, but she needed to get some sleep. Tomorrow was another day, and she could continue her sleuthing then. She turned off the light and slid beneath the sheet and a light blanket. She recalled the wonderful day she had enjoyed with Alan—the weather, the company, the conversation, even the food had been perfect. Leah smiled and buried her head in the pillow. Her life had suddenly taken a new turn, and she had a feeling it was a turn in the right direction.

Chapter 4

Monday at noon Leah caught a cab and arrived at Nola Randolph's office a few minutes ahead of her appointment. Nola was sitting behind her desk, phone at her ear. She motioned for Leah to take a seat while she continued to talk, obviously to a client. "You have to understand that the information I pass on to you does not come with action on my part. That's for the authorities to handle. It looks like your husband is already under suspicion, so I would suggest you let him face the consequences. Call the officer whose name you have, and stop covering for him, unless that's what you really want to do. If it is, I don't know why you hired me. Gotta go. A client just came in. Good-bye." Nola hung up the phone, rolled her eyes, and got down to business immediately. "I see you have a file folder for me. Let's have a look, and while I'm looking, you can fill me in on a few of the basics, especially anything about your parents." Nola was already going through pictures, laying some aside and putting others back in their envelopes.

Leah gave her analysis to explain the lack of helpful information she had brought with her, as well as thoughts she had about why her mother might have said what she had on the day she'd died. Without looking up from the paperwork Leah had given her, Nola remarked, "Too soon for that. Let me look through all this, and then we'll get down to some what-ifs."

Ten minutes later Nola had arranged a series of the pictures on her desk and had Leah's fact sheet in front of her. "Now then, do you know any of these people? I suppose these are your parents," she said, pointing to the wedding photo and the beach photo. "I assume the child is you, but you say you don't recognize any of the other people in the photos. Look closely at the ones on the porch. Anyone look familiar, or see any family resemblance to either of your parents?" Nola looked up.

"I don't think so, but one of the men holding on to the railing has a slight resemblance to my father. I'm really not sure." Leah felt helpless, and she was sure Nola Randolph would think this little exercise only proved how silly this whole thing might be.

Nola was still looking at the paperwork Leah had included. "I see that your father was in prison for some sort of robbery but released without finishing his sentence. I think my first task will be to search all sources in Duluth to get a more complete account. We'll try to find Lizzie for you, as well as to discover why your mother was apologizing. I think that's all I need from you at the moment. Now, I've got a lunch date with an old friend. I'll call you as soon as I get any information. Thanks for bringing this in." Nola indicated the material and the pictures strewn across the desk top and then picked up the papers once again.

Leah realized she was being dismissed and left the office. As she pushed the button for the elevator, she thought, *well, that was short and sweet. Maybe not sweet, but certainly short. I guess I thought she'd ask me more questions. But what do I know about how a PI works?*

At street level Leah stepped out of the elevator and discovered she had time to grab lunch, so she stopped at a food stand and purchased a ham sandwich and a can of Coke. Because it was a warm and beautifully windless day, she decided to walk back to the office. When she reached her cubicle, she saw Alan coming down the hall.

He smiled when he saw her and said, "I was hoping to have a minute or two just to say hi and tell you again what a great day Saturday was for me. I suppose you've had lunch. I'm on my way to get something and then go to court by two thirty. Any chance you could join me? For lunch I mean."

"I'd love to, but I'm due at a meeting in fifteen minutes. I enjoyed Saturday too. It was a special day with that great win."

Leah smiled on her way to her meeting. She was pleased that Alan had come looking for her to say hello and that they had been able to have a brief conversation. The rest of her day was busy, and she was late arriving home that evening.

Tuesday came and went with no word from Nola. But then Leah didn't really expect results that quickly. Wednesday was her date night with Alan, so Leah dressed carefully that morning, not as casually as she often did on an ordinary weekday. That evening they enjoyed a meal at a restaurant along the lakeshore since Alan had driven his car that day. At the end of the evening he took her home, and once again they talked endlessly over tea and cookies.

Thursday was rather uneventful, and Friday was filled with meetings and some research in the firm's library, and at noon Leah pulled out a sandwich she had brought from home and poured herself a cup of the coffee that was available all day. She was enjoying lunch at her desk when she noticed she had several messages. The first was a reminder of a meeting, and the second was a request for an old brief she had that now someone else needed. The third was from Nola. The message had just come in a few minutes ago according to the log, so Leah immediately returned the call, hoping to catch Nola in her office.

"Randolph Private Investigations," Nola answered.

"This is Leah Anderly. You left a message, so I'm calling back to—"

Nola cut in. "Oh, yes, Leah. I've found some of your family. If you've got a fax machine I can send everything to you, or I can e-mail or mail it to you. Once you get it and have a chance to look through everything, get back to me with feedback. Okay?" Nola paused. "So what's your choice? How do you want me to send this?"

"Fax is fine. I have a machine here at my desk." Leah gave her the number, thanked her, and just that quickly Nola said good-bye and hung up. Leah had to smile. She would have to get used to Nola's abrupt manner. She was certainly speedy and quite efficient. Leah had work to do at her desk, but she kept one eye on the fax machine, which had been quiet all day. At two thirty the machine made its usual noise, letting her know something was coming in. In a minute eight pages of print came spilling out. Leah hurried to gather them up and then told the receptionist she was going to take a break. She went into an empty conference room where nothing was scheduled until four o'clock. It should be quiet there, and she wouldn't be disturbed.

At first Leah just skimmed through the first page or two. Most of what was there was a repeat of information she had given Nola about her parents. However, Nola had added a few more details, such as the names of her grandparents and their birth and death dates, but her grandmother McDermott had no death date listed. *Odd,* she thought, since supposedly her mother's parents had both perished in an accident years ago.

At the bottom of the second page things got more interesting. There were names of aunts, uncles, cousins; places of residence for all of them; and in some instances, birth, death, and marriage records. She was amazed to see the names of people she had never heard of but who were obviously related to her. All of them were Anderlys. The third page delved into past history for her parents, with two more pages devoted to her father's trial and incarceration, as well as new information about his release.

Page six followed up with places of residence for her parents before and after their marriage. The last known place of residence before they'd moved to Chicago was Saint Paul, Minnesota, where they had lived for almost two years. Their home had been a rental in a middle-class neighborhood, and according to Nola's research, they had left abruptly, leaving behind furnishings and unpaid electric and gas bills. This surprised Leah because her parents had been meticulous about bill paying. She would have bet her life they would not have left possessions behind and certainly no unpaid bills. However, the data was supported by the landlord, Gerald Mylam, who still owned the property. Nola had logged a phone call for $2.69 to Gerald. According to Nola's notes, he had said, "I'd like to get those bills paid, even if it is twenty years ago!"

The remaining pages were even more troubling. Nola had Googled the names Lizzie and Elizabeth for the years her parents had spent in Saint Paul as well as when they'd lived in the Duluth area. Several articles Nola had included detailed the abduction of a young child named Elizabeth McGregor, called Lizzie by her family. The disappearance had occurred just before Leah's parents had left Saint Paul. What did this mean? Leah reread the articles again, this time more carefully. The child, Lizzie, had been with her mother, sister, and one of her older brothers in a park. The sister had been keeping an eye on Lizzie but apparently had been distracted. It was undoubtedly during that brief period of time that someone had grabbed the child and spirited her away. At first the authorities had believed Lizzie had just wandered off, and they had begun a search of the large and partially wooded park. No trace had ever been found of the little girl, and though a sizable reward had been offered for information about her whereabouts, no one had come forward with anything helpful. Lizzie had vanished into thin air, according to Clarice Davis, the reporter who had written a series of articles for several weeks after the abduction/ disappearance.

The last page was a brief summary of Nola's conversation with Ms. Davis, who still believed an abduction had taken place. She believed that if the child had been killed, a body would most likely have surfaced in the weeks and months afterward.

Leah read Nola's final notes: "Leah, I think there's a very slight chance you might be this young girl. I do believe your mother may have known her and perhaps her parents. There's still a mystery here about what connection your family may have had with the McGregors. Your parents and the McGregors apparently lived six blocks from each other, so they may have been acquainted. I could follow up, but you might want to travel there yourself and try to unravel this mystery. Of course, you might not wish to proceed at all. There's no way of knowing what might be revealed. It could be benign. Maybe your parents were friends with the McGregors, or your mother still felt bad about Lizzie's disappearance. Perhaps she had not been as supportive as she would have liked, or who knows what might have caused her to cry out for forgiveness in regard to Lizzie. If you decide you want me to pursue this, I will, but it would mean a trip to the Twin Cities and would add to the expense list. As of now, you owe me $795. Get in touch, or better yet, come in Monday at noon, and we'll talk about the best way to proceed."

Leah was in shock. All this information told her one thing loud and clear: her parents had not been truthful in many ways. Why would they cut off communication with relatives in the Duluth area? What was her parents' relationship with Lizzie? Leah was baffled. She realized she had spent almost half an hour in the conference room, so she quickly gathered up the papers and put them back in the envelope. Jess, who occupied the cubicle next to Leah's, said that Leah had missed a couple of calls and that Alan had stopped by and wanted her to call when she returned to her desk.

The missed calls were nothing urgent, and Alan wasn't at his desk, so she left him a message: "I heard you stopped by. I'll be at my desk until five thirty." Leah wondered what Alan had on his mind. Business or pleasure?

At five thirty she was still trying to finish a report to be included in the Quinlin file. Alan peeked around the corner of her cubicle. "Hey, time to quit, young lady," he said, smiling.

"I guess it is," she replied, stuffing the report into the file folder and putting it into the out basket. "What was on your mind when you stopped by? I was taking a little break, so I missed you."

"You missed me! I'm delighted that you miss me when I'm not with you. What I had on my mind was you. Specifically I'm hoping you'll go somewhere with me right now." Alan hadn't stopped smiling since he'd come into her cubicle.

"And where is this somewhere you had in mind?"

"I have to deliver some papers for signature in Evanston, and I thought you could ride the train with me. At the station we'll pick up my car and then make the delivery together. We can grab a bite to eat and perhaps even walk around the Northwestern campus."

"Now that's an offer I can't refuse. But why are you doing delivery-boy duties? Don't they usually send some peon on those kinds of errands?" Leah said with a teasing grin. "But I would love to take you up on the invitation. I haven't been on campus for ages."

"Then it's settled. I'll grab the papers and be right back, or if you're ready to leave, you can come with me, since my office is closer to the elevator. It will save time, and I'd like a nice long evening with you, Miss Anderly."

Alan and Leah were lucky to catch a train only seconds before it headed north. They settled into seats near the back of the train, crowded with commuters heading home for the evening. They shared what they had been doing since their Wednesday-night dinner date. As Leah divulged the contents of Nola Randolph's report, Alan put his arm around her.

"Wow! That's quite a revelation," Alan said. "I'm sure you're having a hard time processing everything. I know you loved your parents and felt you had a wonderful upbringing, so their being less than honest has probably shaken you. Am I right?"

Leah nodded, her emotions in danger of bringing tears for the first time since she'd read Nola's report. "I'm trying to make sense of all this, and so far I haven't been able to. I'll be meeting with Nola again, and maybe she can provide a little insight. She's still waiting for additional information, so I hope what she discovers will make things clear and provide a reason for my parents' estrangement from their families. But let's not talk about this anymore. I'm going to try to put it away until Monday. Tonight I just want to enjoy the evening with you."

Alan took her hand and raised it to his lips. "Leah, I'm here for you. I want to always be here for you. You're very important to me, and I want you to know that."

Leah leaned into Alan, and then a few teardrops did fall, but she recovered quickly. Smiling, she said, "I really appreciate your willingness to listen to me and provide a shoulder to cry on. You're pretty important to me too." Alan kissed her forehead and squeezed her hand. The train began to slow for the Evanston stop, and Alan rose first, picking up his briefcase and moving into the aisle. He extended his hand to Leah and let her precede him out of the train car.

Alan's SUV was parked nearby, and they were soon on their way to deliver the papers. Leah stayed in the car while Alan ran up the steps to a large brick-and-stone house set back from the street. Alan disappeared inside and was gone for perhaps five or six minutes. When he returned, he apologized for taking so long. All he had needed was a signature, but Porter Dawson, the man doing the signing, had wanted to catch up. In fact Alan had been invited to stay for dinner. Mr. Dawson had confided that his daughter was home for the weekend and had said that he knew Alan would want to see her as well. "I told him I had my date waiting in the car but of course thanked him for the invitation. Lucy Dawson is another spoiled brat who's a bit toxic, just like Juneau. What is it with parents who want to arrange their children's lives? I don't get a sense that your parents did that, or am I wrong? Uncle Horace was always inviting, finagling, whatever he could do to set me up with some sweet young thing from the 'right' family. I knew I was capable of getting my own date, but he often pushed me into situations where it would be rude and unacceptable to say no. Well, enough. Let's stop at my place so I can change clothes. This afternoon I managed to spill a full glass of iced tea on my shirt. I could button up my jacket to cover up the stain, but I'll feel better if I can change. Besides, you haven't seen where I live. It's just around the bend." Alan maneuvered the car around a rather sharp curve. To the left Leah could see Lake Michigan, and to the right was a massive pile of stone with turrets on both ends and a long paved drive leading to an oversize oaken front door.

"I'm blown away," Leah said. "This is where you live? It really looks like a castle! How do you find your way around inside?"

A vast vaulted entry welcomed visitors, and Leah could see immediately that no expense had been spared in the decor and furnishings. Through an open doorway she caught a glimpse of a spacious area that appeared to be a living room. Alan explained that it was the reception room for guests and that the living quarters, for the most part, were all on the second floor. "There are two separate dining rooms. One is massive, and the other is for more-intimate gatherings or when it's just the three of us. But it still has seating for a dozen, so it really isn't all that intimate. I've gotten used to it, but when I first came here, I found it difficult to feel comfortable having my meals in such a lavish and cavernous room. I swear it seems to echo when a dish is dropped or someone speaks loudly. I can show it to you later if you like, but now let's go up to my suite," Alan said, leading the way to an elevator beside the front door.

They exited the elevator on the third floor, a long hallway stretching both left and right. "This way," directed Alan, taking Leah's arm and heading left, almost to the end of the hall. He opened a door and stepped back to allow Leah to enter first. She entered a spacious room with what appeared to be Victorian furnishings. Nothing looked all that comfortable. Two chairs and two love seats were positioned to create a conversation area, and off to the right was an alcove with a small table and several chairs. Everything looked stiff and not very inviting to Leah.

"Well, what do you think of it? Ain't it homey?" Alan asked facetiously. "Now you can see why I enjoy sitting on your comfortable sofa and your wonderful easy chair. Uncle Horace bought this house eighteen years ago, just a month before his first wife died, and not much has changed, except in his own personal area. His second wife, Estelle, loved anything Victorian, so she was enamored with the decor and probably only replaced curtains and bedspreads. Now come see my bedroom."

At the very end of the hall was a spacious room with windows that looked out on the lake. A king-size bed stood against the south wall of the room, with an expanse of windows facing east. A dresser, nightstands, and a highboy, all in the Victorian style, made up the rest of the furnishings. A large flat-screen TV was mounted on the wall opposite the bed, so that anyone lying there could easily view the screen.

"I bought the bed as soon as I got my first paycheck. Come with me, and I'll show you the bed I slept in when I first came here."

Alan led the way back down the hallway and opened a closed door to a darkened room. The window was shrouded in heavy velvet draperies, preventing light from getting through. He snapped on the lights, revealing stacked boxes and more Victorian furnishings. There were also two twin-size beds with only metal springs and no mattresses. "You might notice the beds seem a little short. That's because they are. I was six foot plus already as a sophomore when I came to live here, so my feet hung over the end of the bed."

Alan opened another door, and they entered a room with two baby beds. "I was told the former owners used this as a nursery. I don't use either of these rooms anymore. I sometimes had college mates stay over, and they used the twin beds, but I tried to invite only short people," Alan said with a grin.

A third door, which Alan identified as the guest room, was locked. He explained that some repairs were being made because the eaves leaked water into the ceiling. "Sorry I can't show it to you. It's not quite so Victorian, so it's not a bad little room."

"You have more room in your suite than I do in my apartment, but I guess I wouldn't care to trade. Victorian stuff has never tickled my fancy. I suppose everything's authentic and worth quite a lot ..." Leah trailed off, suddenly afraid she had said something inappropriate.

"I wish Uncle Horace would sell everything ... the house and the contents. At least I wish he'd get rid of all this uncomfortable furniture. I don't think he sees it. I suppose he likes having things the same, including the routine around here. Well, I won't go into that. Since Estelle died, I'm sure he's been lonely. He probably finds comfort in having everything as it was when she was alive. Hey, we should get going. You can sit uncomfortably in the so-called parlor, or you can sit on my bed while I get dressed. I have a dressing room and bathroom that I didn't show you, but I will. I don't know if the maid cleaned up today, so there might be towels on the floor," Alan warned.

Leah was blown away by the sheer size of Alan's bath and dressing areas. His closet was bigger than her bedroom, but she noticed that only a fifth of the space was being used. Hangers hung forlornly, and shelves were mostly empty, except one where several pairs of shoes were neatly lined up. "Come sit on my bed. I'll turn on the TV, and you can watch some mindless show while I change. See, I have these wedge pillows to lean against. I can sit and read or watch television in perfect comfort. It's almost as good as your nice easy chair."

Leah settled in against the pillows and watched the ending of an old segment of *Gunsmoke*, which brought back memories of her father enjoying that show. Alan reappeared after only five minutes, sporting a pair of chinos and a T-shirt that said Carter Lake, Minnesota. He was carrying a light brown jacket and pulled it on as he came into the room.

"Where's Carter Lake?" asked Leah as they made their way back down the hall to the elevator.

"Its north of Minneapolis about seventy miles. Dad and I used to go there every summer to fish, and sometimes in the winter we'd do a little ice fishing and cross-country skiing. We'd rent a cabin that was more of a shack I guess, but I loved it. I'd like to buy property there and build a cabin of my own. That's

41

on my agenda, but I don't seem to have enough time to run up there and look at lots. Do you like to fish or cross-country ski?" Alan asked.

"I've never fished, ice or otherwise, and I've never skied, downhill or cross-country. I guess I'm just a city girl who never had a chance to go out into the countryside. When our family drove anywhere, I loved it, and I suspect I'd like cross-country skiing because I love snow, crazy as that might sound. I run and bike sometimes, but that's about it. I wasn't into sports, except running cross-country my junior and senior years."

The elevator pinged, indicating it had arrived at the third floor with someone undoubtedly inside. The doors opened, and Juneau stepped out. She seemed surprised to see Leah with Alan and did not hide her displeasure very well. "I saw your car, so I thought I'd get you to take me out for a bite or maybe to that new bar with the three-piece band. I guess that won't be happening, unless you could find a friend to escort Miss … ah … Miss Anderson, is it?" Juneau looked coyly at Alan as she spoke.

"You're right: it won't be happening. Leah and I have plans, and they don't include a visit to that new bar. You shouldn't go there either, because you got into trouble on your last visit. Didn't Uncle Horace have to come get you at the police station?" Alan asked.

"Oh, that was nothing. It was just a misunderstanding. It's a great place with music and dancing, and the food isn't bad. Sure you won't change your mind? I know a guy I could call who would be delighted to get to know Leeeah," Juneau said with sarcasm.

Alan took Leah's arm, and they entered the elevator. Before Juneau could react, Alan had pushed the button, closing the door, and they were on their way to the first floor. "Sorry about Juneau once again. She's one reason why I'd like to move out on my own. Her rooms are on the other side of the house, but she finds excuses to come see me, especially if she sees my car. She can't drive, although she owns a beautiful BMW convertible that her aunt bought for her. She has three DWIs, so her license has been suspended. But enough about Juneau. Let's go find a place to eat."

Alan took Leah to one of the favorite haunts for Northwestern students, and they enjoyed the atmosphere and the food as well. A stroll across campus brought back memories for both of them, and they discovered they were acquainted with several of the same people who had been in pre-law. "I wish we had met back when we were students," Alan said, taking Leah's hand as they crossed the parking lot on their way back to the car.

"That would have been nice, but we can't change history. Did you enjoy your college days?" Leah asked.

"Most of the time, but I guess I was still grieving the loss of my dad, and I know I regretted having no mother. Uncle Horace tried to get her to visit, but she had my half sister by then, and my brothers were still in the Portland area and were in and out of her house. I did feel left out, but Uncle Horace did his best to make up for everything I was missing. Well, enough wallowing in self-pity. Time to get you back to Hyde Park. It's getting late."

Chapter 5

The next day Leah was looking forward to a quiet Saturday and Sunday to do some sorting and cleaning out of boxes she had stashed in her spare bedroom. Alan had left earlier that afternoon for Philadelphia, where he planned to visit an old college roommate before spending three days of interviews and depositions for an upcoming case in December or January. Her apartment seemed very quiet, so Leah turned on the radio to listen to the Los Angeles Philharmonic Orchestra playing live in the Hollywood Bowl. The music helped her to forget what had been going through her head ever since the previous evening. Alan had said she was very important to him! Was it too much to hope that the two of them could have a relationship that would lead eventually to an engagement and even marriage? She couldn't remember ever feeling this way about previous boyfriends. What she liked best about Alan was his sense of humor and his ability to converse on any subject, something they had done each time they were together. He was also very considerate. Maybe he hadn't been very kind to Juneau Friday night, but she had pretty much deserved what he had said to her. It was seven o'clock when Leah stopped working and made a pot of tea and fixed a sandwich. She was just sitting down to enjoy her meal when the phone rang.

"Hello, this is Leah," she said.

"Hey, Leah, I miss you. I didn't plan to call, but as soon as I got into my hotel room, I saw the phone sitting there, and it said, 'Call Leah.' Of course I'm on my cell, but I guess wired phones and wireless ones communicate. What are you doing? Do you miss me too?" Alan asked.

"What a surprise to hear from you. Yes, I think I do miss you. In fact I know I do because I was just thinking about you. How was your flight? Any problems?"

"No problems at all, which is a surprise. I got a cab right away, so I'm all settled in for the night. I called room service for a little repast. I wish you were here to enjoy it with me. I suppose you've already eaten. It's past seven your time."

"I'm having a cup of tea and a peanut butter sandwich right now. You're probably going to have something much more exciting than that, but the peanut butter jar called to me." Leah smiled as she imagined Alan on the other end of the phone line.

"I'd rather have peanut butter with you than the ham and cheese I just ordered. By the way, my old roomie bugged out on me. His in-laws are having a surprise anniversary party, which was a surprise to his wife as well. He only learned about it this morning, but we're meeting for breakfast tomorrow and will hook up with another classmate from across the river in New Jersey. What are you doing tonight and tomorrow?"

"I've been going through boxes that I haven't looked at since I moved here. I've already set aside things to donate and other things I want to find a place for. I hope to finish the project tomorrow. I guess I won't see you again until Thursday. I think you said you had to be in Philly for three days, or did that include Sunday?"

"It doesn't include Sunday, sorry to say. My flight gets in Wednesday night very late, but how about a Thursday lunch, since we'll miss what seems to have become a traditional Wednesday dinner. I hope you're free on Saturday. I want to take you to a dinner and dance in Evanston. It's a wedding reception for the daughter of one of Uncle Horace's neighbors. I've known them a long time, and the bride and I were good friends and science partners our senior year. She's marrying the guy she dated in high school. They broke up briefly when they both went off to college, but by Christmas it was on again. In my estimation they were meant for each other. I could see that already in back then."

"Are you sure you want to take me? I won't know anyone, and there will be countless young women who will be dying to dance with you. I would just get in the way," Leah said, half in jest and half seriously. She was concerned about being in a crowd of the rich and famous. Maybe she was being too sensitive, but she knew she didn't fit in with Alan's friends who had grown up in families where money was never a concern. She had learned early in life to save and to spend carefully.

"Of course I want you to be my date. The invitation says 'and guest,' and that will be you. It arrived by special delivery this morning. It's a hurry-up deal because the groom is being deployed to the Middle East next month and they want a honeymoon before he leaves. He's a lieutenant in the marines. The other part of my invitation has to do with overnight plans. The wedding is set for five thirty, with a reception, dinner and dancing afterward. Festivities won't begin until seven thirty, so we're looking at a very late night. I'll arrange for the guest room in my suite to be prepared, and I will stay there, and you can have my king-size bed. I know you were eyeing it with lust when you were there with me recently. Am I right?" Alan chuckled, teasing Leah as he often did.

"Well, I don't know. I suppose it will be all right, but I can certainly stay in the guest room. No need for you to give up your bed. I've never slept in a king-size bed before. I'd probably get lost. Really, Alan, the guest room will be just fine. I suppose I should bring my wedding finery and change there."

"Yes, bring clothing for the wedding and something casual for Sunday. If the weather's warm and not too windy, I'd like to take you out on the lake. Uncle Horace has a boat I can use, and we could even try fishing. You said you'd never fished before, so it could be fun. How about it?"

"Sure, why not? Another first in my life."

"My food is here, and I'm famished. Maybe I'll get a chance to call you late tomorrow or Tuesday. If not, I'll see you Thursday for lunch. Good night, sweet Leah. Dream of me."

Leah hung up the phone, smiling. She was already picturing the two of them dancing.

Chapter 6

On Monday Leah left the office precisely at noon. She was fortunate to catch a bus going in the right direction, and in ten minutes she was in front of Nola Randolph's open door. Nola was speaking on the phone and motioned to Leah to come in and close the door, which she did.

Nola finished her call abruptly, which was her manner, both on the phone and in person. "Well, I suppose you're anxious to hear what I've dug up about your Lizzie. Here, take a look at this. Skim it, and then we can talk." Nola handed Leah several pages of material, as well as couple of color photos, which appeared to have been taken recently. There was the gray house with the red shutters Leah had "remembered," and there were lilacs in the backyard, although there were no blossoms, since it was fall. No sandbox was visible, but several other pictures of the back and front yard clicked a hint of memory. The sandbox had been on the right side of the fenced backyard. How did she know that? There was no proof in the pictures, but it came to Leah as she looked at each one for the second time that she may have been in that house and that backyard and that she had seen those lilacs in bloom. When she looked up at Nola this time, she felt as though all the blood had drained from her head. She felt dizzy and more than a little anxious.

"I don't know, but I think I recognize … No … that's too strong a word. I have a feeling that I might have been in this house and yard. Maybe I visited there with my parents, or maybe, as you hinted, I could be this long-lost Lizzie. Oh God, I hope not. What would that mean?"

Leah felt uneasy and almost wished she had not started this search. She looked up to discover Nola studying her intently. "Well, Leah, do you think you could be Lizzie?"

Leah stared at the printed material as though it would somehow give her the answer to Nola's question. Could she be Lizzie? She didn't think she wanted to be Lizzie, but that didn't answer the question.

Nola reached out and touched Leah's hand. It was the first time she had done anything remotely personal. "I think you should go there. Not right away. Give this some time to soak in. There's one thing that wasn't in the papers. Lizzie had a birthmark on the back of her head right at the neck line—a small brownish mark resembling a triangle. Do you have such a birthmark?"

Leah buried her head in her arms on the desk and began to sob.

"I guess that's a yes," Nola said softly as she again reached across the desk, putting her hand on Leah's head. Then she walked around behind Leah's chair and pulled her hair away from her neck. There was the birthmark. "Leah, you have a lot to decide. I'd go to Saint Paul with you, but I'm not good at that sort of thing. I'm an investigator, and I do that rather well I think. It would be better for you to go alone or perhaps with a friend. I know you don't have any relatives you're close to, and besides, it looks like they aren't your relatives after all. But don't go yet. Think it through, and figure out what you're going to say before you go."

Leah raised her head and wiped her eyes. She thanked Nola and assured her she would pay the bill as soon as she received it. Then she turned abruptly and left the office. The street was crowded with people going to and from lunch. Leah saw none of them. She walked all the way back to the office in a daze, trying to compose herself before she had to face her coworkers. There was a ton of work to finish before the end of the day, so she knew she had to get on top of her feelings. By the time she arrived at the door to the building housing the law firm, she had calmed down and decided what she would do and when she would do it. She desperately wished Alan wasn't away. Should she call him in Philadelphia? No, not a good idea. She knew how busy he was, and he might be in court right now. Maybe tonight she would call. By the time she reached her desk, she had made up her mind to block everything out and get her work done. She was doing some interesting research, and to her surprise she was quickly able to concentrate and make progress.

Promptly at 5:00 p.m. she turned off her computer, grabbed her jacket and all the paperwork from Nola, and headed for the bus. She was exhausted when she arrived at her apartment. A cup of tea helped her relax, and then she began making plans for how to deal with this new and startling information. She fixed toast to go with her tea and sat down to watch the seven o'clock news. At midnight she awoke, surprised that she had fallen asleep. Of course it was far too late to call Alan, and anyway her mind was still fogged with sleep. She stripped off her clothes and fell into bed, not bothering to put on her nightgown or brush her teeth. As she drifted off once again, she thought, *Mama would not like it that I skipped brushing.*

At five thirty Leah awoke again, and the whole Lizzie scenario began playing in her head. Why would her parents have abducted her? Why was her birth date not the same as Lizzie's? She still couldn't think of herself as Lizzie or even as someone named Elizabeth. She was Leah! Then she had a revelation. She would call her mother's mother, who Nola had discovered was still alive and living in Wisconsin. Surely her mother had kept in touch. In fact she was sure of it. There had been no letters in the boxes Leah had been sorting through, and she would have noticed a call to Wisconsin on the phone bill. But Leah had seen a prepaid phone card somewhere in the morass of papers she had gone through, so it seemed possible her mother had used it to call the grandmother Leah had been told was dead. This made her determined to get in touch by phone or, better yet, in person, with Grandmother McDermott. Maybe some answers could be obtained there.

Leah managed to make it through Tuesday and Wednesday, although one of her coworkers had asked if she was all right. Leah had wanted to scream, "No, I'm not all right. I don't know who I am!"

When Leah came to work Thursday morning, she walked past Alan's office to see if he was already in for the day. The door was closed, and even through the frosted glass she could tell there was no light on. She was due in a meeting at nine and had papers to gather to carry to the conference room. She was able to focus on the work at hand, but by noon when the meeting broke up, she was ready for the lunch Alan had suggested. A call to his cell went unanswered. *He must be in a meeting,* thought Leah, so she sat down to go through the mail that had been delivered while she had been away from her desk.

By one o'clock there was no sign of Alan, and his cell still went unanswered. Reluctantly Leah took the elevator to the second floor where there were vending machines for sandwiches, drinks, and candy bars. She selected a cheese sandwich and package of potato chips. She would have water with her rather unsatisfactory meal. She sat in her cubicle to consume her lunch and had almost finished when Alan appeared. "Leah, I'm sorry I missed our lunch date. I see you've eaten already. I was virtually held captive by the partners. They wanted to know everything about what went on in Philadelphia. I didn't realize how important they thought it was until they began to question me. Now I have to go back there next week with George Willett. I'm not very happy. I really don't think I'm the one that should be going, since I haven't been privy to most of the stuff they're dealing with. But Uncle Horace says he wants me involved, so I have no choice." Alan shook his head and paused.

Leah could see that Alan was agitated, and she had second thoughts about sharing her own news that had thrown into confusion her identity.

Alan went on, "But our date for Saturday is still on, as I won't leave for Philly until Sunday sometime. Our boat ride is probably not going to happen. I'm really sorry because I was looking forward to taking you out on the water. I've got to run, but if you're free for dinner, I told Uncle Horace that his plan for a family meal tonight will have to take place without me. You and I are going out somewhere. Why don't you pick a place? I have to go. They're bringing in lunch, and we're going to continue to talk while we eat."

Leah only had time to say okay before Alan headed for the elevator and another go-round with the partners. *Well,* she thought, *I don't think I want to be a lawyer with that kind of schedule. I wish Alan wasn't caught up in the frenzy that's apparently going on right now.* She had no idea what the problem in Philadelphia might be, nor did she care to know. There was enough work on her own desk to keep her occupied for the rest of the day and beyond, not to mention her concern about her personal dilemma.

At five thirty Alan appeared at her cubicle, a look of relief on his face. "Free at last! I was afraid they were going to go into a night session with dinner catered in, but thankfully George Willett said he had dinner guests coming, so everything will start up again tomorrow. What have you decided about dinner? What great place have you chosen?" Alan was smiling and looking a little more relaxed.

"I have a place in mind in Hyde Park that I hope you'll like. I'm ready to go if you are."

They took the elevator down to the entrance and walked across the street to the parking garage. Once in Alan's car they began to talk about the latest word out of the Northwestern football program. The best tight end they'd had in years had been involved in a car accident and was hospitalized. Bad news for the Wildcat fans and for the injured player.

As they came closer to the turnoff for Hyde Park, Alan asked where the restaurant Leah had chosen was and if they had reservations. "We're having Crock-Pot stew at Leah's Laid-Back

Bistro. I have homemade bread and I put the stew on this morning. It should be ready when we get there, so we can eat as soon as you like. Is that all right with you?"

"Wow! That's more than all right. I must admit I wasn't looking forward to sitting in a restaurant with lots of people talking and some obnoxious music playing in the background. If we want music at Leah's Bistro, may I choose?" Alan asked as he parked down the block from Leah's apartment building.

"Yes, and you can even set the table if you want to be really helpful." Leah jumped out of the car and headed to her apartment. "Come on, slowpoke," she called, grinning at Alan.

The aroma was wonderful when Leah unlocked her door, and they entered the apartment. "Do you want to eat right away, or would you prefer to relax before we dine? I might even have some cheese and crackers, and there's Coke or Mountain Dew." Leah was trying to read Alan's expression. She was pretty sure he was delighted with her invitation, but instead of responding to her offer of a little predinner snack, he took two steps toward her, pulled her into his arms, and kissed her.

"No, I don't want to eat right away, and I don't need any before predinner snack. I think I found what I really want." He kissed her again.

Dinner was put on hold while Alan pulled Leah over to the sofa. There he put both arms around her and nuzzled her neck. "I've missed you. Oh, how I've missed you. I hate to think of heading off to Philly again on Sunday, and with George Willett in particular. I'm sorry to say it, but he's pretty boring and always talks about his golf prowess. For two cents I'd chuck the firm and get into the kind of lawyering I had in mind when I graduated. Unfortunately I can't do that right now, but soon I hope I'll be able to tell Uncle Horace I'm through with Marsden, Willett, and Desmond. What do you think of that?"

"I must admit there are days I have the same thoughts, but I'm well paid, and I do love the research work. It's all the other stuff I could do without, but I suppose any situation is bound to come with drawbacks. No job is perfect, or so I've been told," Leah said.

"I know what you mean. I've thought about leaving more often these last few weeks than I ever have before. Enough talk for now. Let's get that wonderful-smelling stew on the table. I'm really hungry. At lunch everyone kept asking me questions, so I didn't have time to eat my entire sandwich before someone came in and cleared everything away."

Alan enjoyed a second helping of stew and three pieces of homemade bread. Leah apologized that she hadn't made anything sweet, since she had not realized she would be having a dinner guest. However, she found an unopened carton of Oreos, and with a cup of piping-hot tea, their dessert was quite satisfying.

When they had almost finished the tea, Leah told Alan everything that Nola had discovered about her parents' cutting off ties with their families and then about the abduction of the child Elizabeth McGregor and how it was very likely that she, Leah, was that abducted child.

Alan could hardly believe the story and kept asking questions that she had already answered. She assured him she was having the same trouble. "But the hardest part is accepting that my parents were untruthful. Why do you think they cut ties with their families, and why did they abduct me?"

Alan had held Leah's hand since she'd begun her story, and now he moved closer and put his arm around her, holding her tightly. "Maybe they couldn't have children, and then they saw you and grabbed you on the spur of the moment. After that it might have been awkward or dangerous to give you back, even if they had wanted to. Oh, I don't know. I don't have any idea why they would have done what they did. I wish I could have met them. From your description of your parents I find it hard to imagine something like this happening. What are you going to do? Will you go to meet your other family and tell them you're probably their daughter? Are they still alive? There are lots of questions, aren't there?" Alan looked at Leah, trying to judge what she might be feeling.

"I think I might visit my mother's mother in Wisconsin. She's in a nursing facility just outside of Milwaukee, so that's not far. If her memory is sound, maybe she can enlighten me on some of this. In my mind I keep referring to her as my grandmother, but I guess she really isn't, if this whole nightmare is the truth."

"I'm sorry I have to go back to Philly on Sunday. I could go up there with you, and we could confront your grandmother together. *Confront* isn't the right word, but do you think she knew that her daughter and husband abducted a child?"

Leah nodded. "I'm almost positive my mother was in touch with her on a regular basis. There are no letters and no record of phone calls, but I found a prepaid phone card, so I think Mom used that to call her while I was at work. I'm thinking of renting a car and driving up there on Sunday now that you're off to Philly, but I surely would have loved to have you with me."

"You don't have to rent a car. You can use mine. After our big date Saturday night and your overnight stay, you can drive it home or head off for Milwaukee right from my house. You'll be closer to the Wisconsin state line here in Evanston." Alan offered.

"You're really serious about my spending the night? What would my mother say?" Leah grinned.

"I don't know. What would she say? I've told you that you'll have your own bed and it would make going to Wisconsin much easier. On Monday you could drive to work and leave the car in the parking garage across from the firm, or you could drive it back and forth all week. Your choice. What do you think?"

"It might be a good plan, but I probably won't drive back and forth. Parking space is tight in this neighborhood, so the parking garage would be better. If you're willing to trust me, I'd love to take your car on Sunday."

Alan assured Leah that he trusted her completely, so they sketched out their schedule for Saturday and Sunday. Then

Alan said he really had to leave because he had laundry to do and Uncle Horace wanted a conference at nine thirty. "I can just make it if I leave in ten minutes. Shall we do the dishes? I'll help."

"No, I'll do them after you're gone. Let's just sit here and enjoy the music you put on for dinner. It's still playing, and yes, you chose well."

After Alan left, Leah cleaned up the kitchen, humming to herself. She felt so much better having shared Nola's discoveries with Alan and having had a chance to voice her very real feelings, and yes, even her fears about what might be ahead of her if she decided to make the trip to the Twin Cities. Perhaps Alan could go with her on that journey, but she would have to make the run up to Milwaukee for a visit with her grandmother on her own.

Midafternoon on Friday Alan stopped by Leah's cubicle. "I've only got a minute while we're on a break, but I wanted to confirm that I'll pick you up tomorrow at two thirty, if that's all right. Don't forget to bring along whatever you need for your trip to Wisconsin, as well as your dancing duds. I hope you'll be forgiving if I step on your toes. I haven't danced since college." Alan looked down the hallway and then quickly came around Leah's desk, held her chin in his hands, and kissed her. "Until tomorrow," he whispered and hurried away.

Chapter 7

Saturday morning Leah had an appointment with a hairdresser. She had decided that her plain wash-and-go look needed a little spicing up for the high-class wedding she would be attending with Alan. She borrowed a mid-calf-length strapless dress with a sequined short jacket from her good friend Paula, who had worn it to a wedding last fall. She'd purchased a new pair of sandals to match the dress on Friday over her lunch break. Leah was ready for the big event.

Alan arrived a few minutes early, but Leah had already put her luggage and the carrier bag with her dress near the door. She was tidying up the kitchen after a late lunch when her bell buzzed. She came out into the hall and leaned over the stair railing to make sure it was Alan. He came bounding up the stairs, grinning his mischievous grin. "I've got a surprise for you, lovely Leah." He was holding something behind his back.

"Well, come in, and don't keep me guessing what it is," Leah said, her own smile reflecting his.

Alan extended a small oblong box to her. "Open it. I hope you like it. If you don't, it can be returned."

Leah carefully pulled the paper away from the small box and opened it, revealing a beautiful silver bracelet and a pair of matching earrings. She was blown away. She had not thought Alan might give her a gift, now or anytime soon. She sat down on the sofa and carefully lifted the bracelet from the box.

Alan sat beside her, watching intently as she tried to fasten the clasp on the bracelet. "Here, let me help," he said. Leah held up her arm, admiring the bracelet, and then she removed her tiny imitation-pearl earrings and inserted the silver ones. "Oh Alan, these are so beautiful, but you shouldn't have gotten me such an expensive gift. I don't know what to say, except thank you, thank you so much. I love your gift and will enjoy wearing them tonight." She rose quickly and stood in front of the mirror above the small table by the front door. Her smile told Alan she was very pleased.

"You know, I've never given a girl a personal gift like this before, so I was unsure about the selection. I'm glad you're pleased, and I hope they'll go with whatever you're wearing tonight."

"They'll be just perfect." Leah came back and seated herself on the sofa beside Alan once again, and then she put her hands on his shoulders and kissed him quickly. As she pulled away, he pulled her back and kissed her again and then several more times.

"I could do this all day, but I suppose we'd better go," Alan said. "There's a college game at Soldier Field that will end soon, so we should try to beat the traffic. Are you ready, Miss Anderly, for a fabulous evening of dinner and dancing? I know I am."

The drive to Evanston was uneventful traffic-wise. Leah and Alan kept up a steady stream of conversation as they made their way north. The radio had been tuned to the Northwestern game, but it was halftime for a good portion of the trip, so they could talk without having to keep one ear on what was happening in Columbus, Ohio, where the game was being played.

When they arrived at the mansion, as Leah had privately termed it, there was no one in sight. Alan picked up Leah's bags, and they entered the house and took the elevator to the third floor. Once in Alan's suite of rooms, he announced that he would be giving her his king-size bed and he would be sleeping in the guest room. "My bathroom here is more spacious, and you'll have room to set out all your war paint and whatever else women carry around with them," he said, grinning.

"For your information, Mr. Parkin, I use very little 'war paint,' as you call it, and I'm sure there's plenty of room in the guest bathroom. I know from experience that moving things to another room can be a bit inconvenient."

"Well, I suppose we could share the room. Heaven knows the bed is big enough, and the bathroom has two sinks. One for you and one for me. What do you think?"

"I'll not even comment. I'll stay here, even though I think the smaller bedroom would be just fine. I won't know how to act in such a spacious area as this," Leah said, waving her arm to indicate how large Alan's bedroom seemed to her. "And the view is something I'm not used to either, but I love it."

Alan hung up the garment bag, and Leah removed the dress, wanting to make sure it hadn't gotten wrinkled in transit. "Oh wow! You'll be a knockout in that dress! I hope you didn't buy it especially for this event—"

Leah interrupted, "No, I borrowed it from Paula, who has worn it at least once, so it's secondhand, and I'll be giving it back to her on Monday. The nicest thing I had was too summery for a fall wedding, so I asked Paula to let me borrow this one." Leah smoothed the jacket as she hung it on a separate hanger.

Although Alan's bedroom door was open, a knock came, followed by "Hello, I saw your car, so I knew you were back. Oh, you have company. Again!" Juneau Barkley came into the room, the smell of floral perfume preceding her. Leah found scent, especially in heavy doses, to be offensive. She wanted to rush to the window and open it, but of course she didn't. Instead she said hello, and so did Alan, who then went on to ask Juneau what had brought her up to his space. *Space* was the exact word he used, which surprised Leah.

"I thought maybe you'd escort me to the wedding. Uncle Horace is going, but he's not much of a date. Is your friend staying long, or are you taking her back to wherever pretty soon?" Juneau looked hopefully at Alan, casting a disdainful look at Leah.

"Leah's my date for the wedding, the dinner, and dance. We might blow off the ceremony and just show up for the dinner and dance. You'll have a good time with Uncle Horace, and he'll make sure some young guys pay attention to you. Would you mind closing the door when you go out?" Alan asked, making it clear he wanted Juneau to leave.

"You're not very friendly today. Must be the company you keep. I'll see you at the festivities, but if I were you, I wouldn't blow off the ceremony. Uncle Horace is a special friend of the bride's father and is giving the young couple a generous check to help pay for their honeymoon, or so I heard." Juneau turned and at the doorway stared at Alan before issuing a parting jab. "Leeeah," she said with more than a hint of disdain, "I hope you have a good time and don't trip over Alan's or your own big feet." She slammed the door on her way out.

"Juneau's in rare form, as usual. I've been fending her off most of my life. Our families always vacationed together in the summer, and even after my mother left us, Uncle Horace kept inviting Dad and me. After my father died and I came to live here, I was captive to everything going on in this house. I'm grateful Uncle Horace took me in, but it wasn't easy to tolerate Juneau. By then she had been living here for some time. Let's drop this subject. I promise not to rant again about Juneau. Let's walk down to the beach. There's a lovely cove where we can sit on the rocks or in the warm sand if the wind isn't too strong and blowing spray. Come on, you'll love it."

Alan grabbed Leah's hand, and they took the elevator to the basement level, where Alan told her they had a straight shot to the beach, cutting off some walking. There was no wind, and the water lapped gently against the sand and rocks. They found a wonderful spot out of the wind. Alan sat down and invited Leah to sit in front of him and lean back. He placed his arms around her waist, and they sat that way for a long time, talking and watching the activity on the water, most of it far offshore. However, a huge cruiser came slowly by, and Alan waved. He told Leah the boat belonged to the Desmonds, but that their son and his wife were at the helm.

Alan suggested a walk along the shoreline because he wanted Leah to see some of the huge estates along the lake. He reassured her that it was all right since he knew almost everyone who lived in the area. They strolled along the shore, Leah delighting in the sun-drenched landscape with its waving sea grass and the blue of sea and sky. Soon, however, it was time to turn back and get ready for the wedding. They would have to skip the ceremony since they had spent more time at the lakeshore than they'd realized, and it was a twenty-minute trip to the church where the wedding was taking place. Instead, Alan suggested they should dress and go directly to the country club for the dinner and dance.

Back in Alan's room, Leah jumped into the shower for a quick wash-off, having picked up sand on her legs and feet. He headed off to the guest-room bath to shower. When he returned in half an hour, he was fully dressed in his tux but was carrying his socks and shoes. Leah was still in her robe and was working on repairing the hairdo her stylist had spent a long time getting just right. Alan leaned against the doorjamb and watched as Leah fiddled with comb, some spritz, and the hair dryer. "Do you have to do that every morning before you come to work? I mean, do you spend a lot of time getting your hair just the way you want it?"

"Oh no, I just wash my hair and then let it air-dry if I have time. Otherwise I do use the dryer, but I don't bother with these little curls and wispy strands. That's all the style, you know, so I was told this morning when I had the hairdresser fix me up so I would be presentable for high society."

"I suppose I've never noticed exactly how your hair looks when you come to work, but you always look just great to me, so I was surprised to see you working so hard to do ... what is it you called it? Curls and wispy strands? You look beautiful,

Leah, but I think I like the way you looked when I came by your cubicle and saw you for the first time several months ago."

"I didn't think you noticed me. I remember you coming by to introduce yourself, but I was pretty sure I hadn't made much of an impression. I had just knocked over a houseplant someone had given me, and there was dirt all over the desk and the floor, and I was trying to clean everything up."

"I thought you were delightful and had a great sense of humor. That's something I value in people. You made some joke about starting a garden on your carpet, or something like that."

"I was embarrassed that you came along just then. I liked you right away because you didn't look at me in a disapproving manner. Mr. Willett came in once when I was putting on my tennis shoes, which I do when I get ready to go home. Walking in heels to the bus or train and then home afterward isn't comfortable. But he disapproved, I could tell. Well, I'm finished with my hair, so I'm going to get dressed now. I won't be long."

"I'll be waiting right here, but if you need any help, I'm your guy. I'm good with zippers and buttons and even—"

Leah cut him off. "No help needed, thank you." With that she closed the door. Ten minutes later she emerged completely dressed, except for her shoes.

"Woo, woo, you are one hot-looking babe," Alan said, whistling to show his approval.

"I'm not sure I like the idea of being called a 'hot-looking babe.' Sounds a bit risqué to me. I was hoping for 'Leah, you're looking quite nice this evening.' That would be better I think." She laughed.

Alan got off the bed where he had been stretched out and came up to Leah.

As he put his arms around her, she said, "Watch the hair … and the dress, and be careful because I don't have my shoes on. I've got a sore ankle, so I'm waiting until the last minute to put them on. I see you don't have your shoes on either. What's your excuse?"

"No excuse. I just like going shoeless. Here, sit on the bed, and I'll give you a foot massage. Maybe that will make your ankle feel better." Alan began to rub Leah's foot, with special attention to her ankle.

After a minute or so she said, "Ah, Alan, it's the other foot," and began to laugh.

Alan kissed the foot and grabbed the other one and repeated the treatment, which Leah agreed had indeed been helpful. They both sat on the bed, side by side, and Alan turned on the TV. The big wedge pillows behind them were wonderful supports and so very comfortable that in a matter of only a few minutes Alan had fallen asleep. Leah studied him as he slept. She noticed how long his eyelashes were and how, even in sleep, the dimple in his left cheek was faintly visible. He also seemed to have a hint of a smile on his face. She leaned back, and before long she too dropped off to sleep.

The ringing phone on the bedside table woke them both. "Hello," Alan said, still feeling somewhat disoriented. "No, we'll be there … We still have plenty of time, Uncle Horace. Sorry about not being at the wedding, but we thought we'd not be missed … Okay, sure. Yes, I will; I promise. See you in about twenty minutes."

"I guess I'm in the doghouse for missing the wedding, but Uncle will get over it. In fact he's already pretty much let it go. I'm supposed to apologize to the bride's parents, which I promised to do. Did you sleep too?" Alan asked, seeing Leah still lying back on the wedge pillow.

"I'm afraid I did. I think we're both running on fumes from lack of sleep. You especially, having flown from Philadelphia and then working twelve-hour days and even a couple of evenings. I suppose I'd better check my hair again. Napping probably didn't help my hairdo at all."

Leah fixed a few strands of hair, and they both put on their shoes and agreed that they were presentable for high society. "Time to face the music," Alan said. "Hopefully we can just dance with each other and ignore everyone else. That's what

I'm planning to do, but I may have to dance with the bride's mother. Uncle Horace mentioned that. Come on, beautiful, let's roll."

The reception was already under way, although not all the guests had arrived, including the wedding party. Picture taking was happening somewhere. Alan escorted Leah to the table where the punch was being served. They both chose the nonalcoholic punch and then piled some very tasty-looking tidbits of seafood, cheese, and even caviar on small plates. Leah had never had caviar before, and after tasting it she wasn't sure she liked it. Alan showed her how to put only a little on a cracker, saying, "It's better in small doses. I'm not all that fond of it either, but hey, it's expensive, so we have to pretend to like it, or they'll think we're rubes from the backwoods." They found a quiet corner where they sat and nibbled the food and sipped punch.

Dinner began a little late, but it was a fine meal, and almost immediately the band started playing. They saved the dance music until the newlyweds had finished their dinner and appeared for the traditional first dance, followed by the parents dancing with their respective children: father with daughter and son with mother. After that the floor was open for anyone, and Alan pulled Leah up for their first dance. She was feeling a little anxious since she had not danced in a long time, but they seemed to glide right along with the music, and she discovered she was really enjoying herself. After three straight dances Leah was ready for a break, so they made their way into a solarium that looked out over the golf course. The light had long ago faded, and a pale gibbon moon flitted in and out of a few clouds, casting shadows on the lawn.

"Nice wedding celebration, don't you think?" Alan said. "The meal was good too." Leah nodded, still looking out at the moonlit landscape. "What are you thinking about?" Alan asked. "You look like you're far away somewhere."

"Oh, I was just thinking about how different this celebration is from what my parents must have had. What about your parents? Did they have a big wedding and a huge party afterward?"

"I don't think so. They were married in a church, but I suspect it was a small affair in comparison to this one. My mother and Uncle Horace came from a middle-class family, and money was always tight. Uncle Horace of course made his fortune rather quickly. You know my parents met at Northwestern, where Mom had a scholarship. Dad's family was quite wealthy, although he cared less about money than my mother did. I used to think the breakup was all my mother's doing, but Dad probably wasn't blameless. Of course my mom's drinking problem was the biggest thing they had to deal with." Alan paused. "Sorry I got off on all that. When I get married, I'd like to do it quietly with only very good friends present and a small party afterward. Or maybe forget the party altogether. What about you? Are you an advocate of big weddings or not?"

"Honestly, I haven't given it a thought. I know some girls plan their weddings long before they even have a candidate for a husband. I think I might concur with your small-wedding idea. Maybe it's because neither of us has a huge family that we see having a few friends in attendance as a good idea. Right now I'm in limbo. Do I have one family or two? I wish this whole ordeal was over."

"I'd really like to go with you tomorrow. I'm sorry I can't, but I want to hear from you when you find out anything. Maybe we can talk tomorrow night after you get home and I'm in Philadelphia. I'll call you."

"I look forward to that," Leah said. Then Alan suggested they return to the festivities and do more dancing. The music had picked up tempo, but they were able to adjust and seemed to be doing as well as most of the other couples. At the end of the number, as they were waiting for the band to begin another set, Juneau came up behind Alan and linked her arm in his. "I'm claiming the next dance, so, Miss Leeeah, maybe you ought to find yourself another partner."

Leah decided not to react and instead said, "Go ahead, Alan. I'll sit over there near the solarium. Enjoy!" Then Leah walked away, much to Juneau's surprise. Leah heard her make another snide comment to Alan about his "snooty" date.

Watching Juneau and Alan dance amused Leah. She could see that Alan was an unwilling partner and that Juneau was annoyed with him. Alan was being less than gracious, if body language and facial expressions were good indicators. Juneau tried to dance closer to Alan by putting both arms around his neck and pressing her body against his. He, however, reached up and removed her hands, and began dancing farther apart than before. As soon as the band segued into the second song of the set, Alan steered Juneau toward the sideline, where Uncle Horace was talking with a couple who looked to be in their late sixties. She couldn't hear what was being said, but it seemed to Leah that Juneau was complaining to her uncle that Alan was not a willing dance partner. After a few exchanges, Alan turned away, giving the couple and Uncle Horace a slight nod, and then made his way back to Leah.

"Free at last! Juneau is really ticked off because I wouldn't listen to her prattle about you. Uncle Horace tried to soothe her and asked me to take her over for a drink at the bar. That's the last thing Juneau needs. She's already well on her way to a Sunday-morning hangover. Come on, let's dance."

A half hour later the band took a twenty-minute break, but before and after that Alan and Leah danced every dance. At a few minutes past midnight Alan suggested they ought to leave, since Leah had planned an early departure for Wisconsin. The crowd had thinned somewhat, but there were still twenty or thirty people on the dance floor and more sitting at tables scattered around the edges of the dance floor, nibbling on snack food and drinking.

When they reached the mansion, Alan parked the car so that it was headed down the driveway to make it easier for Leah to negotiate the semicircular drive in the morning. When they reached the third floor and Alan's suite of rooms, both of them

Dona Buchheim

66

agreed that they were too tired to sit and talk, and neither of them wanted anything more to eat or drink, which was how they usually ended their evenings together.

"Why don't you get ready for bed, and I'll tuck you in and then go off to my lonely little guest bedroom," Alan said. "Meanwhile I'm taking off my shoes, turning on the TV, and watching the late-night sports show to see who won and who lost today. Take your time, so I can see most of the report. I don't have TV in my lonely little bedroom." He grinned, once again teasing Leah.

Leah undressed, donned her nightgown, washed her face, and brushed her teeth. Alan had said to take her time, so she did. When she came out of the bathroom, Alan was sound asleep, his head on one of the pillows and his bare feet tucked under the folded coverlet at the end of the bed. She smiled. He looked almost angelic. She hated to wake him, knowing how tired he had been all day, and then they had danced most of the evening, so he was obviously exhausted.

I think I'll go over to that "lonely little guest bedroom" and let Alan have the big king bed. He'll know where I've gone come morning, she thought. She gently pulled the coverlet over him before she tiptoed out. Once in the hallway, Leah realized that she had no idea where to find the guest bedroom. When Alan had given her the tour, they had not actually gone into the bedroom, and Leah's memory failed her as far as knowing which one of the multiple doors was the correct one. She tried the first door and discovered a room full of boxes and books and old furniture. Baby beds took up space in another small room. The next door led to the room with the twin beds, but there were no mattresses … only springs, some of which were broken and poking up in various directions. The guest-bathroom door stood open, but an adjacent door was locked. She stood there in the hall, trying to figure out where the room could be. She had no memory of its location. She went back into the living room and gave a cursory glance at the small settee, but discarded the idea of trying to sleep there. It was too short by half and hard as a rock. None of the straight-backed chairs were the least bit comfortable. The hardwood floor and its rather threadbare oriental rug would not be a suitable bed either. She returned to Alan's bedroom and looked around for somewhere to lie down. The bed was the only option.

"Okay, Leah," she said to herself, "it's a big bed, and if you crawl in and hug this edge, it will be okay." Then she giggled, remembering a story she'd read a long time ago about bundling. Young couples who were courting would often spend a night or two in the same bed, with a board in between them. She had no board, but there were those wedge pillows, so she picked up two of them and laid them down the middle of the bed. Then she crawled in on the side opposite of where Alan lay sleeping. She could hear his rhythmic breathing, and somehow it was soothing and reassuring, and she soon fell asleep.

At three in the morning Leah heard a slight noise and saw a light under the bathroom door. Alan must have awakened. Should she feign sleep or say something when he came out? The toilet flushed, followed by the sound of running water, and then the light turned off. She heard Alan's footfalls on the hardwood floor and then a plunk, plunk, signaling the tossing of the wedge pillows onto the floor. Then Leah felt Alan stretched out behind her. He wrapped his arm around her waist, spooning her and kissed her neck. She turned her head and saw a smiling Alan, lit by the moonlight coming through the window.

"Oh, you're a sly one, Leah Anderly. Here you are so warm in my bed, and my feet are so cold from that tile floor in the bathroom. See?" He stroked her legs with his cold feet.

"Stop! That's freezing." Leah laughed. Alan also laughed, and he pulled her around so they were facing each other. He kissed her cheeks and then her lips. As they drew closer together, she realized he was no longer dressed in his tux or anything else except his boxers. What should she say or do? Even in the dark she could see Alan was looking at her, their faces only an inch or two apart. He kissed her again, and she knew she would say nothing, didn't want to say or do anything to stop what was now inevitable. Instead of speaking, she put both arms around Alan's neck and drew him in for another kiss.

Chapter 8

Leah and Alan awoke when the morning sun came pouring in through the east window and fell in long shafts on the bed they shared. It was obviously going to be a beautiful day. "Good morning, lovely Leah," Alan said, his eyes and his mouth smiling down at her as he raised up on one elbow. "You're gorgeous, you know. Absolutely, wonderfully gorgeous. Did I tell you I love you? Well, I do. You know, don't you, that we now have to be married. I'm ready to propose officially, since you refused to allow me to do that in the middle of the night. I'll get down on one knee and say all the right words and mean them. Speak, lovely Leah."

"I love you too, Alan, but as I said last night, the proposal has to be traditional because someday when our children ask us about our engagement, I don't want to say it was in bed, the first time we declared our love in a very beautiful way. But I think we both ought to get dressed before this little performance takes place. And I'd like a shower. Shall I go first?" Leah asked, running her finger along Alan's cheek.

"The shower's big enough for two, so come on. It'll save water, and I know you're all about being eco-friendly." Alan rolled out of bed and then came around to the other side, where Leah had turned to get up. He pulled her into his arms, kissed her, and then led her into the shower. There was much laughter, and Alan conceded after they had finished that they probably had used more water than if they had showered separately.

Alan made a pot of coffee and fixed cereal for them. "Sorry, I'm out of bread, but I have these wonderfully healthy Pop-Tarts. Strawberry or blueberry?"

"Strawberry please." Leah was enjoying Alan's attempt at breakfast hospitality, and she admitted she had not had a Pop-Tart in years. Over breakfast they laughed and talked again about the wedding celebration of the previous night, and when they had finished their second cup of coffee, Alan knelt down on one knee in front of Leah and said, "Leah Anderly, I'm hopelessly in love with you and want you to be my wife. Will you marry me?"

"Alan Parkin, I accept your proposal, with all my love."

"When shall we do this surprising thing? How about next weekend?" Alan said with a grin, knowing it wasn't even remotely possible. "I do want it to happen before the year is out. We're just three weeks away from Thanksgiving, but maybe a New Year's Eve wedding would be fun. What do you think?"

"I like the idea of a New Year's Eve wedding, but what sort of wedding? Would it be something like we talked about last night ... a small gathering of friends and of course your uncle and then a meal somewhere afterward? What are your thoughts?"

"Your thoughts are my thoughts. The fewer frills, the better. But I guess I had the impression that brides always wanted their wedding day to be the highlight of their lives, with all the bells and whistles."

"Alan, you can get up off your knees now. The floor is hard, and it can't be comfortable kneeling there. Sit across from me. All right, now I'll tell you ... I'm not interested in all the bells and whistles. You, Alan, will be the joy of the celebration of marriage for me. Everything and everyone else is secondary. But if you want bells and whistles, I won't say no."

"I do believe we have a meeting of the minds here. Simple is good. So New Year's Eve? And where?" Alan asked, reaching across the table for Leah's hand.

"New Year's Eve would be lovely if we can pull it off, but there's Philadelphia. Will you be finished by then? And as to where, I'd like to be married in my little Methodist church down the street, but if you have somewhere else that's important to you, I'm willing to negotiate." Leah looked expectantly at Alan and added, "Why don't we put off making any decisions until next weekend? We can each give some thought to what we'd like and decide details later."

"I suppose that's the sensible thing to do. I just know I want to spend my life with you, and come hell or high water, that's going to happen. I suspect Uncle Horace will be a hard sell, but I'll tell him this afternoon before I leave for Philly."

"Sad to say, I have to think about going north to Wisconsin, and you have to hang up your tux. I saw it lying on the floor of the bathroom, right where you stripped it off in the middle of last night."

Leah came around the table and put her hand on Alan's shoulder and leaned in to kiss him. He pulled her into his lap and said, "So you noticed I had shed my duds. I planned to go to the guest room, but there you were in the bed, looking so sweet, and well, we both know what happened next. I feel a little guilty this morning. I took advantage of the situation, but you didn't say no. Did you want to say no? I hope you didn't."

"I thought briefly about it and questioned the wisdom of what I knew we were about to do, but I didn't say no, and I'm not sorry."

"I'm not either, and I didn't question the wisdom of it either, because I knew I loved you and wanted us to spend the rest of our lives together, which we shall do. Uncle Horace may sputter and rant and tell me I'm making a mistake, but he doesn't know you at all … only as an employee, and even in that area he's clueless about your value to the firm. Oh, Leah, we have so much to talk about, but it's time to get you headed to Wisconsin. I wish we were both going."

Chapter 9

Leah left only a half hour later than she had planned, and by nine thirty she was carefully negotiating the long driveway to the street at the bottom of the hill upon which Horace Marsden's house perched in all its splendor. Traffic was light, and she easily found her way to the main road leading north into Wisconsin. She arrived at the Sunnyside Nursing and Long-Term Care Facility earlier than anticipated. After parking Alan's car, Leah sat there surveying the well-maintained building and grounds. There were several brightly colored lawn chairs and a few tables with striped umbrellas on a cement patio. Fall flowers in a profusion of color grew in circular beds on either side of the front entrance, giving a feeling of welcome to the place.

Leah entered the facility through a wide front door that opened into a hallway that stretched to what appeared to be the dining area. To her left was a reception desk, and positioned nearby were several easy chairs. A young woman wearing a bright-green dress came down the hallway from the right. "Hello," she greeted Leah. "Are you here to visit one of our residents?"

"Yes, I'm here to see Corinne McDermott. I'm her granddaughter, but this is the first time I've been here. She knows I planned to come."

"Oh yes, she mentioned a visitor. Let me see if she's ready for guests. Be right back." The young woman strode off back down the hallway from which she had come and disappeared into a room halfway along the corridor. When she returned, she smiled at Leah and said, "Come with me," as she turned and led the way into a room with easy chairs and sofas, a piano, and several tables with chairs pushed in around them. A half-finished jigsaw puzzle lay on one of the tables, and cards were stacked on another. "You can wait here, and someone will bring your grandmother to you. It won't be long. She was just getting her hair combed." The young woman turned and, with a parting smile, disappeared around the corner.

Leah studied the room. So far she was pleased with everything she saw, both outside and inside. She hoped the care was as good as the physical building and grounds. In only a few minutes, a wheelchair appeared, pushed by a young man who looked to be in his mid to late twenties. He smiled at Leah as he approached, pushing her grandmother. "Good morning. You must be Leah. Corinne told me about you. I hope you have a great visit." Then to Corinne he said, "Use your call button when you're ready to go back to your room. If you get tired, I'll come get you."

Corinne nodded and watched her attendant leave. Then she studied her granddaughter intently for a few seconds before she spoke. "My dear granddaughter, it's so good to see you again. It's been twenty or more years since I last saw you. You've grown!" she said with a chuckle. "I'm so pleased you found me and that we can talk. I'm sure you have lots of questions."

"I do. When did you see me for the first time? How old was I, and where was it?" Leah asked.

"You were just past three. Actually, you were somewhat older than that, because your mother, Grace, gave you the birth date of the first Leah who was four months younger. She had been born to your parents in Whitney, Minnesota."

"Tell me about the first Leah."

Corinne paused and settled herself more comfortably before going on. "I'll tell you about the first Leah in a minute, but to answer your question, the first time I saw you was right after your father abducted you. Your parents were heading to Chicago, and on their way south, they stopped at our house. Your grandfather and I lived just north of Madison, Wisconsin, at that time. We were shocked to learn what your father had done. I asked him why, and he said it was because your mother was so unhappy. The first Leah, their daughter, had died the previous year, and though they'd tried to have another baby, they had been unsuccessful. Two miscarriages, followed by radical surgery to save your mother's life, made it impossible for her to have more children. She was heartbroken, and your father couldn't stand to see her suffer. Adoption was out of the question because of his criminal record, even though his guilt in the whole matter had never been properly settled and wasn't likely to be."

Leah was stunned. "I had no idea about any of this. I wish my mother had told me, but I suppose she didn't know how to begin. What was the cause of death of the first Leah?"

"She had a weak immune system according to the doctors. Right from the beginning she suffered from infections that often hospitalized her. Her death was attributed to pneumonia. She's buried in a little cemetery on the edge of the Iron Range in Minnesota. Your parents lived there briefly just before Leah's death. I can give you directions if you ever wish to visit the grave site."

"I can see now why my mother was always so concerned about my health. Whenever I'd get the sniffles, she'd hover over me until I got well, but fortunately I was a very healthy child and never spent any time in the hospital and had no serious illnesses."

"Your mother was grateful for your good health, and so was I. The next and last time your grandfather and I saw you was when we came to Chicago a year later. Grace had been sick, and I was worried about her. She had a severe case of bronchitis that turned into pneumonia. We stayed for a week to care for you and for her, but when we left, it was agreed there would be no more visits, and we were sworn to secrecy about your whereabouts. It was the first anniversary of your kidnapping, and your dad had seen an article about your abduction in the Chicago paper that reported you had not been found, dead or alive. Harold, your dad, didn't want to take any chances that he might be found out or that, more importantly, they might find you. His family had no idea where he was or that an abduction had occurred. I didn't see how it would matter if we visited. We weren't going to tell anyone, but we went along with it. Grace and I called each other on special occasions, and in the last years since your father's death, we talked at least once a month and more often when she developed cancer. I wanted to come then, but of course I wasn't physically able. I have severe arthritis that keeps me in this chair, but my mind is still sharp. At least I think so. I asked Grace several times if it might be a good idea to tell you the truth about your origins, but she said she wasn't ready to lose you, so I stopped asking. Now, do you have more questions?"

Corinne studied her granddaughter to see what reaction this bizarre story was producing.

"I guess I'm wondering why Dad didn't tell his parents or at least let them know where he was living and that he was all right."

"That's another story. Your dad's father was an SOB, pardon my saying so, but it was true. His mother, his father's second wife, was a dear sweet woman. Your father's father and his first wife had two sons and a daughter. The first wife died in a house fire while he was out in the field and the children were in school. I always wondered about how it started and if he might have had something to do with it. He and his first wife didn't get along, which was no secret, and their children, the boys especially, were a handful. In high school they got in all kinds of trouble. When he married a second time and your dad was born, your grandfather seemed to be fine, doting on his new wife and baby son. But it wasn't long before he turned abusive again. I guess I didn't mention that he regularly beat his sons and his first wife. I never heard if the daughter had been ill-treated, but she left home at sixteen to get married, so it makes you wonder."

Corinne paused once again. "Are you going to find your birth parents, Leah? I only ask because I wonder how it might affect you. I guess I'd like to think you had a good upbringing. You certainly turned out to be a wonderful daughter, and I know Grace and your dad were very proud of you. But if you feel the need to find out about these people who are your blood family, I understand."

"I don't know what I'll do. There's a lot to think about and decide," Leah said.

The two women continued to talk on a variety of subjects. Just before Leah said she had to leave, she confided to her grandmother that she had a serious boyfriend and that perhaps she would be getting married before long. "Just to warn you that you may become a great-grandmother in the future."

"Does that mean you want to continue to think of me as your grandmother? I'd love that. You know, sometimes the ties we have with people who we're not related to by blood can be stronger and more lasting. I hope that will be the case with us. I don't know how long I have left in this world, but I'm not going to dry up and blow away. I have good reason now to stay alive. But you'd better get going, so you get home before dark."

Leah leaned over and kissed her grandmother's forehead. Then she put her hand on her grandmother's shoulder and repeated a blessing she had learned in Sunday school many years ago: "God be gracious to you all your life long. May he give you strength and keep you strong."

On the drive home Leah thought about her visit with her grandmother and what she had learned. She couldn't wait to talk to Alan tonight and tell him everything. The traffic was reasonably light until she reached the tollway, where progress slowed to stop and go for several miles, but she made it home just as the sun dropped behind her apartment building.

She wrote down everything she could remember from her conversation with her grandmother and added her own comments and analysis. Then she made a cup of tea and waited for Alan's call. At eleven thirty she decided his flight had been delayed, so she prepared for bed, and when midnight came and went, she turned out her reading light and went to sleep.

Chapter 10

Mondays were always busy at the firm, and this Monday was no exception. By the time Leah arrived at her desk, she had already picked up four folders of work. The phone rang incessantly until just before noon, so she decided to take her laptop into a conference room, where she would be able to work without interruption. By five she had managed to plow through all the folders and pass them along to whoever needed the information she had gathered.

Leah had driven Alan's car to work and parked across the street in the parking garage. He had said she could drive it as much as she wished, so she thought she might take it home for another night since she really wanted to make a run to Target for some things she needed. The bus connection was fine, but a car would be quicker and more convenient. The car was parked on the third level, so she took the stairs, just for the exercise. Someone was standing alongside Alan's car. The dim evening light made it difficult to see, and for a moment she was frightened it might be someone who would take her purse, the car keys, and then the car. She decided to walk on by, but she recognized the man as one of the maintenance employees at the firm. She was pretty sure his name was Mouskowski, but everyone called him Moose. She smiled and greeted him by his nickname.

Moose appeared to be nervous. He said, "I'm sorry, Miss Anderly, but I have instructions to get the keys to Mr. Alan's car and drive it up to Evanston. Mr. Marsden told me it was probably here. I had a hard time finding it at first, but that nice red color and the license plate helped me locate it. Can I give you a lift to the bus or the train?"

Leah was surprised. No, she was shocked that Mr. Marsden had sent Moose to take Alan's car. No word from Alan had come all day, which was a little strange, since he had said he would call during the day on Monday if they missed connecting on Sunday night.

"No, I'll be fine. My bus stop is two blocks away, so I can walk. Here are the keys. I'm kind of surprised because Alan lent me the car for a trip I took yesterday and said I could use it all week if I wanted to. I almost left it here tonight. I guess I'm glad I didn't. Now at least you can see it gets safely back to Evanston. Good night. See you tomorrow."

Moose nodded, looking a little embarrassed by the whole exchange, and got into the car and when Leah had reached the stairs, he was already driving down the ramp to the street.

The bus ride home gave Leah time to try to make sense of what had just happened. Obviously Uncle Horace had decided he didn't want her driving Alan's car. Fair enough, but why hadn't Alan called? Maybe he didn't even know about it. Well, she would wait until tonight when she was sure she would hear from him.

Leah fixed a bowl of soup and a sandwich and sat down in the living room in front of the TV to watch the seven o'clock news. She was just finishing her meal when the phone rang. "Hello," she answered.

"Hi, Leah, I've only got seconds to say this. Uncle Horace is on a rampage, and he's got George Willett riding herd on me. George wouldn't let me alone for a minute last night, and by the time he had downed his third drink, it was past one in the morning. By eight this morning he was at my door, and we headed to court, except nothing was going on. I'd had only five hours of sleep, and when I questioned him about coming by at such an early hour, he acted as if he didn't know how he had made a mistake about the time for our meeting. I'd tried to tell him there was no court session today. Then he herded me into the conference room at the hotel where some of the lawyers had been meeting. There were three of them there, but nobody was doing much of anything. When I said I had to make a phone call, George said we were not allowed to make calls while negotiations were in full swing, but there was no full swing, no negotiations at all actually. I began to get suspicious. You see, I told Uncle Horace before I left on Sunday that you and I are engaged. He also found out that you had stayed the night in my room. He was livid and told me you were … Well, I won't go into what he said. All of it was garbage. He forbade me to see you or talk to you again, and he said if I didn't promise to do as he said, he would kick me out of the law firm and disinherit me. I almost laughed in his face."

"Oh, Alan, I'm sorry."

"I don't care about the inheritance, and I have for some time thought about getting out anyway. There's too much politics and that old 'you scratch my back and I'll scratch yours.' Hey, they're coming. They don't know I have my cell. I'll call tonight if I can, unless George puts me in shackles. Love you, Leah."

That was weird, Leah thought. *Did Mr. Marsden actually send George Willett along to keep Alan from getting in touch with me? And what was all that about kicking Alan out of the firm? She couldn't believe Mr. Marsden would do that to his own nephew, whom he professed to love like a son. Am I so unacceptable? Is my pedigree so important?* Leah shook her head as she realized she hadn't had a chance to say anything to Alan except "I'm sorry."

The next day Leah left the office late because one of the junior partners had come in at four o'clock with a request for a case study that had to be on his desk before eight that evening. She made it, but just by a few minutes. He, however, was nowhere in sight. There was no one with whom she could leave the papers, so she took them back to her office, tucked them safely away in her filing cabinet, and locked it. She sighed. Somehow it seemed more like busywork to her than a real request for important information. She called the junior partner's phone and left a message, telling him where he could find the file and the key to the cabinet. Then she went home.

There was no message from Alan, although she was not surprised. She ate a quick dinner of chicken potpie and then lay down on the bed to hopefully catch some shut-eye because she was sure that if Alan called, it would be very late. She was right; at one thirty the phone rang. "Hey, did I wake you?"

"Sort of, but I was expecting a late call, so I curled up right after supper and had a little nap. What's going on?" Leah asked.

"GW took me out for dinner with three other lawyers, and afterward they wanted to go to a club. I told them I had work to do, but they virtually dragged me along, and I had to sit through a couple of cabaret acts with scantily clad women, most of whom, if you looked closely, had passed their prime. I sat there thinking about you and about our wedding, and finally about one o'clock they decided to call it quits. George wanted to come in for a nightcap, but I told him I didn't have any liquor in my room. He suggested we call room service, but I said absolutely not. I said I was dead tired, and as he continued to talk, I started undressing. By the time he gave up, I was down to my undershorts and had gone into the bathroom to brush my teeth. I guess he thought it was safe to leave and I wouldn't try to call you."

"I don't know what to say. It's so strange," Leah replied.

"I wish I knew what was going on. Oh, and I have to stay here over the weekend because we are to go up to Boston for a couple of depositions that can only be gotten on Saturday. We're staying through Sunday as well because we were given tickets to the Patriots' game. Then Uncle Horace and Juneau are coming on Tuesday, and we're all supposed to go to the Bahamas for Thanksgiving. He said that there was no negotiating but that once we're back, he'll talk about our engagement and marriage. What could I say? That seemed to be my only option. I could bolt right now, but I'd hate to. What do you think?"

"I suppose do as Uncle says and hope for the best. I hesitate to mention this, but it's your car, so you should know. I drove to work on Monday and planned to drive home and make a trip to Target, but when I got to the garage last night, Moose was standing beside the car, waiting for me. He had orders from your uncle to take the car back to Evanston. I of course gave him the keys. I didn't know what else to do. I hope that was all right. I'm sure Moose is a trustworthy person, and he did say he had orders."

"That's too much! I'm sorry you had to go through the humiliation. Uncle is going to hear about this from me!" Alan fumed.

"Don't worry about it. I'm not taking it personally. By the way, I had a great trip to see my grandmother and learned a lot from her that makes everything clearer, but I think I'll wait to tell you details. It's so late now, and you need your sleep. When do you think we might be able to talk again?"

"Maybe tomorrow night, but Thursday night for sure. We leave Friday noon for Boston, so who knows when I'll be able to call after that. I'll do my best. This cloak-and-dagger business is annoying, and I intend to let Uncle know I resent it. This thing with the car is over the top. I know what he wants from me. He wants me to get involved romantically with Juneau, but that ain't gonna happen! Don't worry, Leah; I'll work it out, and we'll still be married on New Year's Eve, come hell or high water. Good night, love; sleep well."

It was difficult for Leah to get back to sleep. Alan was having difficulties with his uncle, and it was all because of her. But what could she do? She mulled over their conversation and thought of things she ought to have said but hadn't and a couple of things she had said but maybe shouldn't have, such as reporting the taking of the car from the parking garage. Finally, at a little before four, she dropped off to a troubled sleep, dreaming of sinister beings in a dark space, waiting, waiting for her to come around the corner.

Chapter 11

Wednesday came and went, and that evening in her kitchen, Leah waited for Alan's call. At ten thirty the phone rang. She picked up and said, "Hello."

"Hello! Your Philly reporter checking in. I'm free to call you whenever. I talked to Uncle for a long time on the phone today, and we managed to straighten out a few things. I didn't make any waves about Thanksgiving. If that's what it takes … enduring five days with Juneau … I can handle that. How was work today?"

"Very busy. I have a stack of stuff piled up for first thing tomorrow, so I'm planning to go in by seven if I can. What about you? How's your work going?"

"Apace, as George says. I don't know what that means, but I don't think we're making much progress in getting our case laid out. I have ideas, but nobody wants to consider them, so I sit there, waiting for something meaningful to come out of the discussions and the research. I wish they'd let me bring a team from our Chicago office. We'd soon have what we need. Of course I'd want you to be the lead. But it won't happen. Everybody's too busy protecting their own turf. If this thing gets settled before Christmas, I'll be surprised. I want to come back to Chicago and do the kind of work I've been doing there, so when Uncle comes Tuesday, I'll spring it on him. Pray for me, Leah. I'm going to need all the help I can get. By the way, I won't be calling until Saturday; we've been invited

84

to some reception out on Long Island, and I'm to be attentive to the host and hostess. Friday we go to Boston, but Saturday morning I should be free to call."

Leah and Alan exchanged a few more personal words, ending with Alan's promise that they would tie the knot on the thirty-first of December, "come hell or high water," something he'd said several times before. It made Leah wonder whether Uncle Horace was exerting pressure that Alan had not shared. What could she do? Nothing. She would do her work diligently so that no one could find fault with her job performance. They said good night, and the connection was severed. Leah held the phone in her hand until the dial tone sounded. She was missing Alan more than she thought she would, and it didn't look as if they would see each other until early December. She had a feeling the wedding would not come off as Alan promised, but she couldn't put her finger on why this idea had crept into her subconscious. She shook her head, crawled under the covers, and tried to sleep.

As planned, Leah left her apartment the next morning before six. She was the first one on her floor and even had to turn on some of the lights. By nine, when most of the other people had arrived, she had lowered her stack of file folders and sent several off to their respective offices. Some of the work seemed repetitive, but maybe she was being picky. At any rate, there was no one to complain to, so she redid several request forms and copied files that she was sure were being requested a second or third time.

At nine fifteen she headed to the coffee room and poured a cup of hot cappuccino and grabbed a doughnut hole from a package someone had brought to share. She took everything back to her desk and had just taken her first sip when Horace Marsden came into her cubicle. She was surprised since she could not remember that he had ever stopped to see her or even made an appearance on the fifth floor, where she and the other researchers worked.

"Miss Anderly, I'd like a word with you. Please follow me." Horace Marsden turned on his heel and walked across the hall to an empty conference room, with Leah following close behind, wondering what it was all about. He closed the door and sat in one of the armchairs at the head of the long table. Leah remained standing and did not presume to sit unless invited. No invitation was extended.

"I'm sorry to be the bringer of bad news, but we are terminating your employment as of right now. You can go back and collect your personal items, but I want Helena Gross to check over what you take, to make sure nothing belonging to the firm leaves this building. I have here a check in the amount of five hundred thousand dollars, and for that I expect you not to contest this action or speak of it to anyone here employed, and you are not to contact Alan. He will be apprised of this in due time … perhaps on Saturday. I will fly out today, as I have some issues with him as well. You, Miss Anderly, are not a suitable choice for a wife, and I intend to make sure the two of you do not marry. Believe me, I have the will and the power to do this. Alan will fall in line if you stay out of his life. I learned from him that you were spirited away as a young child and raised by your so-called parents. If you think that can be overlooked, you are sadly mistaken. I understand the father that raised you never went farther than the tenth grade in school and worked his whole life as a janitor. That's not the sort of family background I care to have Alan marry into. Do you understand me, Miss Anderly? I have ways to make your life miserable if you decide to fight this, and I will do it. Now, here, take this pound of flesh. I suspect you'll run through this money as fast as you would have run through Alan's inheritance." He opened the door and then turned back as though to say something else. Leah, however, had something on her mind.

"Oh, you've been very clear indeed. You're an SOB, Horace Marsden!" *Where did that come from?* Leah wondered. *I don't care. What can he do to me? I was just fired, and I'm almost sure Alan won't be marrying me.*

Horace Marsden glared at Leah. He was red in the face as he fumed, "You're a no-good slut, and I don't ever want to see your face in this building again! Moose will escort you out! Now!" Horace Marsden walked quickly through the door, slamming it behind him.

Leah sat down in the chair she had been leaning on. She felt weak in the knees. What had she done to elicit such venom from a man she didn't know and who didn't know her? They had never had a conversation before today. She may have said "Good morning" to him a time or two, but that was it. She suddenly felt anxiety for Alan. How would he react? When would she hear from him, if at all? The check was in her hand, and she almost tore it in two but decided not to. Slowly she rose and stepped across the hall to her cubicle to gather her belongings. There wasn't much. In the storage closet she found an empty box into which she deposited her personal items. As she was closing the lid, Helena Gross entered her cubicle. Moose stood in the doorway, a sad look on his face. Leah said nothing to Ms. Gross. She hardly knew her, so it didn't seem necessary to make any comment one way or the other. After checking all her desk drawers, she set the box on the desk and gestured for Ms. Gross to look through it.

"Is this your laptop?" Ms. Gross asked.

"Yes, it is. It belongs to me and no one else." Leah turned on the computer and entered her name and password. The menu appeared. "See, it's mine!"

"How do I know you didn't program one of our laptops?" accused Ms. Gross.

"Because I tell you I didn't. Now get out of my way; I'm leaving. If anyone thinks this belongs to the company, they can sue me or come and get it, but you or whoever makes the claim had better have conclusive proof that it belongs here. Moose, please escort me out." Leah, head held high, walked past a stunned Ms. Gross, and followed by Moose, headed to the elevator that was just stopping. Kyle Jones, one of Leah's team members, was getting off.

"Hey, Leah, we've got a meeting in ten minutes. Where you going?"

"Tell everybody good-bye, Kyle. I got fired and am now being escorted out. You'll find the files you need on my desk. Some of the work has already gone to the respective offices, but you'd better follow up. I sent off the Billings file, the Graham/Hickman file, and both files on the Montague v. US/BC. Good-bye. Have a good life." Leah marched into the elevator, Moose at her heels. Inside, she faced the door and didn't look at Moose. When they reached the first floor, he held the button on the door to keep it from opening. "Sorry, Miss Leah, I don't know what this is all about, but it seems to me it's a bad idea. I hope you can come back and work here again. We'll miss you."

He let the door slide open, and Leah exited the elevator and then pushed her way through the revolving front door. On the street she hailed a taxi. Why not? She could afford it. After all she had a check for $500,000 in her purse!

There was no word from Alan the rest of the week or the beginning of the following week. With Thanksgiving looming she was sure he, Juneau, and Uncle Horace had already departed for the Bahamas. Maybe they'd left the previous Friday. Alan might not call until well after Thanksgiving or maybe never!

With no plans of her own for the holiday, the thought came to Leah that the day after Thanksgiving might be a good time to travel to Saint Paul to meet her "family." It wasn't something she was keen on doing, but it seemed only right that they should know she was alive and well. She called Nola at the detective agency to pick her brain about how she should proceed. Should she call them ahead of time or just show up?

Nola answered on the first ring, and after they had exchanged a brief greeting, Leah told her the reason for the call.

"Hmmm, I guess my gut feeling is just show up. It's going to be a shock to them no matter what, but you being there in the flesh might make it easier for them to accept the fact that you are their long-lost daughter. It could make it easier for you too, hopefully. But what do I know? I've never come across this particular problem before."

Leah knew Nola was about to hang up, so she said quickly, "I got fired, so now I'm unemployed. Don't worry; I already sent you a check, and if there's a cost for the advice you just gave me, I'll take care of that too."

"I'm so sorry, Leah. I'd go with you to Saint Paul, but as I said before, I'm good at investigative work, but the personal stuff isn't something I do well. Let me know how it goes up in Saint Paul, will you?" They ended the call with Leah's promise to report next week on her visit up north.

Thanksgiving was a quiet day for Leah. She shared a meal with her friend Paula, who was also alone, and in the afternoon she watched football and napped on the couch. At five that afternoon the phone rang. Caller ID did not tell Leah who was calling, only that it was from a strange number. She picked up and said hello.

"Leah, its Alan. I have to be brief because I'm at a pay phone and don't have much change. I just heard from Uncle that you've been fired, and I'm livid. He told me some tale about you not working well with the team and being late with assignments and so the decision was made to let you go. He said he gave you a nice parting bonus. You probably were angry and felt like tearing up the check, but I hope you didn't. I don't know how much it was, but if it was to keep us apart, which I'm pretty sure it was, it has to be a chunk of money. Don't give it back or destroy it. Use it. Go back to school and finish your degree if you want to. It looks like I'm going to be stuck in Philly until Christmas. This probably means our wedding won't take place on New Year's Eve. I'm just sick about all this. Oh, oh, I heard a beep, and I'm out of change. I love you, Leah. Stay strong."

The connection was broken. Leah realized that once again she had not been able to say anything, except hello.

She sat there, wondering how things had come to this. How could Alan's uncle have such influence over him? Why hadn't she been given a chance to meet Horace Marsden and for them to get to know each other? "Well, no use crying about it," Leah said aloud. But the tears came anyway.

Chapter 12

Friday morning Leah was up early to catch a flight to Saint Paul that left O'Hare at 8:00 a.m. A timely arrival in Minneapolis–Saint Paul allowed her ample time to rent a car and drive to the McGregors' home. The built-in GPS accurately directed her, and at ten forty-five she pulled up in front of the gray house with red shutters she had seen in her flashback. The colors had seemed brighter in her memory. Leah sat in the car for a moment, trying to formulate what she would say to whoever answered the door. It was a warm day for late November, and through an open window she could see a brief stretch of hallway illuminated by a ceiling light so she assumed someone was home.

Leah rang the doorbell and immediately heard footsteps. A young woman of indeterminate age stood there, seemingly hesitant to swing open the door.

"Good morning. I'm Leah Anderly, and I wonder if Mr. and Mrs. McGregor are at home. I'd like to speak with them about their young daughter who disappeared many years ago."

"Are you another reporter? Mama doesn't need any more supposed sightings or anyone giving her false hopes. I'm her daughter, so why don't you talk to me. I'll come out, and you can say your piece, and then we'll see."

"You must be Charlene. I've recently learned about your family, and I'm here today because it is almost a certainty that I'm the long-lost Lizzie. You may find that hard to believe, but

I believe it now after having a private investigator do some research. This is not some scheme to worm my way into your family or get money from you. None of that is my intention. I came to relieve your parents' minds and let them know their daughter is alive and doing well." Leah thought, *I'm not doing so well with my job or my fiancé!*

Charlene stood there, her mouth literally hanging open. "I don't believe you. Where have you been all these years, and why didn't you come forward sooner? Can you imagine what life is like here? Mama lives for word of her missing daughter, and we all …" Charlene stopped in midsentence and then continued, "Come in. We'll go into the sunroom out back. Mama's upstairs, so you can answer my questions before you meet her. Or if I don't like what you say, maybe I'll suggest you leave."

Charlene led the way, and Leah followed her down a long hall into a sunroom at the back of the house. Charlene closed the door and indicated Leah should take a seat in one of the white wicker chairs arranged in a semicircle. They both sat down with an empty chair between them.

"To begin with, I want to know what happened to you and why you're here now. Mama would have had a happier life if you had come back right away."

"I was taken by a man who had lost a child and whose wife could bear no more children. She was devastated, and he foolishly thought the answer was to abduct a little girl the same age as their child. The man and woman, Harold and Grace Anderly, raised me and loved me. They were my parents. Both of them are gone now, and I miss them very much, especially my mother, whom I cared for in her last weeks of life when she was dying of cancer. I couldn't have asked for a more loving home environment. I have no real memory of living here. I was only three or four, so memories from that time are virtually nonexistent, although I once had a dream or a vision about a gray house with red shutters. I don't know if that counts as a memory. When my mother was dying, she said in her delirium, 'Lizzie, I'm sorry.' That ultimately prompted me to hire a detective to find out who Lizzie was and why my mother was apologizing. My private investigator was very thorough and eventually discovered the story of Lizzie's disappearance, which coincided with the time my parents left Saint Paul. The clincher is that I have the triangular birthmark on the back of my neck. My mother told me it was an angel's kiss from when I was born, so I gave it little thought, especially after I had grown up. That's basically it. If you think it would be hurtful to speak to your parents, I'll leave and not bother you again."

Charlene stared at Leah and was silent for almost a minute, then said, "Let me see that birthmark." Leah pulled back her hair and turned so the back of her neck was visible. Charlene looked intently at her once more but said nothing.

Leah was ready to reiterate her willingness to leave without seeing the parents, but then Charlene spoke. "I think Mama needs to put her demons to rest. She needs to know her daughter is, as you say, alive and well. Wait here until I bring her in. I'm going to try to prepare her a little bit. Okay?"

Leah nodded and watched Charlene depart. She tried to analyze her feelings, but she had none at the moment. Seeing Charlene, her sister, had not stirred up feelings of any kind. Charlene was just someone she was meeting for the first time. There was no connection and she wondered if that was normal. She was even more anxious about meeting Mrs. McGregor, her mother. Would there be any recognition there? Would she experience a memory or something buried deep inside herself? Leah waited almost fifteen minutes before the door opened and Charlene entered, followed by a round-faced woman with salt-and-pepper hair, a prominent nose, and sharp brown eyes. She looked somewhat overweight, but perhaps it was her choice of clothing that created that impression. Leah rose and stuck out her hand, inviting a handshake. But it didn't happen. Instead Marcene McGregor, face aglow, flung herself at Leah, arms enfolding her as best she could. She was a good six inches shorter than Leah. She pulled Leah's face down and began to smother her in wet kisses.

Leah drew back, holding her mother at arm's length, and said, "I guess Charlene told you why I'm here."

"Oh yes, yes! I knew you'd come. I just knew it! Now that you're here, everything will be all right. Oh, I'm so happy. Let's go to the kitchen and have some coffee, and I'll tell you all about your family and how much your return means to us." Marcene took Leah's hand and pulled her into the kitchen, where she took cups out of the cupboard, cookies from a cookie jar, and sugar and powdered creamer from the countertop. "Sit down, daughter," she said, smiling broadly.

Leah didn't feel like the daughter; Charlene was the daughter. She stood for a moment and then sat down, drawing up a chair from the corner. A sip of coffee was all that Leah managed before Marcene began her monologue.

"Lizzie, you have one grandmother who lives in Inver Grove. She's not with it mentally, and Grandpa McGregor passed on. My parents, Elsie and Bren O'Malley, are gone too. Then there's your older brothers, Stephen and Harmon, and of course you've met Charlene. There's also a little brother, Russell. He's around somewhere, but Steve is off playing basketball and Harmon had to go back to work in Milwaukee. Your father is at the store. We own several hardware stores, and he manages them all but works at the one not far from here. Oh, he will be so excited when he finds out you've come back to us."

Marcene leaned across the table and grabbed Leah's hand and kissed it several times. Then she continued, "You have seven aunts and uncles on my side and three on your father's side, plus lots of cousins. I'm going to give everybody living close by a call and invite them to a big party tomorrow evening to celebrate your return. Oh, it will be glorious, and we'll need to call the newspaper. They'll want to do a big story about this remarkable happening, and with pictures too. Oh my, you are lovely, Lizzie … beautiful, but so thin. We'll fatten you up with some good old home cooking, won't we, Charlene?"

Charlene did not respond.

"Drink up," Marcene said. "Have a cookie. Have two cookies. I'm so happy I can't stop smiling."

Leah was overwhelmed. She had not expected this outpouring of family information as the first item of business. Marcene had not asked one question about her life for the past twenty-plus years. At least Charlene had been a little bit curious. *Well, I won't volunteer anything,* Leah thought. *I'll wait for the questions, as I'm sure they'll come eventually.*

Marcene seemed to run out of steam. She sat back, sighed, and began to eat a cookie and sip her coffee, but she continued to look at Leah and smile. Charlene broke the silence by asking, "Did you drive here? And where is home for you?"

"I rented a car after I flew in this morning from Chicago where I live. I'm currently between jobs, so I could get away today, but I have an interview tomorrow afternoon for a position I'm hopeful about, so I'll be flying back early tomorrow morning. You mentioned a party tomorrow night. I can't stay for that I'm afraid."

"But you have to stay! It will be in your honor, and everyone will come; I know they will. Surely you can put off the interview until later. You could stay until Sunday night or Monday, and we could all attend Mass together Sunday morning. Oh my, Father Gorman will be delighted to meet you, Lizzie. I've had him offering prayers, especially on holidays and anniversaries, and now they've been answered. So you have to stay."

"I really can't. My flight back is at eight tomorrow morning ... and I'm not Catholic. You mentioned going to Mass," Leah said, unsure how this bit of information might be received.

"But of course you're Catholic! You were baptized a Catholic, so you're Catholic. All my family are Catholic, except your uncle Fred Berger, who wouldn't convert. I'm sure you'll remember going to church; you were taught very early to kneel and cross yourself, and you were always delighted to be able to do what the grown-ups did. Oh yes, you're Catholic through and through," Marcene announced.

Leah didn't argue. Then she asked, "Have you called your husband to tell him I'm here? I'd really like to see him at the store if you think that would be all right."

"I suppose so. Charlene, maybe you and I can pull together a little party for tonight, and we'll get Russell to take Lizzie down to the store. Oh, won't Gene be surprised. That's a great idea. I'd almost like to be there to see his reaction, but if we're to have a party, we have work to do. Russell! Russell!" Marcene shouted, almost making Leah jump. There were footsteps on the stairs, and a young man of seventeen or eighteen came into the kitchen.

"Russell, this is your sister Lizzie—Elizabeth Jane McGregor. Isn't this the biggest surprise you ever had in your life? Well, go over and give her a hug and a kiss and welcome her into the family."

Russell's face showed his confusion, but he dutifully leaned over and gave Leah a token hug and a peck on the cheek.

"Lizzie wants to surprise her father at the store, so will you take her? Oh, the boys have the car, and your dad has the pickup. But then you have a car, don't you, Lizzie? You can drive, and Russell can navigate. Yes, that will work. All right, it's settled. Finish your coffee, Lizzie, and off you go. Now don't hang around the store too long, because there's work to do here and we can use another pair of hands."

Leah and Russell dutifully headed out to the rental car. Leah, at the wheel, looked over at Russell, smiled, and said, "Well, I guess I'm quite the surprise for you. Sorry you get stuck taking me to the store, but I'm grateful to have someone tell me where to turn. Shall we go?"

"Yeah," said Russell. "Turn left at the corner."

At the stop sign at the end of the block, Russell looked over at Leah and asked if she would mind pulling over once they turned the corner. She complied, wondering about the request.

"Sorry about this, but I've got to know who you really are. You can't be lost Lizzie. Dad said she was dead and gone, so who are you?"

Leah spent several minutes explaining everything to Russell, and when she had finished, he nodded and said, "I guess then you really are Lizzie. So how does that feel to find out you're not who you thought you were?" He looked inquiringly at Leah.

She liked Russell. It was a good question, one Marcene had not asked. *I could have been an imposter, but she didn't even question that I was Lizzie. At least Charlene wanted some facts and looked at my birthmark, but not Marcene,* she thought.

"You know, it feels really weird when I think about it, but you see, I'm not Lizzie ... not really. I'm Leah, someone I've been for most of my life. I don't think I'll ever be Lizzie. I have no plans to start calling myself Elizabeth either, because I'm not her. It's confusing, but I know one thing: I'm Leah and always will be."

"Okay, I get it. You know, I almost envy you. You got away from this crazy family. Well, we mostly have a crazy mother. She drives us nuts, but you were spared that. You ought to know that I'm the replacement child. I was conceived specifically to replace you when it became clear you weren't going to be found or would be found dead. I get reminded of my status every once in a while, but I'm out of school now and looking for a job, hopefully far away from here. I work for Dad, but I hate it. I'd like to be able to create something or be an inventor. I love making stuff out of bits and pieces of metal, wire, wood, whatever, and I want to find a school that will help me learn what I need to get a good job in a creative field. But nobody pays any attention to what I want. It's 'Russell, why don't you do this?' or 'Russell, why don't you do that?' I'm sick of it. Well, we'd better get to the store. Mama might have called Dad after all, and he'll be waiting."

"Russell, will you go in with me and sort of pave the way, tell your dad who I am? I'm not comfortable repeating my story again, especially to someone who is my parent but whom I don't know at all. Would you mind?" Leah asked.

"Sure, I'll do it. I can't wait to see the old man's reaction. He never believed like Mama did, so this is going to blow him away. You can park over there. It's for deliveries, but there won't be any today. Come on, let's go in."

The store was semibusy, with a number of customers milling around and two standing in line at the checkout counter. Gene McGregor sat behind a desk in the back, bending over paperwork. Leah studied him, just as she had done with Marcene. Would she have a different reaction to him than she'd had to her mother?

Gene McGregor saw his son and smiled as he came up to the counter. Russell said, "Hi, Dad. I've got a surprise for you. This is Leah, but she used to be Elizabeth, or Lizzie, McGregor. I can give you a little of her story, but why don't we go back to your office?"

Leah watched Gene's jaw drop as he stared at her, perhaps wondering if Russell had lost his mind, but he recovered and led the way into a small office with a desk, a table and four chairs, and a wall of filing cabinets. Gene sat down, and Russell and Leah took seats across the table from their father.

"Russell, this better not be some kind of joke, because it's not funny." Then he looked expectantly at Leah for an explanation.

Leah took a deep breath and said, "It might be hard for you to believe, but I'm very sure I'm your daughter. Russell tells me you thought I was dead, but as you can see, I'm very much alive." Then Leah proceeded to tell her father what she had shared with Charlene, including the reasons for her abduction. "I understand Marcene, your wife, never gave up hope that I was alive and …"

Leah trailed off in midsentence, feeling as though she was in some sort of dream world and had no idea how to awaken. "Well, that's about all I wanted to say. If you have questions, I'll try to answer them, but I won't be sharing much about the Anderlys, who raised me. They were loving, caring people, and I miss them very much."

Leah sat back after her little speech and watched Gene struggle to formulate his response. He made two starts before he managed to say, "You're right; this is a shock. I can only imagine how my wife reacted. Crazy as it seems, she's been waiting for you to appear, but I guess she was right. You are alive, and I do believe you. In fact I can see a resemblance to my youngest sister and maybe even to myself. It's not just your physical appearance but your nervous toe tapping. That's something I do when I'm in a difficult situation, and your brother Harmon does the same thing. You have no idea what we went through and what we're still going through in some respects. Your mother never got over your loss and has always acted as though you're away on a short trip and will soon be back."

Gene shook his head, not so much in disbelief but perhaps as a failure to process this sudden appearance of a long-lost daughter he'd assumed was dead.

After a moment he went on, "Marcene made Charlene's and Russell's lives difficult at times. Steven and Harmon seemed less impacted, or perhaps they were just stronger. None of her children could ever measure up to what she was sure you would have become. I don't know how she's handling this now, but I suspect she's going to want you to come back to us and occupy your old room." Gene shook his head again. "I just think you should be prepared. She's very persuasive."

"I thought as much. In fact she and Charlene are planning a party for this evening even though I wasn't in favor of it. She wants to invite the press to take pictures of the reunion. If that's part of things, count me out. I'll come to the party but not if the newspaper or TV people are there to record everything for the masses.

"Why don't we go back to the house and sort this out? I can leave Helen in charge here. Russell, you can take … what did you say you're called? Linda?"

"No, I'm Leah. And thank you for not calling me Lizzie."

Gene asked Russell to drive the truck home, saying he would ride with Leah. As soon as they were in the car, he said, "I hope you're a strong person, Leah, because you'll need to be. This isn't going to be easy for you. My wife ... your mother ... is a strong-minded woman who hardly ever takes no for an answer, and I'm afraid we have all been prone to give in to her. It's easier than bucking her persistence and her wrath as well. She's a good woman, really, and she loved you very much. I think she's not willing to admit it, but deep inside she feels guilty about what happened. You disappeared while she was talking with friends, having told Charlene, at age six, to watch you. Harmon too was supposed to keep an eye open if you wandered off, which you often did because you were curious and loved animals and flowers and bugs. So there's a lot of buried guilt in the family. I want you to know I'm delighted you're here, something I haven't acknowledged until now. I hope you and I will have a connection, but I can see how you might be reluctant to commit to this family. I'm afraid we're a little dysfunctional, or at least some of us are. Enough! Let's find out if there's to be a party and head off having the press there. I'll speak to Marcene."

There were several cars parked in front of the McGregor house, and inside Leah was overwhelmed with new relatives and hugs and wet kisses. *These wet kisses must be a family thing,* she thought. The kitchen was already a mess, with mixing bowls and flour on the countertop where piecrusts were being rolled out. Several pots of something were simmering on the stove. Two aunts and three cousins were introduced, and Leah was asked what her specialty was. She was perplexed at first and then realized they were talking about what food she was good at making.

"I'm sorry, but I can't think of anything right now. I'm afraid I'm a little overwhelmed. If you'd excuse me, I'd like to spend some time talking with ..." She hesitated before she said *Gene*, not father, but not Mr. McGregor either.

Gene was right behind her, and he addressed his wife, asking if the newspapers or television people had been called.

"Oh, I got so busy I forgot. I'll do it right now." She wiped her hands on her apron and headed for the telephone.

"No," Gene said. "Leah doesn't want any publicity. It can be announced later that she's back, but not today. No press."

"Don't be silly, Gene; of course we have to tell everyone that our baby girl is safely home. They need to see how beautiful she is and how happy we are to have her back." She picked up the phone, but instantly Gene grasped her wrist and hung up the phone.

"No, Marcene. If you make the call, Leah will leave, and I think she'll think twice about coming back to see us again. Now make your pies or whatever you're doing, and let me have a few minutes to talk with my daughter."

Marcene was clearly unhappy, but glancing at Leah, she must have been able to see that Gene had spoken truth. Leah was ready to bolt, looking like a deer caught in the headlights, temporarily shocked into inaction, but now ready to run.

"All right, all right. I don't agree with this, because the world needs to know. Oh, go talk, but I want Lizzie back here in twenty minutes. Surely you can say what you want to in that amount of time." She turned to the stove and stirred a bubbling dish and then picked up the rolling pin and began shaping a piecrust into a circle.

Gene led Leah into the sunroom. It was away from the activities in the kitchen, and Gene closed the door to keep out the chatter that drifted down the hallway. It was obvious that Marcene and her sisters were a gregarious bunch.

Father and daughter talked for more than twenty minutes, and Marcene, to her credit, did not interrupt them. Leah sketched out some of her life, focusing mostly on her later years of high school, college, law school, and employment. She avoided speaking at length about her parents, although Gene asked several questions about them that she was willing to answer. He then related things about his life and his family of origin and touched a little on his frustration with his wife and children.

"I don't want to sound like a complainer, but it's been difficult and has gotten worse in the last five years. Russell and his mother are always at swords' points, and she accuses me of not being firm with him. Charlene is her mother's tote-and-fetch girl. That's harsh, but Marcene seems to need someone who will do as she commands without argument. Charlene worked for a time in a florist shop, but Marcene wanted her at home, and Charlene has never been able to say no to her mother. Well, it's over now. I hope you'll want to be part of this family, come for holidays and keep in touch …" Gene trailed off.

Leah wondered what Gene meant by "It's over now." *What's over? Obviously the expectation is that I will slip into the family and everything will be fine.* She hardly knew how to respond. She wasn't sure she cared to be part of the family. It was her family, but it didn't feel like it. She hesitated before saying, "I don't know what our relationship will be. I guess when I came up here I was rather naive. I thought I would introduce myself, let you know I was alive, and then see what would develop after that. I wasn't prepared for Marcene. She's pretty overwhelming. This whole dynamic of having brothers and a sister, plus aunts, uncles, and cousins, is something foreign to me. I used to think about having a brother or sister, but I can't say I wanted one. I was happy as things were, and as I've said before, I had a wonderful life and great parents. That may be hard for you to hear. I know it is for Marcene. A couple of times when I referred to my parents and my upbringing, she frowned. But that's my life, and I can't say I would change anything."

Gene nodded once again, either agreeing with Leah or showing he understood her point of view. They sat quietly for a minute before he said, "I think you should go back to Chicago, go to school in January as you're planning to do, but hopefully keep in touch to let us know how things are going. I'm surprised you haven't mentioned a boyfriend, but I suppose you've been focused on your career, and with school looming for another year or two it's better not to have a romantic involvement."

"I didn't say anything about my love life because … well … it's painful to think about and just as painful to speak about. I am … or was … engaged to a man named Alan. Our wedding date was set for New Year's Eve, but that probably won't happen. I didn't tell you that I lost my job. It was because of my involvement with Alan. His uncle was my boss and didn't approve of me and gave Alan an ultimatum. It's complicated. I can't promise I'll keep in touch weekly, but if we take this relationship slowly, I'll try. Once school starts, I'll be busy, and the part-time job I've applied for will further complicate being able to devote time and energy to being part of your family in the way I think your wife wants."

"We'll work on it, Leah. I get the impression that you have no desire to be called Lizzie, or Elizabeth, but Marcene probably will never call you Leah. I understand how hard this is for you, and it's going to be for us as well. Now I'd better let you go into the kitchen and face the relatives." Gene smiled.

"I'd rather not, but I guess I must. I haven't met the two oldest sons. Will they be here for the party?"

"Stephen will be here. He lives in Washington State, and Harmon was here but had to go back to Milwaukee, where he's working as a nurse in a care facility. Marcene thinks men shouldn't be nurses, but he loves what he's doing, and I think he's really good at it. You'll like Harmon. You're a little bit alike and have the same eyes."

Chapter 13

Leah was put to work in the production of the tons of food Marcene said they would need for all the people who would be arriving. When Leah came back into the kitchen after her talk with Gene, the women had already made sandwiches and set out soft drinks for lunch. She had been invited to help herself. The new aunts and cousins bombarded her with questions that she fended off for the most part, and after a particularly personal question, she announced she was not answering anything more. If they wanted conversation, it would have to be about current events, the weather, what they liked to do for fun, or where they were employed. That shut down the conversation for a few minutes, but before long they were going full bore again. They lobbed only a few more questions at Leah, and she batted them away like pesky flies. *How can they be so insensitive and so nosy?*

By three-thirty, guests had begun to arrive, and Leah was excused from kitchen duty to meet and greet the hordes pouring in. At least to Leah it seemed like hordes. It was hard to fathom that all these people were relatives. There was no way she could remember their names, and after awhile she quit trying. Smiling and nodding was as much as she could muster after the first forty-five minutes of constant coming and going. At one point Gene rescued her, finding an unoccupied chair so she could sit down. The crowning irony was when a young man about her age asked, "Do you remember me? We took a

bath together when you were about two and I was four or five."
He grinned broadly, and Leah wondered if he was serious or
just trying to be funny.

"Sorry, I don't remember you or the bath," Leah said and
then without thinking added, "In fact I don't remember anyone
here, including Gene and Marcene."

The young fellow seemed shocked, but was it because
she didn't remember the bath or because she didn't remember
anyone at the party, including her parents? He mumbled
something about her probably being too young to remember
and then sat down on a hassock on the other side of the room.

Marcene came into the living room and announced that
food was ready in the sunroom and everyone should fill their
plates. Tables and chairs had been set up in every conceivable
open space in the house, including the basement. Leah tried
to estimate how many people were there, but it was difficult
because everyone seemed to be moving from room to room. She
gave up counting and filled her plate. The food was excellent,
and she had to acknowledge that Marcene and her family were
good cooks. The noise level raised considerably after the meal
when after-dinner drinks were passed around. She was offered
one but declined. Five minutes later someone else brought her
a drink, and she once again said she didn't care for anything.

Leah talked with countless relatives, all eager to have a
word with her and ask about her life as an "abductee," as one
of them called her. It became more difficult to fend off the
questions, and at eight thirty she found Gene and told him
she had to leave. It was at least a forty-five-minute drive to
the airport hotel where she was staying, and she had an early
flight in the morning. Marcene overheard the conversation
and announced that of course Leah had to stay. In fact, she
must spend the night. "You can't leave now. This party is for
you, and we want you to enjoy every minute of it. There's still
speeches to be made and a royal welcome home for our beloved
daughter who has been kept from us for so many years. No,
you can't leave now. Your old room is ready for you. Anyway,

Lizzie, you have to stay because we're going to have a toast to you. Uncle Fritz is passing out the drinks, and in a minute I or your father will offer the toast. I was hoping Father Gorman could come, but he was busy and begged off. He'd love to see you Sunday at Mass."

Leah looked at the ceiling, frustrated. "I already told you I'm not spending the night. I haven't changed my plane reservations, so of course I'm not going to church with you, and as soon as you do the toast or whatever it is, I have to be on my way."

Marcene was obviously very disappointed but recovered her poise and went in search of Uncle Fritz so they could have the toast. In less than a minute she was back, bearing two glasses of a clear liquid. She handed one to Leah, who at first declined the drink but finally accepted it at Marcene's insistence. Marcene called for quiet in her very strong, pay-attention voice. It took a few moments for the crowd to get the message. More people were coming up the stairs from the basement to squeeze into the already-crowded area on the main floor.

"All right, folks," Marcene shouted, "I propose a toast to my darling daughter who was lost and now is found. She has returned to us, and we will embrace her as our own once again. We hope and pray she will very soon leave Chicago and come to live with us here in her old room. To Elizabeth!"

The crowd shouted, "Here! Here!" and downed their drinks. Leah just stood there, not taking even one sip of her drink. Marcene nodded at her, motioning for her to drink. When she failed to drink or respond verbally, Marcene covered the awkward moment by saying Lizzie was "overcome." Then she took Leah's arm and led her into the bathroom, closing the door.

"You should have sipped your drink, Lizzie. It's not polite if you don't, and after someone toasts you, it's common practice to respond with a toast of your own or to at least say thank you." For the first time since Leah had arrived, Marcene seemed annoyed with her.

"I'm sorry, but I don't drink, and I was not aware of your customs. I'm sorry I've disappointed you," Leah said, and she meant it. Then she gave Marcene a quick hug and pulled open the bathroom door. Instead of heading back into the living room, she slipped into the sunroom, where she deposited her drink. She then left via the sunroom door that led to the backyard, circled around the house, and found her way down the block where she had parked when she and Gene had returned from the store. She laid her head on the steering wheel as tears welled up. It had been an awful day. Why had she come? Nothing had turned out as she'd thought it might.

As she raised her head to wipe her eyes, there was a tap on the passenger-side window. It was Russell. He opened the door and slid into the seat. He patted Leah on the arm and said, "I'll bet you weren't expecting all that and wish you hadn't come here. I wouldn't blame you, but I'm glad you did." Once again he patted Leah's arm, and she took his hand this time and squeezed it.

"Thanks, Russell, and yes, it was a little bit over the moon. I'm not used to so many relatives. The only relative I've known besides my parents is my mother's mother, and I just met her for the first time a week ago. How do you keep everybody straight, and do you get together like that all the time? Or are there smaller, more-intimate gatherings?"

"Mama doesn't know anything about small and intimate. Everything is always large and boisterous. I'm used to it, but I knew right away that it would blow your mind. I really like you, Leah, and if I could be really bold, I'd like to ask a question. It's not a personal one about your parents or your life, but …"

"Sure you can. Ask away, and I'll answer if I can," replied Leah.

"Do you think I could come to Chicago, maybe bring my sleeping bag and sleep on your floor for a few nights? I want to check out a school there that has programs I'm interested in. I've mentioned it to Mama and Dad who haven't given me any encouragement, but I've kind of decided to go down there anyway, to check out the school, and try to land a job. I'd get out of your hair as soon as I could. I don't know anybody in Chicago, so I'm hoping you'll let me stay a few nights." Russell had been studying something out beyond the windshield, but when he finished, he looked over at Leah to gauge her reaction.

"Sure, Russell, you can stay at my place. I have an extra bedroom, so you won't have to sleep on the floor or even bring your sleeping bag, unless you find that more comfortable." Leah smiled at Russell.

"Oh man, that's great. I really appreciate it, Leah, and I promise not to be a nuisance. I hope I can get everything lined up so I can leave the end of next week or the first of the following week. I haven't decided if I'm going to just leave and not say anything until I get settled or if I should tell my parents my plans. I hate to just leave; you've seen what Mama is like. Much as I dislike some of the things she does, I hate to disappoint her or make her unhappy. But I have to get out of here. I don't know what will happen if I don't. Thanks for saying yes. I'll be in touch to let you know when I'm coming, but I'll need your phone number."

Leah wrote down her address and cell phone number. Russell promised not to share the information and said he'd let her know when he planned to arrive in Chicago. He confided that he might try to hitchhike if the weather stayed favorable.

"Don't do that," Leah said. "Here, let me give you some bus money. I just got a big bonus at work, so I can afford it. It's too dangerous to hitchhike, especially if you've never done it before. Please promise you won't hitchhike!"

"I promise, and thanks for the cash which I'll use for bus fare. I'll pay you back once I get a job and can earn some money. I'd better let you be on your way before a lot of people realize you're gone and come looking for you. See you in a week or two."

Leah watched Russell run back to the house. Then she started the car and drove off. She did not glance back to see if anyone had come out to look for her. It was nearly midnight before she was able to return her rented car to the airport and catch a shuttle to her hotel. Her room was small but comfortable, with a king-size bed. She stared at it, remembering the king bed in Alan's room and the night they'd spent together. She wondered where he was right now. The Bahamas, no doubt, with Uncle Horace and Juneau. Juneau worried her. Leah's experience with Juneau confirmed a manipulative nature and a determination to worm her way into Alan's life. Alan had said as much himself. *Well, there's nothing I can do about that or about almost anything else. I just hope I can get the job at the bookstore. I don't want to dip into the blood money from Uncle Horace, at least not yet.*

Chapter 14

The Wednesday after Thanksgiving weekend, just as Leah was leaving her apartment, the phone rang. She turned back to answer it in case it was the employment agency she had signed with to help her find a job. "Hello, Leah Anderly," she said in her most professional voice.

"Well, hello, Miss Anderly. I'll bet you were expecting somebody official. Sorry to disappoint you, but this is Connie Burns at Marsden, Willett, and Desmond. Remember me? We've gone out to lunch before with others from the firm, so I feel I know you well enough to pass along a little information. Ever since you left rather abruptly, the rumors have been flying. I know you were let go by the big guy himself. But that's not why I'm calling. Edith, Mr. Willett's secretary told me this morning when I delivered some papers up there that Alan Parkin is in the hospital in Philadelphia and has been since Sunday. It's supposed to be hush-hush, but of course that didn't stop her from telling me. She doesn't like Mr. Willett, but it's a good job, so what can I say? Well, anyway, we thought you ought to know, since you and Alan were seeing each other now and then. The rumor is that HM got rid of you to break you guys up before it got serious. We liked working with you, Leah, and don't think you were treated fairly. Well, that's it, although I could give you a few more gems from the rumor mill. I hope you take this as information from several friends rather than seeing it as passing on gossip and rumors. I was elected at coffee this morning. I'm sorry about everything you must be going through."

Connie paused, so Leah knew she had to respond. But how? "I remember you well, Connie. You were helpful in so many ways when I first came to work. You gave me tips and steered me past pitfalls that only someone who had been working there awhile would know. Can you tell me how Alan is? Is going to be all right? What's wrong, do you know?"

"Mr. Parkin was in pain for a day or so, and he thought it was some suspicious sushi he had eaten. But then he fainted, probably from the pain, Edith said, and they called an ambulance. His appendix had ruptured, and I guess there was some infection. They operated and removed the appendix, but as far as how serious it is, I don't know. Apparently they're trying to decide whether to have him airlifted back here or have him remain in Philadelphia. Mr. Marsden and his niece flew to Paris to buy a bridal dress and other stuff for the wedding."

Leah suddenly felt very dizzy. Wedding? Alan and Juneau's wedding? She had no time to react, as Connie plunged ahead, saying, "Mr. Willet, who was working in Philadelphia with Alan came home this morning. He called from the airport to say he would be in this afternoon. It seems odd that he would come home when Alan is … when he's … Well, he's in the hospital for crying out loud. Somebody ought to be there! Even his uncle and Juneau took off. I don't understand it."

"Thanks for letting me know, Connie. I really appreciate it, and thank the others too. I suspect it's probably my old team that elected you. I know you weren't part of that directly, but we could always count on you if we needed anything, so thanks."

The call ended with the promise they would find a time to have lunch soon. Leah poured herself a cup of what was by now tepid coffee, but she needed a jolt of caffeine to help her decide what to do. Connie had obliquely indicated that Alan and Juneau were to be married. Leah regretted not asking Connie more about the wedding. Should she call back and ask if she had heard correctly? Should she fly to Philadelphia? Horace Marsden had warned her not to see or talk to Alan again. Running to Alan's side didn't seem wise, but she might try to call him in a few days if she could learn where he was.

The phone rang again. "Hello," Leah answered.

"Leah Anderly? It's Elise Morrison at the Book Nook. After your interview I've decided I'd like to hire you, if you still want the job. Could you start tomorrow?"

"Oh yes, I would like the position. What time shall I come in?"

"Let's say eight, if that's not too early. We open at nine, so that will give you time to fill out paperwork, and then either I or one of the staff will give you a crash course on running the register, how to locate books, and a lot of other things. Does that sound all right to you?"

"I'll be there at eight. Thanks for giving me this opportunity. I'll do my very best to master the ins and outs of working at the Book Nook. Do you need anything from me? A letter of recommendation or anything else?"

"No, I've had a ringing endorsement of your character and ability, so I think that's all I'll need. See you tomorrow then."

"Wow, what a surprise," Leah said out loud after hanging up. "I wonder who recommended me and how anyone even knew I applied for the position."

The good news about her job was overshadowed by what she had just heard from Connie. She was a little surprised she had not cried. Certainly Alan's marrying Juneau was worth crying over, but somehow she thought there might be more to the story. She hoped Alan would call soon. Maybe he'd have an explanation for or even a denial of the wedding, or maybe Juneau was marrying someone else.

Chapter 15

When Leah arrived at the Book Nook, the door was locked, but a handwritten note directed her down the alley to the side door. Elise Morrison greeted Leah with a smile and a word of welcome and then stepped back so she could enter the rather narrow hallway leading to a large work area with a long table and several chairs. Piles of books were stacked on the table and on the floor along one side of the room.

"Pardon the mess. We had to remove these things from our storage area upstairs because of water seepage. These old buildings sometimes have leaks that spring up almost overnight. Thankfully, someone's coming to fix it today. Come in, and you can fill out paperwork, and then we'll start your training."

After Leah had taken care of the necessary forms, she asked Elise who had recommended her.

"Oh, it was Jack Desmond. He and my husband are old friends from college, and we get together a couple of times a year. We went to dinner the night after I got your application for the job, so I just thought I'd ask him about your work ethic and your presence, which are important in a salesperson. He couldn't stop telling me good things about you and said I couldn't hire anyone better, so of course I followed his recommendation. You probably know him from your work at the law office where he's a partner. It's Marshall, Williams, and Desmond, or something like that."

"Yes, my team did research for him sometimes, and I sat with him and his wife at the Illini-Wildcat game back in September."

Elise didn't waste any time getting started with Leah's orientation, and soon Leah was fully engaged in learning the workings of the bookstore. Elise explained the computer and its use. Leah was sure that wouldn't give her much trouble, but the cash register, an old-fashioned one with keys you pressed, looked foreboding.

"Don't worry. You'll soon get the hang of it, and I do love this old machine. Because it's not electric, it never fails; even if we lose power, it keeps on keeping track of our sales. At the end of the day I'll show you how we read the transactions and where we record them. It may be a bit old fashioned, but it works well for me. I'm not so great with the high-tech stuff we use for looking up books we have in stock and checking availability of books from publishers and suppliers. We'll get to that when Nancy Graham comes in at noon."

Most of the morning for Leah was spent watching Elise perform various duties, including ringing up sales, and by eleven o'clock she felt confident enough to take over running the cash register. Lunch was a sandwich she brought from home, along with a cup of the coffee that was available to customers all day long. By five, when Elise told her she could call it a day, Leah was exhausted, mostly because she was not used to standing on her feet since right after lunch.

At home, Leah took a long, hot bath and retired early. During the day she had managed to avoid thinking of Alan and how things might or might not be, but when she crawled into bed, she couldn't hold those thoughts at bay any longer. The tears came, and when at last she was able to quiet herself, she felt better … cleansed perhaps. She prayed for strength to get through whatever was ahead for her, and she pleaded with God to lay a healing hand on Alan.

Leah's current schedule had her coming in early and working until five. Classes would not begin for her until mid-January. Then Elise would adjust her schedule to fit her class times. The Christmas season was a busy one, so Elise was grateful for all the hours Leah could give.

Leah's second day of work was a virtual repeat of her first day, and by Friday she felt confident in performing almost all the tasks she had been taught. She was even getting used to being on her feet, but Elise advised her to take a break morning and afternoon, saying, "Take a load off. We all need to do that."

Friday night Leah ordered in from the small café nearby and curled up in front of the television set while she munched on pepperoni-and-sausage pizza and drank diet cola. Leah cleaned up the remains of her meal and then changed into her nightgown and robe to watch the nine o'clock news. It had just begun when the phone rang.

"Hello," she answered.

"Hi, Leah. It's Alan. I'm sorry I haven't been able to call you for more than a week now. I'm in the hospital with a ruptured appendix. I'm doing okay but am still weak as a kitten. Are you all right? Did you wonder why I hadn't called? I miss you."

"I heard from Connie at the office that you were in the hospital, but I hadn't gotten any update, so I've been worried about you. Are you really feeling better? Your voice sounds different, like you're not quite yourself."

"I'm all right. I had one of those tubes in my throat, and now it's sore; that's the reason I guess. I hope I never have to have something like that again. It's not much fun. But tell me what you've been doing. Did you have a good visit with your grandmother?"

"Yes, it was great! I learned about my background and about relatives I didn't know I had. She explained why my dad grabbed me and spirited me away to Chicago. It's a long story, but I think I understand now. The day after Thanksgiving I flew to Saint Paul and dropped in on my birth family. That was quite an experience. I don't want to go into too much detail, but I think I was lucky to be kidnapped, which is a strange thing to say. My family of origin is a bit dysfunctional …

especially my birth mother. I don't think of her as my mother. She is so … How can I describe her? She's an in-charge person and doesn't take no for an answer. That's what my birth father told me, and I did observe that in the brief time I was there. I rather liked my youngest brother, and the older sister was an interesting case. That sounds like a terrible way to describe her, but I think I could come to like her if we had a chance to talk seriously. Her mother dominates her, however. There are two older brothers, both out on their own now, and I met only one of them briefly and we didn't have much conversation. The younger of the two had already returned to Milwaukee where he works in health care. The sister still lives at home, at age twenty-eight. The youngest brother is eager to be on his own and may come to Chicago to stay with me for a few days while he looks for a job and checks out a college here. Well, it's a different sort of family than the one I grew up in."

"You really had quite a weekend. But Leah, so did I. I don't quite know how to tell you this, but apparently I got drunk Thanksgiving night. I swear I don't know how it could have happened. You know I don't drink, but Uncle and Juneau had the bright idea that we should try this local Bahamian concoction. I refused at first, but they insisted that I at least try it, saying we would have a toast to something or other that I can't recall. I had several sips, and it tasted terrible. I remember setting the drink down, and then the room was spinning, and the next thing I remember is waking up in the early morning with a pounding headache. This is the part I'd rather not tell you, but I have to."

Alan paused, cleared his throat, and took almost ten or fifteen seconds before continuing. "Juneau was in bed with me. I was still wearing my dress shirt and necktie, although it was loosened. I had on my socks, and my undershorts were around my ankles. Juneau was stark naked. She claimed I raped her during the night. I have absolutely no memory of going to bed and certainly not of assaulting her as she claimed. I don't even like her. In fact I pretty much despise her, so why would I want to be intimate with her? It doesn't make sense. Uncle is furious. She took a pregnancy test, and it was positive—she's pregnant. Uncle says we have to be married right away to avoid idle gossip. Leah, I can't marry her. I want to marry you. I don't know what to do. They had the telephone removed from my room, so I couldn't call you. Tonight I persuaded one of the night-shift nurses who has been kind to me to bring me a phone, so that's how I managed to call. She's coming to take it away again when we're finished with our conversation. Tell me what to do, Leah. I'm sick about this whole mess. I can't believe anything happened, but I can't prove it, and I guess Juneau really is pregnant. My suspicious nature wonders if she was already with child and hatched this up to snare me into marriage."

Leah didn't know what to say. Alan's story was not something she had expected to hear when she'd picked up the phone and heard his voice. Finally she was able to gather her thoughts and respond. "I don't know what to tell you, Alan. I think you probably need to talk seriously with your uncle. If Juneau has been seeing someone, surely that might cast doubt on her story that you raped her. I hate that word. And from the little I know of Juneau, I doubt she was raped. If you were passed out, she may well have taken advantage of you. I don't know. You should talk to your uncle and get some answers."

"I just want all this to go away. I should have said no to Uncle and not gone to the Bahamas. I didn't want to, but I've found it hard to go against him ever since I came to Evanston after my dad's death. Oh, let's not talk about this anymore. I know I have to deal with it, but I just had to talk to you. How's your work with the team going, and how is everybody at the firm? Uncle said you're back on the team after the little misunderstanding, so I hope everything is all right."

When Leah didn't respond, Alan asked, "Everything's all right, isn't it? There aren't any problems I hope. Uncle said they had hired a new person but that all was going smoothly."

"No, Alan, I'm not on the team. Your uncle paid me off with a huge check and said that I was never to speak to you or see you again and that I wasn't good enough for you. Don't you remember us talking about this the week before Thanksgiving? I can't remember if I told you, but the check he gave me was for five hundred thousand dollars. I kept it for a few days, thinking I'd take it back and throw it in his face, but then I decided to bank it and use it for education. Don't you remember that conversation? Your uncle promised me if I tried to see you or talk to you he would make life miserable for both of us. I don't want that, Alan. I don't want you to be miserable. I'm miserable enough for both of us. I promised I wouldn't speak with you again." Leah feared that Alan's blackout had somehow effected his memory. Everything was so confusing. Then she said, tearfully, "We'd better hang up. I can't talk anymore, and I don't want you to get into trouble. Please take care of yourself. Good night. I love you." Then Leah hung up the phone.

It was a long night of tossing and turning as Leah mulled over what Alan had said and what she had said. By one o'clock she had pretty much come to the conclusion that she might never see him again. Uncle Horace could keep him tied up somewhere, figuratively at least, for a long time, and if he married Juneau, it would be the end for them. Finally she rose and made herself a cup of Sweet Dreams tea and sipped it while sitting on the sofa. She turned on the TV but left the sound off. Whether it was the silent stream of images on the TV or the relaxing effect of the tea, she leaned back and fell asleep.

Sometime during the night she stretched out on the couch, and she was lying, curled up there, hugging a pillow when the phone woke her. It was six thirty. She rubbed her eyes to clear them and her mind. *Who would be calling this early?*

"Hi, Sis. It's Russell. I'm in Chicago. I took an overnight train. How do I get to your place?"

"Russell, I thought you were going to call before you got here." Leah sighed. "I presume you're at Union Station. Go outside, and there should be lots of cabs because your train just got in. You might have to be aggressive to get one. Go right to the curb, and hang on tight to your luggage. Raise your hand to let the cabdriver know you want a ride and then give him my address. I'll be waiting outside on the sidewalk with money to pay for the cab. Go get in line if that's what you have to do. I'll see you when you get here."

Leah hurriedly dressed, putting on what she would wear to work. There would be no time for a shower now and probably not later either. She donned her heavy coat, gloves, and a scarf for her head and took the elevator to the street level. She stayed inside, peering out the long, narrow window on the side of the door, looking for Russell's cab. When Leah observed one pulling up, she stepped out into the cold with money in her hand. Russell struggled out of the backseat, dragging two duffels and a hard-sided suitcase. Leah opened the front passenger-side door and inquired about the fare and then handed the driver what she had correctly assumed it would be.

"Let me get one of those," Leah said to Russell, picking up the larger of the two duffel bags. "Let's get upstairs. It's really cold this morning, and the wind is coming down the street with a vengeance."

Russell seemed rather subdued. *Maybe he's tired,* Leah thought. She carried the duffel into the small guest room across the hall from her room, setting it on one of the twin beds. Russell followed with the other two bags and dropped them on the floor. Then he sat down heavily on the other bed.

"Oh man, I'm so tired. I hardly slept all night. That old train rattled and banged and shook, and it seemed like it stopped every twenty minutes. And the whistle! That darn thing blew like every five minutes. A guy sure can't sleep with all that going on. But, hey, I'm here, and maybe I can get out there this afternoon and beat the bushes for a job. Any ideas where I should start?" Russell asked, looking expectantly at Leah.

"Let's have some breakfast. I've got to be at work in forty-five minutes. The newspaper is in the kitchen, and you can check the ads and see what appeals to you. I'll help you with directions, but for today you ought to stick to places right here in Hyde Park. We'll deal with farther out tomorrow or the next day. You'll need a bus pass I'm guessing. Come on. Let's grab some coffee and cereal, and you can tell me what's going on in the McGregor household."

Breakfast was soon on the table, and Russell recited the latest drama at home. "Mama had a fit when I said I was leaving, even though I told her I was coming here. I think you might have lost a little of the shine she put on you when you first came to our house. She's still ticked off about you leaving the party so early. Other than that, I guess everything's all right, but a little tense."

Russell also filled Leah in on the latest family gossip and said Marcene was planning to talk to a reporter on Thursday and tell them about Leah's "return from the dead," as he put it. Leah frowned but said nothing. She had expected it would happen and wondered if the Chicago papers would pick up on it and if her name would be plastered all over the *Trib* or one of the other smaller rags in the area. *What will be, will be,* she thought and started to put on her coat. It was time to go to work.

"See you tonight. I work until five, and then I walk home, so it will be almost six before I get here. There's your city map and the newspaper, so go to it. Lots of luck, but don't be discouraged if nothing happens today. The Sunday paper is a little better and has more ads. Oh, here's the keys you'll need. The big one opens the outside door, and the smaller one will get you in the apartment. Help yourself to whatever you find in the fridge or the cupboards. Bye, Russell."

That evening when Leah came into the apartment, Russell was frying something. "Smells great," she said. "What's cooking?"

"Sloppy Joes. I picked up buns and a salad from the deli down the street. I hope it was all right to go ahead and make something. I thought you might be too tired to cook when you got home." Russell looked worried that he had overstepped in some way, but Leah was delighted and told him so.

They sat down to eat almost immediately, and she complimented him on his culinary skills, saying he could cook anytime he felt the urge. After the meal, they cleaned up and then sat down to watch television. Russell seemed restless, so Leah suggested they talk and muted the TV.

It took several tries on her part, but Leah was soon able to get Russell to tell her what he had on his mind. "I hate to tell you this," he said, "but don't be surprised if Mama shows up at your doorstep one of these days. When I left, she said she was going to come and check up on me, and anyway, she wants to see where you live and spend a little time with 'her Lizzie.' I don't know how you feel about that. I don't think you'll get a phone call to warn you when she's coming. She'll just show up. I'd like to have a job and be enrolled in class before that happens, but that may not be possible. She'll probably be parked at your doorstep before the end of next week. That's my guess."

Leah wasn't very excited about Russell's news, but what could she do? She supposed she could call and tell Marcene not to come, but on the other hand, Russell might be projecting his own fears when no visit was planned or at least wouldn't happen soon.

"I don't think she'll show up without calling. She doesn't even know if I have room for her, and now that you're here, I don't have room. Well, I guess if she shows up we'll figure out something."

Leah left Russell with the TV remote and went off to do laundry and write a letter to her grandmother.

Chapter 16

The week flew by for Leah. She worked a full schedule at the Book Nook, and on Wednesday of the following week Elise asked her to put in three or four more hours filling in for someone who was sick. She arrived back at her apartment just after ten p.m., having taken the bus instead of walking because she preferred not to be out on the street late at night, even though most of the way home was through a safe residential area. When she inserted her key in the front door of the apartment building, she heard a car door close and footsteps coming her way. She hurriedly unlocked the door and stepped inside, but then a voice called, "Lizzie, it's your mother. I'm freezing cold and want to get inside where it's warm."

Leah turned to see Marcene carrying an overnight bag and a purse. She was getting out of a car parked almost right in front of Leah's apartment. Leah could hear the surprise in her own voice as she asked, "When did you get here? Why didn't you let us know you were coming? I'm afraid there's nowhere for you to sleep because Russell is using my guest room and—"

Marcene cut her off. "You and I can share your bed, so don't worry about it. And why should I let you know I was coming? You're my daughter, and visits between mother and daughter don't have to be arranged ahead of time. Besides, you came to Saint Paul without letting anybody know." She said the last bit with a hint of sarcasm.

"Yes, I know, but that was different. I wasn't planning to spend the night or even stay as long as I did. Oh, never mind. Come on up, and we'll figure out something."

Leah led the way into the elevator, and Marcene followed, somewhat hesitantly. "How high up do you live? I don't like heights."

"I live on the third floor. Actually, it's more like the fourth floor because the basement level is half above ground, although there's no elevator going down there. Anyway, you don't have to look down, so it shouldn't bother you."

Leah inserted the key in her apartment door and stepped inside to turn on the light. She knew Russell wasn't home because he had called her about noon and told her he had a job and they wanted him to attend a training session that would last until ten o'clock.

Marcene immediately began wandering around the apartment while Leah hung up her coat, took off her shoes, and then went into the kitchen to put on water for tea. Marcene's wanderings took her into the kitchen as well, where she opened cupboard doors, searched the refrigerator, and even peered into the oven. Then she picked up her bag and carried it into Leah's bedroom.

Okay, Leah thought, *let her have the bedroom. I'll sleep on the couch, something I've done before.* Leah followed Marcene into the bedroom and pointed out the closet where she could hang anything she cared to. Then she showed her mother the bathroom, telling her it was the only one and so was shared by Russell and of course by Leah herself. Then she asked Marcene if she cared for tea or coffee.

"Hmmm," Marcene replied. "I'd have thought that would have been the first thing you'd do … offer me something after I'd spent hours sitting in that cold car. Yes, I'll have tea. Constant Comment if you have it, and something to go with it. I can't drink tea without something sweet."

Leah invited Marcene to make herself comfortable in the living room while she made the tea. She tried to think what she had in the cupboard that was sweet and would pass muster with Marcene. Russell had brought some Oreos home earlier, but somehow she didn't think that would do. She rummaged in the freezer and found half a pound cake left over from some dessert she had made several weeks ago. While she microwaved the cake for a couple of minutes so it would thaw, she quickly whipped up instant chocolate pudding to go with it. She put everything on a tray, carried it into the living room, and set it on the coffee table.

"What's this?" asked Marcene, looking at the cake and pudding with suspicion.

"I'm afraid I don't have much of anything on hand, so I thought we'd have this pound cake and some chocolate pudding. It's not what I would normally serve guests, but then I wasn't expecting you. There's Oreos if you prefer."

"Well, I can see you haven't been brought up very well. I always have something ready to serve, either in the freezer or the refrigerator. I can see I'm going to have to instruct you in the fine art of entertaining company."

Leah had to bite her tongue to keep from responding the way she would have liked to. *Be kind, be kind,* an inner voice told her.

"Sorry, Marcene, I'll try to do better next time. If you don't want to eat it, don't feel that you must."

They sat and sipped and ate. Leah noticed that Marcene cleaned up every bit of her cake and pudding. *It can't be all that bad,* she thought. When they had finished the dessert and a second cup of tea, it was well after eleven, and Leah said she needed to get some sleep because she had to be at work by eight in the morning.

"Oh, don't mind me. I'll just sit here and watch TV until Russell comes home. I'm not very tired, because I slept in the car this afternoon."

"I'm sorry, Marcene, but the couch is my bed tonight. I can find a couple of books you might enjoy reading in the bedroom, but I've got to put a sheet down and get a pillow and blankets from the linen closet." Leah rose to get the needed bedding, but Marcene stopped her.

"Don't be silly. We can share the bed. I'll try not to have the TV on too loud, and I'll tiptoe in so I won't wake you when I come to bed. I'm something of a night owl. Gene likes to go to bed early, so we have separate rooms, but since you don't have an extra room for me, we can share. I'll get used to it."

Yes, but I won't! Leah thought. She decided to be firm and not give in to Marcene on this issue. "No, I have to get my sleep, and I'm not used to sharing a bed. I've never had to in my whole life, and I get up early and would disturb you, so let me get some books for you, or magazines if you'd prefer."

Marcene rose a little stiffly from the couch, glaring at Leah, but went to the bedroom and closed the door. Leah had not had time to retrieve anything from her room, so in a few minutes she rapped on the door. "Marcene, I'm going to need my clothes for tomorrow and my nightgown. It will only take a minute to gather what I need."

Leah waited. No response, so she knocked again, a bit more forcefully. "I need my things, Marcene. I'm coming in." Leah knew the door wasn't locked, because there was no lock. She pushed the door open and walked in to find Marcene looking through her dresser drawers. "What are you doing? Don't you have any shame? Going through someone's things isn't the way to act when you're a guest in their home."

"But you're my daughter. I want to know all about you. You don't make it very easy, so I have to snoop to find out what I need to know. I see you have pregnancy-prevention pills. Don't you know that's sinful?" Marcene's expression was a combination of shock and displeasure.

"I take those because I have severe cramps every time I have my period. The doctor prescribed them, and they help. They really help. Without them I would miss a day or two of work every month. You don't have to worry that I'm living the life of a whore. Is that what you thought?" Leah couldn't believe she'd just said what she had, but she was angry.

Marcene dropped the pills as though they were red hot. "How dare you use that tone with me! I'm your mother, and I have a right to correct you when you're wrong and point out sins when I see them. I'll say a prayer for you to come to your senses. We all have to suffer cramps. It's what all women put up with, so you need to get over it."

Leah picked up the dropped pills; grabbed her nightgown, underwear, a pair of slacks, and a sweater from her closet; and then hurried out the door, closing it with a bang as she went back into the living room. She was literally shaking with anger. What could she do about this woman who had barged into her home and begun criticizing her upbringing? Maybe that irritated Leah the most. Her mother had seldom had a harsh word to say about anyone or anything, yet she had been firm in her discipline when it had been required. *How can I get rid of this woman?* Leah asked herself.

Leah was putting a sheet on the sofa when she heard the front door open. Russell came in as quietly as he could, thinking perhaps Leah was already asleep but had left the living room light on for him. Then he saw her tucking a sheet under the couch cushions and asked, "Hey, what's going on? What's the sheet for, and those blankets? You planning to sleep out here tonight or what?"

"Yes. Your mother is here and in my bedroom. She's going to drive me up the wall! She was here when I got home. I had to work late tonight, and I guess she sat in her car most of the late afternoon and evening waiting for me to come home. You know, she doesn't make sense half the time. I suggested she should have called so we could make arrangements for her coming, but she said that mothers don't have to notify daughters … that they can just show up. Well, she did, and you've got to help me get her to go home … tomorrow if possible. Do you start your job tomorrow?"

"Yeah, I do. Gee, Leah, I'm sorry you had to deal with Mama by yourself. I don't start work until eleven and will get off at seven, so I can spend some time with her before work and try to convince her to go home. I wonder if I should call Dad. Too late tonight, but maybe tomorrow. I'm beat, so I think I'll go to bed. See you in the morning. Wake me if I'm not up before you leave, okay?"

Sleep didn't come quickly for Leah. Her mind was racing. She was still concerned about doing well in her new job, and then there was Alan. She didn't allow herself to think about him except on her way to and from work and then perhaps when she went to bed at night. There had been no more word from him, so she wondered if he was still in the hospital. Had he confronted his uncle? Could he somehow avoid marrying Juneau? "No, I won't go over these same old what-ifs tonight. I'll just think about the Alan that took me to Champaign and bought me a purple hat," she said softly in the dark as she pictured the two of them in the stands, wearing their school colors. She smiled.

Marcene did not appear before Leah had to leave for work, but Leah woke Russell to tell him that she was on her way out and that he would have to fix breakfast for his mother and hopefully convince her to go home. Once she was at the Book Nook, the activity and the constant parade of customers in and out of the store kept her busy, and she was able to block out what might be going on back at her apartment. At four thirty Elise suggested she leave a little early. Leah had confided to her some of the drama that had occurred the previous evening, so Elise's suggestion was welcome.

Leah took the bus since it was spitting snow and the wind out of the northwest had dropped the temperatures dramatically since noon, when she had gone out for a sandwich and hot chocolate. When she approached the door to her apartment, she heard the vacuum cleaner. At least it sounded like it. At any rate, the noise was coming from her apartment. She unlocked the door and saw Marcene pushing the vacuum across the living room rug. Marcene turned off the machine when she realized Leah had come in. Then she smiled broadly and said she was doing a little fall housecleaning and hoped

Leah appreciated her efforts, because she had been at it since right after lunch.

Everything in the living room was in a different place, including the television. Marcene had rearranged the furniture! The artwork on the walls was gone, but where it had disappeared to, Leah couldn't tell, as there was no sign of anything stacked in the living room/kitchen/dining area. She was speechless. What should she say? She knew what she wanted to say, but diplomacy seemed to be called for. There had already been enough confrontation with Marcene.

"Well," Leah said, "you certainly have been busy. I guess we can try this new arrangement, but the TV will have to go back where it was. There's only one source for the cable, so we can't get anything except the local stations unless the TV is plugged into that strip." Leah pointed to the baseboard installation that brought cable into her living room.

"Surely you can have an additional plug installed. Gene put in extra outlets for us so I can move things around whenever I get the urge. Any good electrician can do the work. How do you like it? I think it's nicer and makes the room look bigger. Heaven knows you can't do anything about how small all your rooms are, but rearranging and moving things around helps a lot. I put one of the chairs in my bedroom, and another one is in the front closet for now. I haven't figured out a good place for it yet." Marcene looked rather pleased with herself.

Leah decided not to say anything, but as soon as her houseguest left to go back home—soon, she hoped—she would put things back the way they were. Leah thanked her mother and went into the kitchen to start dinner.

On the way home on the bus Leah had decided to fix waffles, eggs, and sausage, something both she and Russell had enjoyed a few nights ago. It was easy and did not require much preparation time. Leah laid out the ingredients and whipped up the waffle batter. Marcene came into the kitchen as she was putting the sausages in the pan to brown.

"What are you doing?" Marcene asked, acting as though Leah had done something outrageous.

"I'm making waffles and sausages. It won't take long. I'm sure you're hungry after your afternoon of furniture moving. Why don't you sit down and enjoy a glass of tomato juice before we have our meal?" Leah said.

"I've never fixed waffles and sausages for dinner, and I don't think you should either. What's wrong with meat and potatoes and vegetables? Don't you have chicken or beef or pork or something in your freezer? I guess I should have checked. Well, it isn't all that late. We can go shopping for what we need right now. I'll even buy. Come on, get your coat. We can take my car."

"Sorry, but I have no intention of going to the store this evening. It's after five, and the traffic will be horrendous. There's nothing wrong with waffles and sausage for dinner. I make it when I want to have something quick and easy. Please, just sit down, and I'll get it ready. You should try it; you'll like it," Leah said, quoting some long-ago TV commercial and putting on a smile she didn't feel in an effort to convince Marcene to accept her choice for dinner.

"Well, I never! When I have guests, I try to accommodate their needs. Guess this tells me something. Go ahead and fix your breakfast, but don't expect me to eat any of it. I'm sure it would not sit well on my stomach at this time of day."

Leah didn't respond but continued her meal preparation, and in less than fifteen minutes she had waffles, eggs, and sausage on the table. She saved batter for Russell, who probably would not be home until perhaps eight o'clock, since his place of work was a thirty-minute bus ride and then a ten-minute walk to the apartment. Marcene ignored her and the food. Leah tried to jump-start a conversation that might carry them somewhere beyond the present. She asked Marcene what sort of work she had done before she was married.

At first Marcene just sat there, arms crossed, looking rather sour. Then she said, "I was my mother's right-hand helper in the house from the time I finished school until I got married. When I was in high school, I did the cleaning and laundry, cooked, did the dishes, and took up sewing for the younger children. You met my four sisters. Well, they were all younger, and somebody had to take care of business. I also had four brothers, but two left home right after high school. We never heard from one of them again, and the other one, Nigel, joined the army and was killed. That broke Mama's spirit, and I had to take over everything. And I did it well … Everyone said so. You should have been raised in a big family; then you'd have learned skills that you're obviously not very good at. I could certainly teach you, but I don't think you even want to learn. We'll let that go. I just want you to know me better so you can be a real part of your family again."

Leah wondered how knowing Marcene better would contribute to being involved with the McGregor family. *How about getting to know me … who I am? Wouldn't that be a logical first step? Nobody but Gene and Russell has asked me anything about my life, and even Russell hasn't probed very much. Marcene seems to want me to know all about who they are and what they think and how they do things. That would be all right and make for good conversation, but it has to be a two-way street,* Leah thought. She didn't respond to Marcene's little monologue at once. Silence prevailed, so she decided to risk a mild reply. At least she hoped it would be mild.

"Marcene, I appreciate that it's hard for you to accept me as I am. I would be glad to tell you about myself and my past life and about my accomplishments and my failures, as well as my hopes and dreams. You can't make me into instant family. The family I grew up in is different from the one you and Gene share with your other children. You can't drag me kicking and screaming into your world. I think you need to get to know *me*, and maybe we can build a relationship on mutual respect and trust of each other. Can you see what I'm saying?"

Leah tried to discern what was going through her mother's mind. Marcene was staring straight ahead and had not made eye contact since Leah had begun to speak. Nevertheless, Leah continued, "I've gotten to know Russ a little already. I think we've found a bond, and we're building on it. It will have to be the same with you and the rest of the family. Think about that, please."

Leah rose and cleared the dishes from the table. She put the untouched waffles and sausages on a plate, covered it with plastic wrap, and put it in the refrigerator. Then she turned to Marcene once more and said, "I'm going to visit a neighbor of mine who recently had surgery. I ran into her husband on my way home this evening. He has to attend a meeting tonight, and he asked if I would keep her company while he's away. If I'm back before you retire for the night, maybe we can continue this conversation."

Marcene still said nothing but rose and went into "her" bedroom.

"Okay," Leah said aloud and proceeded to wrap up some cookies she had picked up from the bakery on her way home. She would take them over to Alice, her neighbor. She left a note for Russell about making himself waffles and frying up more sausage and left to visit her friend.

It was after nine thirty when she returned to her apartment. The lights were off in the living room, and Russell had left a note on the kitchen counter saying he had gone out with a new friend to see a movie and wouldn't be until late. She looked into the refrigerator to see if he had eaten the waffles. They were gone, so she assumed he had. But then she saw the empty batter bowl. In the dishwasher were two more dinner plates, so Leah assumed that Marcene had had second thoughts about not eating breakfast food at dinnertime. She smiled. Maybe it was a sign of capitulation, but she doubted it. As she prepared for bed and snuggled under the covers, she smiled again. "Chalk one up for Leah," she said.

There was no sign of Marcene when Leah left for work, and Russell was still in bed as well. She didn't leave a note, assuming Russell could handle his mother, if in fact handling was required. The day passed quickly for Leah because they were very busy at the Book Nook and she had a tutorial session on how to order books. The job she loved the most, other than waiting on eager customers, was opening the boxes of new books that came almost every day. So many of them called to her, and she had laid aside several to purchase with part of her first paycheck. *This could be a dangerous job,* she'd concluded, *requiring real self-discipline. It wouldn't be difficult to spend half my check on books.* She'd managed to limit herself to five, with a promise not to add to the stack until after payday.

It was already dark when Leah arrived home a little past six, having walked on this particular evening. When she opened the door to her apartment, several different smells, all of them good, assaulted her senses. She could detect the wonderful aroma of bread, as well as some sort of meat. She caught a whiff of something pungent. Cinnamon? Nutmeg? Maybe a combination. It was apparent Marcene had been cooking and baking.

"Hello," Leah called as she came through the door and stripped off her coat. "Something smells good."

Marcene came out of the kitchen, a smile on her face. "Oh yes, I've been very busy all day. I've made all sorts of things for your freezer, so you won't find yourself short of good stuff for unexpected guests. I made meatballs, Russell's favorite meatloaf, a tuna casserole, three loaves of pumpkin bread, a chocolate cake, and two kinds of cookies, and for supper we're having my specialty, which is corned beef and cabbage, even though it's not Saint Pat's day. And I made two pies for the freezer and an apple-raisin for us tonight."

Leah was astonished at the long list of baked and cooked foods Marcene had made. But why, Leah wondered, had she gone so overboard? In the kitchen the counter was filled with all the items Marcene had mentioned, plus two loaves of what appeared to be Irish soda bread.

"What in the world am I going to do with all this?" Leah asked, looking at Marcene and wondering if she realized that two people couldn't begin to eat everything spread out in front of her, at least not anytime soon. The freezer had been pretty full before, and it would be difficult—perhaps impossible—to find enough free space for all the food arrayed on the counter. "Thank you for your effort. This is above and beyond, and I do appreciate what you accomplished, but some of this will grow old and stale before we can consume it," Leah said. She was still in shock, trying to understand what Marcene had been thinking when she went on the baking and cooking binge.

"Don't you have a freezer in your storage area? Surely you have more space than just the top part of your refrigerator? I wanted you to see what you should be doing at least once a month or even more often. Then you won't be taken by surprise when guests come, like you were when I arrived. You can buy a small freezer that won't take up much room. We could run out yet tonight and pick one up, and it would be a good investment for you so you're not caught short again. Now I think I'd like to have that corned beef and cabbage I made. Russell doesn't like it, so we don't need to wait for him. Why don't you set the table, and I'll get the food in bowls. I hope you have a little something to go with this. A little Irish beer would be nice, but if you have wine, we'll make that do. I didn't see any nice wineglasses. If you don't have any, I'll put that on my list of things I want to get you for Christmas. Come on. I'm hungry after working all day."

Leah was close to laughter, but she managed to suppress it. It struck her as hilarious that Marcene would think it appropriate to make all that food without first checking. She was just beginning to realize how different Marcene was from Grace Anderly, her mother. Part of the difference might be ethnic since Leah had had no experience with Irish traditions, but for Marcene, food was important, and being prepared was essential. Leah smiled. It was just too funny, but her laughter would have been difficult to explain.

The corned beef and cabbage was all right, but it wasn't one of Leah's favorites. She dutifully ate what she could and remarked it was nice to have some leftovers for the weekend.

Leah invited Marcene to go into the living room and watch TV while she cleaned up the kitchen. Mixing bowls and pots and utensils of all sorts were stacked in the sink. Leah didn't care. She wanted to be alone, and this was a way for her to have solitude and at the same time acknowledge that Marcene had worked hard all day and deserved a rest. Leah put a pillow behind Marcene's back, turned on the TV, and handed her the remote before returning to kitchen duty. Early that morning Leah had moved the TV back to its original spot, so it was properly installed and ready for use once again.

It took an hour and fifteen minutes to clean up the dishes and the kitchen and find spots for all the food. In the end, Leah took one pie to the friend she had visited the previous evening and then distributed several of the pumpkin-bread loaves to other neighbors. The freezer and refrigerator were full, but Leah was able to put some items outside on the kitchen window's ledge, where they could survive in the cold December air. It wasn't the first time she had used the window ledge for emergency purposes. Upon completing her cleanup tasks, she went into the living room and discovered that Marcene was sound asleep. She debated just leaving her there but decided to awaken her and see her safely to bed. In the morning, Saturday, she didn't have to be at work until noon, so she planned to talk to her mother about leaving then or most certainly on Sunday.

Chapter 17

The phone jangled loudly before seven on Saturday morning. Leah rolled out of her bed, which was not hard to do on the couch, and reached over to answer. "Hello," she said sleepily.

"Hello. It's Gene. I wanted to let you know that I just landed at O'Hare and will get a taxi to your place as soon as I can. I've come to rescue you. Russell called me yesterday and said you had probably had enough of Marcene."

He chuckled and then said, "You know, she left without telling me, and because I was at a convention of hardware people in Des Moines, Iowa, I didn't find out she was gone until Russell called. I traded in my Des Moines to Minneapolis ticket for one to Chicago, and here I am. I'll drive back with her today, but I can't say I'm unhappy to have an excuse to see you. I'm also delighted to get to see where you live and have a little while to chat before we leave."

"I look forward to your coming. You're right; it's been a bit dicey here. As Russell told me several times, his mother can be pretty forceful. She cleaned my living room and rearranged all the furniture and told me I should get additional cable-television plugs so the TV could be moved from one place to another." Leah laughed. It had become a source of amusement to her now, replacing the anger and frustration that had been her first reaction. She'd realized that getting angry didn't change anything, and in one respect, it was funny. Leah also related

Marcene's baking-and-cooking frenzy of the previous day and assured him they would have enough food to provide a hearty lunch before he and Marcene left for the Twin Cities.

Marcene still had not come out of her room at nine thirty, and Leah was pretty sure that Gene would be arriving soon. Should she knock on the bedroom door or just let her sleep until Gene arrived? She decided to wait. Almost at once, the bell rang, letting her know someone was asking to be buzzed in down below.

Gene looked thinner than Leah remembered, and she discovered she was not unhappy to see him, perhaps because he was the answer to her prayer. "Welcome to Hyde Park," she said, holding the door open for him. "Come in. Have you had breakfast?"

"I had a breakfast sandwich on the plane, but if you have coffee, I'd love that."

"How about some pumpkin bread your wife made? I haven't had any yet, but it smelled great when I came home yesterday. Come into the kitchen and sit down, and I'll make a fresh pot of coffee. Your wife is still in bed, but I think I hear some activity now."

Gene sat down, looking around at the apartment and commenting about what a cozy, comfortable place it was, although he said he realized that the living room still bore the mark of his wife's rearrangements. He said that Leah would probably put the furniture back once they were gone.

"I probably will," conceded Leah. She wondered if furniture arranging was an ongoing activity at their house. Marcene came out of the bedroom, fully dressed. Her hair was nicely combed and pulled away from her face, which Leah thought to be a better style than just letting it hang down as she had done the last two days.

"I thought I heard your voice, Gene. What are you doing in Chicago? You're supposed to be in Des Moines for your meeting."

"I was, but Russell told me you were here, so I thought I'd fly in and we could drive home together. It's a beautiful sunny day, so it should be a lovely drive. I hear there's new snow farther north but nothing on the highways. Are you ready to go back?" Gene asked.

"No, I don't think so. There's so much I still want to do here. Lizzie and I haven't had the sort of conversation I've been looking forward to, so I think I'll need at least another three or four days before I'm ready to leave. You can take the car, and when I'm ready, Leah can drive me home. We can rent a car. It's close to Christmas, so it would be a good time for her to come and see how a real family celebrates the birth of our Lord. My work here isn't done yet, Gene."

"Marcene, there's no work for you here. I want you to come home with me. The house is always so quiet without you, and I'm sure Charlene hardly knows what to do with herself with you not there." Leah thought she saw this little exchange as more tongue in cheek than passing on news from the home front.

"You think so? You miss me? Well, I find that hard to believe, but I suppose the house has gone to pot, and Charlene isn't much of a cook. If you think I'm needed, maybe I will go, but I'd like Lizzie to come too. Russell has a job now, so he's busy, but maybe he can get off for Christmas and come up north then."

Once again Leah was amazed at Marcene's thought processes. Did she think that Leah didn't have a job to keep her in Chicago? Did she think Leah could just leave whenever she wished? It was mind-boggling. It occurred to Leah that her birth mother might be a sexist who was stuck in outdated gender roles from back in the thirties and forties. The humor of it struck Leah once again, but she suppressed even a grin.

The coffee was ready, so Leah poured three cups and laid out the pumpkin bread and some butter. She offered Marcene cereal and fruit, which was refused, politely. There was a change in attitude here, and Leah wondered what accounted for it. After finishing several slices of bread and several cups of coffee,

Marcene disappeared into the bedroom to pack, inviting Leah to help her. However, Leah declined, saying she wanted to be able to visit with her father for a few minutes.

Gene was clearly eager to speak with Leah, and as soon as she sat down with him in the living room, he asked, "Will you and Russell be coming for Christmas? I'm sure Marcene has already talked about it with you, but I want you to know all the family would be delighted to have you there."

"I appreciate the offer, but I have plans to spend Christmas Eve and part of Christmas Day with my grandmother at her care facility. I have to work the day after Christmas because it's the beginning of the store's after-Christmas sale, so I'll be coming back to Chicago midafternoon on Christmas Day. I'll encourage Russell to go home for Christmas Eve and Christmas Day if he has the time off. If he does, would you talk seriously with him, Gene?"

Gene raised an eyebrow but nodded.

"You know, he doesn't think you listen when he tells you his ideas and what he's interested in. He's a great kid, and I think he has a lot of potential. He's enrolled for a mid-January class in what they call industrial artistry. I'm not sure what it's all about, but he's very excited, so if you could listen and encourage him, it would be great. He doesn't think anyone cares about him. His phrase is 'Nobody gives a damn.' I'm sure that's not true, but I thought you should hear it from me. Listen to him, will you? He's not a kid anymore, so give him a chance. Don't put him down, even if you think he's not making the best choices. He needs to try his wings and get a little encouragement. That's my opinion." Leah hoped she had not offended Gene.

Leah's words seemed to surprise Gene, but he nodded several times. "I guess I've been less than supportive of Russell and the things he's interested in, probably because they don't interest me. I was hoping I'd have one son who would want to help me run my stores, but it doesn't look like that's going to happen. I'll listen, Leah. Thanks for reminding me, because I get used to tuning people out if I don't have an interest in what they're saying. My wife's a good example of that attitude. Maybe I'll even try a little harder there too."

Gene gave Leah a loose hug and said, "I'll get the old Chevy warmed up. Marcene will appreciate not having to get into a cold car."

Russell emerged from his bedroom, still in a pair of sweatpants and a rather disreputable T-shirt with a hole in one sleeve. "Hey, Dad. I'm glad you came. You taking Mama back today?"

"Yes, we'll be leaving as soon as she finishes packing. Everything going all right, son? I'd like to hear about your new job, but I think for Leah's sake I should get your Mama out of here as soon as possible." He smiled at Russell and looked over at Leah, who was smiling as well. Then with the promise that father and son would have a chat soon, maybe at Christmas, he left to warm up the car.

The door closed on Gene, and Leah heard the bedroom door open at the same time. She wondered if Marcene had been waiting for Gene to leave before she came out.

"Lizzie, we'll expect you and Russell for Christmas Eve. We have such wonderful traditions I think you'll enjoy. Try to bring gifts for the immediate family and also for Uncle Fritz and Aunt Louise. They were your baptismal sponsors, so they're special. Cards for the rest of the aunts and uncles will be fine, but a box of candy for each family would be nice. I know Gene's downstairs already, so I'd better go. Come give your mother a hug and kiss."

Marcene took Leah's arm and pulled her into a tight embrace, and once again Leah was forced to endure a series of sloppy kisses. Leah, to her credit, was able to smile and say good-bye and thank you to her mother. Once the door was closed, however, Leah breathed a sigh of relief and immediately stripped her bed and gathered towels from the bathroom to include in the first load of laundry. She also pulled the sheet and pillowcase from her sofa sleeping spot. It would feel good to return to normal. Work at the Book Nook would begin at twelve, so the repositioning of the living room furniture would have to wait until tomorrow.

Chapter 18

With less than a week until Christmas Leah had a lot to do and little time to do it. On her lunch hour and after work she went shopping. She felt obligated to give Gene and Marcene, as well as Charlene and Russell, gifts, but she had only said hello to Stephen, so she thought a nice card would suffice. Though she had not met Harmon at all, she would send a card to him as well. A special gift for her grandmother was also on her agenda, and after much searching she found a lovely music box. A dancer on top twirled around when the key underneath was wound. She was sure one of the aides would be happy to assist her grandmother in the winding process since her arthritis would keep her from doing it herself.

The days passed quickly, and on December 24, Leah and Russell took the train to the downtown station, where they boarded another train that took them to the airport. As part of Russell's Christmas gift, Leah had given him an airline ticket to Minneapolis–Saint Paul. He was to board at 10:00 a.m. and would return the following day on the last flight out of the Twin Cities. Before they arrived at O'Hare, Leah quizzed Russell about the trains he would need to take on his return. She hoped he had it all straight.

"Hey, don't worry," he said. "I'm not a punk kid anymore. I'm a city boy. I got this down cold. See you very late tomorrow night. You drive carefully, okay?" Russell hugged her, and they parted company, he to his gate and she to rent a car for her road trip north.

Traffic on the tollway was heavy, with most of it heading in the same direction she was going, but after she exited onto a two-lane road, she virtually had the pavement to herself. She arrived at the nursing care center just before one in the afternoon, having stopped for lunch a few miles from the facility. One of the things Leah had failed to do was to call ahead for a motel room, but she was sure the people at the nursing home could recommend a place nearby. She hoped to be able to take care of that piece of business before seeing her grandmother.

Leah parked the rental, a compact car that she very much enjoyed driving. There was no one at the desk when she entered, so she sat down on one of the chairs in the reception area and picked up a magazine. In less than a minute a young male nurse came striding down the hallway. He smiled when he saw her, and Leah returned the smile.

"I'll bet you're here to visit my favorite resident. Corinne told me that her granddaughter was coming and that she was a very beautiful young lady, so you must be the one. I'm Harmon, but as you can probably see from my badge, I'm Harm to the residents." Harm stuck out his hand, and it was then that Leah saw his last name: McGregor! Harmon McGregor! She thought, *Oh, my God, this is my brother! What should I do? What should I say?*

She hesitated only a moment, however, before she said, "I'm Leah Anderly." She waited to see if he recognized the name, but he didn't seem to react, except to look a little puzzled by her hesitation to greet him.

"Sorry if I was a bit too forward, but I like to get to know the relatives of the residents. That's how we usually refer to the patients. Corinne is special to me, and we've become good friends. You know, you look familiar. Have you been here before?"

"I was here once before, but I don't think we met. Maybe we saw each other in the hall. I don't remember." Leah knew she had to identify herself. They would meet one day soon anyway, and if she failed to acknowledge him now, it would be awkward when it did happen. "Harmon, Harm, have you been in touch with your family since Thanksgiving? Oh, I don't know how to say this, but I know who you are, and I guess I have to tell you who I am, but I don't quite know how to do it." Leah paused and looked down at the floor and then at Harmon once again.

A look of recognition crossed Harmon's face. "Leah! You said your name was Leah. You're not *the* Leah are you? The lost Lizzie?"

"I am the lost Lizzie, for want of a better description. I had no idea you worked here when your parents said you were in Milwaukee working in a care facility. I missed seeing you the day I revealed my identity to your parents. I heard you had to leave to return to work. I met your older brother, and you probably know that Russell is living with me now. Just this morning I put him on a plane to the Twin Cities to spend Christmas at home. If you're going up there, he can tell you all about me. I like Russell very much, and we get along great ..." Leah trailed off, not knowing how to stop.

"Ah, bratty little brother Russell. He gave me fits in my teens, and I suppose I wasn't very nice to him sometimes. I hope he's behaving himself. I heard he has a job and is starting school in January. Good for him."

"Yes, he's all set for school. I'm not sure he should keep his current job. They're paying him in cash, and he gets no pay stub. As a student of the law, I know it could be trouble down the way for him if he continues to work there, and if they're into other illegal stuff, I wouldn't want Russell to get caught up in that. I haven't spoken to him about this yet, because we just finished dealing with a four-day visit from your mother. Well, I won't go into that. Don't worry; I'll look after Russ. He's my brother, you know. I guess you are too, but I'm having a hard time with all this family I've discovered I have. I'm an only child and haven't had any experience with siblings, so it's been a difficult few weeks trying to sort things out." Leah hoped she wasn't rambling too much, but she wanted to explain a few things to Harmon to get off on the right foot with him.

Harmon was grinning. "I think I know what you're saying. I'm part of that goofy family, and I've had my share of problems with every one of them, but probably Mama has been the biggest challenge. I get the message that her visit was a little trying. I can only imagine. The few times we've talked recently she's gone on and on about how you're going to come back to live in your old bedroom and take up your rightful place in the family, whatever that means. Your rightful place for years was 'poor little lost girl,' and Mama's was 'poor Mama who continues to suffer that loss every day.' I used to wish they'd find your body so we could bury you and the drama would stop. Sorry. I shouldn't have said that. Do you know Mama blamed me for your disappearance? Charlene too. Only Stephen escaped because he was helping Dad at the store that morning. Then poor Russ came along. He didn't get blamed, but he wasn't the girl that Mama wanted, and he certainly wasn't anything like you had been. To hear Mama tell it, and we heard it over and over and over again, you were smart, beautiful, and of course absolutely perfect, and the rest of us fell short. She'd say that if you had not been lost, you would have continued to be all those things." Harmon paused and looked intently at Leah. "Hmmm, maybe Mama was right. You did turn out to be beautiful, and from what Russell says, you're going to finish your law degree and be a famous lawyer, so you're smart too."

Leah couldn't help it: she started to laugh. "Wow. I didn't realize how much all of you siblings must have hated me. I can only say I'm sorry I caused you trouble of one sort or another. Right now I'm thinking of resigning my position in the family, but I want to keep Russ. Your dad isn't too bad either, but I don't think he's aware of the feelings all of you have about me and about the whole disappearance business. I suppose I can't include Stephen in that, because I had only a very brief conversation with him. We were introduced, and he was commanded to hug and kiss me, which he did, rather reluctantly I thought. Then he disappeared, and I didn't see him again. That probably means he has the same feelings as the rest of you. Charlene certainly let me know what my disappearing did to her life. I guess I feel a little guilt, but hey, I had nothing to do with it, and I don't remember a thing about life with the McGregor family."

"Why don't we start over? Hi, I'm Harmon McGregor. I work here, and I like to play basketball in my free time and ice-skate in the winter. I love to read mysteries and westerns, and I have a new girlfriend. You're the first to know. Your turn, Leah."

"Okay. Hi, I'm Leah Anderly. I work at the Book Nook, a bookstore in Hyde Park, a suburb of Chicago. I used to be a paralegal, but after January first I'll begin my studies to finish my law degree while working part-time. I love college football, especially if it's Northwestern University playing. I also like to read almost anything, and I love to walk and run and swim. I was engaged, but not any longer. I guess that's it."

"Where are you staying? Do you have friends in the area, or are you going on to Minneapolis–St Paul? Mama thinks you are, but Dad said you wouldn't be coming."

"I don't have a motel yet. I was hoping to make a reservation once I arrived. Any recommendations? And no, I'm not going to the Cities for Christmas. I plan to spend today and part of tomorrow with my grandmother. She told me she made arrangements for me to have a special dinner with her here this evening. I hear you do holidays up royally."

"We do. I'm working today and tomorrow but get New Year's off. If you don't have a place to stay, why don't you come home with me after my shift ends at nine tonight? The Ritz it ain't, but it's clean because I just went over it with a lick and a promise yesterday," Harmon said with a grin.

"Oh, that would be an imposition," Leah said.

"Not at all. Actually, I think it would be an ideal time to get to know my new old sister, so please accept my invitation. I'm serious when I say I want you to come."

"All right. Maybe I can get some insights about how to handle your mother, and maybe you can also tell me more about Charlene and Stephen. I hardly know them at all. You can also regale me with stories of your adventures. Russ says you were quite the lothario in high school and college … the campus jock that every girl was dying to date. That's all I know about you, so if there's something of more substance that you would care to reveal, I would be delighted to hear it."

They both laughed, and Harmon set the time and place where Leah was to wait for him after his shift ended. Then he escorted her to her grandmother's room but didn't go in, saying he was needed to help an aide with a dementia patient.

"Merry Christmas, Grandma," Leah called as she came into the room, carrying several small packages and one larger one. "I come bearing gifts, but we'll wait until later to open them. How are you? You look well."

Corinne was sitting in her wheelchair, bent over a newspaper. Leah leaned down to hug her and kiss her forehead. Then Leah drew up a chair from the corner and sat in front of her grandmother. "What are you reading?" Leah asked, trying to see what it was from an upside-down angle.

"You made the Milwaukee paper this morning: 'Saint Paul Family Receives Unexpected Christmas Gift.' It's about your abduction and then about you coming back to them, although they make it sound like it just happened yesterday and was a sort of Christmas present. There's a picture of your mother and sister with a cake that says, 'Welcome Home, Lizzie.' Are you going there for Christmas, or will you be with me today and tomorrow?" Corinne was obviously a little shaken by the article in the paper but maybe more shaken by the possibility that her granddaughter would not be staying to celebrate Christmas.

"I'm staying here, Grandma. It's pretty typical of Marcene to continue to plan for my coming for Christmas even though

I told her I wouldn't be there, because I want to be here with you. Let me read what it says, if I may."

Leah scanned the article, which seemed to focus more on what had happened twenty years ago and the effect it had had on the family and on Marcene in particular. Leah's name was not mentioned. She was referred to as Lizzie or Elizabeth, for which she was grateful. Gene had probably insisted on that omission. The last sentence hinted that the "abductee" did not want publicity and that her name had not been released for that reason.

"Now this is a Christmas gift … having my name left out of the story! Even if the Chicago papers pick it up, I'm not identified, so I shouldn't have reporters on my doorstep wanting an interview. They would be looking for something to pull on the heartstrings, such as how awful my life was until I found my real parents. I hope this is the end of the drama. You know my younger brother, Russell, is staying with me, and we're getting along well. You'll never believe it, but just a few minutes ago I met another brother of mine. You know him. Harmon McGregor. He was the only immediate family member I hadn't met, so we didn't recognize each other. Then I saw his name tag. That gave me a shock! I like him, though, and I felt an almost-instant connect. That didn't happen with any other family members. What do you think about all this?"

"Harm? He's your brother? Oh for goodness' sake, now that is a surprise. I like him very much. He's a wonderful nurse and talks to me when he takes my vitals. Many of the aides don't. We talk about the latest news and always chat about the Green Bay Packers and the Vikings. He's a Vikings fan, and I'm not! But it's all good-natured teasing. Well, well, he's your brother. This is good news as far as I'm concerned, to know you have a fine fellow like Harm as a brother. My, my," Grandmother said, smiling and shaking her head in disbelief.

They spent the rest of the afternoon talking, and Leah sat quietly while her grandmother took a short nap. Then an announcement was made over the PA system that dinner would be served in ten minutes, so Leah offered to push her grandmother's wheelchair. The hallway was crowded with five or six wheelchairs being pushed or self-propelled, and an aide was directing traffic at the door to the dining room. There were place cards for the residents and their guests. Leah spotted Harm in a far corner of the room, and when he saw Leah, he immediately came their way. "Your places are over here," he said, pointing to the left, near the bank of windows that looked out on the frozen pond.

They found their spots and were delighted to see that Harm was seated with them. He smiled and confessed that he had managed to arrange their seating. All the staff on duty would be eating with the residents, except those serving or working in the kitchen. Heaping plates of turkey and dressing, potatoes with gravy, and green beans with bacon were delivered to each guest, and there were bowls of cranberry sauce, coleslaw, and cottage cheese on each table. They were encouraged to help themselves or ask for assistance in serving up the various salad choices.

At the end of the meal, bread pudding with a delicious sauce was served to those who still had room. Leah was effusive with praise for the meal and the efficiency with which it was served. Harm was delighted with her appreciative words and promised to pass along her compliments to the chefs. He told her a host of volunteers had helped prepare and serve the meal. As the tables were being cleared, Leah's grandmother said, "I'd like to lie down for a while, if you don't mind, Leah. It's my evening routine. A little rest now allows me to stay up later for TV or whatever is going on. And it is Christmas Eve, so we must be ready for that, although I'm sure you don't believe in Santa Claus anymore," Corinne said with a smile.

Leah agreed a little rest was in order. It would give her a chance to sit in the comfortable rocking chair and catch forty winks herself. Both of them dropped off before long, although Corinne had tried to carry on a conversation, thinking it might please Leah. At seven thirty Grandmother awoke, and when

Leah told her the time, she said, "You've come all the way from Chicago, and here I am, sleeping the time away."

"I slept too, so don't worry about it. Why don't you open the gifts I brought?" Corinne opened the first small package and was delighted to find the music box with the dancing ballerina that reminded her of how much she'd loved to dance as a young girl. The other small package held several hair clips and Corinne was delighted with those as well, saying the clips would help keep the hair out of her eyes. The large package was a pale-pink bathrobe made of fleece. The rest of the evening they talked about family, and Corinne related stories Leah had never heard before. She promised herself she'd write them down once she returned home. At nine Leah announced that she was to meet Harm at the front entry. She wondered aloud if Grandma would think it inappropriate for her to stay with him in his apartment, but after all, they were brother and sister.

"How nice that he's already looking after his newfound sister. Now if he was just my nurse and not your brother, I would have second thoughts on you going there." Grandma's eyes twinkled as she said this.

"Oh, Grandma, I can see that you must have been full of mischief when you were young. I don't suppose you'd have done something like that—stayed overnight with a boy … or young man I should say."

"Now wouldn't you just love to know? If my father had found out, pity the poor boy. You're right of course; it wasn't done in polite society. But these days, anything goes I guess. Well, I'm glad you'll have a chance to get acquainted with your brother. Run along. I'll see you tomorrow."

Harmon was a few minutes late and said, "Sorry I'm late, but there's always some last-minute thing to take care of. I'm ready now, so you can follow me in your car. It isn't far, and I'll make sure I don't lose you in the traffic jam. Just kidding about the traffic. Come on."

It was less than a five-minute drive to Harmon's place which was not an apartment as Leah had assumed but a small house with a wide front porch that curved around one side. A detached garage had room for two cars, and as Harmon drove in, he waved Leah into the other stall. The garage was spotless, and there was little in it except the two cars. A snow shovel and a rake hung on one wall, and a shelf at the back held a few tools, all neatly laid out or hung on the wall.

Harmon led the way into the house via the back door at the end of the side porch Leah had observed. Inside, a small entryway contained hooks for hanging coats, and a short bench held a pair of winter boots and some very dilapidated tennis shoes. The door from the entryway into the house had a window with a neatly hung lace curtain that obscured the view into the room. Leah couldn't help wondering if Marcene had been there. But no, she had not observed this level of neatness in Marcene and Gene's house.

Harmon opened the door, and they entered the kitchen. "I have to warn you that it's a bit of a mess in here. I'm in the middle of remodeling. The floor isn't finished, and they messed up on the color of the sink. See, everything is white but the kitchen sink! Is it pale pink or pale yellow? Depends on the light, but right now it looks pink to me. They're coming on the twenty-eighth to change it, but at least they left me with a sink. They were going to take the wrong one away, but then I wouldn't have had any source of water except in the bathroom. I'll show you to your room later. I just got the bed and dresser a week ago, so you're the first to try them out. I'll get sheets and blankets, but first let me turn up the heat and take off my uniform. There's the living room, so make yourself comfortable. I won't be long."

Leah was impressed with the house, which seemed bigger on the inside than it had appeared to be from the outside. The living room ran almost the length of the front of the house, with an alcove to the right. The bedrooms were obviously upstairs because she heard the sound of Harmon's footfalls on bare wood above her. The living room was sparsely furnished, but what was there was attractive and comfortable. A large flat-screen TV was fastened to the wall, and Leah immediately remembered Marcene's furniture rearranging, including the moving of the television set. She smiled as she pictured Marcene trying to unscrew this TV from the wall.

Harmon was wearing a pair of jeans and a University of Minnesota sweatshirt when he came downstairs. "Why don't I show you the guest room, and if you like, you can change too? But that's just a suggestion, not a command." Harmon smiled.

The room Leah was to occupy had a slanted ceiling on one side, and the bed was tucked into that area. She hoped she wouldn't raise up in the night and bump her head, but she decided there was plenty of room. Double windows looked out on a small backyard, where she could see the remains of a summer garden, with stocks of something rising out from under the inch or so of snow. The bathroom was between her room and Harmon's. Leah decided to change into a pair of sweatpants and a purple Northwestern pullover with white stripes on the sleeves and the neck. When she finished dressing, she joined Harmon in the kitchen, where he was making noise with pots and pans.

"What's cooking?" asked Leah.

"I have some homemade soup that I'll heat up, but it's half-frozen, so it may take awhile. Are you hungry? We ate quite early, so I thought we could have cheese and crackers and even a little beer or soda. We had a pretty large meal, but I thought we might need a little something on the light side before bedtime."

"I would like a glass of water, but I can get that myself if you point me to the glasses."

Harmon reached into the cupboard and pulled out two glasses. He filled them with ice and then ran water into them from the kitchen sink. "Shall we take our drinks into the living room where we can be more comfortable, or do you want to sit at the kitchen table? Your choice, Leah."

"Let's sit in the living room. I love your sofa and chairs. They're very comfortable."

They sat down and sipped their water. Leah was amazed to be sitting with yet another brother. Only a month ago she'd had no siblings, and now she had four and was going to stay at the home of one of them. She smiled.

"What are you thinking about?" Harmon asked. "Are you thinking what I'm thinking, that this is weird? Eight hours ago we didn't know each other, but here we are. I guess we ought to be telling each other things about ourselves. I'd love to know about your interests and your work and whatever else you want to share. I'll give you some insight into my likes and dislikes and maybe mention goals I have. Why don't you go first?"

Leah began telling Harmon about her life, especially the years from school age onward. She didn't go into her work at the law firm in any great detail, only to say she had enjoyed what she did. She said her goal now was to finish her degree. But as soon as those words were out of her mouth, she had a revelation, though she didn't know where it came from.

"You know, I may go a different direction and forget the law degree. I may start work on a master's in social work. I think I'd like working with kids or maybe with young women who are having a tough time in life. I saw how you relate to the elderly, and I admire your work and how you seem to enjoy what you do. I guess I'd like to work in an area where I could help people who wanted and needed help. I'm not cut out to be a nurse, but there are other areas where I could fit in, or at least I hope so."

Harmon expressed enthusiasm for Leah's desire to explore social work in some capacity, but she replied that it had only just now popped into her head to go in that direction. They spoke about options for her at some length, and then he told her about his struggle before settling on a nursing career.

"I wanted to be a doctor, but the long years put me off, so I took some business courses and then even thought about becoming a teacher. But in the end I applied for acceptance into the nursing program at Fairview in Minneapolis and luckily got in. I may go back for a specialty later on, but I'm happy with where I am right now. I have a lot of responsibility for the nursing program here, yet I still manage to work directly with the residents, which I enjoy."

A wonderful aroma was wafting into the living room. Harmon said the soup was probably hot, so they carried their glasses back into the kitchen, refilled them, and Harmon dished up the soup, added some bread, cheese, and peanut butter to the simple meal, and Leah pronounced it perfect.

There was ice cream for dessert, and Harmon also put on the coffeepot, saying he enjoyed having a cup or two after his meal. They carried dessert and coffee back into the living room, where Harmon turned on the TV to a Christmas Eve concert that was beautifully done. They sat quietly for a good share of the program, and then Harmon said, "I suppose we should have gone to church tonight."

"I suppose we should have, but I enjoyed the choir and the orchestral offering on the program we just saw. It was all very well done, and those young people, all college students, were obviously enjoying what they were doing. Such talent! Do you go to church most Sundays, or do you only attend when you visit your parents? I wonder because I've observed your mom is big on regular church attendance. She even tried to get me to go when I was there right after Thanksgiving … when you bugged out and didn't come and meet me," Leah teased.

"I guess I don't go very often, but I do work two out of four Sundays. I could go on Saturday nights, but I don't. Mama is big on church, and I guess I had it shoved down my throat when I was growing up, so now I'm more selective about when I attend. I like hearing good music. I play a little piano and bought a Clavinova. It's over there in the alcove, but I don't seem to find as much time to play as I thought I would. I'd probably go to Mass more often if there was more music. What about you? Are you a churchgoer?"

"I do go quite regularly … but to a Methodist church, not a Catholic one … and believe it or not, Russell went with me once. He enjoyed the music too. It must be a family trait, because that's the part I like the best. I enjoy the singing, especially in a church with a good choir. They lead and help the rest of us feel comfortable belting out the words to a song like 'Amazing Grace.'"

Leah and Harmon continued their conversation until after midnight, when Harmon said, "Maybe we ought to call it a night. I have early duty tomorrow, starting at 8:00 a.m., but I usually try to get there before that to see if anybody had a bad night or needs a little TLC. You can sleep in as long as you like. I'll set out cereal for you, and there's a couple of bananas. Well, you'll figure it out. I'll let you use the upstairs bathroom, and I'll use the half-bath down here."

Leah said good night and trekked up the stairs, and after brushing her teeth and washing her face, she immediately crawled into bed. It had been a long but delightful day. She fell asleep almost at once and was able to relegate Alan to the far recesses of her mind.

In the morning Leah spent several hours visiting with her grandmother, and at noon they enjoyed a sumptuous meal in the dining room. However, Leah warned Grandma that she had to leave no later than two o'clock. She wanted to avoid driving late in the day when traffic would be heavier, and since it was spitting a little snow, she was even more anxious to get on the road. Half an hour after lunch Leah said her good-byes and by one thirty was in the car, heading back to Chicago, with the snow coming down a little harder. Harmon had not been able to sit with them at noon but came to say good-bye to Leah. She thanked him again for his hospitality and told him she hoped to be able to reciprocate at some time in the future.

The snow tapered off thirty minutes down the road, and soon the highway was clean and clear for the rest of the way. Leah arrived at the airport at three fifteen, turned in the rental car, and boarded the train back to Hyde Park. She fixed an early supper of a sandwich and a cup of tea and took it into the living room. She turned on the television but left the sound off. She thought about Alan, wondering what he was doing and if he was thinking about her. Were Alan and Juneau together? She didn't want to think about Juneau at all, but it was hard not to. Were they married? Not likely, as Alan had probably not gotten out of the hospital until a few days ago. There had been no word from anyone at the firm since three days before Christmas, when Jeremy had sent her an e-mail wishing her a merry Christmas and saying he hoped she would stop in soon to see everyone. Not likely. She would not be welcome at the office, but she would like to know how her old team was and whether the Quinlin case had gone to trial. At eleven she prepared for bed and crawled under the covers. The sheets and the air felt so cold, even though she'd raised the thermostat twice.

Leah thought perhaps it was feeling cold all over that made sleep illusive, but in truth she knew it was Alan. She tried to put him out of her mind, but he was right there, invading every effort to focus on something or someone else. A deep sadness had been creeping over her ever since she had heard that he and Juneau might get married and that there was a child on the way. *How will I ever get past this? There's no happiness in my life.*

Then she remembered something her mother had said on more than one occasion, but one particular incident … her father's death … stood out. Leah, who had held herself together through his illness, had broken down and sobbed. Her mother had also been crying but through her tears had said, "I know you're not happy, nor am I, but we should always be able to find a little joy in every situation. We can be joyful that your father is free of the pain that wracked his body and joyful that we had him in our lives for as many years as we did and joyful that he's with the angels, probably singing his favorite hymn, 'Rock of Ages.'"

Leah tried to think what joy she might find in the loss of Alan and the ending of her engagement, as well as being fired, all still tender spots in her soul. *Well, I suppose the fact that I experienced falling in love, really falling head over heels in love, and having someone love me in return might be a source of joy. Maybe beginning a new career might be a jump-start for joy too.*

On the drive back to Chicago she had solidified her idea about pursuing social work rather than finishing her law degree, and she realized she was looking forward to exploring something new. Right at this moment, however, the specter of joy seemed elusive.

Chapter 19

January blew in with a vengeance, dumping eight inches of snow on Chicago on New Year's Eve, with even more along Lake Michigan. Hyde Park, with its close proximity to the lake, received a foot of the white stuff. Leah and Russell didn't venture out until the second of January, when they both had work schedules to keep. Leah also stopped by the registrar's office at the University of Chicago on her lunch hour for the purpose of changing her class schedule and her plan for the future. The law would be put aside. She would concentrate on a new and better way of helping people, or so she believed.

Classes and work kept Leah busy, and the same was true for Russell. They had fallen into a comfortable routine, each claiming certain tasks as their own. Russell quit his first job after Leah talked to him of her concern about how he was being paid. An instructor in one of his classes helped him secure a position at a small machine-tooling shop whose owner was a supporter of the Greater Chicago Technical College where Russell was enrolled. It proved to be a good place to work, and the pay was better.

Russell and Leah kept in touch with the McGregors in Saint Paul, although not as often as Marcene would have liked. Charlene and Leah had begun e-mailing as a means of communication since it was easier for Charlene, who often had difficulty expressing herself. Leah tried to help Charlene see that always acceding to Marcene's commands wasn't necessarily a good thing for either of them, and she encouraged Charlene to go back to school or get a job.

The Book Nook served as an alternate universe for Leah and a welcome break from the classroom and paper writing. She and Russell sometimes shared space at the kitchen table, working on papers or presentations for their respective courses of study. Russell's presence in her life made Leah realize that at least one really good thing had come from her tracking down her family of origin.

Classes were very satisfying for Leah, but when spring break arrived, she was glad for a chance to have a respite from studying. On a particularly warm and sunny day she dragged her bicycle out of the basement storage area, pumped up the tires, and pedaled her way to the bike path along Lake Michigan. Bright pink tulips, purple hyacinths, and white lilies of the valley vied for her attention, and the greening grass along the lake beckoned. She stopped her ride, dismounted, and sat down facing the water. It was unusually calm with almost no spray where the water hit the rocks. The ground, however, was still slightly damp from the previous evening's rainfall, so Leah was forced to abandon her spot and continue her ride. Still, it had been delightful to enjoy the juices and joys of spring.

That evening she and Russell made plans for a trip to Saint Paul for Easter weekend. "We can drive up early Saturday and come back late Sunday. Is that okay with your schedule?" Leah asked as they lingered over their evening meal.

"Sure. I guess I'm ready to see everyone again. Dad e-mailed that Harmon and Stephen are going to be there, so we should show up, but two days will be enough for me," Russell said as he rose to clear the table.

"Two days sounds right for me too. I'm hoping it will go better than the last time I was there. I'll do my best not to make waves or say the wrong thing. I'm glad we're going together, because it will make it easier for me," Leah said.

On Saturday they left Chicago before seven in the morning. The trip was uneventful, and when they arrived, only Charlene was at home. Marcene and the boys were out shopping for groceries, and Gene was at the store. Before they had time to take their bags upstairs, Charlene took Leah aside and said she would soon begin work at a neighborhood bank. She had not told anyone else about it and wanted some advice on how to break the news, particularly to Marcene. Together they came up with a plan for announcing it at the beginning of their meal on Sunday noon, when a prayer of thanks was traditionally offered. Leah suggested that Charlene begin by saying, "I'd like to add a prayer of thanks of my own, and I hope all of you will be pleased for me. I will be starting a job at the State Bank next week."

On Sunday after Mass, the family gathered for the noon meal, and after their traditional prayer, Charlene made her prayer/speech. Marcene reacted immediately. "A job at the bank? You never said anything about that. What kind of work? I need you around here, so how can you even think of going off to what's probably a menial job? You can't be a teller. You can't even add fractions when we bake something. You need to remember your limitations, Charlene. No, you could never cut it at any bank!"

Charlene was visibly shaken by her mother's vehement outburst. No one said anything. *Well,* thought Leah, *somebody has to say something,* so she said, "Charlene, why don't you tell everyone about this great opportunity? Tell them about the training you're going to receive and what it could lead to in the future. I applaud your initiative, and I think we should have a toast to Charlene and her new job." Leah raised her water glass. "To Charlene and to her success at the State Bank of Saint Paul!"

Everyone looked at Leah and then at Marcene, as though waiting for a rebuke. But Harmon chimed in, "To Charlene. Good for you! May you have success and make a pile of money."

Then the rest of the family, in turn, toasted Charlene, all except Marcene, who sat there with her mouth open and a look of disbelief on her face. Charlene was smiling and acknowledged the good wishes.

No one said anything else, and they began passing the food. When everyone had their plates full, Marcene pushed back her chair, pointed her finger at Leah, and shouted, "I wish you had never come back from the dead!" Then she left the room. They could hear her footsteps on the stairs and the slamming of a door.

Leah kept looking at Gene. Why didn't he speak? He should have said something before, but certainly now was an opportunity to address the problem they all knew existed in the family. The elephant had left the room, but no one was saying anything. Leah rose and stood behind her chair. "We have a problem here. I believe your mother—no, our mother—is mentally ill, and we should do something about it. Somebody has to talk to her and get her to see a doctor for an evaluation. I don't know what goes on here day in and day out, but Charlene has told me things she has observed, and it doesn't take a rocket scientist to figure out something's wrong."

"Right, something is wrong, and it's been wrong ever since our sister came back from the dead, as Mama just said. I don't want to point fingers, but it seems to me that you, Leah, or whatever you want to be called, are the problem. Lizzie wasn't good enough for you I guess. Ever since you came back, things have gotten worse, or so I hear. You didn't show up at Christmas as promised, and Mama had gifts and your favorite kind of cookies waiting for you. The least you could have done was come for a day." Stephen glared at Leah as he spoke.

Harmon weighed in then, saying Leah had been visiting her grandmother at Christmas. He had not told anyone about Leah's having stayed at his house, nor had he shared any of their conversation. Now he defended her. "Steve, you don't even know Leah. She stayed at my house, and I was glad for the chance to talk with her and find out about her and what her hopes and dreams are."

"You mean she stayed overnight? That wasn't a good idea," Steve said.

"Why not? We had a good time, and I got to know her better."

"Asking a single woman to spend the night doesn't seem like a good idea to me. What will your neighbors think? But then, you've never used very good judgment when it came to women." Stephen took a sip of his wine and glared at his brother.

"My God, Steve, she's my sister. It's not like I invited her in for … for sex!"

"Okay, that's it! I resign from this family. I'm getting my stuff together and leaving. You can talk about me all you want. I don't give a damn. Russell, are you staying or coming with me?" Leah asked.

"I'm coming, Sis. Let's blow this place."

Leah and Russell left the dining room and in less than five minutes came downstairs, bags in hand. Leah led the way out the door, followed by Russell, who looked back at his father, perhaps hoping he would say something, anything.

They quickly threw their luggage into the trunk of the rental car and slid into their respective seats. As Leah was buckling her seat belt, Harmon opened her door and put his hand on her shoulder. "Don't go off like this, Leah. I agree with you completely about Mama needing an evaluation. I wish I knew where Dad was. He's hardly said two words to any of us since church, and that whole scene at the table didn't get any response from him either. Please, don't go yet."

"I don't think staying will be in anyone's best interest, least of all mine. I think I finally see the hate some members of this family have for me. Maybe *hate* is too strong a word, but I think you all wish, deep in your souls, that I had not come back from the dead, as your mother said. I'm not Mama's sweet little girl … the one you began to resent the minute she—I— disappeared into thin air, and I suspect that resentment continued to get stronger with the years. I was always thrown in your faces as the poor lost child who would have been more beautiful, more successful, smarter, more amazing than any of you could ever be. That's what you had to live with because your mother chose to wallow in her loss. Now I'm back, and she wishes I wasn't, and if you're all honest, you wish the same thing. I complicate things. I'm sorry, and I guess from now on I'll just try to stay out of your lives."

"Don't count me in what you just said," Russ announced. "I think you coming back to us was the best thing to ever happen to me. I'm sticking with you, Sister, and I probably won't ever come back here either."

Harmon laughed. "Here we are, having a crazy conversation. Yes, it is crazy. I like you, Leah, and I'm delighted to have you as a sister. If you weren't my sister ... well, who knows? We might have hit it off in a whole different way. Now that's sick, isn't it? I only say that because I think we're all a little sick, and we got the infection from you-know-who. No, Leah, not you, but from our mother. Do you really believe she's sick? She's sometimes mean, always bossy, sometimes sweet, and always vindictive. Is that what mental illness does to a person? I wish I'd paid more attention to that segment of my nursing education. Well, if you're not going to stay, travel safe, but keep in touch, both of you." Harmon closed the car door, backed away, and headed to the house.

It was a long ride back to Chicago, but the radio kept them company. Neither Russ nor Leah seemed interested in rehashing the weekend, and by the time they arrived at the airport and turned in the rental car, Leah had been able to put things in perspective; at least she hoped so.

Chapter 20

Spring turned fickle, allowing cold and even a few flurries of snow to fall on May 10. Leah was ready for summer, so when it finally came, she was delighted to be able to swim in the lake, run or bike along Lake Shore Drive, and get together with friends. She was taking a heavy load during the summer term that involved research and a paper due by the end of August. She'd already started writing and had checked out multiple books and monographs related to her chosen subject.

One beautiful evening in mid-June, after a run along the lake and then a shower and a change of clothes, Leah sat down to read through some of the material for her paper. The telephone jangled. "Hello," Leah said.

"Leah, its Gene. I have bad news. Marcene went in for her annual medical exam and mammogram five weeks ago. The results were suspicious, so three weeks ago she went to a specialist, who confirmed her doctor's diagnosis. She has stage four breast cancer. Her lymph nodes are compromised, and it's probably spread to her stomach and her pancreas. She's not dealing with this very well, and I suppose none of us are."

"Oh, Gene, I'm sorry to hear this. What do you plan to do?" Leah asked.

"I've been trying to figure it out. Charlene has moved out and lives with a friend in Minnetonka. The bank transferred her to their branch there, and she has pretty much cut herself off from us. I think she has a boyfriend. I hope so, for her sake.

Harmon was home this weekend, but he can't leave work right now except on days off, and Stephen is in Seattle working on his PhD. We desperately need someone to be with Marcene during the day. She can't do much of anything any longer, or refuses to might be a better way to say it. She's very weak, and they don't think she's going to last long. Chemo or radiation are possibilities, but the specialist says it's too far gone now and there won't be a cure. Chemo will only make her sick. She cries all the time and won't eat anything except cereal."

"That sounds like a difficult situation for everyone. I'm so very sorry for you and of course for Marcene."

"I hate to ask, but is there any chance you could come up to be with her, at least for a few weeks? I've asked a couple of her friends, but they all have the same story. She's been so nasty to them over the last year or so that they don't want to come over, even for a visit. She's also managed to alienate her sisters. I feel bad that I didn't question her about her lack of energy and appetite, and then there was the pain she had, usually right after eating, which may be why she wants only cereal. I should have realized something was wrong, but she's been complaining about imaginary aches and pains since you were taken, so I've learned to disengage. Could you come, Leah?"

The news of Marcene's cancer was shocking and unexpected. Leah tried to remember if Marcene had displayed any symptoms at Easter, just two months ago, but she couldn't recall anything raising a red flag. "I'm taking an independent summer course, but I might be able to come up after a lecture by a visiting professor on Friday. Attendance there is a requirement. If I can bring some books and work at your house, I suppose I could do it. Could the rest of the family come for a week or so if or when I have to return here for a lecture? I can't miss any of those, but I won't have another one for three and a half weeks. You know Russell was just promoted, so it isn't likely he can get away."

Leah paused, trying to figure out if she really should go. She felt sorry for Marcene. The big C scared and often devastated families when the diagnosis was made.

"Could you come Saturday?" Gene asked. "We really need you. I hate to impose this on you, but I don't know who else to ask. I hired two different caregivers already, and both were in and out in less than two days. You know what she can be like. Can you come?"

"All right, Gene, I'll come with the understanding that I can go home for the next lecture and that I'll have time to read and work on my paper while I'm there."

"Of course. We'll figure it out. Thank you for saying yes. Marcene will be glad you're coming I'm sure. She's gotten over Easter. We all have. I'll send you the money for plane fare, or would you rather rent a car and drive up?"

"I think I'll fly, but if I have to go back and forth a time or two, maybe I'll rent a car. I'll make the reservation and let you know what time I get in. Hopefully it will be Saturday."

They said their good-byes, and Leah sighed, sat down at the kitchen table, and thought about the implications of her agreeing to care for her mother. She was sure it would be nothing like caring for Grace, whom she still thought of as her mother. Marcene was her birth mother, but there was no bond there, not like the one Leah had experienced with Grace. She sighed again and then said out loud, "Leah, you're a glutton for punishment, but what else can you do? You owe her and Gene your life, so you have to do this."

Leah's plane was on time, and Gene was waiting for her. "Thanks for coming," he said as they walked toward the parking area, got into the car and started driving. "Harmon is at the house right now. He wanted to pick you up, but I told him I needed a little time to talk to you before we get to the house where everything may be chaotic. It's been hard for all of us, but Marcene is probably the one who's having the most trouble adjusting to the reality of our lives. I'd been planning to divorce her and even moved out briefly in late May, but I came back when she got the diagnosis. I don't think anybody else knows about my divorce plans. I hadn't even said anything to Marcene. I feel ashamed I guess, but I want a life, which I haven't had in years. I hope to marry a woman who works for me part-time. She's a widow with two young children, and she's a lot younger than I am, but neither of us has a problem with that anymore. I was hesitant, but she made me realize that loving someone isn't determined by age or even circumstance sometimes. Now I'm being the dutiful husband, and I feel guilty, knowing Marcene is going to die and that I will be free to marry Janet. A divorce would have been hard because of our religion, so I guess I spared her the scandal and humiliation."

Leah was stunned. She had not imagined that Gene was that unhappy. However, she had observed that the household pretty much revolved around what Marcene wanted and what she expected of everyone. Leah hardly knew what to say. Finally she reached across the seat and put her hand lightly on Gene's hand. They were quiet for a few minutes, and then Leah said, "I can't blame you for wanting more from life than you've had, but I guess I'm glad you came back. Will you marry soon after Marcene's death?"

"Oh, we'll wait perhaps six months, but I'll probably spend more time at Janet's house than at mine. I'm going to sell our house because it's too big for me, and Janet doesn't want to move into what was and would probably always be Marcene's home. We'll live at her place for a while and then build something. Her house doesn't come with a history like mine does. Her husband died five years ago when they were living in Michigan, and then she and the girls came here to be near family. Ah, we're home. I guess it won't be home for any of us much longer."

Gene carried Leah's bag inside and deposited it in the front hall, and they both went into the sunroom, where a hospital bed had been brought in for Marcene. Leah was shocked to see how emaciated Marcene looked. At Easter her hair had been light brown with streaks of gray. Now it was dull gray, lifeless, and uncombed, but something could be done about that.

Taking Marcene's hand, Leah leaned over and kissed her mother's forehead. Then she stood back and smiled. "Marcene, I'm here to take care of you. Is that okay?"

"Oh Lizzie, I'm glad you came. I knew you would. Now I think I might even get well with you here to help me. That other daughter of mine is worthless when anybody is sick … always has been and always will be. You know your room is ready for you. Gene, take our daughter upstairs to unpack. I'm kind of tired, and I don't think I want to get up. What I need is a little rest, so go, but come back later."

Almost at once Marcene closed her eyes and appeared to fall asleep.

Leah followed Gene into her childhood bedroom, where he set down her luggage. "Marcene seemed to rally when you came in. I think she's pleased you're here, and so am I. You know what to say and do. She needs a shampoo, but I'm not much good at that, and Charlene hasn't come over since she and her mother argued a few weeks ago, so yes, it's good you're here."

Leah settled into her old bedroom, even though Gene said she could have her choice of rooms, now that none of the family lived there any longer. The canopy over the bed almost hung in shreds, but somehow it seemed right for Leah to sleep there. Even the stuffed animals pleased her, and she picked up each one, wondering which had been her favorite. Maybe she would ask Marcene. Until this moment, embracing the room and her long-ago past had not been something Leah had cared to do. She had even been adamant about not doing it. At Easter she had slept in Charlene's room.

After unpacking, Leah went downstairs to ask Gene what he saw as her responsibilities in caring for Marcene. He replied that he would hire someone to clean the house and that he himself would help with meals and take care of certain household chores. Leah's responsibility would be strictly to care for Marcene.

"I'll do my best," Leah said. "I cared for my mother when she was dying, so I have a little experience. Will you be spending time with her in the evenings?"

Gene looked down and then said, rather hesitantly, "I had not planned to spend much time here. We really don't have anything to talk about anymore, and she still manages to find fault with me. I'm not sure I could be a calming influence, because she usually starts something and I don't seem able to fend it off without angry words."

"I understand, but maybe you could find some safe ground, like reminiscing about the good times you must have had back when you were first married or when your first child was born. Maybe that would comfort her. Well, I'll leave it to you."

"I'll do my best, Leah, but I have to get back to the store. See you at dinner tonight. I'll bring food from the deli, so you don't have to worry about cooking anything."

As Gene went out the front door, Harmon came in, having gone to the pharmacy to fill several prescriptions for his mother. "Hey, Leah. I'm glad you're here. Are you feeling okay about this? Can you do it? Just wondering, because I've been here two days now and can't wait to get back to work at the nursing home." Harmon hugged his sister, and they made their way into the sunroom, where Marcene was still napping.

"Sleep is good for Mama," Harmon said. "Let's have lunch. I bought a couple of sandwiches at McDonalds, if that's okay with you?"

"I haven't had a McDonald's hamburger in ages, and how about a Coke with it?" asked Leah. Harmon led the way into the kitchen, and they sat down at the table. Leah was feeling a little conflicted that their father had shared with her and not the rest of the children about his plan to divorce their mother and that he had even moved out for a brief period. And then there was his relationship with Janet. This information should be shared with all the children, or at least she thought so. To Gene's credit, he came back when Marcene received her diagnosis. Should she tell Harmon? "*Not my place to do that*," she thought. They ate without much conversation, but as they finished Leah said, "I think we were both pretty hungry, at least I was, so thanks for picking up burgers … they hit the spot."

"Leah, I think I should tell you that I believe Mama might not last very long, just to prepare you. I took her pulse and blood pressure this morning, and the readings weren't good. Her breath has the smell of death about it. Does that sound weird? Well, it's something I've noticed working in a care facility."

Harmon rose and cleared away the wrappings from the burgers, put their glasses in the dishwasher, and then said, "I really hate to go, but I've got night duty. I exchanged shifts with a friend who is attending a wedding this weekend, so I need to head back to Milwaukee. I'll drive up again when I have two days off in a row, but I don't know when. I'll probably come around the Fourth of July. Don't get discouraged, Leah. Make Dad and Charlene give you a break. Gotta go. My bag is already in the car. Come give your brother a hug and wave to me from the front steps, okay?"

The house was very quiet after Harmon left, but not for long. Marcene soon awoke and called out for Gene.

"Gene's gone, Marcene. Remember? I'm here now to help out. Do you want anything? How about something to eat or drink?"

Marcene seemed to be trying to say something but was having difficulty, so Leah bent over the bed. "Water ... water," Marcene croaked.

Leah brought a glass with a bent straw and held it for Marcene to take a drink. Much of what she sipped ran down her chin, and Leah wiped it away with a Kleenex. She continued to encourage her mother to drink until she was satisfied that Marcene had swallowed enough to do her some good. Her voice did sound better when she spoke once again. "Get me Cheerios with milk and lots of sugar, and I want to sit up. Hurry up, will you? I'm hungry. It must be way past noon."

"Cheerios coming up, and yes, it's almost two o'clock. You were having a nice nap, and sleep is good for you too."

"I wasn't napping. You and Gene left, but I wasn't asleep. I don't like being alone all the time. What happened to Harmon?"

"Harmon had to go back to Milwaukee. He peeked in on you, but you were sleeping. He left your medicine, so you can take it with your meal."

"No medicine! I don't need that stuff ... doesn't do any good anyway. I need a gin and tonic. Now that would do me some good." Marcene tried to pull herself up to a sitting position but fell back down from the effort.

Leah quickly went to Marcene's side to adjust the hospital bed to a near-sitting position. She straightened the coverlet and then hurried out to the kitchen to get the Cheerios. When she returned only a few minutes later, Marcene was sitting there with her eyes closed. Leah debated whether to rouse her and then decided that getting some food into her stomach was a good idea.

"Marcene, here's your lunch." Leah set the food down on a nearby wheeled tray table and maneuvered it into position so her mother could eat the cereal and hopefully also the cheese and crackers she had included.

"Take those crackers away. Can't eat them. Where's my drink?" demanded Marcene.

"Sorry, but I don't know if you're supposed to have alcohol when you're taking medicine. Anyway, I have no idea how to make a gin and tonic. Do you need help with the cereal? I can—"

Marcene cut her off with a vehement no and lifted a spoonful of several Cheerios to her mouth. The milk dribbled onto her chin, and Leah jumped up immediately to wipe it away. Tears formed in Marcene's eyes as Leah took the spoon from her hands and began to feed her. There was no more conversation, and when Marcene had eaten all she could, Leah took away the tray and asked if she wanted to lie down again.

"Yes, Daughter, I think I do. I don't like this! It's not how I thought I'd get you back, but you're here, and I'm glad about that. I can't seem to summon the strength to have the conversation with you I've had up here in my head for so long. I'm so tired, and I don't like that. I wish I could get up and make bread or a cake, but I'm stuck. Will you play music for me, Lizzie? It's soothing, and God knows I need soothing."

Marcene closed her eyes, sighed, and made a shooing gesture, which Leah took to mean that she should get busy and put a CD in the machine.

"Any requests? What's your favorite?" Leah asked.

"Play one of those old Frank Sinatra records. Always liked Frank."

Leah found a disc that seemed to fill the bill. Frank was the featured singer on it, although he was singing duet with someone Leah had never heard of. She sat down beside the hospital bed and listened all the way to the end. Marcene smiled a time or two as though the music brought back good memories. Once she even tried to sing along, but her voice cracked, and she stopped. When the CD finished playing, Leah tried giving her another drink of water, this time with a little more success. After that, Marcene slept, so Leah went upstairs to unpack and then prowled around the kitchen to see what might be stored in the cupboards, refrigerator, and freezer.

Gene came in with a bag of chicken and mashed potatoes and gravy from the deli just as Leah was pulling a pie out of the freezer. She was thinking of baking it for their dessert, but Gene said he had brownies, a favorite of Marcene's. Gene stayed all evening, and Leah could hear him talking softly to his wife but couldn't tell what they were saying. It seemed best to stay out of the room if they were reminiscing about their early life together, although she would have loved to hear their conversation. It might have helped her to understand them better and to figure out what had brought them together.

The following week passed slowly with Gene away at the store, even on Saturday, but he spent most evenings with his wife. Sunday he was with Janet, so Leah was left alone with Marcene, who seemed to have put away her early annoyance with Leah. They were able to have several short conversations. Leah had already heard about Marcene's life before her marriage and came to the conclusion from their further talks that being thrust into the role of housekeeper, cook, and babysitter at an early age had warped her view of the role of women. *Perhaps we are all products of our upbringing,* Leah thought. Yet she knew from conversations with friends that some of them had rebelled against unhealthy attitudes while others had found a path to adulthood that combined acceptance with independence. It made her hope that her new course of study would provide psychological insights into this and other areas of human behavior.

As the next two weeks wore on, Marcene began to sleep more and more, and on Monday, the visiting nurse observed that Marcene was probably only two or three weeks from death. The nurse instructed Leah to make her mother as comfortable as possible and give her the meds whenever the pain began.

That Friday marked three weeks Leah had been there taking care of her mother. Marcene had begun to lose her ability to speak clearly, and since week two of Leah's visit, she had no longer been able to walk to the bathroom, even with assistance. The doctor suspected the loss of speech might be due to a ministroke but decided against further testing to determine the cause because it would involve going into the hospital and Marcene had been adamant about not being hospitalized again.

On Saturday night Leah was alone with her mother. Gene had taken Janet and the girls to a movie. It was a little past eleven, and Marcene groaned and tried to turn over, or so Leah thought.

"Marcene, do you have to go to the bathroom? Shall I get the bedpan? Or do you just want me to help you turn over on your side?" Leah asked.

"Kuz Mama," Marcene murmured. Leah was surprised that her mother was making an effort to speak, as she had all but stopped communicating except with gestures.

"What did you say?"

Marcene laboriously lifted her right arm and touched her lips. Her left arm had stopped functioning a week ago, likely due to the ministroke.

"Do you want a drink of water?" asked Leah, reaching for the water glass on the bedside table.

"Kuz Mama," she repeated and touched her lips once again.

"You want me to kiss you, is that it?"

Marcene made a guttural noise and for the third time touched her lips. The effort seemed to have exhausted her. She let her arm fall, and her head rolled slightly to the left. Leah leaned over, and taking Marcene's right hand in hers, she kissed her on the forehead, on one cheek, and then the other. When she raised up, Marcene had a faint smile on her face, but her eyes were closed. Leah listened. Was her mother still breathing? Yes, there was a slight rise and fall of the chest. Leah sat down in the chair and kept watch. She had a premonition about what might be happening. Should she call Gene? He would be home soon, so she decided to do nothing. At a little before midnight, the rise and fall ceased, and when Leah put her hand under Marcene's nose and then her over mouth, she felt no breath. She checked Marcene's pulse. Nothing. Then she telephoned the doctor for instructions. Just as she was dialing Gene's cell phone, he came in the front door.

"Gene, your wife is at peace now. It happened just a few minutes ago. I thought of calling you earlier when I sensed she might be at the end of her life, but even if I had, I don't think you could have gotten here in time. I've called the doctor, and he'll be over to confirm the death and do the necessary paperwork. Do you want to call everyone now or wait until morning? Should I have called the priest? Is it too late to do it now? I wish we had talked about this before so I would have known what to do, but I guess we didn't really think her time would come so quickly."

"I'll call Father Gorman. He won't mind coming out late. I think last rites are appropriate even if the person has already expired, but since I didn't grow up Catholic, I don't know for sure. As for calling the family, we'll wait until morning. Nobody can do anything tonight, and I don't want Harmon or Charlene driving over here so late. Stephen's so far away, in more ways than one, so another day won't matter. Same goes for Russell and Marcene's sisters. Why don't you go to bed? I'll wait up for the doctor and the priest. One of us ought to get some sleep."

The funeral would have pleased Marcene; at least that was Gene's analysis when everything was over and the last guests had left the house to return home. All Marcene's sisters had come, as well as her sister-in-law. The McGregor children had all been present, and Harmon had delivered a fine eulogy. Afterward he'd confided to Leah that he had tried to portray his mother as she had been before the event that had changed all their lives: the disappearance of Lizzie. Charlene had wept uncontrollably, which had surprised all the family members, since for years Marcene had treated her as her personal maid who had been expected to anticipate the required response in all situations. The rest of the family had not shed any tears publically, but Leah wondered if they might have, at some point, grieved privately. Marcene was their mother after all, and even with all her faults and failures, she had commanded a certain respect.

Gene had still not told the rest of his children about his plan to marry, so the morning after the funeral Leah spoke to him about it. "You need to tell your kids about you and Janet," she said. "I think they'll understand. I think Russell and Harmon will, and I believe Charlene will too. I don't know about Stephen, since he's a bit of a mystery to me." Leah heard footsteps on the stairs, and since Stephen was the only one who had not yet come down, she knew it was him.

"Good morning, Dad, Leah," he said as he came into the kitchen, where they were sitting at the table, cups of coffee in front of them. Stephen poured himself a cup and sat down too. He sipped the hot brew but did not look at either of them. When he raised his eyes, he said, "I plan to be around for a while. I can work on my thesis here, and I have the University of Minnesota library close by if I need it. I want to make sure the estate is handled properly and that Mama's wishes are carried out."

"There is no estate, at least not yet," Gene said. "Your mother and I had a joint will in which whoever survived the other would have title to everything. Only after I'm gone will there be an estate. I should tell you that I plan to sell the house since it's too large for me and there's probably no one in the family who wants it anyway. You all have your separate lives in other places, except Charlene, and she will soon have her own house when she gets married. If you want any mementos to remember Mama, we can talk about that, but everybody will have to sign off on what anyone else wants."

"It sounds like you've had this all thought out for a long time. Were you just waiting and hoping Mama would die so you could sell the house right out from under us? We all grew up here, and it's been home as long as I can remember. Don't we get to have a say in what happens?" Stephen was glowering at his father.

"Well, I guess the answer to that is no. You don't have a say in whether or not I sell the house. I didn't want to have this conversation until all of you were present. Charlene will be here in a little while, and Harmon and Russell are at the store, getting some supplies for lunch. So let's postpone further conversation until they're all here. I have to go over to my office and sign paychecks. I should be home before noon, so let's talk then, all right?"

As soon as Gene left, Leah tried to get a conversation started with Stephen, but looking everywhere except at her, he said, "I don't feel like talking, and anyway, I don't know what we have in common, so I'm going back upstairs to read. I'll come down when everyone's here." With that, he rose, leaving Leah sitting alone at the kitchen table. She was trying not to feel hurt by his put-down. That's what it felt like at any rate. She thought perhaps he was still grieving, so she tried to put his words aside and concentrate on how and when she could make her escape. That was how she was beginning to think of it, an escape back to an alternate reality without the drama and rancor that seemed to penetrate the air molecules here in the house. She sighed, put her cup into the dishwasher, and went into the sunroom to tidy up and return some things to their right places.

When Harmon and Russell returned from the store, Leah told them their father had a few things he wanted to share with them over lunch. "I was going to leave for Milwaukee in a little while, but I suppose I'd better hang here and listen to what Dad has to say," Harmon said, looking a little disappointed. His fiancée was due back from a visit with her parents, so Leah knew he was anxious to return home. Russell too was eager to return home, for much the same reason: his girlfriend. Leah, on the other hand, had no one drawing her back to Chicago, but she would be pleased to return nevertheless.

Leah and Charlene, with some help from Russell, put together a nice salad-and-sandwich luncheon while Harmon and Stephen returned chairs and tables borrowed from the church parish hall for the after-funeral gathering at the house. Gene was a little late returning from the store. He looked more relaxed than he had earlier, and Leah hoped he would be able to find the right words to explain what he planned to do, without offending his children.

The conversation was cordial during the meal, and when they had finished, Gene began. "I'm going to put the house up for sale as soon as I get some cosmetic repairs taken care of. I know all of you will be leaving soon, so I don't expect you to get involved in this project. The yard is the biggest concern. None of the usual spring and summer spruce-up has been done and no flowers planted, but I'll get someone to do that. Steve doesn't want me to sell, and maybe some of the rest of you don't either, but as I said to him, this isn't negotiable. This house is too large for me with its six bedrooms and three baths, not to mention all the living space, plus a huge basement, so the house will go. If any of you want a keepsake, it can be negotiated. I won't be taking anything with me except my personal stuff. I'll stick around long enough to get the repairs done and hopefully see the house sold before I move out, but even that's not a certainty."

Gene paused, and Leah knew what was coming. She crossed her fingers that there wouldn't be any angry reactions. She vowed to be still and not get into the fight if there was one.

"In about four or five months, I plan to marry Janet Cameron. You all know who she is because she's been working part-time for me in the office for five years. I had planned to divorce your mother, but when she got sick, I changed my mind and stayed here, and now I'm glad I did. You all know your mother and I had a stormy relationship that only escalated with time. I wonder now if I had insisted that she see a psychiatrist, if things would have been different. I didn't help the situation by retaliating in kind when she went on one of her tirades. If we could have had a real discussion instead of a fight … well, who knows? I hope you'll all accept this news without trying to lay blame on me, Janet, or Marcene. There's plenty of blame to go around I guess, but I love Janet, and she loves me. Even though there's almost eighteen years' difference in our ages, we have been able to see that it's not important. Her kids are great, and we get along well. I've been able to bond with them, and I look forward to being their father and maybe doing a better job with them than I was able to do with you. So that's all I want to say. I hope—"

Charlene interrupted, "How could you, Dad? I suppose you've been sleeping with her since … well … who knows how long, and poor Mama not knowing a thing was wrong." Charlene wiped away tears and blew her nose.

No one else spoke, and then Russell said, "Congratulations, Dad. I really hope you'll be happy with Janet. I like her and always have."

Leah could tell that Harmon was tapping his toes under the table, a sign he was anxious about his response. He said, "Dad, I guess I'm not totally surprised about you seeing someone or about wanting to leave Mama. There were lots of times as a kid that I thought about running away. I got so tired of the yelling, the blaming, and the laying on of guilt for real or imagined sins. By the time I got to high school I stopped trying to figure out this family. I was just waiting until I could get away. Maybe you had some of those same feelings. I'm glad you have someone to share the rest of your life with, and I join Russ in extending congratulations." Harmon patted his father's shoulder.

Stephen hadn't said one word, but his face told anyone who looked closely that he was conflicted. "I don't know what to say," he said. "My Catholic upbringing tells me I should be angry and throw accusations like Charlene did, but I know things weren't great around here. It just came to me that I, being the oldest, was able to escape before things got so bad. For years I thought all mothers were like ours. I stayed with a college friend at his home for a couple of weeks and observed how differently they interacted and treated one another. I'm sorry, Dad, for what I said this morning, and I too congratulate you and wish you well."

Gene wiped a few tears from his eyes and nodded. Leah knew that nod. It didn't mean agreement necessarily but acceptance of what Stephen was saying. She had planned to stay silent since she often felt like an outsider, but then other times she had felt accepted, so why not say what was on her mind?

"Gene, Dad, I want to thank you for how you let me find my own way into this family. I'll never forget that you have not once called me Lizzie … that I've always been Leah to you. You knew me right away, like a father knows a daughter. You knew what I needed to do and who I needed to be. I'm just sorry I wasn't able to bring myself to call you Dad until just now. But you know the reason for that, and you accepted it. You accepted me for who I was, something your wife couldn't do, but I understood that, and in the end it didn't matter. So I join my brothers in saying congratulations and best wishes for a long and happy life with Janet. I look forward to meeting her."

Conversation about when everyone was planning to leave kicked things back to normal, and in the middle of a discussion about how far, exactly, it was to Chicago, Charlene offered her own version of an apology. "Sorry everybody for spouting off. I've got things on my mind. You know Cleve and I are getting married soon, and I have so much to do before the big day. I do hope you all can come. Congratulations, Dad. I gotta go now. See you at my wedding." Charlene pushed back her chair, picked up her purse from the kitchen counter, and walked out the back door.

The three brothers and Leah looked at one another and then started laughing. "Leave it to Charlene to break the tension, without even knowing she was doing it," Harmon said. Gene looked puzzled. "Oh, Dad, it's just we all know Charlene pretty well. She's like a flag at the airport; she flutters whichever way the wind blows. She's fine, even if her apology was more about her than about apologizing. We've heard that song and dance before," Harmon explained.

Chapter 21

Leah and Russell were soon involved in work and school after returning to Chicago, and before Labor Day Russell moved out of the apartment to live with his girlfriend, Reba. Leah still hadn't met Reba, so she insisted both of them come to Sunday dinner. Reba Graves turned out to be a lovely young lady that Leah liked immediately, and before the day was over, they were talking like old friends and teasing Russell, who thought they were ganging up on him.

The apartment seemed deadly quiet with Russell gone, and Leah was missing him more than she thought she would. She had not realized until he'd left how he had filled a void in her life. She had a brother! Well, she had three brothers, but Russell would always be special. For a moment a memory of Alan came to mind, but she was able to push it aside as she busied herself gathering a few things Russell had forgotten in his bedroom closet. Then in a back corner she saw her purple-and-white felt hat, slightly crushed from having had a box pushed up against it. Leah pulled it out, straightened the brim, and poked her hand inside so it once again looked almost as good as new. She sat down on the bed, holding the hat in her hands, and thought about the wonderful time she and Alan had enjoyed together. The drive to and from Champaign and then sharing food and conversation at her apartment were still special memories. She couldn't help but wonder if he and Juneau were living at the mansion in Evanston with Uncle

179

Horace. There had been a picture of them in the society pages last January when they had married, and later there had been an announcement that Mr. and Mrs. Alan Parkin were the parents of a baby boy. Leah tried to think back to when that had been. May or June? She wondered what they had named the baby and if they were happy. A baby! Would she ever have a child? Would she ever find someone like Alan again? "Stop it!" Leah said to herself as she shoved the hat into the back of the closet once more.

Classes were into their third week, and now Leah was working only part-time at the Book Nook. On her way home she started to think about her decision to go into social work. Should she have stayed with law? She had not touched the money Horace Marsden had thrust into her hands so many months ago. She didn't want to dip into it, but without the little extra that Russell had contributed toward household expenses and with her not-so-well-paid job at the Book Nook, she was going through her bank account at an alarming rate. Tuition was expensive, and books were unbelievably high priced. Maybe it was time to use the blood money. Alan had told her to use it for education. What was she saving it for anyway? "Not tonight," she said out loud as she put the key in her door. "Tomorrow I'll think about the future."

The future caught up with Leah before she was ready for it. Her faculty advisor called her into his office after his class two days later. "Leah," he said, "I want to encourage you to get cracking. We need social workers out there, and you're going to be a good one. Right now I have a request for an intern at a downtown agency that deals mostly with women and children, but they also have a food pantry and a drop-in daytime shelter for the homeless when it rains or snows or is cold. I see you as the perfect candidate, and you could easily write your thesis based on your experience there. What do you think? Can you be a full-time student and handle the internship? You'll get academic credit for your work there. Think about it, and get back to me as soon as possible. The internship would start the first week of October. I don't have the date in front of me, but we'll talk in a couple of days, all right?"

Leah agreed to think about the opportunity and promised to make a decision soon, perhaps as early as tomorrow afternoon. That evening she walked home after work, giving herself time to think more clearly about the internship and cutting off her source of income, since she would have to quit her job. There was a very small stipend for the internship, but there would be more expenses involved in going downtown every day, like bus or train fare, in addition to her normal school fees. She went to bed that night still conflicted about what to do, but her inclination was to go for broke. She could get a loan when her bank account ran low, or, as she had told herself several times before, she could dip into the blood money.

The next afternoon she met with her advisor and told him that she wanted to be considered for the internship and that she would need to know the starting date so she could give notice at the Book Nook. In a matter of minutes her life was decided for the next three to six months. The internship would be for the first quarter but could be extended beyond that, depending on whether she and those in charge of the program wished to continue it. "If you don't screw up," her professor told her, "you've got it for the whole time. I believe it's a good place for you to learn about social work. Book learning is necessary, but experience in the real world is where you learn the most."

On October 4 Leah began working at the agency. It meant walking a tight line to assure that she did her best in academia and in the internship. She soon discovered that the agency was, as Ben Barman, the director described it, an insatiable monster. There was always more work than there was time to do it, and many evenings she didn't get home until nine although her schedule called for finishing by five. Then there were pages to read and notes to take, but she managed to balance everything reasonably well.

The last day of October marked the end of the fiscal year for the agency, and so it was crunch time for those trying to keep all the programs afloat. One morning there was much rejoicing when Ben Barman announced someone had made a substantial gift to help see them through the winter and even beyond. Winter was always a time of concern because the needs of their clients were greater. Coats and hats and gloves were needed, and the traffic in and out of the soup kitchen always increased in November.

On Monday Leah was informed of a hurriedly called staff meeting. The only item on the agenda was an announcement by Ben Barman. He was beaming when he told those assembled that the firm of Marsden, Willett, and Desmond had pledged $750,000 to be presented at a special gathering on Friday. The presentation was already arranged, and photographers and journalists would be present. "I want all of you to be here, unless you have an appointment you can't break. Mr. Parkin and Mr. Canady will be here for the presentation, and I hope all of you will thank them personally. They will stay for lunch with our clients as well as the staff, and I want you here for that too. Make a note for Friday at eleven thirty. Okay? That's it for now."

Leah wondered if she could blend into the woodwork the day of the presentation. Much as she would like to catch a glimpse of Alan to see how he looked, she didn't think she was ready for a face-to-face with him. Even after almost a year her emotions were still a bit raw when it came to Alan Parkin. She hadn't been able to wipe him out of her memory bank or even to banish him from her thoughts. It wasn't that she spent a lot of time thinking about him, but he was still there, lurking in the back of her mind. Little things would remind her of him ... how he had smiled at her, their conversations, their laughing at crazy things. The incident with the purple hat also came to mind.

Leah hoped to be assigned to the lunch detail and spend her time in the kitchen, but Mr. Barman said he wanted all the social workers up front during the presentation. He also wanted one of them to speak a brief word of thanks in addition to what he would have to say. Tuesday afternoon as Leah was ready to leave for her class session at the university, Mr. Barman took her aside and asked if she would be the one to speak the word of thanks on behalf of the social workers.

"But I'm not even a social worker yet. I'm just a lowly intern," she replied. "Someone else would surely be a better choice for the job."

"Well, you used to work at Marsden, Willett, and Desmond, so I thought we could take advantage of that connection as a sort of human-interest touch. I know you're good with words and could do this with your eyes closed. Come on, Leah, don't make me beg. Janice Porter wants to do it, but I can't in good conscience allow that. If the press is there, and they will be, we can't count on her to put a sentence together without saying 'you know' or 'umm'! Sorry, but I really need you. Bess Trotter would do it, but she's out with a case of shingles. Please do this for me"

What could she do? Finally Leah agreed to speak "a few words."

"And don't forget to shake hands just before the presentation. No, do that afterward. Shake the hand of whoever speaks or maybe both of them," Ben Barman suggested.

Leah spent the next three days crafting what she would say and worrying about having to face Alan, but by Thursday night she was satisfied with what she had written, having practiced in front of the bathroom mirror several times. Friday morning Leah took special care in selecting appropriate attire. She didn't want to embarrass the agency, especially if her picture was in the paper. She hoped it wouldn't be. That morning she left the apartment a little earlier than usual, in order to speak to Mr. Barman about what she planned to say, to make sure it was all right. He wasn't there, and by the time he did arrive, it was only five minutes before the presentation. Leah looked out the window facing the street and saw Alan and Greg Canady getting out of a taxi. She had met Greg but didn't know him well. Maybe he would be the one presenting the check, and she wouldn't have to shake Alan's hand.

Confusion reigned with clients and staff trying to find places to sit. Extra chairs had been placed in the dining area, and those were filled first, with the rest finding places at the tables that were already set up for lunch. Leah hung back and decided to stand behind those who had occupied the extra chairs. In the area at the front was a podium with a microphone, and Alan and Greg were led to the first row of chairs in front of the podium where they sat down. Ben Barman motioned to Leah to come forward. She had hoped she could enter from the side where she was standing and then disappear again through the kitchen door, which was right behind where she was currently positioned. But now she had to make her way to the front. She didn't look at Alan, keeping her eyes on the *Caring for People Since 1979* banner that hung behind the podium.

Leah took a seat at one end of the front row. Alan and Greg were sitting on the opposite end and Mr. Barman took a seat next to Leah. She didn't think Alan had seen her. *Oh,* she thought, *I shouldn't have said yes.*

Introductions were made, and Alan rose, stood at the podium, and spoke briefly about the important work the agency was doing. He talked a little about the firm and its policy to support community programs, explaining that this year they had decided to choose this particular agency to receive a substantial gift. He said that contributions had been received from every single employee at Marsden, Willett, and Desmond and that the senior partners, Mr. Marsden, Mr. Willett, and Mr. Desmond, had each contributed $150,000. Then he handed the check to Mr. Barman, who accepted it with effusive thanks, speaking highly of the firm of Marsden, Willett, and Desmond.

Alan sat down and then Mr. Barman introduced Leah, saying "Our spokesperson for the staff is our new intern, Miss Leah Anderly, who actually used to work at the firm of Marsden, Willett, and Desmond."

Leah rose, stepped in front of the podium and looked straight out at the assembly and spoke her brief word of thanks, highlighting some of the programs the money would be funding, including the program aimed at assisting homeless women with children. When she finished, there was applause, and she walked over and shook Greg Canady's hand and then Alan's hand. She couldn't help herself … she looked directly at him and did not drop her eyes as she shook his hand firmly. She tried for a smile and thought she had probably pulled it off. There was shock registered on his face, especially in his eyes. She pulled her hand away and walked back to the kitchen door and disappeared inside. She was shaking, but she had done it, and she hoped she had not betrayed how she was feeling inside.

The kitchen staff immediately put the serving line into operation, and the invited guests were the first ones to pick up their plates. Leah, behind the servers, observed Alan looking toward the door through which she had disappeared. Then he turned and obviously spotted her, because he raised a hand and smiled. The smile was the old smile Leah remembered. But what did it mean? Nothing, she decided. She wouldn't try to avoid him, but she wouldn't spend any more time talking with him than was absolutely necessary. Alan put his tray down on one of the tables. Then he came into the kitchen and stood right in front of her. "Hello, Leah. Would you sit with us? I'd like to know what you're doing here and why you aren't in law anymore."

"I'll sit for a minute, but I have a class this afternoon, so I'll have to duck out soon." That wasn't entirely true; her class wasn't until four. She didn't pick up any food but sat down at Alan and Greg's table.

"Greg, have you met Leah Anderly? Once, a long time ago, she worked at the firm, in research mostly."

"Well, Alan," Leah said, "you make it sound like it was years and years ago. It really wasn't all that long ago. Only last year at this time I was working there. But I suspect, Greg, you know I was fired. So now I'm doing something very different. I'm at the university, working toward a Master's in social work, and I'm interning here. It allows me to work with clients while

I'm still learning. It's a great opportunity, and I'm enjoying it." Leah decided to get the jump on Alan's questions about why she was here, although she didn't really tell the whole why of it ... not exactly.

"I'm surprised," Alan said. "I thought you were the very best researcher we had, and well, I assumed you'd want to finish your degree. What turned you off law?"

"Oh, a number of things. I discovered the law doesn't have a heart sometimes, and I wanted to work where people are treated as human beings with value. Everyone has value. I didn't always see that in the law, but I enjoyed the work while I was involved in it. I won't look back though. Looking back only makes you unable to see what's just ahead, and I hope for good things still out there, waiting to be discovered. Sorry, but I have to leave. Nice seeing you again, Alan, and you too, Greg." Leah rose, and so did Alan. He reached out and put his hand on her shoulder.

"Don't go," he said. "I thought we could talk about what you've been doing since ... well, it's been a while since we talked. I've missed our talks. Would you—"

Leah didn't let him finish. She gently pulled away and said, "I really have to go. Maybe sometime you can tell me what you've been doing since I left the firm."

Leah turned abruptly and strode out the door and onto the street. Tears came, and she hated herself for getting emotional. She was grateful she had been able to extricate herself before something was said that would have opened the floodgates while she and Alan were still in conversation. There was no future with Alan. He was married and had a child. "Stop it, Leah," she muttered as she boarded a bus heading south. "Just stop it. It's over. Get it through your head once and for all!"

Chapter 22

Lovely fall temperatures lasted into December, but by the end of the second week of the month, the weather turned cold and wintry. Sleet and snow covered the streets, making them slippery, so Leah took the bus to the university. Christmas break would begin with her last class of the day, and she wanted to see her advisor. He was sitting at his desk when she arrived at his office door. "Come in, Leah," he said, rising to pull out a chair from several stacked together in a corner of his cluttered office. "Have a seat, and tell me what's on your mind."

"Nothing earth shaking, but I was wondering if you've had any word about the internship program continuing on into the next quarter. If it doesn't, then I need to look for a part-time job. The internship doesn't pay a lot, but it helps. I don't want to go into debt if I can help it."

"I thought you had already been notified that the program is to be canceled at the end of the year. The agency's board of directors opted not to continue it for the present. Instead they're using money from the Marsden gift to pay for the hiring of additional staff. Some on the board apparently feel they're not getting their money's worth from the internship program. I don't agree, but I have nothing to say about it. Ben Barman is livid. He knows more than anyone else how valuable the program has been. I thought that huge gift would have put them on safe financial footing, but to hear the board talk, they're next to being bankrupt. Sorry, I didn't know you hadn't been told. Ben's probably trying to find some funding to keep you on, but you ought to ask him today if you're going down there."

"I'm going there as soon as my next class is over. I was hoping I could stay on doing what I've come to enjoy. I too think it's a good program that has yielded some positive results. Thanks for telling me. I'll see Mr. Barman today and find out if the board has changed its mind. I've got to run. Thanks for everything."

Leah was disappointed but not totally surprised. There had been rumors about the board not liking the intern program and being concerned with fiscal frugality. She wondered where exactly the huge gift was being spent. When she arrived at the agency at three thirty, Ben Barman had already left for the day, but the associate director, Greta Hulstad, was at the desk, helping a young mother with an infant fill out papers. When they had finished, Leah asked Greta what she knew about the internship program.

"Oh, it's probably history, to hear Patsy Digman talk, anyway. She's on the board and stops in here once or twice a week. She said the board voted itself a 'bonus,' at least that's what she called it. They serve without pay but are reimbursed for expenses they incur on behalf of the agency. She says several board members felt a once-a-year bonus was needed to keep good people on the board. Grant Leffler resigned, saying he couldn't afford the time or money anymore, and that got the wheels moving, so she said. You know Patsy is in our corner, Leah. She wants to keep the program and even expand it, but she's like the voice of one crying in the wilderness. Isn't that from the Bible somewhere? Well, that's as much as I know. Patsy told me not to say anything, but I guess I did anyway. She's trying to solicit funding on her own, but she doesn't want anybody to know about that either."

The phone rang, and when Greta turned to answer it, Leah walked out the front door and kept going until twenty minutes later when she reached the offices of Marsden, Willett, and

Desmond. At the front desk she asked if it was possible to have five minutes with Mr. Desmond before the end of the day. She provided the receptionist with a brief description of what she wished to talk about with him, saying she was willing to wait.

The receptionist made a phone call and said Mr. Desmond could see her at four thirty but had someone coming in at five so they would need to be finished by then. Leah said she wouldn't need any more time than that. She waited, spending the time people watching. Leah hoped Horace Marsden would not come strolling by, or else she might once again be escorted out! The law firm was very busy with much coming and going the whole time she was waiting. At 4:40 Leah was told to take the elevator to the eighth floor and someone would direct her to Mr. Desmond's office. Leah knew where Mr. Desmond's office was but didn't say so.

The inner door opened almost at once when Leah stepped into the outer office and gave her name to the secretary. "Leah, I'm delighted to see you. Come in." Jack Desmond was cordial, and for that Leah was grateful. He offered her coffee, which she declined. Then she told Jack Desmond what she had learned from Greta an hour ago. "I don't know if you have any interest in looking into this, but since your firm contributed such a large amount of money to the agency, I thought you ought to know what some of that money is being used for. I have no idea how much, but even a dollar would be considered compensation, and that goes against the board's bylaws. I would prefer that Greta Hulstad's name not be used. She should not lose her job because of speaking up about this, and if you could keep my name out of it, I'd appreciate that as well. Around here I'm persona non grata. Is this something that bears looking into, do you think?"

Maybe I shouldn't have come, Leah thought, *but if substantial sums are being given to board members, that's not right.*

Jack Desmond leaned back in his chair, and looking directly at Leah, he said, "It takes a little courage to come here. I suspect you haven't been inside this building since old

Horace booted you out. When I heard about that, I was upset, but one doesn't go against the Big Guy, as a lot of people call him behind his back. Hardly anybody knew why you left, and I don't know if Alan knew either for a long time. As for doing something about the board's decision … I don't know. I'll ask a couple of other people, and maybe we can make a few phone calls and prevent this so-called bonus from happening. I don't know about reinstating the internship program. That's probably not something we can do anything about. Thanks for coming in. You know, I gave you a great recommendation for your job at the Book Nook. Elise is a good friend, and she really hated to see you leave. If you want to get back into the paralegal business, I know a firm who's hiring. Horace Marsden and George Willett might not like my doing that, but right after Christmas Horace will be off to Bermuda for four months, and George is losing it. He has dementia, sad to say. He's working less, and what he does sometimes has to be redone by someone else. You didn't hear that from me, Leah."

"Sorry about that. Dementia is tough for spouses and families to live with," Leah said.

"If you want to get back into law, there's a firm in Oak Park looking for a good paralegal. Say the word, and I'll let them know they ought to call you."

"Thanks, I appreciate your support on all fronts. I won't be going back into law, even though I had planned to get my degree when I first signed up for classes at the university. I think I've found my niche, and I'll be sticking with social work. I hope you have a wonderful Christmas." Leah left, wondering what might come of her conversation with Jack Desmond. His remark about having recommended her for the job at the Book Nook made her decide to stop by and say hello to Elise.

Leah arrived just before six, and the Book Nook was crowded with customers. "My favorite employee! How's the internship going? We miss you and wish you were still working here. Any chance you could come back? We're really busy right now."

"The internship is ending, sorry to say. The board decided it wasn't cost effective, so if you're serious and could use another clerk, I'd love to work for you again." Working at the store hadn't been on her mind when she came in, as she'd assumed Elise had a full staff with Christmas coming.

"Oh, Leah, you just said the most beautiful words. You're hired! When can you start? How about tomorrow evening and then all day Saturday and Sunday afternoon if you can manage. I know you have papers and reading to do, but give me as much time as you can. This is great! And I won't have to train you! I don't think we've added anything new and different, so you could hit the ground running."

"I can come in around six tomorrow, and yes, Saturday and Sunday afternoon would be fine. I'm out of class now for the holidays, so I'll give you whatever you need until after the New Year. I'm glad I stopped in to say hello."

Elise and Leah chatted for a few more minutes, but then the place erupted when a crowd of students came in, all needing last-minute gifts for friends and parents and grandparents. Leah jumped in to help a couple of customers with their selections, staying until past seven. Then she hurried home because Russ and Reba were coming over for pizza.

Russell arrived first, grinning from ear to ear. "Hey, Sis. I got a raise today, and I bought Reba a ring for Christmas. I hope you won't give me grief about getting engaged. I know you think I'm too young, but we want to be married. If I had my way, we'd get hitched on Valentine's Day, but Reba wants a summer wedding ... maybe on the lakefront. What do you think?"

"Russ, it's really none of my business what you do. I care about you, and if this is what you really want to do, I'm in your corner. You and Reba should be sure about this move because once you combine your stuff and figure out who pays for what, it gets sticky if one of you wants to back out or, maybe even worse, change the rules. But I trust your judgment. You've grown up so much since you came here a little more than a year ago. But hey, I still miss having you make chili for me on cold winter nights," Leah said, tousling Russell's hair.

"I promise we'll invite you over for chili and other meals too. I miss you too, Leah. You've been like a sister to me. Oh yeah, you are my sister, but it's just that you're so not like Charlene that sometimes I forget. I'm going to change my duds, and I need to take a shower if there's time before dinner. Then I'll set the table, okay?" Russell disappeared into the bathroom, and Leah smiled, thinking about the first day her little brother had showed up at her door. What a change that had made in her life!

Reba rang the bell just as Russ was coming out of the bathroom. They enjoyed the pizza Reba had brought, and the conversation flowed. Leah teased Russell good-naturedly about whether he was still leaving his socks and shoes lying around everywhere. After their meal and a quick cleanup, Russ and Reba sat down to work on a financial budget they could live with. They had informed Leah that they were always coming up short at the end of each month, so plans needed to be made. "I'll leave the two of you to your task ... and good luck. I have studying I need to do." She went to her room to read over tomorrow's assignments and perhaps also to decide what she would do about Christmas this year. Reba and Russ would be spending the holidays in Peoria with Reba's family. Leah thought she might visit her grandmother as she had done last year. According to Harmon, Corrine was having some unexplained pains, and her spirits had been a little low, so she decided to call Harmon for the latest update on her grandmother.

"Hi, Harmon. I thought I'd call to see how Corinne is and whether it would be a good idea to come to visit over Christmas."

"Didn't the director of the nursing home call you? She should have. I know you're listed as next of kin, so you should have been contacted. Leah, your grandmother died this afternoon about five thirty. I'm really sorry you had to find out like this. They came to get her a little while ago. Oh man, I'm going to ream out Mrs. Chambers for not calling you."

"I wish I had been there with her. I wonder if … Let me check if there was a call on my cell. It's been turned off most of the day, so maybe she called and couldn't get me." Leah pulled out her cell phone, and yes, there was a message asking her to call the nursing home as soon as possible.

"Don't get on Mrs. Chambers' case, Harmon; she did call. I just didn't get the message. I suppose I should call now. Did you say they had taken her away to a funeral home? Do you know if she is to be cremated or buried? We didn't talk about it. Oh, I wish I had been there."

"I'm sorry, Sis. Let me ask and call you back. Knowing Corinne, I suspect she prepaid everything and wrote down all her wishes, so Mrs. Chambers will have that information. I'm in the car, pulled over to the side and blocking somebody's driveway, so I've got to hang up, but you'll hear from me soon. Bye, Leah."

When Leah put the phone back in the cradle, a sadness washed over her. Her grandmother had only been part of her life for a year, and there were still stories for them to tell each other. She wondered about the funeral. She assumed there would be one, but she would wait to hear from Harmon. Russ and Reba were bent over a notebook when Leah returned to the living room. She informed them about the death of her grandmother and then retired to her bedroom to prepare for bed, even though it was only nine fifteen and she never went to bed that early.

The phone rang a little before ten, and Russ picked it up. In a few moments he rapped on Leah's door to say Harmon was calling with information about her grandmother.

"Hi, Harmon," she said. "What do you have to tell me?"

"The doctor said she died very quickly from a massive stroke. He said it was fortunate she didn't survive, as she would have been severely impaired. Mrs. Chambers said Corinne's wishes were for a short service here at the home. She will be cremated, and her ashes will be buried beside her husband. I didn't ask where that was, but I assume it's not far away. She wrote down verses to be read and hymns to be sung and even wrote her own obituary. You know, Leah, your grandmother was a most remarkable woman and a strong one too, not physically, but in every other way. The chaplain will do the service, and I'll get a little trio together to sing one of her favorite songs. Will you be coming up for the service? If you do, you know you can stay with me. Katy lives with me now, but the guest room is yours. The service will be Monday afternoon if that fits with your schedule. If not, it can be changed. I'm so sorry, Leah, for both of us. She was like a grandmother to me too."

"I think I can manage Monday. Classes are over, so I'll drive up that morning, stay with you if that's all right, and then leave again the next morning. I'm working at the bookstore again. With Christmas so close, Elise wants me there whenever I'm free, but I know she'll understand about the funeral. Thanks for the details. I'll see you Monday morning at the nursing home. Good-bye, Harmon."

Chapter 23

Monday morning before eight Leah was on her way to Milwaukee, having discovered only recently that she could rent a car in Hyde Park and didn't need to go out to the airport for a rental. At first she had to fight heavy traffic, but when she took the turnoff for Milwaukee, the stop-and-start flow improved. She arrived at the nursing facility just before eleven. The young woman on duty at the front desk told her that Harmon was with a resident, but she paged him, and he came almost at once.

"Leah, I'm glad you're here. I made an appointment for you with the chaplain. He wants to go over the service with you and have you fill in some blanks. He's in the conference room, so I'll take you there now if that's all right. Or do you need a few minutes?" Harmon had put his hand on Leah's arm, and at his expression of concern, she turned to bury her head on his shoulder.

"I'm okay, really, but it just hit me that my grandmother's not here. I can't walk down the corridor to her room and sit with her to talk about ... Well, we talked about a lot of things over the last year. I'm ready to see the chaplain, but I'm not sure I can fill in any blanks. We were still in discovery mode, as Grandma said a number of times."

Harmon escorted Leah to the conference room and introduced her to the chaplain, Matthew Jacobsen, who Leah thought might be in his late sixties or even seventies. He had a shock of white hair and stood perhaps six feet tall. He reminded her a little bit of her father, although his hair had not been as white as Pastor Jacobsen's. They exchanged greetings, and he invited Leah to sit at the table across from him. Harmon excused himself since he was on duty.

"You have my sympathy, Miss Anderly. I know about you from my visits with your grandmother. She was so excited to tell me about you and the remarkable story of how you came into her life. I think your finding her after so many years made a big difference for her. Every time I visited, she was full of tales of what you were doing. She was awed by your wanting to have a relationship with her even though the two of you were not related, but she always amended that to say you were relatives by choice and that was an even stronger bond. Blood relatives, she said, were supposed to love each other. Well, you probably had the same conversation with her yourself."

Pastor Jacobsen paused and reached across the table to pat Leah's hand, as he had observed tears forming in her eyes.

"You miss her already, don't you? Let me tell you what I have planned, but first a question: Do you wish to speak at the memorial service? Corinne left rather extensive instructions about her funeral, and one thing was to keep it short and to tell the truth. I think you and I can do that. Could you speak, or would it be too difficult?" Pastor Jacobsen had been looking at Leah all the while they had been talking, and she sensed as well as saw his compassion and that he had cared about her grandmother.

"Yes, I'll say a few words and keep it short, or Grandma might haunt my dreams." Leah laughed nervously and then went on, "I haven't spoken to anyone who could tell me the arrangements for burial. I know she will be cremated and buried next to her husband, but is the burial scheduled? I'm sure she must have said what she wanted."

"Yes, she did. She left instructions that if she died during the winter, her burial would be postponed until spring. I believe it will be sometime in May. She didn't want any inscription added to her husband's tombstone, saying it wasn't necessary.

To quote Corrine, 'Nobody will come looking for me after I'm gone, but Leah will know where I am if she wants to visit me.' The funeral home will take care of that, and if you want to be notified of day and time, I'm sure that can be arranged. Now I have some people to see, and I expect you will want to start collecting your thoughts about what to say this afternoon. The service is set for four-thirty in the dining room. The residents eat at five, so she chose four-thirty because then everyone would already be in the dining room for their dinner. I plan to arrive by four if you have any questions for me. You have my sympathy, Leah. Death is a big deal, even if sometimes we try to tell ourselves it isn't. I'll see you this afternoon."

Leah sat there, realizing how deliberate her grandmother had been in her planning to make sure no one had to make decisions or be inconvenienced. She thought about what she would say. She took out a notepad from her purse and began jotting down ideas. It was apparent almost at once that she would not be able to say everything she would like to and keep to the time schedule her grandmother had laid out for them. When Harmon came back from his rounds to check on her, she had decided what would be included in her eulogy. She supposed it wasn't really a eulogy, but hopefully it would describe the grandmother she had come to know and love.

"Would you like to go to my house? I've got a computer there if you want to use it and print out something. I know Matthew was going to ask you to speak, and I was sure you'd say yes. Did you?" Harmon asked.

"Yes, I did. No question about that, and I would like to go to your house. I think I can find my way, but just to be sure, remind me where I turn."

"No, I'll drive over with you, and we'll grab a bite to eat there. I can bug out for an hour or so, and maybe we can talk. I always enjoy talking to you. Shall we go?"

As before when Leah had come to visit her grandmother, Harmon was a good host. A lunch of soup and sandwiches was perfect as they talked across the table.

After discussing the funeral, Harmon said, "I want to change the subject if I may. I want you to know that Katy and I are engaged and will be married in the spring. As soon as we select the date, I'll let you know. I want you to be there. I hope you'll want to be there, and I also hope you're okay with our living arrangements." Harmon had a concerned look on his face as he spoke those last words.

Leah smiled. "Harm, I'm fine with whatever you choose to do, and I'm sure I'll like Katy very much when we meet, so congratulations. You can count on me to be there. Have you told your dad? I don't see him getting upset about your moving in together, because he was coming and going with Janet long before your mother died. Russell is living with his intended as well. I don't know about Charlene or Stephen and what they might think, but it's your life, and you probably don't even have to say anything to them if you don't want to. They don't come to visit you here anyway."

The funeral came off as Corinne had intended, including staying on schedule. There were two scripture readings: Psalm 8 and Titus 3:5–8. The pastor had a fine six-minute sermonette, and Leah was able to speak about her grandmother without shedding any tears. To her surprise, Harm spoke as well, on behalf of the staff. That Corinne had been well loved by everyone there was obvious. As soon as the service ended, the evening meal was served, so Leah, Harm, and Katy had dinner with the residents. It amused and touched all three of them when a gentleman of advanced years made his way to their table, his walker scraping against the tiles.

"Miss Leah, I feel as though I know you," he said. "Your grandma loved to talk about you and showed me pictures. Corrine surely did set store by you. If we had been a few years younger and in just a little better health, I would have asked that woman to marry me. Maybe I should have anyway. It would have been somebody to talk to at night when the lights went out. I always liked that with my wife. We talked at night. Well, those days are gone, and you can't bring 'em back. You young folks make the most of things now, while you can, and drive careful going back home. I know your grandma worried until she got a call that you made it back safe and sound."

Leah and Katy left soon after the meal, and Harmon followed an hour or so later, after helping settle a dementia patient who wanted to "go home" but of course couldn't.

Katy, Harm, and Leah had a quiet evening, and Leah especially enjoyed getting to know her future sister-in-law a little better. They discovered they liked some of the same things, and she was astonished to learn that Katy had attended Northwestern, although only for one year. She had transferred to the University of Wisconsin in Milwaukee when her father had died. They talked about wedding plans, and Katy asked Leah to be a bridesmaid. Leah was surprised, but she was delighted to be able to say yes.

In the morning Leah left when Harm and Katy did. She ran into a little traffic on the toll road, but she was able to return the rental before eleven and not have to pay for an additional day. She walked home, changed clothes, and then caught a bus to the Book Nook. It felt good to be back working among her friends, the books.

Leah stayed on until after eight, and because she hadn't been home long enough to do any shopping, she decided to stop at the Corner Café for supper. She sat down at the counter, and as she was waiting for her meal, she grabbed a copy of the *Chicago Tribune* lying nearby. She scanned the front page and then turned to the second page, where a headline startled her: "Horace Marsden, Well-Known Attorney Dies." She read quickly through the article and learned that Horace Marsden had died of a heart attack the previous day. It listed his various accomplishments and his connection with the firm that bore his name. Listed survivors included a sister, a sister-in-law, three nephews and two nieces. Services were to be on Saturday at a mortuary in Evanston.

Leah couldn't believe Horace Marsden was dead. He had seemed invincible to her, especially that day when he'd fired her and told her to get out and stay out of Alan's life. Somehow that seemed like an eternity ago. She thought about attending the funeral but decided it wouldn't be a good idea. She knew herself well enough to know she wanted a glimpse of Alan, but if Juneau was there, it would be better to stay away. What did it mean that Juneau was living in Florida? Was it a temporary thing? And there was no mention of the baby. That seemed strange, but maybe great-nephews didn't count. She laid the newspaper back down on the counter and hurried home, where she had unpacking to do.

Chapter 24

Christmas would be a quiet day for Leah. Russell and Reba had gone to Peoria, Illinois, to spend Christmas Eve and Christmas Day with Reba's parents. It was Russell's first time meeting his prospective in-laws. Gene, Janet, and the girls had flown to Cancun for the holidays, and Charlene and her new love interest, Roger, were traveling to Florida, where the young man's parents and grandparents lived. She had canceled her wedding with Clive when she'd met Roger. He was the assistant manager at the bank where she had been transferred in October. Leah worried about Charlene's quick decisions, both jobwise and boyfriend wise, but she realized that Charlene had not dated much in high school and hardly at all after that. She had become Mama's tote-and-fetch girl, as Gene had described it. Leah had no idea what Stephen would be doing. She never heard from him, and Harmon and Russell heard little or nothing. Leah couldn't help wondering where Alan would be spending Christmas. Florida perhaps?

Although she had not planned to put up a tree, on Christmas Eve morning she dug out the decorations and the old artificial tree her parents had purchased when she'd been in junior high school. It was no more than three feet tall, but it fit perfectly on one of her end tables. She removed the lamp that was sitting there and began decorating the little tree. It didn't take long, and when she plugged in the light cord and stood back to survey her work, she was pleased. It wasn't much, but it gave the living room the feeling of Christmas. At ten she left for the Book Nook.

Business was brisk until about four when suddenly the store was completely empty of customers. Elise sat down on a stool behind the counter, sighed, and said, "Leah, I think we can call it a day. Go round up Keith and Morgan, and tell them to go home. Then would you like to come upstairs and enjoy a little eggnog with us? I think my ball and chain is home by now. How about it?"

"Thanks for the invitation, but I'm really tired. I'm not used to standing for as long as I did today. I guess I'll have to toughen up again when I start working more hours on the twenty-sixth. I'd just like to go home and have a hot bath. I plan to attend the Christmas Eve service at Rockefeller Chapel this evening. I've heard it's very lovely." Leah hoped Elise would not be offended that she was turning down her gracious invitation. Leah had earlier told Elise that she would be alone, which likely had prompted the invitation.

"I understand. I hope you have a lovely Christmas, and I know you'll enjoy the service at the chapel. Off you go, Leah. I'll see you on the twenty-sixth, say about nine?"

It had snowed a little during the day, so Leah pulled on her boots, shrugged into her coat, and headed out the door. At four thirty it was still light, although the sky in the west was pink and promised a lovely sunset. The bus pulled up just as Leah came out of the bookstore, so she hopped on and in a few minutes was at her stop, two blocks from her apartment. She was already digging for her keys as she neared the door to the lobby of her building. Out of the corner of her eye she saw someone exit a car parked across the street and come toward her. Probably one of the residents she supposed.

"Leah," a voice behind her said.

Leah turned and was astonished to see Stephen crossing the street. "Stephen? What are you doing in Chicago?"

"Well, I thought I'd see if you were home and if maybe we could have dinner tonight. It's Christmas Eve, and I thought because everyone else in our family is involved elsewhere … I thought … Well, I thought you might be home."

"Wow, what a surprise. What brings you to Chicago?"

"I had a job interview a few days ago, and then I decided to stick around and take in a couple of shows and see the sights. I haven't been in Chicago since college days. I thought about calling you earlier, but I wasn't sure I should." Stephen looked at his feet as he finished his sentence.

"You should have called. But I'm glad you're here now. Let's go in where it's warm. I have chicken in the Crock-Pot, and there's enough for two." Leah led the way into the foyer of her building, and they took the elevator to the third floor. "I wasn't expecting a guest, so excuse any mess. I know I left the Christmas decoration boxes stacked in the hallway. Well, never mind. It's not important, is it? What's important is that you're here. I want to hear all about what you've been doing. You said you had a job interview, so that must mean you're thinking about relocating."

Leah inserted the key in her door and preceded Stephen into her apartment. She flipped the light switch, which turned on the hall light and also the Christmas tree lights, transforming the apartment from its early-evening gloom.

The appealing smell of the stew permeated the air, and Stephen commented that he had not experienced that kind of aroma for a very long time … perhaps not since childhood. "Well, it's just plain food," Leah said, "but why don't you take off your coat and sit down while I put some coffee on and find something to go with the stew?"

In only a few minutes the meal was on the table. Leah had not realized how hungry she was until they'd entered the apartment. She was as tantalized by the aroma as Stephen had been. He was also hungry and tucked into the stew. Neither of them spoke for several minutes.

Then Leah asked, "Where was your interview, and are you serious about coming back to the Midwest?"

"I interviewed at Loyola University, and yes, I'm interested. When I left college for grad school in Washington, I thought I was going to a place where I would find what I was looking for, but I never really did. For that reason I'm seriously considering this move, if they offer me the position. I think they might. I've already had two phone interviews, so this was the third, and I believe it went very well. They're desperate for someone as soon as possible, as they had a death in the department, so two of the courses I would be teaching have not been offered this fall. They would like someone who could begin now on a part-time basis and then full-time next September."

"I don't know what your field is, Stephen. Is it in the humanities or math or what?"

"I was in the math department in Washington, but I've also been teaching a class in computer programming, sort of a hobby of mine. Initially I did some of that on the side, and then a year ago, the dean asked me to teach the advanced course they wanted to offer. I might do something similar at Loyola, if they decide they want me. I'm afraid I've already burned my bridges in Washington, because back in October when I had the first phone interview, I gave my notice to be finished at the end of the fall term. Probably not a very smart move, but I have some savings, and I know I can get a job as a programmer or hang out my shingle for a while until something comes along."

This information was news to Leah, who had not known Stephen's field of interest or what his gifts were. "I admire anyone who can find their way around a computer, and I would think programming could be a lucrative career choice. Have you considered working exclusively in that discipline?"

"I have an interview with IBM on the twenty-seventh, and I'll see what they have to say. My problem is that I haven't worked a real job in that field but only helped out here and there at the request of two programmer friends. I'll see what happens and whether it could work for me. Can I have another bowl of this great stew?"

Leah smiled, got up, and filled Stephen's bowl once again. She was delighted he enjoyed it but even more pleased at his sharing something of himself. They finished the meal and cleaned up the kitchen, and then Leah invited Stephen to attend the service at Rockefeller Chapel with her. She said that the service was not a Roman Catholic one but that perhaps he would enjoy the music. He agreed to accompany her. Leah changed clothes, and since Stephen had a rental car, he offered to drive. Parking was a little difficult, but they finally found a place only a block away.

Inside the church, the organ was already swelling to a crescendo on a rendition of "Hark the Herald Angels Sing." They found seats halfway down the long, cavernous chancel and settled in for the rest of the organ prelude. Then the choir processed in, and in the balcony area a brass quintet played. A string group in the front was not visible from where Leah and Stephen were seated, but they could hear violins playing the first hymn, "O Little Town of Bethlehem," when the worshippers were invited to rise and sing. The service ended with the "Hallelujah Chorus."

Stephen was impressed with the architecture as well as the music. He also praised the preacher, acknowledging that this was the first time he had been to a Protestant church since he'd been fourteen and his family had attended a confirmation service for a friend of his. As they drove back to Leah's apartment, Stephen announced that he should be going back to his hotel.

Then, to Leah's surprise, Steven asked her if she would be his guest for Christmas dinner. The hotel where he was staying had recommended a restaurant that provided excellent holiday meals at several times during the day.

"I'd love to, Stephen, but I invited my friend Connie to come over about five o'clock for a meal. Of course you could join us if you like." Leah hated to say no to his invitation. She hadn't eaten at a fine restaurant for a long time, and she had not been looking forward to cooking tomorrow.

"Why not invite her to join us? We can call for reservations as soon as we get back to your place, and then you can call your friend. I'd like that, Leah. Would you ask her?"

"Of course. We'll do just as you suggested. How thoughtful, Stephen, to include my friend. I think you'll like Connie. We worked for the same law firm some time ago, but we've both moved on since, and she now works at the University of Chicago Library."

Dinner downtown was a treat for Leah, and she enjoyed the conversation as well. Stephen seemed more outgoing after the salad course, and by the time the waiter came with the dessert menu, he was sharing stories that had them laughing. Everyone passed on dessert, and they left the restaurant to drive back to Leah's apartment. Leah said they should play cards or a game or something, and Stephen offered to drop Connie off after the evening's entertainment.

Coffee and Christmas cookies at Leah's was as far as the entertainment went. No one seemed interested in game playing, but the conversation continued until past eleven, when Connie said it was probably time to wrap it up, as she had to work in the morning.

"Thanks, Leah," Stephen said as he and Connie were at the door, ready to leave. "I'm sorry I didn't think to bring you a Christmas gift. I didn't buy a single one this year. I just sent cards to everyone. I hope you got mine."

Leah nodded. "Yes, I did, and I enjoyed the beautiful picture of Mount Hood on the card. Someday I'd like to see it for real, but that won't be for a long time. I have to finish my degree first and get a decent job so I can afford vacations. Well, good night you two. Call me before you go back to Seattle; I'm interested in what develops with the job."

After her guests were gone, Leah cleaned up the coffee cups and only then remembered she had three gifts under the tree that were just sitting there, waiting to be opened. The first package she opened was from Gene and Janet; it was a Royal Stewart tartan throw. From Russell and Reba she received a pair of silver dangly earrings that she knew would go well with a necklace she had gotten at the Book Nook with her employee discount. Harmon and Katy had sent a beautifully illustrated book of poetry by both American and British authors, and she began paging through it at once. She loved poetry and had at one time tried to write free verse, but she'd discovered that everything she wrote seemed to want to rhyme, so she had given up that idea. But maybe rhyming verses were acceptable. Some of the old-time poets wrote that way, and their works had endured.

She went to bed early since she too had work on her agenda in the morning.

The next week passed quickly for Leah because she was so busy. She wondered once toward the end of the week if Stephen would call. She had neglected to find out where he was staying, so she couldn't call him. She had his home phone number in Seattle, but that did her no good at all now.

New Year's Eve came, and Leah couldn't help but think that this very day might have been her wedding anniversary if things had worked out and she and Alan had married as they had planned. "Don't think about it, Leah," she said to herself. She tried to put it out of her mind, but she was having a little difficulty doing so. What was Alan doing tonight? Would he think about the date and remember their thwarted plans as she was doing? The phone interrupted her thoughts, for which she was grateful. She hoped it was Stephen, but no, it was Elise.

"Leah, would you like to come to our house and see in the New Year with us? It will be a very small group, and I'll see you get a ride home when the party's over."

"That would be lovely, Elise. Can I bring anything? I have tons of Christmas cookies, and I could whip up some dip for veggies."

"Sounds good, but don't spend a ton of time putting something together. I'm sure we'll have plenty of food. Come about nine o'clock. I can come for you if you'd like, or I can have Jack and Harriet pick you up."

"Don't worry; I'll get there all right, but a ride home would be nice. Thanks for the invitation. I look forward to it."

After ending the call, Leah got busy putting together ingredients for the dip and found an unopened box of Bugles to include along with Christmas cookies. Then it dawned on her. Elise had said Jack and Harriet were going to be there. That would undoubtedly be the Desmonds. Maybe she should have declined the invitation. It would be awkward now to call and cancel. *Oh, just go, Leah, and stop worrying that Alan might be a topic of conversation.*

It was a clear night, and there was very little wind, so walking to Elise's house was actually a pleasure. The brisk air was invigorating, and she needed the exercise. It was a few minutes past nine when Leah presented herself at Elise's door, the last of the guests to arrive. Elise introduced her to two other couples and several singles, all grad students like herself. Dr. Jamison of the history department and his wife were there, and the grad students present were all working on degrees in history. Leah had seen one of the young men in the bookstore just the other day, so she struck up a conversation with him.

"Tell me how you're coming with your dissertation. I'm curious because I have all these notes and must start writing soon. I suspect social work and history don't have much in common, but paper writing is sort of a universal thing. Any tips you'd care to pass along?" Leah asked.

"You might be surprised how different disciplines sometimes overlap, and I'd be willing to bet we could think up things they have in common. I guess I'd rather talk about something else. I'm sick of my dissertation. Tell me what you do for fun, Leah. That's your name, isn't it? It was kind of noisy when Elise made the intros, so I didn't quite catch it."

"Yes, I'm Leah, and you are …? Sorry, but I missed your name."

"I'm Nick Jankowski, and I'm from Milwaukee. You know … home of the Brewers and also some pretty fine beer. Do you drink beer?"

"No, I prefer Coke or Mountain Dew. Are you a beer connoisseur?"

"Not really. Actually I seldom imbibe, but I enjoy a brewski on a hot summer day. Beyond that I stick with the soft stuff too. It causes raised eyebrows sometimes, especially among guys I meet for the first time. They find it hard to believe I don't drink beer. What do you like to do for fun, Leah?"

"Fun! I can hardly remember. My schedule has been so busy I don't have time for much of anything. I enjoy walking and running and biking, and in summer I swim in Lake Michigan. Oh yes, I enjoy detective shows on TV. What about you?"

"I'm into soccer. I play on a league team in fall and spring. In winter I try to work out or play basketball, and I like sports on TV. I guess movies are also something I enjoy from time to time. Did you see the Harry Potter series?"

"Sorry, no. I haven't gotten into the movie going habit, but recently I saw one on TV that I liked. It was an old black and white, but I don't remember the name of it."

"Oh hey, I love those old black and whites. The plots are often predictable, but I still like to see how the hero comes through in the end. There's a place downtown that shows old movies a night or two a week. I haven't been there but have heard about it. We ought to go. Would you like to do that? Go to a movie with me?" Nick looked hopefully at Leah.

"Oh, I don't know. Won't you be too busy? We just met, so I don't know." Leah was conflicted about saying yes, but saying no to a friend of Elise's made her hesitate.

"I'm sure we can carve out a little time to see a movie. Say yes. It could be fun, and we might even become friends. How about it?"

"Well, why not? What night works for you?" Leah asked. They compared schedules and finally settled on the day after New Year's. "I'll drive over and pick you up. 7:00 p.m. then, day after tomorrow."

Leah wondered if she had made a mistake, but it was too late now. The rest of the evening was spent playing several ridiculous parlor games, and of course there was a mountain of food. At midnight Elise and Ed brought out party hats and horns for everyone, and with the television tuned to the local channel, they participated in the countdown to midnight. Nick had made his way to Leah's side, so when the clock struck the final gong, indicating the New Year had arrived, he pulled her into his arms and kissed her. She was more surprised than anything, but it was rather pleasant, so she didn't protest. Everyone was kissing everyone, but mostly on the check. Elise passed champagne around to toast the New Year, but Leah knew there would be two glasses with sparkling grape juice: one for Ed and one for her. The party ended, and Leah had not had to field any questions about Alan from the Desmonds. However, they were driving her home, so perhaps it was still to come.

Jack Desmond pulled the car around and told Leah she should sit in the front. It was a two-door car, and he pointed out that it would be easier for her to get out once they reached her apartment. Harriet climbed into the back.

"Well, Leah, how have you been? Sorry we didn't get to talk much at the party. I'm wondering if you've heard anything from Alan. We're worried about him at the firm. He left the day after his uncle's funeral and said he wouldn't be available until at least February 1. I think his marriage went south, and Juneau may have already married someone else. I don't know that for a certainty. Have you heard from of him?"

"No, I haven't. It's been a long time since I talked to him … probably late October. I noticed Mr. Marsden's obituary said Juneau was somewhere in Florida. Is she living down there now?"

"We have no idea. She was at the funeral, but I heard Horace had bought her a place in South Beach. I'm worried about Alan, as I said before. I know the two of you were close last year, so I wouldn't be surprised if he gets in touch with you, especially if he and Juneau are splitting up. Well, here we are. Happy New Year, Leah. I wish you well in your studies, and if you hear anything from Alan, let me know. Will you do that?"

"Thanks, Mr. and Mrs. Desmond, and yes, if I hear anything, I'll be in touch. Thanks for the ride, and happy New Year to both of you."

Leah jumped out of the Desmonds' car and hurried to her apartment. Why did Alan Parkin have to keep intruding in her life? She was not ready to believe anything about the possible breakup of his and Juneau's marriage. Knowing Juneau, it was not likely she would let go of Alan very easily. She wished she had asked about their child, but it hadn't seemed like a good idea. As she was putting her key into her apartment door, she saw a long, narrow box leaning against the doorjamb. She picked it up after noticing her name written in longhand on the outside and carried it inside. She opened it and then removed the green florist paper inside, uncovering one long-stemmed yellow rose.

"Oh no!" Yellow roses were her favorite, but few people knew that, although Alan did. A note inside read, "One yellow rose for what might have been." There was no signature, but Leah knew it had to be from Alan. But why? It seemed cruel to send her a reminder on this day, one year after they had planned to be married. She slumped into a chair, held the flower to her nose, and breathed in the aroma. If he wanted to communicate with her, why not call? They had always been able to talk to each other, so if he wanted to say he was sorry or try to make amends and start over, he could have found a better way to do it. Leah was feeling betrayal all over again, and she was angry. She shredded the flower into tiny bits and threw it in the wastebasket. Then she went to bed.

As a way of taking her mind off Alan, she thought about Nick Jankowski. Maybe it was a good thing to go out with someone once again. "Give it a try, Leah," she said. "Maybe Nick will be someone you want to get to know better."

Nick Jankowski picked up Leah for the movie as planned, and Leah enjoyed what turned out to be a rollicking romantic-comedy mystery that had them laughing out loud. On the way back to Hyde Park, Nick said, "Why don't we pick up a couple of sandwiches and some Cokes from Subway and take them back to your place? The night's still young, and I'd love to get to know you better, Leah."

Reluctantly Leah agreed, although she would have preferred being dropped off at her front door and say good night there. She had gotten a prickly feeling about Nick in the theater when he'd "accidently" brushed his arm across her chest while trying to help her with her coat. He'd also taken her hand at one point, but she'd pulled away.

As soon as they were in Leah's apartment, Nick made himself at home, flopping down on the sofa while Leah unpacked the sandwiches and put ice in glasses for the Coke. She set everything on the kitchen table and ignored Nick in the living room. When it was ready, she called, "Nick, come out to the kitchen for your sandwich."

"Let's have our little repast in here. It's cozier, and I love your Christmas tree." Nick had turned off all the lights except for those that adorned the little tree on the end table.

"No, I prefer not to serve food in there, so come sit at the table."

Nick reluctantly ambled into the kitchen and slid into a chair adjacent to Leah, rather than taking the one across from her. They began to eat their sandwiches, but after only a few bites, Leah excused herself and went into her bedroom. In the back of her dresser drawer she had a small container of pepper spray, and she put it into the pocket of her cardigan, hoping Nick wouldn't notice. Back at the table she tried to start a meaningful conversation and was somewhat successful when she began to talk about sports. The Bulls, the Bears, and even the White Sox, which of course weren't playing in January, provided some discussion, but the chatter stopped once Nick finished his sandwich. Leah was still working on hers, although she wasn't very hungry. She laid down the remaining half and said she thought it was time to end their evening. Nick protested but finally rose and picked up his coat from the easy chair in the living room. Leah was standing at the door, a forced smile on her face. She wanted him gone. Why exactly, she didn't know, but he made her uncomfortable.

At the door Nick grabbed Leah and encased her in a tight hold, trying to force her head back so he could kiss her. She tried to push him away, saying, "No, Nick. I'm not ready for this. Please leave." He ignored her request and began walking her backward into the living room. When they were in front of the sofa, he lifted her up and almost threw her onto the cushions. She managed to extract the pepper spray from her pocket and struggled to get a good angle to ensure that his eyes would get the full force of the spray. Then she pressed the button. He screamed when the stinging mist hit his face, eyes, nose, and mouth. Leah kept depressing the button, closing her eyes and holding her breath. She was fairly successful and had only a slight stinging in her left eye. Nick fell to the floor in obvious pain. Leah jumped up and ran from her apartment to Jeffery Collins's door. He was a policeman, and Leah was hoping he was home and would get Nick out of her apartment. Fortunately he was there, and he immediately grabbed his coat and followed her back into her living room. Even before entering the apartment they could hear Nick's screams, so Jeffery suggested Leah get some water and a cloth so they could wash at least some of the spray out of his eyes.

"He won't be driving his car tonight," Jeffery said as he helped Nick up.

Leah handed Nick's jacket to Jeffery, who unsuccessfully tried to pull his arms into the sleeves. "I think our lothario is suffering from something else besides pepper spray," Jeffery said. In the process of the struggle to get Nick's coat on, a half-empty bottle of vodka fell out of his pocket. "Here's the culprit," Jeffery said, picking it up and setting it on the kitchen table. "I'll take him home, unless you want to press charges."

"I guess not. He's a grad student, and if he gets into trouble, he might not graduate. I wouldn't want that. I thought he was a nice guy, but something about him tonight made me uncomfortable. He left the movie twice, first to get a drink of water, he said, and then to go to the john, but I suspect it was to drink some of that vodka. He told me he didn't drink when I met him a few nights ago at a party at my boss's house. Thanks for coming to my rescue. Will you be all right with him by yourself?"

"Oh yes. I'll put the cuffs on him when I get him to my car. I hope he can tell me where he lives. I don't suppose you know."

Leah shook her head. "I could call my boss, but she might not know either. I think he can probably tell you his address, but I hope he forgets mine!"

"I'll put the fear of the Lord into him. I'll tell him if he so much as says one word to you, in person or by phone, we'll pick him up and he won't like what happens to him. Good night, Leah. I hope this won't affect your night's sleep."

Leah went back into her apartment and locked the door. One thing was clear to her: she wasn't ready to start dating again!

The next day Leah realized she had not had any word from Stephen about his job interviews. She assumed he had gone back to Seattle, but she was a bit miffed that he had not called before leaving Chicago. She might call him at home tonight after work, but right now she was due at the Book Nook. Late in the afternoon she was delighted to see Connie approaching the register. A customer needed advice about a gift for a ten-year-old nephew, so Leah led her over to the children's section while motioning for Connie to wait. As soon as Leah had finished with the customer, she greeted her friend with a hug and said, "Long time no see. What have you been doing since Christmas? I haven't seen or heard anything from you. Of course I didn't call you either. You look great. What have you done with your hair? I like it."

"Oh, I've been pretty busy. Students coming back, wanting books, that sort of thing. Have you heard from your brother? I was just wondering," Connie said.

Leah thought she detected a certain hesitation in Connie's question. "No, I haven't heard a word from Stephen. I was hoping he'd call before going back to Seattle, but I've not heard anything from him, so I don't know if his job interviews went well or what's going on. Sorry."

"Can we go into that back room where we had tea the last time I was here? I think I need to talk to you." Connie had a somewhat-strained expression on her face.

Leah signaled another clerk to cover for her, and she and Connie went through the door to the back room. No one was there, so they sat down, and Leah offered Connie tea or a soft drink. Connie shook her head.

"You should have heard this from Steve. I don't know why he didn't want to tell you himself, but he's still in Chicago. He's going to teach a seminar at Loyola, and in the meantime he's still on the hook with IBM, but nothing has popped there yet. I told him to call you, but obviously he hasn't. I'm sorry, Leah. You're probably disappointed in him. He is your brother and should let you know what's going on in his life." Connie's concerned look made Leah wonder what the rest of the story might be. She hoped it wasn't anything serious.

"It sounds like you've been in touch. I guess that's a surprise in itself, but that's all right. I've got no problem with his talking to you. You know, I hadn't spoken more than a couple of words to him until he showed up at my door on Christmas Eve, so I don't expect him to think he has to tell me what goes on in his life. I guess I'm glad he felt like calling you. I know you're a good listener, Connie, and a good friend."

"I hope you'll still think that, Leah. Steve and I went out four times last week, and this week we were together for New Year's Eve and New Year's Day. Ever since he took me home Christmas evening, we've been together a lot. In fact, he came in that night, and we talked until two in the morning. We just hit it off. I've felt rotten not telling you, but he didn't want me to. I still don't understand why." Connie wore a worried look.

"You and Stephen?"

"He likes to be called Steve. He told me that on Christmas night. I've never met anyone quite like him. He's a deep thinker and so kind and thoughtful. I'm afraid that I've fallen head over heels for your brother. Why do you think he didn't want you to know about us?"

"I'm not sure, but I should tell you that he comes from a pretty dysfunctional family—not all of them, mostly his mother. He probably told you she died last summer. I think he's reticent about telling me he's dating you because of who I was … who I am. I was the lost McGregor child, spirited away and never heard from until recently. Poor little Lizzie! All the McGregor kids suffered through their growing-up years with the loss of Lizzie hanging over everything. Mama saw to that. I told you the story of my abduction and my return, so he might have fears that I'll screw up his relationship with you, but I wouldn't do that. I'm delighted that you and Steve are seeing each other. I think he needs someone like you in his life."

"What should I do?" Connie asked.

"Nothing, dear friend. Just be who you are. Let me take care of this. I'll need his phone number, and I'll call him tonight, unless you two are going out on a date."

"Not tonight. I have to go to my aunt's birthday party, and Steve wasn't ready to meet family. I hope he won't be mad that I gave you his number."

"Never fear! Leah will make no waves and will in fact smooth the way for you. I promise. You know, I'm getting pretty good at this sister thing if I do say so myself. Now I've got to get back to work, but we'll get together soon, all three of us!"

Leah didn't get home from the Book Nook until nine o'clock even though her shift was due to end at six. Elise needed help with a shipment of books, so Leah agreed to stay on to help. The first thing she did upon arriving home was to put on the kettle for tea. Then she dug Steve's phone number out of her purse and called him. *I must remember to call him Steve. I don't remember anyone but Harmon calling him that. He was always Stephen. Hmmm.*

"Hello, Brother. I ran into Connie today, and she gave me your number. So how's the job search going, and where are you living these days?"

"Leah, I guess I owe you an explanation, or an apology. I got the job at Loyola and will start very soon teaching a seminar. Beyond that nothing else has come up, but there are several things on the back burner. I rented an efficiency not far from Loyola, which is fine for now. I suppose Connie told you that we've seen each other a few times."

"I think it's probably more than just a few times, from what Connie said. Hey, Steve, I think it's great. Connie's a good friend and a fine person, so I couldn't be more pleased that the two of you hit it off. Don't worry about me. I won't do anything to embarrass you. I promise. I'm not Lizzie, you know. I'm Leah, and we're two very different people. I know what Lizzie did to all of you, and I have no wish to follow in her footsteps. I just want to be your sister and your friend." Leah hoped she was explaining herself adequately. Steve hadn't said anything for a couple of seconds, so she wondered if she had struck the right note.

"You know, Leah, you're not a McGregor. Oh, I don't mean that really. What I should have said is that you're not like any of the McGregors. We're all a little impaired in one way or another. I know you get along well with Harm, but as time goes on, you may see a couple of his quirks. Since the end of high school I haven't spent much time with him, so he may have outgrown the childish stuff he used to pull. I should have taken what you said to me on Christmas Eve as gospel truth, but I didn't think I could trust you. The McGregors haven't always been reliable. Dad wasn't, and Mama certainly wasn't. I don't keep in touch with any of the family. It's just easier because we're all dragging around so much baggage; at least I know I am. I hope we can be in touch since I'm going to be staying in Chicago. I'd like to get to know you better. What do you think?"

"I think I'd like that. Call me when there's news on the job front or just for the heck of it. I might be hard to find because I'm working on my thesis and have a crazy schedule sometimes, but leave a message, and I'll call back. Okay?"

Steve agreed that keeping in touch was a good thing, and they ended the call. Leah was amazed at the abrupt change in her older brother's attitude. She agreed with Connie that he was perhaps a deep thinker and maybe a deep feeler as well, not something she would have suspected from the way family members had sometimes described him. "It's a beginning," she said to the four walls.

Chapter 25

Leah continued to plow ahead on her thesis, and she worked almost full-time at the Book Nook. Her bank account, however, was dangerously low. She had not touched Horace Marsden's blood money, but she needed to pay last term's tuition before it was due at the end of the week. She also needed warm clothing for winter, so even though she would have preferred to postpone using the money, she decided to transfer $100,000 into her checking account. There were weddings coming up and a baby due, so there would be other expenses when those events occurred. Gene had called just a few days ago saying that he and Janet were expecting. He had seemed apologetic when he'd delivered the news. Leah had almost laughed but had caught herself in time. He was, he'd said, almost sixty, and what business did he have producing a child at this time in his life? But there would be a baby in late summer! She had congratulated him and told him that he had a wonderful opportunity to once again guide a child into adulthood and that maybe it would be easier this time around. He'd laughed then and said he certainly hoped so.

By the second week of January, Leah was well into writing her dissertation and as a result had been forced to cut down her hours at the bookstore, much to Elise's chagrin. Leah needed to spend more time at the library for additional research, and she discovered that it was easier in the early part of the day. In the evening she wasn't as sharp and had a harder time maintaining her focus on the printed word. Today she was scheduled to work at the Book Nook from two until closing. When she arrived, there were hordes of customers milling about, and Leah jumped right into the help mode the minute she shed her coat. By the end of the evening the traffic in and out had slowed down. After locking the door, Elise invited Leah to stay for a cup of tea. As they sipped their tea, Elise asked, "What's going on in that pretty little head of yours? You seem to be miles away."

Leah sighed. "It's my future. I'm trying to decide a lot of things. Where do I want to work? Here in Chicago or elsewhere? As soon as I finish my thesis, I'll be on the fast track for my diploma, so it's time I start thinking about the future. If I leave Chicago, I'll really miss you and our conversations and friendship, but I have to move on with this career that I've chosen for good or ill."

"You'll figure it out, Leah. For selfish reasons I hope you'll stay in Chicago. You've become the daughter I never had, so I would miss seeing you. I know it's a tough decision, but I'm sure you'll make the right one. Do you ever have second thoughts about giving up law?"

"Not really, although it would be easier for me to apply for a paralegal position because I'd know what I was doing. This social work business is new, and I'm untried, which makes it's a little scary, but I think it's the best path for me right now."

Elise frowned. What did the "right now" mean? She hoped her dear friend would find her life's work and whatever else she was seeking. "Leah, I hope you'll find happiness in your new profession. I know you said you were quite happy as a paralegal until you lost your job, but I firmly believe you can find happiness in social work because you're a person who cares about people."

"Thanks, Elise. I hope social work will be the right choice. As my mother used to say, 'Find joy in what you do.' Happiness is elusive sometimes, but joy is a deep-down feeling that can come even in difficult times. I suspect I'll have difficult times starting out and finding my way, but I'm looking forward to it. Really I am."

"That's a good mantra: finding joy in your work. I do, although I'm not always happy about some things, like surly customers, publishers who don't follow through as promised, and all the stuff we deal with here. I'll have to remember what you said about finding joy in my work and maybe complain a little less, especially to Ed. It's not his fault if special orders are late or if Mrs. Stockbridge from down the street barks at me. Good advice, Leah, good advice."

When Leah left the Book Nook that evening, she thought about what Elise had said. It would be hard to leave Chicago for many reasons, but the memories of her former position at the law firm and of course her memories of Alan were rooted here, so a new environment might be good. She had put off any decision, but now it was January, and she was still trying to decide where to apply. Leah had discovered in December that with some law school courses that transferred, she already had enough credits to graduate and only needed to finish her thesis, so it was time to get serious about looking for work.

Should she stay in Chicago? There were good reasons to stay and a few good ones to go somewhere else, where memories might fade. Gene had suggested she consider the Twin Cities. He gave her the name of someone he knew who could give her leads for a job. Her professor in the sociology department had also offered his assistance and had mentioned two places she might try. Somehow she had not been excited about moving out into a new field of work. Was it anxiety about being prepared or something else?

"Leah, it's time to get your life going in a new direction," she told herself. "The best solution to inertia is to get off dead center." She decided to do some research and make a few calls. The computer helped her discover several openings in Chicago and the Twin Cities and several other places she had not previously considered. Starting in a completely unknown environment would mean making new friends and discovering new and exciting things, which appealed to her. What she needed was a professional opinion. Tomorrow she was due at work by nine thirty and would finish at five. Maybe her advisor would still be in his office at the end of the day, or she might call him at home since he had said that would be all right.

The next evening after work Leah's advisor gave her a list of possible opportunities. He suggested she get busy, telling her, "These things take time." That night she continued to surf the web, but in the end, only a couple of the job listings appealed to her. She sent off résumés and transcripts to three places: one in Saint Paul, one in Milwaukee, and one in Chicago. She heard back from the Milwaukee agency first. The news wasn't good. She was one of seventeen applicants, and they were planning to lop off ten of those, including hers. The agency in suburban Chicago called next and arranged an interview, but she didn't care for the job description once it was described fully to her over the phone. It sounded more like clerical work, and she wanted to be involved with women and children.

The Saint Paul agency called one day in the late morning, just as she was leaving for work.

"Hello, Leah Anderly." She had begun to answer the phone in that manner to save time by letting potential employers know who was speaking.

"Miss Anderly, this is Dick Huggins with Interfaith Mission Agency in Saint Paul. You applied for a position here, and we'd like to interview you. I'll be in Chicago tomorrow, and if it would be convenient for you, we might conduct an interview there, or you could come here if that would fit your schedule better. Are you still interested?"

"Yes, I am. If you're coming here, that would be fine. I'm working at a bookstore, and we're very shorthanded, so getting away for several days would put my boss in a difficult position, but I know she would be more than willing to let me have time off for the interview. In fact, we have a room at the Book

Nook where I think we could meet." Leah hoped she hadn't overstepped by offering a meeting space.

"That would be just fine. I'm coming to the University of Chicago to see an old friend. Is the bookstore downtown? I remember a Book Nook, but I can't recall where it is."

"We're just a few blocks from the University, so it should be convenient for you. What time would you like to meet? I'm sure my boss will be willing to let me have time off whenever it suits your schedule. If you like, I'll arrange for the room when I ask for time off," Leah said.

They agreed upon 4:00 p.m. the following day, and as soon as their conversation ended, Leah called Elise to make the necessary arrangements. As expected, there was no problem in using the room at the Book Nook.

She was scheduled to begin work at 10:00 a.m. the next day, but she decided to leave a little early and drop in on Professor Housten, who had been her favorite professor in the social work department. He was in his office when she rapped on his door. He was delighted to see her. When she announced that she had an interview for a job that afternoon, he congratulated her, saying he was sure she would do well.

"But that's why I'm here, to ask if you know what sort of questions I might be asked. This social work business is new for me. I know many of the questions I'd be asked if I were interviewing for a position in a law firm, but this is different."

"Yes, I suppose it is. First of all, be honest. If you don't know the answer to something, say so. Keep your answers as succinct as possible, but be ready to elaborate. Some like long, well-developed answers, but most prefer a short answer with the chance to expand on your initial response. You know the material we covered in class very well, and you have good sense. You can figure things out, so if you can project that in the interview, you should be fine. By the way, where is this place you're being considered for, and who is the interviewer? I might have run across him or her at various professional meetings," Professor Housten said.

"He's with the Interfaith Mission Agency in Saint Paul, and his name is Dick Huggins. He said Dick, but I suppose his name is really Richard."

"Dick Huggins? I know him well. In fact he's dropping by later to see me. We haven't been together in probably five years now. He was in Denver then. I didn't realize he was in Saint Paul. Well, well. You know, Leah, if you decide after the interview that you might want the job, I can almost guarantee you'll get it because I'm going to make sure he knows from me what a fine student you are. Well, well. Imagine that! Dick Huggins! And his name really is Dick and not Richard. Good luck, although I don't think you'll need it. Between the two of us we'll convince old Dick that you're the one … that is, if you decide it's the place you want to be."

The phone rang, and Professor Housten waved for Leah to stay a moment. "Hello. Oh yes, I didn't forget. I'll be sure to pick it up on the way home. Yes, I'll be there. Love you too." The professor hung up the phone and said, "In case you didn't figure it out, that was my wife. We're going out to dinner, and I'm to pick up her dress from the dry cleaner's. Now I have a faculty committee meeting, so I'd best be on my way. I'll walk out with you. I didn't want you to leave until I had a chance to wish you all the best as you begin a new career. Let me know how things go with the interview. I'm sure you'll get the job, and working with Dick will be a good thing. He's a great fellow."

Leah's interview went very well, and Dick Huggins impressed her. He seemed to be impressed with her too and tentatively offered her the position, pending approval by the board of directors. He told her the board had agreed to follow his recommendation, so the approval was just perfunctory. He also confided to Leah that the last time the board had insisted on a candidate, one he had not wanted to hire, the decision had been disastrous. Now, he said, they were content to do away with the board interviews and allow the director of operations to make the final decision.

"I think I'd like to work at Interfaith Mission, but I'll wait for an official offer. The pay is fine, and the job I would have, working with women and those with young children, is just what I was hoping to do. I'll wait to hear from you, and thanks for the interview."

Dick Huggins chuckled. "You know, Leah, if I didn't offer you the job, there would be hell to pay with my friend Bernie Housten. I think he just uses his initials, BJ Housten, but his name is Bernhardt Joshua Housten. Don't tell him I told you, okay?" Leah said his given name would never pass her lips. They both laughed, and Dick Huggins said he hoped they would soon be working together.

Chapter 26

Leah moved to Saint Paul on the last day of January. The agency was very anxious to have her begin as soon as possible because they had been shorthanded for some time. She had not finished her thesis, so her diploma would be held until that was completed. Her new boss said it was not an impediment to her employment.

Living in a new city had its challenges, but before long Leah became familiar with the streets and highways and how to navigate them. She became the owner of a secondhand Volkswagen and was living temporarily with Janet and Gene until she could find a suitable apartment.

Carol Michaels, with whom she became acquainted on the first day of work at Interfaith Mission, had been very helpful with information and advice about Leah's new job and also with practical matters, such as shopping, dentists, and doctors.

Leah and Carol were planning to attend a conference in Chicago the first week in March, and Leah offered to drive, saying she knew her way around Chicago. They could park the car and use public transportation while attending the sessions, which were to be held in several different locations. Carol, however, had a last-minute phone call from her mother saying her father was to have surgery the next morning in Duluth, so she canceled her plans and drove up to be with her father. Leah thought about flying or taking the train to Chicago, but the agency had assumed she and Carol would be driving, and she already had accepted the mileage allowance, so she decided to drive. It would be better anyway, giving her more freedom to stay where she wished, which was with Elise. Once she knew Carol wasn't coming with her, she called Elise to see if the offer of her guest room was still good. It was, so she canceled their hotel reservation. Leah looked forward to having some time with her former boss and good friend.

Leah left the Cities Sunday morning and arrived in Hyde Park in late afternoon.

"Hey, come in," Elise said when she answered the door. "You look like you're ready for a cup of tea. Let's bring your bag in, and while you take it upstairs, I'll put the kettle on."

Leah was delighted to see Elise, and they began to exchange stories of what they had been doing since last being in touch. "I miss having you reign over the used-book area at the store. Remember how we scrambled to get that going? Now it's turned into something of a moneymaker, which I didn't think it would. I believe you helped convince me it was a good idea, and you were right. Any new and brilliant ideas how I can increase sales and not have to work myself into a frenzy?"

"None, I'm afraid, since I hardly ever have the chance to frequent bookstores. I've had no time to read really, because I'm still not finished with my dissertation, but hopefully in another month it will be ready to send off."

The doorbell rang, and Elise excused herself to answer it. When she returned to the kitchen, Jack and Harriet Desmond were right behind her. "Leah, I think you know Jack and Harriet. I didn't expect to see them today, but Jack says they were in the neighborhood and wanted to stop by. I suspect they wanted to come keep me company since Ed is off on a long business trip to Italy."

Jack Desmond greeted Leah warmly, as did Harriet, who said she was delighted to once again see the infamous Leah Anderly. Jack laughed and explained, "My wife was finally told all the sordid details about how Horace Marsden kicked you out, and the story is still circulating about how you put old Horace in his place and what you told Ms. Gross when she questioned you about the ownership of your personal computer. I think you also ordered her out of your way as you left your cubicle. I love that story."

Leah was surprised. No, she was shocked to learn that all this had been noised around the office. Maybe more people knew what had happened and how it had happened and even why it had happened than she had thought. "I guess I was a little testy. I even said worse things under my breath on my way home," Leah confessed.

Turning to Elise, Jack said, "You're right, we stopped by to see if you wanted to go to dinner, knowing that Ed was away. We came over here to visit Harriet's aunt Kate, who has a sprained ankle and was complaining about it. We thought we could cheer her up, but it seems she made a remarkable recovery and is off playing bridge somewhere. I really doubt the sprained-ankle story. She's sometimes prone to exaggeration. Not for the first time we've come running for no real reason." Harriet laughed, so Leah guessed that Aunt Kate's ailments might be a ploy for attention.

"So would you two join us for dinner somewhere nearby? I think you mentioned a place on Hyde Park Boulevard that just opened and has gotten good reviews. We could call for reservations at, say, six? What do you say, ladies?" Jack looked expectantly at Elise and Leah.

"I'd love to go out. I was going to order in Chinese for Leah, but I suspect she would enjoy going somewhere and be able to order what she likes. Are you okay with dinner out, Leah?" Elise asked.

"Sure, I'd love it, but I should change my clothes. These old jeans and this not very respectable sweatshirt aren't acceptable dinner attire. It won't take me long," Leah promised..

In less than thirty minutes the reservation had been made, and Leah and Elise had both changed their clothes. The ride to the restaurant took only ten minutes, and by a few minutes to six they were seated at their table.

The restaurant wasn't busy. Perhaps it was too early for most people. Consequently, they were given immediate seating. They ordered beverages, and everyone gave the waiter their choices for dinner. As they waited for the food to be delivered to their table, Jack, Harriet, and Elise spoke about what each of them had been doing recently, as well as catching up on the activities of their children. Leah listened with interest, eager to learn more about Jack and Harriet in particular.

"Leah, you haven't said a word, no doubt because we've dominated the conversation. Tell us about you and what you're doing—and not just your work but your social life and any love interests too," Jack said with a smile.

Leah described her job and said she enjoyed her work very much but was still in the learning mode. "As far as a social life, there's not much time for leisure activities, and I haven't met anybody that would remotely fit the category of love interest. I suppose I'm over the hill anyway. Isn't everything after twenty-five a slide downward?" She smiled when she said this, but it did make her wonder if there was anyone out there who might fit the description of love interest.

Their food was delivered, and they ate while continuing to converse. When the waiter came to ask about dessert, Jack said he wanted a piece of lemon pie. "I never get pie at home anymore!" he complained.

"That's because you're supposed to watch your weight and your blood sugar. I just want to keep you healthy, but if you want pie, go ahead and have pie," Harriet conceded.

No one else cared for dessert, but they all enjoyed coffee and more conversation. Jack had just forked the last bite of lemon and crust into his mouth when he put his hand to his forehead as though to say, "How could I have forgotten this?" Then to Leah he said, "I was just up in your neck of the woods, literally. I drove up to see Alan. Did you know he's living in a hut up in the north woods and plans to stay up there? He bought the property some time ago, either right before or after his marriage started going south. Anyway, he's trying to finish it up, but he's got a long way to go if I'm any judge of things. It looks like a sturdy-enough structure, but inside there are no walls or doors to speak of. He pointed out a couple of improvements he'd made, but I couldn't see it as such. Well, I'm not the outdoor sort of guy, and living in a cabin doesn't appeal to me."

Leah listened carefully, more than a little surprised to hear that Alan wasn't at the law firm and instead was up in some hut in the north woods, wherever that was.

Jack Desmond continued, "But, Leah, what I was going to say is you ought to drive up there. It can't be all that far from the Twin Cities. I think we made it in well under two hours, but I wasn't driving, so I can't say for sure. My brother lives in Minneapolis, and we get together for golf once or twice a year, but this trip was specifically to see Alan. Gary, my brother, picked me up at the airport and drove with me to see him."

"I didn't know Alan was living in Minnesota. I thought he was in Evanston with Juneau and the baby, and I had no idea he wasn't with the firm anymore," Leah said.

"Oh, he and Juneau split a long time ago. I don't know where she is, but I don't think she's in Evanston. Alan told me the house might soon be up for sale, but there's not likely to be much interest in it. The place is too big for most people, and the Victorian motif is still there. I don't know if you were ever in the house, but if you were, you'd know that the decor would appeal to only a few people. But getting back to Alan, I think he might be depressed … about the accident I mean. He gets around pretty well, but you can tell he hates being a cripple. That's not my word but his. I think he would benefit from a visit, and I know you and he dated for a while, so you've got a little history. Give it some thought, Leah. I'm really worried about him. I wish he'd come back to work, but he says he'll probably never work as a lawyer again. God knows he doesn't have to with all the money he no doubt inherited from Horace, though I guess most of it is tied up in probate and will be for a while. Think about it, please. You might be able to get through to him where I couldn't."

Leah was astonished. She hadn't heard about any accident ... and Juneau was a surprise too. She hesitated and then asked Jack what sort of accident Alan had been involved in.

"Oh, you didn't hear? It was just after the first of the year. Alan had a green light and had just driven into the middle of the intersection when a semi plowed into the left side of his car. His lower left leg was crushed. They couldn't save it, so he had an amputation and after that a lot of recovery and therapy. Now he's got a prosthesis, but it didn't look to me like it fit exactly right. I told him he ought to check it out, and he said he might. He has a local doctor, but I think he ought to go to Minneapolis to see a specialist as well as someone skilled in the art of prosthesis fitting. I also believe he ought to see a psychiatrist to help him get his head on straight. He was getting around very well I thought, but I believe his mental state is more the problem than his physical, so for that reason you might be good medicine for him. As I said before, think about it, Leah."

Jack and Harriet Desmond dropped Elise and Leah at Elise's house and headed north to their home in the Highlands. Leah said she was tired and would be going straight to bed. Her early-morning rising, the drive down, and then the evening's conversation had taken its toll, and she wanted to crawl into bed and think about what Jack had said about Alan and what had happened to him.

Leah wondered why it was that just when she had been able to stop thinking about Alan, at least most of the time, there he was, right back in her mind and thoughts. She couldn't imagine Alan having to deal with the loss of a limb, and she was sure it had been and still was very difficult for him. Should she drive up there? Jack Desmond had given her far more credit than the situation warranted. She didn't think she was capable of the kind of therapy that Alan needed, and she was sure her suggesting to Alan that he see someone who could help him mentally wouldn't sit well with him. She remembered the self-confident Alan, the Alan who knew who he was and what he wanted to do and what a good lawyer he was. Now he had given up law completely. What a waste! But what could she say or do to convince him of his value to the firm? She might remind him of his once-upon-a-time thought about doing storefront lawyering and representing those who were unable to hire a high-priced lawyer.

Dropping off to sleep wasn't easy, but she finally was able to think of other things. She thought about Russell, whom she hoped to see tomorrow night, and about Harmon and his fiancée and even about Charlene, with whom she still had an up-and-down relationship, though it was improving. Gene was happy as could be, but they seldom talked anymore. Even though they lived less than a thirty-minute drive from each other, Gene had not come to see her since she had moved into a small efficiency near her office. She had stayed with Gene and Janet for only a week before she'd found a suitable place, and she had not gone to visit them since. She wished Gene well, but because he would never quite fit into the role of dad, and he probably knew that, it didn't seem crucial to keep close contact. And then there was Steve. He never called, never visited any of his siblings. He had sent her an e-mail saying he had hopes of a full-time position but had not specified what it was or with whom, and a recent phone call on her part had been short because he had been on his way to a computer-programming job. She didn't know if he and Gene talked to each other. With this load of family, Alan, and her own thoughts and feelings on her mind, she said a prayer for all of them and for herself and then fell asleep.

Chapter 27

Spring promised to come early to Minnesota. Ice on the lakes was breaking up, crocuses were blooming, and the air had a balmy feel to it. It was only the fifth of April, but the general mood was one of delight that winter seemed to have retreated north to Canada. Easter was five days away when Debra, a coworker of Leah's at the agency, invited her to spend Easter "up north." Debra and her fiancé were outdoor types and drove to Debra's family's cabin whenever they had a free weekend. It was swimming and fishing in the summer and cross-country skiing and ice fishing in the winter. Leah had never spent any time at a lake and wasn't sure about making the trip, but she finally agreed to go. Debra and Randy were planning to leave at seven in the morning on Thursday and offered to take Leah with them, but she had to decline because of an appointment at eight thirty. Debra had hinted that a friend of Randy's might join them. Leah wasn't sure she wanted to be part of any matchmaking, but if she had her car, she could always leave early. So it was arranged that she would come up Thursday after her meeting, arriving there in plenty of time for dinner.

Tuesday evening Leah tried to decide what she should take with her. They were to attend church on Sunday, so she'd need one nice outfit, but had been assured that the rest of the time would be supercasual. Debra had also told her to include warm clothes, since temperatures up north often dropped dramatically at night. There were no guarantees they would have four full days of sunshine such as they had been enjoying in the Cities. Additionally, there was undoubtedly still some snow on the ground, so Debra urged her to pack boots for hiking. The phone rang just as Leah pulled a suitcase from the back of her closet.

"Hello," she said upon answering it.

"Hi, Leah. It's Elise. I just had a call from Jack Desmond. He heard a rumor that your friend Alan is not doing very well. Apparently one of Jack and Alan's mutual friends stopped by to see how things were, and Alan was less than welcoming and was totally uninterested in what was going on back here in Chicago. That worried Jack, so he wanted me to call and remind you that if you haven't gone to see him, maybe now would be a good time to do so. I don't like to be the one to pass along suggestions about what someone else ought to do, but, well, Jack is an old friend, and I know he's concerned about Alan. So for what it's worth, if you go that direction, maybe you could stop by for a few minutes. I have no idea how close he lives, but I have the directions to his place and a phone number." Elise then proceeded to provide the directions and the phone number.

"I don't know if I can do what Jack wants, but I'll think about it. It just so happens that I'm driving north to spend Easter weekend with friends, and I suspect Alan's place might be on the way, based on the directions you just gave me. Of course I share any concern Jack has for Alan, so tell him I'll try."

The two friends talked a little more about what each of them had been doing since they'd last been together, and then they said good-bye, with the promise to keep in touch and to have a wonderful Easter.

Leah hadn't given much consideration to stopping to see Alan, even though it had crossed her mind. Jack Desmond's request, being made a second time, put the idea back in play. She got out a map of Minnesota and ran her finger up the highway she would be traveling on her way to spend the weekend with Debra and Randy. The lake and the side road where Alan lived were about ten miles off the main road, and from there it would be close to an hour more of travel to her destination.

Okay, I suppose I can do this. But is it a good idea? Leah pondered the pros and cons and finally decided it would be all right. She figured she didn't have to stay very long, especially if Alan wasn't eager for a guest. She wondered who had stopped by and been rebuffed. She continued putting clothing into the suitcase, leaving room for last-minute selections and toiletries. Thursday was only a day away, with still enough time to change her mind about stopping to see Alan.

The schedule Leah had for Wednesday kept her moving from one meeting to the next, and by six o'clock, when her last appointment ended, she was ready to go home and put up her feet. She stopped to pick up a pizza at Godfather's, as she didn't have anything planned for dinner and it was already too late to shop for groceries and cook something at home. Leah sat in front of the TV set, eating pizza and drinking Coke. She didn't eat in front of the TV very often, but her feet hurt since she had been in two meetings where she had been required to stand most of the time. By nine thirty she had checked everything she had packed, adding a sweatshirt in case of cold temperatures. Tomorrow morning she only needed to put in her toothbrush and toiletries. She programed her GPS for Alan's address and then crawled under the covers. Even though she felt physically drained, her mind wouldn't turn off. Was it a good idea to see Alan? Should she have called him to say she was coming? Maybe she should just drive on by. Quite frankly, she even had second thoughts about going north at all, ever since Debra had mentioned that Randy's friend might be there. It could be a long weekend, especially if she and the friend didn't hit it off or, worse yet, if he turned out to be another Nick Jankowski!

The alarm clock jangled annoyingly at six thirty the next morning, and Leah jumped out of bed, surprised she had slept so long. She usually woke on her own by five thirty or six but always set the alarm for six thirty just in case. After a quick shower and a hurried breakfast she was on her way to the Interfaith Mission offices for her eight-thirty appointment. She arrived a little after eight and cleaned up odds and ends that had been left for that when-I-get-around-to-it time. At eight forty-five she checked her appointment calendar and asked the receptionist if there had been a cancellation. The answer was in the negative, so Leah called the client with whom she was to meet. A sleepy voice answered and said that the client had left town and that, quite frankly, he didn't care if she ever came back. Then the connection was broken. *Well,* thought Leah, *I guess I may as well leave early. Obviously I won't be seeing Shelby. I hope she's okay.*

Traffic was light, and Leah enjoyed being out on the open road. Trees weren't budding yet, but forsythias brightened up several front yards, and a few willows along a stream promised the arrival of spring. A weak sun was trying to break through the cloud cover but not having much success. About an hour into her journey, Leah observed the sky behind her darkening. Thick clouds were drifting in from the west and south, but the northern sky ahead of her was somewhat brighter. Leah checked her gas gauge and discovered she would soon need to refuel, so she pulled into a gas station with a convenience store attached. After filling her car, she went inside for a cup of coffee and to use the restroom. She overheard someone, probably a local, asking if there was snow coming. The reply was "I doubt it. It's too warm. Might get a spit of rain though." Leah hoped that was accurate information, but even rain would not be all that welcome. She slid back into the car and turned on the radio to try to find weather news to confirm or deny the local forecast she had heard. A music station playing golden oldies, as her mother had called them, kept her humming along to some songs and actually singing along with others. She remembered her mother's love of music, especially music from her childhood and young adult years.

The GPS warned Leah that in two miles she needed to make a right turn on County Road K, so she kept a watchful eye open. In exactly two miles, there was the sign for the road she was to take. She slowed and carefully executed the turn. She was committed now to visiting Alan. A signboard at an intersection with a gravel road listed the names of eight people who apparently lived in that direction. She saw Parkin listed and cautiously continued. The road was narrow, with trees on either side, and occasionally she caught a glimpse of water and ice off to the right. She began counting the houses, and when house number six appeared, she became a little anxious. There would be only two more houses before reaching number eight and undoubtedly the end of the road, since the sign had said it was a dead end. House number seven had a small hand-painted sign with the house number and *Parkin* in capital letters. A short lane led to a log house, with the lake in the background. She'd found it!

The structure looked to be fairly new, as the wood was still light-colored and had not weathered, although it was possible it had been treated to retain its natural look. There was a second story with a steeply sloping roofline, and off to the side was a large garage with a vehicle parked inside. It was difficult to see if the garage had a door, but there was obviously room for another car or even more than one. She pulled up in front of the house, checked her hair in the mirror, and then got out of the car. She sighed. She sincerely hoped she was ready to see Alan.

There was no bell, so Leah knocked on the door, which was very substantial looking, with no window or screen door. She was just ready to knock once again when the door opened. Alan stood there, looking like the Alan she remembered, except he was now sporting a short, well-trimmed beard that suited him. He wore a plaid flannel shirt, open at the neck, with a T-shirt showing underneath. She avoided looking at his feet but did observe he had on khaki cargo pants. She smiled. He looked to be in shock. "Leah!" he said.

"Hello, Alan. I was just in the neighborhood, so I thought I'd drop in for a visit. I hope that's all right." She smiled again, hoping her rather-tepid attempt at humor would be obvious.

Alan smiled in return. "Come in. I must say you're probably the last person I expected to see when I opened the door. How did you find me? Not too many people know where I live." Alan closed the door behind her and led the way into what appeared to be the living room, although, as Jack had said, there were no dividing walls. The area was spacious, and beyond a sofa, a coffee table, and two chairs, Leah could see kitchen cupboards, a stove, and a refrigerator, as well as a small round table with three chairs. When she stopped in front of the sofa, she looked to the left and saw a bedroom, with a king-size bed, but again there was only the hint of a wall. There was a dresser and, along one side, what was undoubtedly a built-in bookcase.

"I like your home, Alan. I'm curious about the ladder over there. Does that lead to the second story I saw from the outside? Jack Desmond told me you had done a lot of work on this place yourself, and he's the one who told me where to find you. In fact, he encouraged me to drop by. So here I am."

"Jack would do that. I'm sure he told you all sorts of tales about how I've become a hermit and won't come back to the firm or even to Chicago. Well, I like it here, and I like the privacy and the fact that I don't have to see or talk to anyone if I don't want to. Most of the time I don't. But I'm glad you came, Leah. Let me take your coat. To answer your question, the ladder is temporary, and it does lead to a rather large loft area with a bed, and that's about it. I was just going to have some lunch, so why don't you join me? I make a mean pot of chili."

"Chili would be nice, but I don't want to impose. I guess I should speak my piece and say what Jack wanted me to say. I'm supposed to convince you to come back to work at the firm. I don't know why you left, so I'm not speaking for myself, but I thought you should know why I stopped by."

"I see. Well, the invitation to lunch is extended. Will you stay? I suppose you're curious about what I've been doing, especially why I've hidden away up here in the frigid northland.

Jack may have his opinions, but he doesn't know me. I think you might know me better than anybody in my life right now, and even you … especially you … would be surprised. I may tell you my story, and I may not. But let's eat. I've been working all morning, and I'm hungry. Please sit, and I'll dish up the chili."

Leah sat and watched as Alan deftly ladled chili into two large bowls, filled a plate with crackers, brought out bread and cheese and butter, and then placed everything on the table. She avoided looking at his feet or his legs, just as she had done since he'd appeared at the door. He didn't seem to limp, and as far as she could see, he was moving about quite normally.

"Dig in, Leah. I made the bread myself. I've become quite self-sufficient since I've been up here."

"How long have you been here?" Leah asked, before taking a spoonful of the chili.

"I came up permanently about two months ago, but I bought the land more than a year ago and had this log house erected last summer. It's a kit, but everything comes with it, including the cupboards. I had to buy the appliances and the furniture of course. You might have noticed the king-size bed. I suppose you remember that I had one in Evanston that I bought and paid for myself. I thought I could get along with a regular bed, but I couldn't help remembering that big bed in Evanston. So I bought this one and had them move the regular-sized one up to the loft. I obviously can't go up and down the ladder very well, especially trying to haul anything with me. I'm sure Jack told you about my accident, or maybe you read about it in the paper. I'm mad as hell about it, Leah. It somehow seems so very unfair. I'd just been through hell of another kind, and then this." Alan gestured toward his left leg.

"Alan, I'm so very sorry. I can't begin to imagine what it must be like … what it was like when it happened." Leah wanted to say more but decided to save her thoughts for later, if it seemed appropriate, rather than to say what was on her mind and heart right now.

"Oh, everybody's sorry, but sorry won't bring back my leg or my life as I knew it. I get along pretty well; at least that's what everybody says and thinks. But do you know that just going to the bathroom in the middle of the night is a pain in the butt? I've got to strap this damn device on just to be able to take a pee. Sorry for my not-so-nice choice of words. It's like having a piece of machinery that you have to take with you everywhere. I tried hopping into the bathroom one night, but I fell down, and that hurt like hell. The foot and ankle that I lost still hurt. I mean that literally. I feel pain where they used to be, and it's real. The doc calls it phantom pain, but it's real—very real." Alan stopped his angry tirade and looking above Leah's head, he said, "Sorry. You came as a friend, and I'm not behaving as one. I'm being a little shit who can't take what's thrown at him … just bitch, bitch, bitch."

What should she say? How to say it was an even more difficult choice. Finally she said, "Alan, is there anything, anything at all, that I can say or do that would help you bear the pain of all this? You've had so many losses in your life. Now you've lost part of your leg. I'm not sure what to say, but I'd give anything if I could make your pain go away. I'd even take on some of it myself if I could."

Alan had laid his head on his arms while Leah had been speaking. When she finished, he raised up, a look of surprise on his face. "You don't mean that, do you? That you would be willing to share my pain if you could? Nobody has ever said anything remotely like that. I get so tired of people telling me how sorry they are. Most of the time I doubt they really feel sorry deep down. I remember when Greg Canady came up here. He said I should be grateful I had a lot of money to ease my pain. My God, Leah, can you imagine thinking that money could ease anyone's pain? I'd give up every penny I have if I could only …" Alan paused. "No, I won't say any more, because it would sound self-serving, and anyway, it's not possible to change what is. Somehow I've got to learn to live with what is, not what could have been. Do you know what I mean?"

"I think so. I've got a few ifs in my life too. I should tell you about the outcome of my quest to discover who Lizzie was, or is, but it might be a better idea for me to be on my way. I have an hour or perhaps a bit less to drive, and I see it's snowing. My little VW isn't equipped to handle a lot of snow. I'd like to come again. Maybe I could stop by on my way back home, and we could catch up." Leah hoped she wasn't pushing things. Alan might not care to be reminded of life as it had been. As he'd said, he needed to learn to deal with the here and now. Just then her cell phone rang.

"Oh, sorry, I'd better answer that. It could be Debra wondering if I'm getting close to their cabin. I didn't realize how long we've been talking." She picked up and said, "Hello. Oh, hi, Debra, what's up?" She was silent for a few moments. "You're kidding? Really?" More silence. "So do you think the snow will stop and you'll be able to get up to your cabin?" Silence again. "I see. So I'd better turn around and head back." A long silence. "I get the picture. Well, I'll ask Alan about a motel nearby where I can stay until the storm is over. You really think I can't get back to Minneapolis?"

Debra evidently had more to say, and Leah listened and then said, "Okay, see you Monday," and ended the call. Turning her attention back to Alan, she said, "Well, guess what. Minneapolis is in the midst of a huge blizzard, and they have already closed Interstate 90 on the south and west sides of the city and have encouraged everyone in the area to stay put. It's some sort of freak storm that started in Kansas as rain but hit a cold front. Now it's turned to snow, and there's wind with it, so it's drifting. Lots of roads have become impassable after only a couple of hours of snowfall. Debra said she and her husband didn't get started as early as they'd planned. By the time they loaded the car, the snow was coming down pretty hard, and they have been advised not to travel north at all. We aren't getting anything substantial here, are we?"

Alan had gotten up from the table and was peering out the window. "Looks like it's coming our way. There's maybe four inches on the ground already. Let me call Frank and see about the forecast. He's my neighbor down the road in number eight. We're the only two houses occupied for the winter, so we look after each other. Frank and Mary are in their eighties but love it up here and don't go south for the winter like many do."

Alan was on the phone for only a few minutes before informing Leah that there was a gale blowing out there and that as much as ten inches of snow was predicted.

"Oh, that doesn't sound good. Where can I find the nearest motel and get settled in? It sounds like I'll probably be there for a couple of days. I suppose there are a number of places around here since it's a tourist area, right?"

"Wrong," said Alan. "This particular lake is populated almost strictly with private homes. There is one resort on the other side of the lake, but they close in October and don't come back from Florida until the end of April. The nearest motel that's decent is a good thirty miles from here. It would be unwise to travel with the wind blowing like Frank says it is. He's quite the weather maven and keeps me posted on incoming storms. I guess because they had drop-in guests this morning he forgot to call as he usually does. I think you'll have to stay right here with me. You can have the loft. It's pretty nice up there, even though there's no furniture except the bed and a small table with a lamp. It will be warmer up there than down here. I try to bank the fire in the fireplace so that it stays burning overnight, and sometimes I throw on additional logs toward morning. I've also got the pellet stove, but I'm running low on the pellets, so I'll have to be judicious in how much I use it. This house is pretty airtight, but when the wind blows, it can get chilly."

"Are you sure it's all right if I stay? What I mean is, won't it be an imposition?"

"No, and you don't need to worry. You won't be in any danger, if that's your concern." Alan didn't meet Leah's gaze as he said this. Then he added, "Sorry, that didn't come out the way I intended. I just meant … Oh, I think you know what I meant. I do want you to stay, and I think you'll like the loft. Now, how about moving into the living room where we can be more comfortable, and you can tell me about your adventure when you went to meet your other family? I'd like to hear all about it."

Leah recounted for Alan her one-day trip after Thanksgiving to Saint Paul and her meeting with her birth parents and three out of four of her siblings. She told him that she had visited them several times in the months after that first visit and that when her birth mother had become ill, she had been the one to care for her.

"That's quite a story. I'm surprised your return to the family wasn't all over the news. It seems like the Minneapolis papers would have wanted to tell the story of your abduction and then the reunion. Or was it out there, and I missed it? I confess I haven't always kept up with the news of the day, but I think I would have noticed a story like the one you just told me." Alan had been listening intently, and Leah could tell he was surprised that she still had a relationship with the McGregors, especially since she had said that the Anderlys were her parents as far as she was concerned and that she had not been able to feel any great kinship with her birth parents, especially her birth mother.

"It was in the papers, right around Christmas, but my name was never revealed, thanks to Gene, my dad, who knew how I felt about having my life splashed all over the news. I don't know how he did it, but he managed to control how much they reported about me personally, and it was never printed in the Chicago papers as far as I know. I'm grateful for that."

"That period of time, just before and after Christmas was a very bad time in my life. I had the accident on the second of January and moved up here as soon as I was released from the doctor's care. Actually, I released myself before they really wanted me to go. It was one of the worst times of my life, and I don't think I looked at a newspaper or turned on the TV or the radio for several weeks. Too much stuff hitting me with too many memories and too many regrets. I thought about jumping in the lake and ending it all." Alan chuckled as he said this. "But of course it was frozen solid. That's kind of the story of my life right now. I'm never at the right place at the right time. Sorry, sorry. No more of that, Alan," he said, obviously chastising himself.

"If it's not too hard to tell it, I'd like to hear your story about Juneau and your son, unless you'd rather not," Leah said.

"Let's wait until tomorrow for that little tale of woe. At least some of it is a tale of woe. We're going to have all day and maybe the next day as well to talk, so we should save a little of the drama for then. Let's get your things out of the car and drive it into the garage. There's no door, but I've got a tarp that pulls down and keeps the worst of the snow out. If your car sits outside, it's likely to be totally covered by morning."

Leah brought in her suitcase, and Alan told her to climb the ladder and then he would hand her suitcase up to her. Climbing the ladder with a load of anything was not a good idea, he said. She discovered the loft to be a cozy room with a lot of charm. Alan also handed up linens and blankets and an old quilt. She made up the bed and then put her suitcase on a folding chair that had been leaning against one wall.

A large window looked out to what Leah thought might be the southeast. Snow was hitting and sticking against the window. It was a wet snow, laden with moisture. Her father, who had grown up on a farm, used to say when such a snow fell, "The farmers will love this. It's great for the summer corn or beans crop."

"Are you going to stay up there all day?" Alan called up the ladder.

"I'm coming. But I want to change into something warmer. I didn't know when I left this morning with the temperature at a balmy fifty degrees that it would get this cold. I'll be down in a minute." As soon as Leah had changed, she carefully made her way down the ladder and discovered Alan standing right there. "I think I've got the hang of this ladder. And I love the loft. It's warm and cozy up there and spacious too."

"Glad you like it. My dad and I rented a place like this a few times, and I always slept in the loft area. It wasn't as spacious as this cabin, but I was in heaven looking out the window and watching moonbeams play on the lake. Those summer trips up here were wonderful. Dad was a busy man during the year, but on vacation he was with me every moment, and I loved it. He was a lawyer too, although his firm in Indianapolis was a lot smaller than Marsden, Willett, and Desmond. He built it up from the ground himself and was quite successful, although family money helped him get started. I guess I didn't get a chance to share much with you about my father."

"No, I guess not. I knew you had a good relationship with him. That must be a satisfying memory," Leah said.

"Yes, it is, after I stopped being mad at him for dying. I was just a kid, and Uncle Horace was actually understanding about that and helped me get rid of some of the anger. I wish he … Uncle Horace, that is … could have … Oh, never mind. I won't go into that. Maybe tomorrow."

Leah once again saw the pain in Alan's eyes and wondered how that might relate to Uncle Horace. She would not ask, even tomorrow, unless Alan decided to talk about it. Then she would let him tell it and not probe.

"Well, Miss Anderly, we ought to think about what we want to make for our dinner. Maybe we can make it a joint effort, if you're game. How about fish? Do you like fish?" asked Alan.

Once again he had shifted abruptly from one mood to another, from pain or regret of something in the past to the here and now. Leah wondered how much effort that cost him. She vowed to try to keep the conversation from drifting into any painful areas, but perhaps there was a minefield of stuff out there about which she had no idea.

"Sure, I like fish," she said. "What kind do you have? I hope we don't have to go out and catch our supper."

"I have walleye in the freezer, and if you've never had that before, you're in for a treat. I'll fix the fish if you can put together something to serve with it. Go crazy with what's in the cupboard and the refrigerator. There's ice cream and cookies for dessert." Alan had already gotten up from the sofa and was headed into the kitchen, just a few steps away. Leah followed and began checking the boxes and cans in Alan's cupboards, choosing some dehydrated hash brown potatoes and a can of green beans to go with the fish. The meal preparation provided additional conversation and some laughter. When Alan opened a can of beer, Leah was surprised. She knew he didn't drink and had assumed that would still be true. She was even more surprised when he mixed the beer with flour, a little cornmeal, and melted butter to make a batter into which he dipped the fish before frying it. She pronounced it the best fish she had ever tasted, and they ate every morsel. They agreed that their joint-effort meal was outstanding. The ice cream and cookies were left for later.

"How about a movie?" Alan asked. "I think the snow will have made my satellite reception impossible, but I have a lot of DVDs, some I haven't even had a chance to look at. I always buy up a bunch when I go shopping at Walmart. I suppose you think I shouldn't patronize them, but hey, they're all we've got unless I drive more than an hour to get to a city with other options. Here's one I'd like to see. Frank told me he and his wife saw it years ago. It's in black and white. I kind of like those old ones. What do you think?" Alan looked to Leah to see if she was interested in his suggestion.

"Whatever you want. I'm not much of a movie expert, and growing up we almost never went to the movies. Recently I've seen a few movies on late-night TV, but I'm usually so tired I fall asleep before they're over. You pick one, and I'm sure I'll enjoy it." Leah momentarily remembered the night she and Nick had seen an old black-and-white movie in Chicago and what had happened afterward.

Alan fiddled with the TV remote and then with another remote for the VCR. The beginning credits played, and then the title of the movie appeared: *The Grapes of Wrath.* Leah said she had read it a long time ago, but had not seen the film. Alan brought quilts for them to cover with, and each sat in a corner of the sofa, the quilts pulled up over their laps and later over their shoulders. The house was cooling off. Alan stopped the film once to make popcorn and to put on more logs to keep the temperature more comfortable in the cabin. Finally, at the end of the film, Leah suggested they call it a night. It was past eleven. The wind was howling outside, and the snow was still coming down. Inside, however, it was now toasty warm.

"You can use the bathroom first. I'll go in the bedroom and won't peek. As you can see, there's no door to the bathroom, but you can draw the curtain I've hooked up. It isn't a perfect fit; it leaves big gaps on each side and is too short by far, but it should do the trick. If you want a shower, there are large towels in the cabinet beside the sink. I'll probably get into what I usually sleep in, so don't be surprised when you come out and see me in my cutoff sweats and an old T-shirt. Off you go."

The whole business of sharing a bathroom without a door turned out to be no big deal. When she came out, Alan was sitting on the sofa, trying to get a picture on the television without much success. A message on the screen said that the signal had been lost. "I just thought I'd try once more to get a little news about the storm. Maybe tomorrow. Good night, Leah. I hope you won't have trouble climbing the ladder in that long nightgown." Alan grinned. He was teasing her. For the first time since she'd arrived, she saw the laughing eyes of the old Alan, and it made her smile. Maybe her visit was a good thing. Maybe she had made him forget, at least for a few hours, his anger and sense of loss.

"I'll be fine on the ladder, so don't worry. Good night, Alan. See you in the morning." Leah hitched up her nightgown and climbed easily up the ladder and disappeared from Alan's view. In bed she snuggled down with the covers pulled up close.

The house turned quiet, save for the sound of the wind rattling tree branches outside. Leah was going over the day in her mind. It seemed an eternity since she'd left the Twin Cities. She thought about the enjoyment of preparing the evening meal together. It was a good memory for her to hold close, and she fell asleep clinging to it.

Leah couldn't see the clock, but she thought it must be after two in the morning when a crash outside her window woke her. She was startled and jumped out of bed, almost hitting her head on the sloping ceiling. She made her way to the window. It was still plastered with snow, but there were several spots that were not covered where she could peer out. She saw nothing except swirling white flakes.

From below she heard Alan call, "Leah, are you all right? I heard a noise like something might have hit the house." Leah could hear him moving around down below.

"I'm fine, and I can't see anything out of this window up here except snow and blowing snow. Could it be a tree that fell or a branch? I think something hit the house, but I'm not sure what or where. Shall I come down, and we can investigate?" she asked.

"Maybe it would be good if you came down. You might be able to help me determine what happened. I should go outside to see if we sustained any damage. Can you find your way? The lights seem to have gone out. It could be the electric line has been compromised. Let me light a candle before you try to come down the ladder."

Leah didn't pay heed to what Alan had said and began to feel her way to the ladder. She put one foot tentatively on the second rung from the top and began to descend. She missed the next step and fell to the floor. Her cry of pain brought Alan rushing back into the living room. He had been in the kitchen to get candles and matches and was just returning, carrying one lit candle and a handful of others.

"Are you hurt?" Alan asked. "Oh God, why did you try to come down before I came with the light? Let's have a look. You've scraped your leg it seems. Where does it hurt, and can you move everything? Let me help you."

"I think I'm all right. Let me see if I can get up. I think I feel a little blood on my leg, but that's probably all it is. I'm okay! I'm okay! I think I can get up. My ankle hurts, but I don't think it's broken. It was stupid of me to try coming down the ladder before you brought the light. I'm sorry."

Alan was down on one knee by this time. "Lean on my shoulder, and we can get up at the same time. If you can't stand, grab on to me. I don't want you to fall again."

Slowly they managed to rise to their feet, and while Leah grimaced from the pain in her ankle, she was sure there were no broken bones and no serious injury, other than a slight sprain. Alan helped her to the sofa, and she sat down. He took a seat next to her and pulled her foot into his lap. He ran his fingers over every part of it, asking where the pain was and if he was being gentle enough.

"I'll be okay, but if you have some gauze and tape, I probably should wrap up this scrape." There was a long scratch down the side of her leg. It had drawn blood but did not seem to be bleeding profusely.

"I have a first aid kit. Be right back," Alan said, and in less than fifteen seconds he returned, the already-opened kit in his hand. He pulled off a length of gauze and cut it with the scissors. Then he applied some sort of ointment to the scrape, covered it with the gauze, and taped it around her leg. "Tomorrow we'll check that ankle again, and if necessary, we'll tape it up. There's an old ankle wrap here somewhere that should give you support if you need it. Now sit tight while I check outside to see what happened. I'll be right back, so don't go away," he said with a grin.

Alan was gone for five or six minutes, and when he returned, he reported that a large limb had fallen against the side of the house right near the loft area where Leah had been sleeping. It didn't seem to have caused any damage, but daylight might reveal more. "You know, if it had come just three feet over to the left, it could have crashed right through the window in your bedroom. Thank God it didn't. I wondered about that tree last fall, and I guess I should have followed my instincts and had it cut down. All right, we're okay, so we'd better try to get some sleep. I think the wind might be dying down. I hope so. You climb in my bed, and I'll sleep on the couch tonight. Maybe by tomorrow night you'll be fit enough to climb the ladder, but not tonight. You're going to keep your feet on the ground floor. Come on, climb in."

"I can't take your bed. The couch is too short for you. Let me sleep there, and you take the bed. Please. I insist. I'm fine, really,"

"Don't argue with the doctor. Come on." Alan pulled Leah up from the couch and led her over to the king-size bed, where she dutifully slid under the covers. He tucked the blanket around her shoulders and then leaned down and kissed her forehead. "Good night; sweet dreams."

"Oh Alan, why don't you put a couple of sofa cushions down the middle of this big bed and climb in on the other side? You shouldn't have to spend the night on the couch because I was foolish enough to fall down the ladder. I know this is sort of a repetition of what happened the night I stayed with you in your uncle Horace's house, but I know nothing will happen this time. Please. Just get those cushions. We can talk for a little while longer until we get sleepy. I'm not a bit sleepy yet. Please, Alan."

Alan said nothing. He just stood there beside the bed looking at Leah. "Oh my lovely Leah, you don't know what you're asking. The last time I had no intention of ... well, that was then, and this is now. I promise you that you will be safe here, and I'll keep that promise." Alan took three cushions from the sofa and placed them under the covers down the middle of the bed. Then he blew out the candle, sat down on the side of the bed, and unfastened his prosthesis. "You know what I'm doing, don't you?" he said. "Maybe even if I had the idea to come over on your side of the bed, this would be a big turnoff for you. Good night, Leah. Until morning then."

Leah didn't say anything for a few minutes, but then she reached across the pillows and put her hand on Alan's shoulder.

"Alan, your bad leg doesn't bother me at all. If we, which we're not, but if …" She hesitated. "Don't assume, okay? Good night now." Leah took back her hand and pulled the covers up around her neck and tried to let her mind find rest, which was not easy to do. An hour later, when she heard Alan's rhythmic breathing, she too fell asleep.

It was still snowing Friday morning but not as heavily, and the wind seemed to have died down. The electricity had come back on, and Alan was already in the kitchen when Leah awakened to the smell of coffee. "Do you have a bathrobe I can borrow?" she asked him. "I'm going to see if I can climb the ladder this morning so I can get properly dressed."

Alan appeared at the bedside, a slight smile on his face. "So you want a bathrobe. Sorry, I don't own one, as I have no need of one up here, living the bachelor's life. Before you do any climbing, I want to see if your ankle is all right. Slide your legs out of bed carefully and then stand up. You might be a little stiff this morning from your fall, so go slowly." Alan watched as Leah stepped gingerly onto the floor.

"Ooh, the floor is cold, but I think I'm okay. There's no real pain, only a little twinge in my shoulder. I can climb up into the loft, so you go on back to the kitchen. I'll join you in a minute."

"I'm staying right here until you're safely up and down the ladder. I'll close my eyes, if that's what you're worried about."

"Okay, okay." Leah took a cautious step onto the first rung of the ladder and made it easily to the top. She looked down and saw that Alan had his eyes closed. She smiled and then disappeared into the far corner of the loft. "You can open your eyes now. I'm safely up, and I know I can come down again too."

She heard Alan say something unintelligible. Leah dressed quickly, selecting some extra layers of warm clothing to take down with her, in case they went out in the snow. She hoped it would stop snowing so she could experience the landscape and the lake, now covered with piles of the still-falling flakes.

When Leah began her climb back down, she was very careful to make sure each foot was securely planted on the ladder rungs. On the last rung, she discovered that Alan was standing right there, ready to catch her if she missed a step. She said, "See, I told you I could do it, but thanks for playing fireman, just in case."

Breakfast was scrambled eggs with deer sausage and toast with the best jam Leah had ever tasted. Alan said that Frank had made it—no, not his wife ... but Frank. It was gooseberry jam, and Frank had picked, stemmed, and cooked the gooseberries from bushes that grew wild in the area. Alan vowed to learn how to make jam next summer. In July there were raspberries and blueberries for the taking and all growing wild nearby. He also informed Leah that the power outage had not been a downed wire from the falling limb. It was probably coincidental that the lights had gone out at the same time the tree branch had hit the house. When he had gotten up at four, the lights had been back on, and he had gone around turning all of them off. Leah had not heard him rise or been aware of the lights being extinguished.

After breakfast Alan announced that they might take a run along the lake on the snowmobile, provided the temperatures warmed a little when the sun rose higher. While they had been eating, the snow had stopped falling, and the clouds had parted sufficiently to allow rays of morning sun to come through the east windows.

"I've never been on a snowmobile, so I think it might be fun. I'm not sure I have appropriate clothing, but I'm up for the adventure."

Alan's phone rang. "Probably Frank, checking to see how we made it through the night." He picked up. "Hello ... Oh, we're fine. I suppose your lights went out last night too. My house guest had a little mishap in the blackout when she fell climbing down the ladder from the loft. No serious injury ... You would say that! ... Tonight? Well, I guess the snow has stopped, so why not? We can come over on the snowmobile, or if I get out with the plow, we can walk over on the road. What time? Can I bring anything? … Okay, Frank, we'll see you at five o'clock." Alan hung up the phone and saw Leah watching him. "I suppose you wonder what that was all about. Frank loves to tease me. I won't tell you what he said. We're invited for a little chitchat before we eat, so we're to come at five. We'll probably be back here before nine because they don't stay up late. I hope it was all right to say yes to the invitation."

Leah nodded.

"They love to have people come over. I'm sure you'll be in for a lot of scrutiny, so be prepared. Frank has been trying to get me interested in several young women in the area, but I've not been cooperative. He probably thinks I'm weakening and that you might be a new love interest, so be prepared for a little good-natured kidding and maybe some questions. Are you still okay with going?"

"Of course. I can take a little ribbing, and Frank sounds delightful. I won't promise to give him the whole truth and nothing but the truth about myself, but it might be fun if he has a sense of humor."

A snowmobile ride down the lane and along the lakeshore was bone chilling for Leah, and she regretted not purchasing long johns. But who knew the weather would turn so cold and there would be so much snow? It was past noon when they returned to the cabin. They had more of the chili that Alan had made, and after the kitchen was cleaned up, Leah said she really needed a nap, blaming the storm that had awakened her during the night and then her difficulty in falling asleep afterward.

"Were you anxious that I might toss those pillows last night and invade your space?" Alan was teasing her again, and she was glad to see it. When she had arrived yesterday, it had been hard to equate the Alan she'd seen with the one she had known when they'd both worked at the law firm. But last night and now today, she saw the old Alan emerge, at least occasionally.

"No, I trusted you. We'd better not get started on the subject of our sleeping arrangements of last evening, and you'd better not tell Frank either," Leah said, grinning herself.

Leah napped, and then they stayed inside until it was time to head over for dinner. Frank and Mary were gracious and welcoming to Leah. During dinner Frank asked Leah how she knew Alan.

"I met Alan at work. I used to be a paralegal in the same firm where he was a lawyer. The team I was part of worked on cases with him. We're both Northwestern University graduates, so that was something for us to bond over."

"Oh, I was hoping you were his long-lost girlfriend, come up here to drag him back to civilization. Our Alan has become something of a hermit. If you have any influence with him, you ought to convince him to go back to that law firm. We're not trying to get rid of him, but I'm just saying he's got too much up here," Frank said, pointing to his head, "to waste it in the woods."

"Don't start, old man," Alan said. "I like it here. It's peaceful, except when you start on one of your rants. I'm afraid you might be stuck with me for a while longer."

When coffee and dessert were served, the conversation returned once more to Leah. "What do you do now? Are you still living in Chicago?" Mary asked.

"No, I live in a suburb of Saint Paul, and I'm a social worker. I work with young and sometimes not-so-young women who are up against it or have children and no husband. I like my work, but I get discouraged because there's so much pain out there. Hopefully my agency is able to help alleviate a little of it through what we do with these women."

Then Frank asked, "Do you have family in Saint Paul? Is that what brought you up there?"

"Yes, I guess you could say I have family there, but it's complicated. What about you two? Do you have family nearby?" Leah was trying to turn the conversation from who she was and who her relatives were. It would be too difficult to tell that story, and she didn't wish to at any rate.

"Oh, it's just the two of us. Got a son in DC and a daughter in Dallas. We don't see much of them. They're too busy. One grandson is at the University of Minnesota, but he doesn't get up here much. Thank goodness for e-mail and the telephone." Mary smiled at Leah and said, "I hope when you get married your children stay close by. It's hard to be so far away and not see them but once a year."

"Why don't you visit them?" asked Leah.

"Too old, and besides, we have to stay around here to look after things, including this fellow." Frank patted Alan on the shoulder.

"Okay, I think it's time we said our good-byes," Alan said. "Leah and I have a few stories to tell each other before she goes back to civilization, so if you'll excuse us, we'll be going. Thanks for the good food and the conversation."

"Hey, you can't go yet. We have to play Hand and Foot," Frank said.

"Stop with the Hand and Foot. We'll play some other time. Come on, Leah, let's jump on that snowmobile and head home."

Leah expressed her thanks for the evening, and after extended good-byes she and Alan agreed to come by tomorrow and also on Sunday morning for Easter Brunch. Mary reminded Alan that he was to bring his famous cream puffs, and he assured her he would.

Temperatures had dropped since their arrival, and by the time they made it back to Alan's house, Leah was chilled through and through. "I didn't bring enough cold weather clothing," she said as they parked the snowmobile in the garage and hurried into the house.

To help them warm up, Alan made coffee, even though they had already consumed several cups at Frank and Mary's house. Then he said, "I've decided that tonight I'll tell you the Juneau-and-Colin saga. It's not something I like talking about, and I wasn't going to do this, but I think I have to. You need to know all of it, not just the bits and pieces. Let's grab our cups and get comfy on the couch, shall we?"

Leah picked up her coffee cup and also the quilt she had used previously. For some reason she was feeling cold all the time. This was not normal for her, so she hoped she wasn't coming down with something. They both settled in. She offered to share the quilt with Alan, but he waved it off. Then he began speaking about his marriage and the birth of his son.

"You already know that Juneau and I were in bed together the morning after Thanksgiving and that soon after that she tested positive for a pregnancy. I suspected something fishy, but since I was out cold when it supposedly happened, I couldn't prove my suspicions. We were married the eighteenth of January, although Uncle Horace had wanted us to tie the knot at Christmas or even before. You know I had a ruptured appendix and was in the hospital for more than a week and then was at home recuperating for another ten days, so having the wedding at once wasn't possible. Then Uncle suggested New Year's Eve as a good time for the wedding. I refused, adamantly. I think you know why, Leah. I stood my ground, and so the eighteenth was chosen. I suggested we have a quiet wedding, but both Uncle and Juneau wouldn't hear of it."

Alan paused in his narrative to sip his coffee. He laid his head back on the sofa for a moment and then continued, "We had a very short honeymoon in Cancun, and Uncle Horace came with us. Can you imagine that? I think he was afraid I would bolt, and believe me, I thought about it. It was probably the most unusual honeymoon in the history of marriages. We arrived on a Sunday night. Juneau and I had the so-called bridal suite, and Uncle was in an adjoining suite, with a short hallway between the two. It didn't take long for Juneau and I to have an argument, and there was Uncle, coming into the room to try to settle the dispute. I don't remember what it was about. I was still on meds, and now that I think back, I suspect Uncle was the one who saw to it that I was given tranquilizers to keep me less than alert. I know I didn't feel normal, and I suppose I didn't act normal either. Juneau was all over me, but I was incapable of making love to her. Whether it was the meds or my feelings of dislike that accounted for it, I don't know. I discovered a day or so later that, after I fell asleep each night, Juneau went out to the bars in the resort and spent time with a series of men, or boys. I came back one afternoon from a walk on the beach, where I had gone to try to clear my head, to find Juneau in bed with a young lad who had delivered sandwiches and some sort of fruit salad. Juneau wasn't even apologetic. She told me to get used to it if I didn't pay more attention to her. We came home at the end of the week, and I tried to bury myself in work and managed to do that for a while. But I couldn't keep that up indefinitely."

Alan leaned back again and closed his eyes for a moment. "Things with Juneau went from bad to worse until one day I made her sit down and listen to me. It was the middle of March, and I had decided I was going to try to make our marriage work, for the sake of our child. By this time her belly was swollen, and she couldn't attract her usual stable of young men. So she agreed to stay at home at night, and for a few months things were better. Not good, but better. By the middle of April her stomach was so big I knew she wouldn't make it to the due date, which was supposedly the end of July. I should have figured things out before then, but I didn't. What did I know about pregnancies? What did I know about anything really? Well, the baby arrived on May 3, and while Juneau tried to convince me it was a premature birth, that didn't sell, because our son weighed eight pounds. He also had jet-black hair and beautiful olive skin. I knew at once I wasn't the father. I had been shanghaied! I ranted at Uncle Horace, who I knew had to have known that Juneau was pregnant long before Thanksgiving. He tried to tell me that he was sure we had been together well before then and that of course the baby was mine. He hadn't seen the child yet, and when he did, it became clear to him as well that I couldn't be the father."

Alan stopped again in his monologue and looked over at Leah, who had been taking it all in silently. Surprise and even shock were evident on her face.

"Quite a story, isn't it, how one fool got himself so screwed up? But the thing was, when we brought that little baby home, I looked at him and thought, *He's not to blame for this. He's so innocent.* And right then I decided I would be a father to him, the best father I could be. Juneau confessed she had no idea who the father was or his name or his nationality, just that he was a sexy guy. She was pretty sure they had only been together one night, and after that she had never seen him again. He may have been a student or just in town visiting. Who knows?"

Alan continued, "Juneau had no interest in caring for the baby, and we hired a twenty-four-hour live-in nurse. The nurse insisted on weekends off, so weekends I became the caregiver. I got up in the night with Colin, which is what we named him. I changed him, fed him, burped him, and took him out in his carriage and later in the stroller. We bonded, and it wasn't long before he knew me and got excited when I came into the room. Then one day in early fall, when he was six months old, Juneau told me she wanted out of our marriage. She had found someone else, and because of his religion we would need to get an annulment rather than a divorce. I agreed to pursue that avenue, and it was easier than I thought. With enough money and the right contacts willing to testify to almost anything, the annulment went through in record time. I assumed I would take Colin since Juneau and her new boyfriend spent no time with him and Juneau seldom participated in his care. What I didn't know was that she had been in contact with a Catholic agency and was planning to turn Colin over to them to be adopted. Juneau isn't Catholic, but she attended Catholic school through high school. Her parents thought the discipline would be good for her, and even after she came to live with Uncle Horace, he kept her there. By the time I was told about the adoption, it was too late. The annulment had stated that 'husband is not the father of the child,' so I had no claim to Colin and couldn't do a thing about Juneau's behind-the-back negotiations with the adoption people. She also managed to get a sizable chunk of money out of Uncle Horace to grease the skids to make sure the adoption went through without any difficulty."

"Oh Alan, I had no idea about any of this. I wondered why your uncle's obituary didn't list a great-nephew, and I suppose that's why. But did your uncle approve of the decisions Juneau made? Was he all right with going ahead with the annulment and the adoption?" Leah asked.

"Not at first, but I guess the more he thought about it, the more logical it seemed to him. Juneau and her baby were an embarrassment. In the end, he financed the purchase of a house in Florida for Juneau and the new husband-to-be, who, by the way, wanted nothing to do with Colin, so that put more pressure on Juneau. And Leah, I didn't even have a chance to hug Colin, kiss his chubby little cheeks, or say good-bye to him. The adoption people came to get him while I was on an overnight trip to Boston in late November. I tried to get him back, but I didn't have a legal leg to stand on. In the end Uncle Horace convinced me not to make a public fuss, which he said was bad for the family name! I'm sorry I let Uncle be such an influence in my life. Maybe if he had died a few months earlier, the adoption wouldn't have happened, and he wouldn't have been able to orchestrate some of the things he did. I might have had a chance to keep Colin. I just hope and pray he has a loving family. They told me he does. The couple had been unable to conceive, and they were over the moon when they saw Colin and knew he would be theirs. The agency of course wouldn't reveal their names, but for weeks I kept a watchful eye on every infant that looked to be around six months old. The day after Uncle Horace died I stopped working at the firm. My accident happened on the way up here, and you can probably imagine the rest. I was already a mess from the loss of Colin, and my work was suffering at the firm, although I usually managed to do what was necessary. I had a couple of people who covered for me a few times. I'm still trying to work my way through all this. So far I haven't done very well."

Alan stopped talking and stared straight ahead. Leah didn't know what she should say, so she let the silence soothe them both for a minute or two. Then she decided to say what had been forming in her mind since she'd come to see Alan. "I think you've had a life filled with loss and grief, Alan, and it's not easy to navigate something like that. My agency offers a class called "Loss and Grief," and all sorts of people come to it. Some get help, but not everyone is ready to let go of their losses. I know you lost your mother at an early age—not to death but to another man—and then she left you to move elsewhere. Your brothers too were a loss I'm sure, and then your father died when you were still young and needed him. Now this, losing a wife, a son, an uncle, and then part of your leg. It's more than anyone should have to bear in such a short span of years. I'm certainly not suggesting that you have to take our class, but if you could somehow allow someone to help you make your way through and out of the losses, it might be helpful. But what do I know? I'm so very sorry that you have these burdens laid on you." Leah reached across the expanse of the sofa and took Alan's hand and cradled it in both of hers. She didn't know what else to do, but she knew the human touch was one gesture that could convey shared sorrow and sadness more than a thousand words could ever do.

"Thanks," Alan said, pulling his hand away. "I know you're sorry for me, but you can't fix anything. It is what it is, and I have to deal with it whether I want to or not. I think I'd like to go to bed now. Do you mind if we call it a night? I presume you're able to climb the ladder if you're careful. I'll use the bathroom first and then crawl into bed and turn my head to the wall while you get ready."

Alan rose from the sofa and went into the bathroom. He didn't even bother to close the half curtain. She heard him brush his teeth and then urinate and flush. When he came out of the bathroom, he was wearing only his undershorts. He ignored her as though she were part of the furnishings and then laid down on the bed and drew the blankets up close.

Leah could see only the top of his head as he lay there, his face to the wall.

For Leah sleep was elusive. She kept replaying over and over the story Alan had told her. It seemed more the stuff of fiction than fact. Yet she knew it was true, although colored slightly by Alan's wounded psyche and by his disappointment in how his life had unraveled over time. She tried to think how she ought to have responded. Had she said enough? Or too much? What exactly should have been her response? It was hard for her to blame Alan. Still, he had not stood up to his uncle as he might have done. His current mood was troubling to her. Should she confess her still-strong feelings for him, or would that only complicate the situation? He obviously needed help, but she couldn't be the one to provide it. An hour later, still in a half-awake, half-asleep state, she offered a prayer for guidance and also for Alan's healing, physical and mental and perhaps even spiritual.

Chapter 28

After a restless night, morning came for Leah with no clear idea of what she ought to do. The house was quiet, and a quick glance at the clock told her it was only five thirty. It was still dark outside, although a faint fading of the night sky visible through the east window in her room promised daylight would be breaking soon. Leah could detect no stirring below, although she thought some sort of noise had roused her out of a light sleep a few minutes earlier. She lay quietly, once again mulling over Alan's story and her possible response today.

The quiet continued until about six thirty. Then she heard the front door open. Apparently Alan had gone out; that must have been the noise that had roused her from sleep. She heard him cross the floor to the kitchen and then the running of water. In a few minutes the smell of coffee wafted up, and she decided it was time to come down and face the day. She dressed hurriedly because it was chilly in the loft bedroom. Alan was removing plates and cups from the cupboard as she entered the kitchen.

"Good morning. You were out and about early this morning. What's the weather going to be like today? Or is it too early to tell?" Leah asked, trying to strike the right note after last night's story session.

"It should be fine because it's clear and cloudless, although right now it's cold. I think it will warm up as the day progresses. How about scrambled eggs and a little bacon?" Alan hadn't really made eye contact with her, but he now glanced in her direction.

"Eggs and bacon are fine. Can I help with something?"

"You can break the eggs if you like. You'll find eggs in the refrigerator, and there's a bowl on the counter. I usually make a three-egg omelet for myself, so add as many more as you like for yourself. I'll do the bacon." Alan pulled two frying pans out of the cupboard and handed one to Leah.

They worked without much conversation. Leah asked for salt and pepper, and Alan inquired if she wanted wheat or white toast. When everything was ready, they sat down opposite each other at the small kitchen table.

"Dig in," Alan said as he scooped eggs onto his plate and stabbed several slices of bacon. They ate quietly, politely passing toast and jam to each other. Alan rose and refilled their coffee cups. Then he pushed his chair back slightly, and holding his coffee cup as though to take a drink, he said, "Leah, I'm sorry I wasn't a very good host last night. I think telling my story out loud for the first time was harder than I thought it would be. I've kept everything inside, and I run over it in my mind, but I've not told anyone but you. Frank and Mary know nothing about this. I don't know why I didn't tell them, and I certainly didn't tell Jack Desmond about my rotten life when he was here. I suppose I'm feeling ashamed, guilty, and yes, mad as hell about some things. But I had to tell you, Leah. I owed you that, and now in the light of day, I guess I'm wondering how you feel. Can you forgive me for everything I did and even more for what I didn't do?"

Leah had been watching Alan as he spoke, and although he hadn't avoided her gaze, their eyes had not met. As he finished, however, he looked at her—hopefully, she thought—no doubt expecting an answer.

"You don't have to apologize, Alan. So much of what happened was just how life can be sometimes. For that matter I didn't handle things all that well either. I could have tried to get in touch with you, but I suppose I was nursing my own hurts and consequently let wounded pride get in the way. You were right to marry Juneau. Who knew that she was lying? And if you hadn't, you would have missed knowing and loving Colin. I hope you can forgive yourself and start building a life again. I know you're a great lawyer, and if you don't want to go back to the old firm, you could connect with another one or even start your own. I hope you will go back to law, if not right now, then maybe in a few months." Leah couldn't think of what else to say. She was afraid she had already said too much.

"I know you want the best for me, and I don't doubt your sincerity, but the law is not my passion anymore. I can't think much beyond today or tomorrow, but thanks for your words. Now, however, I want to change the subject. I'm going to try to be a better host today and tomorrow. I'd like to take you on a shopping trip to Walmart. I doubt you go there very much, if at all. They have everything there. I can lose myself in all the various aisles and often come home with stuff I have no use for, but the prices are so great." Alan smiled. "Actually, I'm joking, but I do have shopping to do, and while we're in town, I want to take you to a special place for lunch. It's not like anything you'd find in Chicago or Saint Paul. It's warming up out there, and the sun is breaking through, so it could be a nice outing."

"I'd love to see Walmart, and yes, I've been there once, but it was a long time ago, before my dad died. We drove out when they had a grand opening. What's the mode of dress for such an adventure?" Leah asked, glad to have a change in subject and even in mood.

"What you have on will be fine. We'll leave before ten if that's all right with you."

Leah agreed to the plans and helped clean up the breakfast dishes. They ended up leaving the cabin a little before nine thirty.

In the car Leah asked Alan where he had gone that morning.

"Sometimes I just need to get out in the fresh air. It helps me clear my head, and I even try to run a little. It isn't easy with my fake foot, but I'm getting better at it. If and when I decide to check out the latest in prostheses, I'm told there's a new deal that's more flexible yet won't collapse on me, and I heard about one for wearing in bed. It's a bitch … Oh, sorry … it's not much fun to strap on my foot/leg in the middle of the night to go to the bathroom. I haven't felt like making the trip into Minneapolis, so I haven't checked into it. Maybe I will; I don't know."

The Walmart store was about twenty miles away, and while the roads were mostly free of snow, Leah and Alan were slowed by the plows clearing the verges. Leah enjoyed following Alan around the store, and she came away with a pair of sunglasses. She had several at home but had not brought any along, and the sun on the snow was blinding, so it seemed like a good purchase. Alan bought supplies in the hardware department and also purchased groceries. They stowed everything in his Jeep and then drove to the restaurant Alan had promised would be something special.

From the outside it wasn't obvious that the building housed a restaurant. The name painted across the board over the door read Chip's Block. Alan told Leah he had no idea what it meant. He had not inquired the two times he had eaten there. Inside, booths lined the walls, and a long counter with stools defined the bar area. Alan suggested they sit at the bar, as he said it was where they would get the real flavor of the place.

The menu was handwritten on a ragged-looking piece of white cardboard, and it was also replicated on a chalkboard behind the bar.

"What's good?" Leah asked, trying to read the chalkboard without much success. It seemed to be written in a code of some sort.

"Well, last time I had the Leftover Stew, but we can't order that today, because it's not Monday."

"What do you mean, 'it's not Monday'? What does that have to do with anything?" Leah asked, puzzled.

"See the M-O behind it? That means Monday only. I was told it contained all the leftovers from the weekend put into one big pot and made into stew, and surprisingly it was delicious. It had an interesting flavor but a good one. Let's see … Today is Saturday, so why not try the special, Swiss Flat Hen. Frank told me it was good with a bowl of Duck's-Breath Soup. Are you game?" Alan asked, smiling perhaps at some private joke.

"Okay, I'm game. Swiss Flat Hen it is and the soup to go with it. Can you interpret for me just exactly what we're going to be getting?"

"The Swiss Flat Hen is an egg-cheese sandwich on the most delicious bread you'll ever taste, or so Frank said when he told me about this place. I think the duck soup is just that: soup made with duck meat. But I guess we'll see when we get it."

Alan placed their order and included coffee as well. Leah looked around and discovered the decor was very different from most restaurants where she had eaten. There was definitely a woodsy theme, with stuffed ducks and geese, a deer head, and several owls perched on branches above the bar, looking down with their yellow eyes at the patrons below. The napkins, in a small basket, were a hodgepodge of various holiday themes. The top few were from Valentine's Day, but underneath she saw some Christmas and even a couple of Thanksgiving ones. She laughed and said, "I didn't think I'd see this. Look, Valentine's Day, Christmas, and Thanksgiving still being celebrated. I love it, and now I can't wait for the food to arrive."

Leah and Alan enjoyed their egg-cheese sandwiches, and the duck soup, while a bit unusual in appearance, nevertheless was very tasty. Slices of duck meat, various vegetables, and a dark broth made Leah think of the many cups of beef bouillon she had consumed as a graduate student at Northwestern, but the taste of this soup was much different and far better. Before they left, Leah inquired of the waiter where the name of the restaurant, Chip's Block, had come from.

The waiter, a somewhat grizzled fellow, grinned and replied, "The boss's dad owned the place and called it the Café down the Block. The boss worked fer his Pa when he was a kid, and everbody called him a chip offa the old block. His nickname was Chip, so it had a sorta double meaning. When he took over some years ago, he decided to call it Chip's Block. Don't make a lotta sense to me, but everybody round about seems to get a kick outta it. Guess it makes sense in a crazy sorta way."

Leah thanked him for the information, and they left the restaurant. Alan was shaking his head and chuckling, and Leah confessed she was puzzled. The explanation hadn't made a lot of sense to her either.

Leah and Alan strolled along the main street, peering into several shops but not going into any of them. Then Alan suggested they drive around the lake. He said there was a large lagoon on the eastern side that often had a little open water even in the winter because it was spring-fed. There they might see wildlife coming to drink or looking for food. The only wildlife they ended up seeing was a large flock of geese flying over the lake, on their way north for the summer no doubt.

They returned to the cabin, and while still in the Jeep, Leah turned to Alan and said, "Maybe I should think about returning to Saint Paul today. The roads seem pretty good, and you didn't expect a weekend visitor. I hate to miss playing Hand and Foot, but—"

Alan interrupted, "You can't leave me now. If I have to play that game with them, just me alone, they'll shellac me royally. If you're there, they'll be polite. At least I think they will. Besides, they would be disappointed if you didn't stay for Easter brunch. I know Mary misses female companionship. She gets pretty tired of Frank and me talking about man stuff." Alan grinned.

Leah laughed. "Man stuff, eh? Well, I do like those two, so if you're not ready to be rid of me just yet, I guess I'll stay."

"I could probably get used to having you around … Well, better not say anything more about that. Let's get the groceries into the house. The milk needs to be refrigerated before it turns sour."

Leah helped carry in the grocery sacks and even put some things away. While they unpacked the food items, Alan tried to explain the Hand and Foot card game to Leah, without too much success. He finally said, "You'll figure it out once you start playing." That didn't inspire much confidence in Leah, who didn't believe she was much of a card player. When everything had been stowed in cupboards and in the work area in the garage, Alan suggested they rest for an hour or two and then go over to Frank and Mary's for an early dinner and Hand and Foot.

Leah climbed up into the loft and was soon asleep. Her night had been short and interrupted as she'd mulled over Alan's story, so she was grateful for the quiet time. She promised herself she wouldn't start in again on what she should or should not have said. Instead she lay down, covered right up to her nose, and thought about their trip to Champaign and the fun it had been, especially buying the hats. Northwestern winning the game had made the day memorable as well. She slept soundly and awoke to the telephone ringing. She could hear Alan speaking indistinctly but could only make out a rather forceful "No!" and "Absolutely not! I'm hanging up now." She heard him slam the phone down, mutter something she couldn't decipher. She decided to stay in the loft a little longer. When she heard the door slam, she knew Alan had gone out, so she climbed down the ladder and waited for him to return.

What was that all about? Leah wondered. She climbed down and went into the bathroom to comb her hair and put on fresh lipstick and then wandered into the kitchen to pour a cup of coffee left from breakfast. She heated it in the microwave and sat down in the living room.

Alan was gone half an hour, and when he came into the house, he seemed to have shed his anger. Maybe the fresh air he had talked about earlier had done its magic on him once again. "Hi, did you have a good walk ... or run? I really slept well, so I'm glad you suggested we rest. I think I'm ready for Hand and Foot," Leah said with a little more lightness than she felt. She was worried about Alan, but it wouldn't be wise to probe. If he wanted to tell her about the phone call, that would be fine, but she didn't want to ask or even suggest that she had heard anything of his conversation.

"Yes, it's not bad out there. It must be almost fifty degrees, and the snow is melting. We'll probably have to drive the Jeep over to Frank's because it will be too sloppy for the snowmobile and walking would be out of the question. It's already a quagmire in a couple of places. I see you've having coffee. Any left?" Alan went into the kitchen, poured what was left in the coffeepot into a mug, and zapped it for a minute or so before joining Leah in the living room.

They sat quietly, sipping coffee, and then Alan asked, "Did you hear the phone ring? I hope it didn't wake you, and I really hope you didn't hear me. Well, I guess it doesn't matter if you did. It was Juneau. She managed to worm my number out of Canady when she found out he had been to see me. She said she wants to come here. Can you imagine Juneau in this place? She'd freak out. Besides, I don't want to see her ever again, so I told her if she came up here, I was going to leave and go somewhere else. She couldn't survive up here. She has no idea what it's like, and she probably thinks it's kind of spa-like with places to shop nearby and great restaurants to visit. I can just imagine what she'd think of Chip's Block." Alan snorted in disgust.

Leah had to smile. She too couldn't picture Juneau in this setting. It rather pleased her that Alan had felt comfortable taking her to Chip's Block and that they both had enjoyed the experience.

"What are you smiling about?" Alan asked, a bit defensively perhaps.

"Oh, I was just picturing Juneau in Chip's Block, that's all. That's enough right there to bring a smile. You're right; she would be out of her element, just as I would be in some of the places where she feels very comfortable. Ah, viva la difference."

Alan laughed out loud. "Right indeed, viva la difference! Oh, look at the time. I need a shower, and then we have to think about trekking over to Frank and Mary's. I saw him a few minutes ago, and he wants to play cards before we eat, so we're to get there posthaste. Do you want to shower as well?"

"It wouldn't be a bad idea, since I didn't this morning. Do you want to go first, or shall I?" Leah inquired.

"You know, I remember a certain moment just like this. Do you recall the solution?"

Leah knew she was probably blushing, but she tried to answer in a diplomatic way. "I seem to remember that a lot of water was wasted that day, so perhaps we ought to be ecologically sound this time. You go first, and I'll go up the ladder and gather together what I want to wear to Frank's. Is that okay with you?"

"Sure, it's fine. I'll not be long." Alan disappeared into the bathroom. *Disappeared* wasn't the right word of course, because with no doors or walls, it was hard to disappear anywhere in the cabin, except when going up into the loft, which was what Leah did. When she heard Alan call to her that he was finished, she took her turn in the bathroom, with Alan's promise he would be in the kitchen with his back turned.

They left for Frank and Mary's house as soon as Leah's hair had dried. They were warmly greeted once again, and after they had shed their coats, Frank and Mary invited them to sit down at the kitchen table and begin playing the card game that Alan didn't particularly care for and that Leah knew little or nothing about. Mary was a patient teacher, and by the second round, Leah was getting the hang of it. Frank was obviously having a wonderful time, and it was a delight to watch his face and listen to his banter as he played one winning card after another. At five thirty Mary called a halt to the game, and they cleared the table for their evening meal. Leah and Alan stayed for a little dessert and coffee, but then Alan said they had to leave because he had things to do for brunch the following day.

"I'll wait until morning to make the cream puffs, but I'll make the filling tonight and put together a salad as we already discussed. Thanks for the dinner and the walloping at cards," Alan said with a smile. "See you tomorrow."

At the door, Frank told Leah she did all right at Hand and Foot for a first timer. When they were back at the cabin again, Alan began to set out ingredients for the cream puff filling and for the salad.

"Can I help?" Leah asked, standing behind one of the kitchen chairs. Alan looked so organized and efficient she almost hated to volunteer, especially since she had no idea what would go into the filling or how to make it.

"Sure. You can cut up the cabbage and the green onions. The recipe is right here." Alan pulled a small recipe card from the inside of one of the cupboards. Leah studied it and began to follow the directions, with an occasional "Is this okay?" or "Am I doing this right?" At the end of an hour, everything was ready, although the salad ingredients would not be combined until the morning. Alan said he planned to rise early to whip up the cream puffs so they would be fresh for their noon meal. Leah was amazed at how much he seemed to know about cooking. It didn't match up with her first impression when she had gone to the mansion in Evanston and they had eaten Pop-Tarts for breakfast.

"Where did you learn to be such a good cook?" Leah asked as she sipped tea he had made.

Alan sat down across the table and replied, "I'm self-taught, I guess, but I've had lots of advice from Frank and Mary. I got started cooking when Juneau and I had one of our many fights. I complained that the rice wasn't tender and the meat was overdone. She got angry and told me the new chef came highly recommended. I made some remark that I could probably do as well as he was doing, and she promptly went into the kitchen and fired him. When she came back, she announced that I was henceforth in charge of meals. Uncle Horace was spending a couple of weeks in the Bahamas, so I couldn't very well ask him to do something about our problem. I had my work at the firm that saw me off before seven some mornings and arriving home sometimes as late as seven or eight in the evening, but I took a week off, until we could get someone new. After she fired the chef, Juneau flounced out of the house, and I didn't see her again until the next evening. The chef came out of the kitchen right after Juneau left and told me he wanted his pay, plus a good-size bonus 'for services rendered'! If I didn't comply, he said he would tip off the society editor about what was going on right under my nose! I had to give him what he wanted. I protected Juneau, which was something I had already done a few times. At that point we no longer shared a bedroom, and I saw her only at meals, although she often didn't show up there either. Well, enough about that. Actually, I've learned a lot about cooking from trial and error."

The conversation lagged a bit after that. Leah suggested it was time for her to retire since an early rising was on the schedule. Alan nodded and said good night, and Leah went off to prepare for bed. She was still having some anxiety about how she had responded to Alan's story the previous evening, and perhaps she should not have asked about his cooking, since it once again aroused unpleasant memories for him. Under the covers she decided she couldn't possibly anticipate Alan's mood based on what was said or left unsaid. *Tomorrow I will not initiate any topic, new or old. I just hope my coming here wasn't a big mistake.*

Easter morning promised blue skies, and already at seven in the morning the snow was melting in sunny spots. Alan was busy in the kitchen, stirring up the cream puffs, Leah surmised. When she came down, fully dressed for the Easter church service, she asked Alan if he had an apron or at least a dish towel she could tie around her waist so she wouldn't get anything on her clothing before church.

"You don't need to do anything. The salad won't be put together until just before we go to Frank and Mary's, and the dessert is in the oven. There's coffee, and we'll have toast and juice this morning if you're okay with that, since we'll be having a rather substantial brunch at eleven thirty or noon."

"That's fine. I just thought there might be something I could do to help, but it looks like you have everything under control. Toast and juice are fine. I can make the toast. Oh, I see you've already put the bread in the toaster." Leah sat down with her cup of coffee, and Alan poured the juice and set it in front of her. Leah wasn't used to being the one waited on and was having a little struggle with herself. She wanted to protest that she could be helpful, but she decided not to. It was Alan's house, and he was doing just fine.

When the cream puffs were done, Alan removed the pan from the oven and with a sharp knife cut a slit in each one. Leah couldn't help herself and asked why he did that.

"To let the stream out. If I didn't, the inside might get soggy. This helps them dry a little so they're crisp on the outside and not mushy on the inside, where I'll put the filling."

"I've learned something new today. I may try making cream puffs when I get back home. Thanks for the culinary lesson. I can't wait to eat one of these at brunch."

Alan seemed pleased by Leah's comments and then excused himself to get ready for church. Leah sat in the kitchen, her back to the bathroom, as Alan showered and got dressed. When he came out, he was wearing a pair of light-gray slacks and a navy-blue blazer. Under the blazer he wore a white turtleneck shirt. He looked wonderful. Leah had a notion to tell him that he cleaned up well but decided instead to give him a genuine compliment. "Alan, you look nice. I like the turtleneck. It's a good combination." She thought, *That's a pretty lame way to tell him he looks good, actually better than good! Handsome is the word that comes to mind, but remember, Leah, you're going to watch what you say today.*

"Thanks. You look pretty good yourself. I like your earrings." Leah was wearing the earrings and bracelet that Alan had given her before they'd gone to the wedding celebration, which seemed so long ago now. The bracelet was hidden by the long sleeves of her navy-blue dress, a recent purchase that was a departure from her usual selections. There were ruffles around the collar and the ends of the sleeves, as well as at the waistline. It was more frills than Leah usually wore, but the dress had been on sale, and she loved the feel of the silky material.

"Thank you. Do you remember the earrings and the bracelet?" She lifted her arm to reveal the bracelet dangling there.

"I remember. The dress I don't remember. It isn't the sort of thing you usually wore." Alan paused as he inspected Leah's attire very carefully. "I think you should wear dresses like that more often. We'd better get going. Are you ready?"

The crowd at the small Lutheran church in the nearby village was large, and by the time Alan and Leah walked into the sanctuary, the seats were almost filled, except for the very front pew, so that was where they sat, along with Frank and Mary. Frank and Mary normally drove farther afield to worship at a good-size Methodist church, but that church had only a sunrise and an 11:00 a.m. service today, so it didn't fit the planned brunch schedule. The pastor, a young man who couldn't have been much older than Leah, had a lovely singing voice, which they could hear, sitting so close to the front. His sermon went on a bit longer than usual, according to Alan.

On the way back to Frank's house, Alan critiqued the sermon. "I guess I have a hard time with the whole idea of finding joy in all life, no matter what. I think that's what Tim said, that the joy of Easter permeates everything. Or maybe he said it should permeate everything. I don't believe it. It doesn't, and it can't. I'll have to have a discussion about that with him sometime this week. We often talk. Well, he talks mostly, and I listen and usually disagree. Oh, forget I said anything. Let's get back to the house and start having some great food."

Frank and Mary had fixed roast leg of lamb, something Leah had enjoyed only a very few times. There was homemade mint jelly from Frank, and a special potato casserole was out of this world. The salad Leah had fixed from Alan's recipe was also excellent, and she made a mental note to copy the recipe before she went back to Saint Paul. Dessert was also excellent. Leah loved the cream puffs, calling them better than any of the ones she had purchased at bakeries back in Chicago. As soon as they had finished, Frank brought up Hand and Foot once again, but this time Leah jumped in with a polite refusal, saying she had to be on her way home to the Twin Cities. Her family was gathering for dessert at her father's new home, and two of her brothers and her sister would be present. Leah said her good-byes and thanked the host and hostess and even managed a word of appreciation for the lesson in Hand and Foot. "It was so gracious to include me in three meals, and I enjoyed our conversation and the warmth I felt here in your home," Leah said with sincerity.

"Well, you just come on back anytime. I hope you do come again to see our friend Alan. He gets lonesome, and I think he needs a little female companionship. So don't be a stranger now. Come back when this snow melts and we have some nice weather." Leah hugged them both, and then she and Alan drove back to his cabin. She had already brought everything down the ladder from the loft, and all she needed to do was put her suitcase in the car and grab her boots from the breezeway.

"Thank you, Alan, for your hospitality. I dropped in, and then the storm came, and you were kind enough to offer shelter and a bed, not to mention the fine meals you made for me. I owe you. So if you come to the Cities sometime, I will soon be able to reciprocate. I'm in the process of buying a small house, and it has a guest room sans the ladder." Leah smiled. "I would be very pleased to see you knock at my door if you come south." Leah turned to the front door, set down her suitcase, and then opened the door and stepped out on the front porch. When she turned to pick up her suitcase, Alan had it in hand. He walked around her and deposited it in the backseat of her car. Leah threw in her boots and closed the door. Alan had backed away and was once again standing on the porch.

"Good-bye, Leah," he said. "Thanks for coming to see me. Who knows, maybe I'll surprise you and stop by on my way to wherever. But don't count on it. I think I've found my place, at least for quite a long while. Drive safely."

Leah raised her hand in a slight wave and then slid into the driver's seat, put on her seat belt, and started the engine. But then she unbuckled and got out of the car. She climbed the steps until she stood right in front of Alan. "Alan Parkin, I've got to have a hug before I go." Leah put her arms around Alan's neck, and with her cheek against his neck she said, "Take care of yourself. You're still someone I care about, and I want only the best for you. Good-bye, friend." Leah turned and got into the car, shifted into drive, and drove off without looking back. The smell of his cologne as she'd hugged him had been so familiar, and an ache in her chest made tears form. By the time she reached the main road, the tears had dissipated, and she was able to see the highway ahead of her. She wondered if Alan would ever come to see her. She knew she would not come to see him again. The so-called ball was in his court now, where it had to be, but she couldn't help thinking that she might never see or hear from him again.

Chapter 29

Leah arrived home a little after four in the afternoon and immediately changed out of her Easter finery into something more casual for the dessert and coffee at Gene and Janet's new house. Even before the gray house with the red shutters had been sold, Gene had begun construction on a new place that was near Janet's old one so that the girls, Cara and Deanne, could stay in the same school. Leah had seen it only from the outside, so she was anxious to have a look inside. She was also eager to see Harmon and Russell. Occasionally she met Charlene for lunch, but Harm and Russ were off in Milwaukee and Chicago, and they hadn't been together recently.

Leah decided to arrive early to allow time for a house tour. She left a little before six for the seven o'clock dessert. Gene answered the door and welcomed her warmly.

"Janet's upstairs with the girls. They're putting on their Easter finery for the little gathering tonight. We made them change as soon as we got home from church, so they're anxious to show off their duds to all of you. Russell and his girlfriend are here, and in fact they spent last night with us."

Russell, hearing Leah's and Gene's voices, came striding into the foyer. "Hey, big sis, come here and get a hug." Russ almost lifted Leah off her feet. She wondered if he had grown another inch or two since she had last seen him. *Surely his growth spurts should be over by now,* she thought.

"Hey, brother mine, it's good to see you. Where's your sweetie?"

"She's upstairs with Janet and the girls. I think they're doing hair or something, but they ought to be down soon."

Gene invited Leah on a quick tour of the downstairs area and the basement, where there was still only a cement floor, concrete walls and a vast open space. However, he said he had plans to finish it into an area the girls could use when they had friends over. He planned to do most of the work himself. "I'm cutting back at the store. I have a good assistant manager, and he's handling more of the day to day, so I've cut my time there dramatically. Janet still does the bookwork, but we may find someone else to do that so we can enjoy some traveling, especially at school vacation times and of course in the summer." The doorbell rang, and Gene said, "Oh, that must be Harmon. I'll let him in."

It was indeed Harmon and Katy, who shed their coats and joined Leah and Russell in the living room. Leah and Russell greeted the newcomers with hugs.

At that point the girls and Janet and Reba came downstairs, beaming. All four were dressed in their Easter outfits, and Reba had given the girls very sophisticated upswept hairdos. The hairstyles made them look much older than they were, which seemed to please them immensely. Janet's new look was a bouffant style that had everyone shaking their heads, and Reba had curled her own usually straight hair until she looked like Shirley Temple … at least that was what Gene said.

Over dessert everyone talked at once, and Leah had a hard time keeping up with the various conversations. She realized again that the McGregor family was a gregarious bunch and that no one stood on ceremony when it came to talking. If you wanted to be heard and had something important to share, you just talked a little louder.

Amid the din, Harmon banged his fork against his coffee cup to get everyone's attention. "Family here assembled, I have an auspicious announcement to make. Katy and I set the date for Memorial Day weekend, so I hope you can all come for the wedding. It will be small and will be held in the nursing home where we both work. We wanted the residents to be able to be there, so I guess in that respect it will be a large wedding. We're not inviting extended family or very many friends, but all of you are invited, and we hope the date works for you. It will be the Saturday ahead of the Monday holiday, so mark your calendars." Harmon sat down to applause and congratulations and best wishes.

Leah smiled and remembered when she and Harmon had first met. She felt Katy was a very lucky young lady to be marrying her brother, and she knew he would be a wonderful husband. She and Harmon had kept up e-mail and phone conversations since their first meeting, and the bond they had now was very strong. Leah was so pleased to have two brothers like Russell and Harmon, both of them special to her in different ways. She couldn't help wondering about Steve. He was still in Chicago, but as far as she knew, she might be the only one who was aware of that.

Leah left later than she'd planned. Her days up north were on her mind, and she really wanted to get home and unwind, but the company of her family … yes, she now counted them as family … kept her there until Russ and Reba left to drive back to Chicago. She worried about them on the highway late at night with the weekend traffic clogging up the roads. Russ assured her he had toned down his driving quite a bit since his teen years. There was laughter and good-natured joking about the validity of that statement, but in the end Leah told herself that worrying about people wouldn't keep them safe. Trusting in their abilities and offering a prayer for their safety was all one could do.

Back in her own little apartment, Leah threw in a load of laundry before crawling into bed, hoping to wake in time to get it dried. Then she managed, for the first time in the past few nights, to fall asleep almost at once.

Leah's workload seemed to increase with the warming of the weather, and the rest of April she worked ten and twelve-hour days just to keep ahead of things. All the extra work served one unintended purpose: she was usually dead tired when she got home at night and was able to drop off to sleep as soon as she hit the bed. Alan was still lurking in the back of her conscious mind, and occasionally, someone or something would remind her of him, and of course then she wondered how he was. Was he digging deeper into what she had decided was depression, or was he doing something about it? A few days after her return home she'd dropped him a brief note, thanking him again for his hospitality and letting him know she had arrived home safely. She also recounted her Easter evening gathering with her McGregor family at Gene's house, and she repeated her invitation for him to stop by when or if he came to the Twin Cities to have his prosthesis checked or to visit his doctor. She tried to word her offer of hospitality to avoid showing concern about the prosthesis or what she perceived as his growing isolation. She ended with greetings for Frank and Mary. After three weeks she had not had a reply, although she supposed her note didn't require one, unless Alan was planning a trip south.

The last weekend in April, Leah was able to complete all the paperwork on the little house she had contracted to purchase, and the first weekend in May she moved in with the help of Harmon and Katy, who drove up from Milwaukee to give her a hand. Gene and the girls helped as well. Janet, now almost five months pregnant, poured lemonade and offered cookies and sandwiches to the workers, but was not allowed to lift anything at all.

The beginning of May, Leah was at last able to finish her thesis and send it off to the university, with the hope that it would pass muster and she would get her degree in June, although that didn't seem likely. Things in academia didn't usually move that quickly.

The end of May, Leah and the rest of the Saint Paul McGregor families traveled to Milwaukee for Harmon and Katy's wedding. Russell and Reba also came from Chicago, but Stephen had sent his regrets. It was a beautiful day, and the service, held in the dining room, afforded the guests a lovely view of the lawns and flowers and the little lake in the background. The staff had prepared a delicious meal, which was served at 5:00 p.m., the regular dinner hour for the residents. A three-tiered wedding cake was cut and served to all the guests along with ice cream and coffee or tea.

"Harmon, this was a beautiful wedding," Leah said. "It seemed right that you had it here, knowing how much these folks love you. I suspect they'll be talking about this for the next six months or more."

"I'm sure they will. Let me say again I'm sorry for reneging on our request for you to be a bridesmaid. We should have had family as attendants as we'd planned, but asking Ralph, Gus, Alice, and Linda to stand up for us pleased them so much. Didn't they look great? Gus even wore his old tuxedo, and Linda, wearing her old bridesmaid dress from her sister's wedding, was so pleased to be part of the festivities. I suppose a few of the other residents were a bit miffed we didn't ask them. We could have asked the whole lot of them to be part of the wedding party, but that didn't seem wise. Now we're off to California for a week. Katy's grandmother couldn't come because of health problems, so we'll see her and also enjoy some fun on the beach, if it's warm enough. Thanks for coming to the wedding."

Leah watched Harmon stride off to find his bride. He was so happy, and she was happy for him. It made her realize that having siblings was a pretty cool thing

Chapter 30

The first weekend in June, Leah spent parts of three days with Charlene, helping with the implementation of wedding plans. They reserved the church and talked to the priest, who said Charlene and Roger needed to come in for premarital counseling. They reserved a reception site, hired a caterer, and went shopping together. Charlene picked out a wedding gown, and Leah chose a dress that she would wear as one of the bridesmaids. At the end of that excursion, Charlene said, "I miss Mama right now. I haven't missed her before, not really, but with my wedding coming up I picture her in the thick of the planning. I'm glad you were here to help me, Leah. I've never been very good at this sort of thing, as I was told more than once. But, hey, we all have different gifts. Isn't that what you said back when you encouraged me to get a job and move out of my parents' house? Best advice I ever had. I guess I'm saying I'm glad you're part of this family. I wasn't sure of that for a long time."

"Thanks for saying that, Charlene," Leah said, and she meant it. It had been a heartache for her to think that her return to her birth family had caused pain for some of them, probably for Charlene most of all. Then she asked, "Are you inviting Stephen to the wedding, and if so, will he come?"

"Yes, I sent him an invitation, but I haven't heard anything. We were close enough in age that we could have been good buddies, but it never happened. Harmon and I were less than two years apart, so we were naturally closer, and then of course you were born, and I became Mama's little helper. I've figured it out, Leah. Mama bullied all of us, and we let her. Maybe Harmon didn't; he managed to find activities that kept him busy, so he didn't get sucked into stuff like the rest of us did. From the time he started school, he was a joiner. Cub Scouts, Boy Scouts, and sports of all kinds, both in school and the community got him out of the house. In high school he had a job that kept him away over the dinner hour, and that's where lots of stuff happened. Assignments were made, punishments were meted out, and guilt was poured on all of us, Dad included. You know I wasn't very happy about his marrying Janet, but he really is a different guy. He's my dad now, a job I think he vacated a long time ago. Hey, I'm quite the psychologist, aren't I?"

"Yes, I think you've got it figured out. I'm proud of what you've been able to accomplish. And I like Roger very much. You should have a wonderful life together."

"I guess I can confess now. I went to see somebody and got help in sorting out a lot of garbage I was carrying around. I'm glad you're doing what you're doing, Leah, helping women and kids especially. I wish I had the gift, but I suppose we have to do what we do best. I like my job at the bank, and I think I do it pretty well. I'm getting a promotion next month. You're the first to know."

Leah was amazed. "You know, Charlene, that's the first time I've heard you speak so eloquently about yourself and about your life. Good for you. I'm glad too that we're sisters. And I'm delighted you asked me to be a bridesmaid. I'm also pleased you decided to have an August wedding instead of a June wedding. We just finished sending Harmon off into the state of wedded bliss, so having a couple of months to whip this wedding into shape is a good thing."

They ended the day with tea and scones at a little café in the mall where they had been shopping. Charlene insisted on paying, and Leah didn't argue. This was a new Charlene that had come out of hiding, and Leah was glad for it.

The next Saturday, Janet asked Leah to accompany her and the girls on a shopping excursion to find appropriate attire for Charlene's wedding. Charlene had asked Deanne and Cara to take care of the guest book at the reception and hand out programs at the wedding itself. They were very excited to be included, and their love of fashion only made the prospect of shopping for fancy dresses more delightful. Leah met the three of them in downtown Minneapolis at noon to have lunch before starting their search for appropriate attire.

"Hey, girls," Leah said as they joined her at a table where she was waiting. "Are you ready to try on lots of gowns, or do you know what you'd like to wear? Of course we have to stick with Charlene's color scheme—you know that, don't you? By the way, where's your mother?"

"Mom's talking to a friend she hasn't seen in years, so she sent us to wait with you. She saw you sitting here," Deanne said. She looked at Cara, and the two of them giggled.

"What's funny? You two know a good joke or something? Come on, let me in on it so I can laugh too," Leah said, looking at her stepsisters.

"You tell her," Cara said, looking at Deanne.

"No, you do it," replied Deanne.

"Okay. We have news. We're not supposed to tell, but it's just too good. Anyway, you're family, so we can tell you, right?" Cara said, nodding wisely.

"Well, Mom and Dad—that's what we call him now—well, they're going to have a baby, and it's a boy! Isn't that hilarious? They told us last night, and we've been happy and laughing about it ever since. We really don't know anything about baby boys, but we think it could be fun."

"Wow! That is big news. It sounds as if you like the idea of a brother. You said you were happy, right?" Leah was pretty sure Gene and Janet had intended not to tell the family the sex of the new baby, although she couldn't figure out why. The way the girls had framed the "secret" also made it sound as if they had just learned their mother was pregnant. Leah wondered if that was the case. Gene had told her more than two months ago, so it seemed strange they had not shared the news with the girls before this.

"Mama had some kind of test, and they actually took a picture of the baby inside her tummy. They told us yesterday at breakfast that it's going to be a boy, and then we got to put our hands on her tummy and feel something move around. It was weird, and I wasn't sure I liked it. But we think a baby brother would be pretty cool. What do you think?"

"Definitely cool."

"We saw his picture, but we're wondering how they could tell it was a boy. Don't all babies look pretty much the same?" Cara asked.

Oh dear, thought Leah, *I'm not sure I'm prepared to answer this question.* She said, "Well, the doctors are good at telling boys from girls. You ought to ask your mother about that."

"We did, but she didn't tell us anything. We thought because you work at a place that helps people who are going to have babies—as least that's what you said—you would know the answer," Deanne said.

"You know, girls, doctors are so smart, and they can tell these things just from looking at pictures like the one you saw. What did you see? Did you see hands or feet? You probably saw the baby's head, right?"

"Right. It looked kinda big, and his feet were really little. I could see his nose, and there was a long string. How did that get in there?" Cara asked.

"Well, you can discuss all that with your mother or maybe your dad. I see your mother coming, so we should decide what we want for lunch." Leah breathed a sigh of relief to be off the hook. She would alert Janet later about her daughters' questions.

"Hi, Leah. I ran into a friend I hadn't seen in some time. Have you ordered yet? I guess not. You don't even have water," Janet said as she sat down.

They ordered lunch, and the girls wanted dessert afterward, so Janet allowed them to go to the dessert buffet to make their selections. Leah took the opportunity to say to Janet, "I think I should tell you that your daughters have let your secret out of the bag. They assumed it was all right because Gene is my father. They told me you're having a boy, which means a half brother for me." Leah smiled.

"Oh dear, oh my. I didn't think they'd say anything. I … we … weren't ready yet to go public. Are you disappointed in your father for marrying someone still in her childbearing years and then not figuring out how to prevent getting pregnant?" Janet was very flustered, and Leah tried to reassure her.

"Janet, Gene told me about the baby two months ago, and what you two do is nobody's business but yours. If this wasn't planned, so what? Babies come along at the most inconvenient times, but I'm sure you'll welcome him, and so will the rest of the family. Your daughters are delighted with the idea of having a baby brother, although they may change their minds once he arrives. Well, you know all about that, having had two children. You should probably tell everyone soon. Don't wait any longer, if you were thinking about doing that. Most women would probably guess just by looking at you, even though you've been wearing clothing that I suppose you assume hides your condition. You definitely need to tell Charlene. She'll probably spout off, but don't worry; I'll have a talk with her. We're getting along very well now, and she's such a happy bride that I don't see her fussing for very long. Here are the girls. Please don't chastise them for betraying your confidence. I'm happy for all of you."

The shopping trip was successful and accomplished more quickly than Leah had dared hope. By four thirty she was back home, where she changed into gardening attire and began pulling weeds in her flower bed. She smiled when she thought about the excited little girls, and she hoped Gene and Janet were excited too.

Chapter 31

Charlene's wedding on August 15 was lovely, and after the midafternoon reception, everyone was invited to the bride and groom's home, where they had a lovely outdoor buffet supper. The weather cooperated, and the temperature was in the eighties. With a canopy protecting the diners, it was very comfortable, especially with the breeze blowing off Lake Minnetonka. At nine o'clock, as Leah was walking to her car to go home, Stephen caught up with her.

"Will you give me a ride to the hotel downtown where I'm staying? I came with Harmon, but they left already. It isn't out of your way, is it?" Stephen asked.

"Hop in. I'm glad to give you a ride. We haven't had any opportunity to exchange more than a few words, so maybe you can fill me in on what's happening in your life."

It had been several months since she had heard anything from her brother. She had assumed after his move to Chicago that their relationship had turned a corner, but he'd stopped e-mailing and had never called her at all. She was always the one to initiate phone contact. As they sat side by side in the car, Leah tried several times to get a conversation going with him, and then decided she would tell him something about herself that he didn't know. In fact there were countless things he didn't know about her. "Steve, you might be interested to learn that I studied law at Northwestern University, with the idea of becoming a famous trial lawyer like Perry Mason." She looked over at Stephen to see if he was at least smiling at her audacity. He wasn't.

She continued, "I didn't graduate. I ran out of money and had to get a job, but I was lucky to be hired by a prestigious firm in downtown Chicago. I worked as a paralegal, doing research with a team of others. It was very satisfying because we could see if our work bore fruit by the way a trial turned out. I worked only six months and then was fired." Once again she looked over at her brother, and this time he had turned toward her and had a look of incredulity on his face.

"Yes, big brother, your little sister was fired. I was told to leave immediately, and I was even ushered out. But before I was allowed on the elevator, someone examined the personal items I had gathered together to take with me, to make sure I wasn't making off with any company secrets or something equally ridiculous. And do you know the reason I was fired? No, of course you wouldn't. I was dating the big boss's nephew, and the big boss came down from on high to deliver the termination blow because he deemed me unfit in every way possible. I didn't have a pedigree, and I was reminded that my father, Harold Anderly, had been a lowly janitor at Carson Pirie Scott Department Store and had not finished high school. I could go on about other ways where I didn't measure up. Not long after that I gave up on law and became a social worker. The law didn't seem to have a heart at all. So that's why I do what I do today, for better or worse. So what do you think about that?" Leah hoped she would at last get a response from Steve.

"Gee, that's some story. I had no idea. Sorry you got fired. I came close once when I goofed up on my first day of my first real job. I started working in one of Dad's hardware stores, and I made the mistake of failing to be polite to the customers. I was observed more than once being sullen and even downright rude to people asking for assistance or inquiring about something on sale. I really didn't want to work there, but Dad and Mama expected that I would put in my time. I was a senior in high school that year. The previous year I had also worked at the store, but Dad had kept me in the back room working with inventory and doing grunt work. At the store where I was sent that second summer, the assistant manager was pretty hard-nosed. He had a talk with Dad, who had a talk with me, and I went back to work with a new attitude." Steve smiled then for the first time that day; at least Leah thought it was the first time.

"Being the boss's kid probably wasn't easy, was it? And I suppose you finished out the year, went off to college, and didn't have to work there again."

"Wrong. I finished the year, but the next two summers when I came home from college, I was right back at one of Dad's stores. The summer of my junior year I got smart and stayed at college to take summer courses that helped me graduate midterm the next year. I think working at the stores Dad owned helped me to become more responsible and to take work seriously. Now I actually think I could go into the hardware business if I had to, although I like what I'm doing far too much to make that kind of change, unless something drastic happened, like Dad becoming incapacitated and needing someone to take over temporarily or even permanently, God forbid. Not my first choice, but I could do it if I had to. Would you ever go back to law if an opportunity presented itself?"

"Good question. I doubt it. But I guess one should never say never. I truly believed back when I started law school that I would make law my life's work and happily so. But things happen ..."

"Whatever became of the old boyfriend? Didn't he have anything to say about the whole firing deal?" Steve asked.

"How should I answer that one?" Leah said. "Well, he married someone else, and there was a baby, but things didn't work out for them. In fact the marriage was annulled after a year, and then he had a tragic accident in which he lost the lower part of his leg. Now he's fighting depression, so it isn't a good outcome for him. I guess I'm grateful I was able to get through my disappointment without too much damage.

Russell helped me more than he will ever know. He came to live with me just before all that happened, and he was someone to talk to at night and over breakfast. I helped him learn how to navigate Chicago, and he's like a native now. He probably knows the city better than I do. He's a good kid. Well, he's not a kid anymore. He's going to be married himself before long. Here's your hotel. Before you get out, can you tell me what happened? Why you haven't kept in contact? The first two months after I moved to Saint Paul we were still e-mailing, but then no word from you. What happened?"

"I thought Connie would have been in touch. I didn't want to be the one to say anything. She was your friend after all. But I guess she didn't tell you what happened. Am I right?"

"Connie and I haven't seen each other or talked for ages. I heard that she was going to be taking a leave of absence from her work, but by the time I was able to get in touch with her, she couldn't talk very long, because she had a friend at her door whom she had invited over. She didn't explain the reason for the leave of absence, so I didn't press her. It was her business, and anyway, she had guests. So did you two have a falling out or something?" Leah turned in her seat and watched Steve, who was avoiding looking in her direction.

"I don't know how to say this. It's hard for me because I'm not very proud of myself. Connie is pregnant, and I haven't been exactly a pillar of support for her. I blamed her for not taking precautions as I'd assumed she had, so when she told me, I sort of flipped out. First thing I thought was, what will Mama say? Isn't that crazy? She's dead and gone, but there she was, interfering in my life from the grave. I knew it was ridiculous to have those thoughts, but they came anyway, and I didn't fight them very hard. I just blew up, and Connie walked out. We were at a restaurant when she told me. She had just been to the doctor that afternoon, but she hadn't informed me ahead of time about the appointment. I was left sitting there, feeling like a fool and still angry. When someone walks out on you, it's a humiliating thing ... at least it was for me. I didn't call or go to see her. I just sulked and told myself I had good reason to be angry. I guess this isn't what you expected to hear, was it?" Steve turned then to look at his sister, his face showing sorrow and something else Leah couldn't quite identify.

"So … have you talked to her at all? When is this baby due?"

"I called her last week, but she hung up on me, which made me angrier. I actually don't know when the baby is due. Probably sometime in November, but it could be earlier or later. I'm mad at myself now, and I want to tell her I'm sorry and to make things right. I thought we'd be married sometime in the future, but when this baby news hit me, I wasn't ready to speak up and do the so-called right thing. I could hear Mama's voice in my head. 'Girls are the responsible ones when there's a baby before marriage,' so of course that was my defense: it was Connie's fault, not mine. I just wish … I wish … but it's too late now."

"It's never too late, Steve, provided you want to marry Connie. It's not the end of the world if you don't, but you need to find a way to talk to her, and not over the phone. Surely you know where she lives, so you could go there and be persistent about having a conversation. That's what I think." Leah stopped and waited for Steve to articulate what she saw in his face. Perhaps it was anxiety or even fear.

"I suppose I'm a coward at heart. I know what I should do, but I'm afraid. I never thought about being a father. Not once in my life did I think I would be a good one, so it wasn't on my radar. I know where babies come from, but I guess I wasn't prepared for this to happen to me. Sometimes I wonder what's wrong with me."

Steve looked so forlorn Leah wanted to hug him and pat his back and tell him everything would be all right, but since that wasn't physically possible, all she did was reach over and take his hand and squeeze it, saying nothing for a few moments.

"Steve, go find Connie at the first opportunity. Don't put it off because you're afraid of being rejected again. If you love her, tell her so. If you don't, tell her that as well, but give her your support through the pregnancy, and promise to be a father to the baby, no matter what. Do you think you could do that?"

"I don't know. I hope so. I wish you were in Chicago. You could do this better than I could. I'm afraid I'll blow it. I do care for Connie, and I want to do what's best for her and the baby."

"Well, tell her that. It's a good place to start, and don't be afraid to show your feelings, whatever they are. Not expressing how you feel only makes a relationship more difficult. Oh, don't take what I've said too literally. I'm hardly one to be giving advice about love and marriage, but talking to Connie is number one. You've got the plane ride back to decide how you really feel and then to formulate what you plan to say that won't hurt her or make things worse. I guess that's the advice I have for you: don't make things worse! I've got to go. I'm blocking the alley. Call or e-mail, Steve, okay?"

"Thanks for the ride and the story and also the advice. You seem more real to me now, Leah. You know, I didn't like you when you came to check us out that Thanksgiving weekend. I don't know why. It was probably irrational, and I can't even articulate what I was feeling, but this past Christmas I felt we were on the way to being friends, if not brother and sister. I'll be in touch, I promise." Steve got out, grabbed his bag, and walked purposefully toward the hotel entrance

As Leah pulled away from the curb, she glanced in the rearview mirror for a glimpse of her brother, but he had already disappeared into the hotel. She desperately hoped she had given him good advice and that he could find the right words that would touch Connie's heart. "I'm pretty sure she loves him," Leah said out loud. "But I guess sometimes love isn't enough when things happen that get in the way."

Chapter 32

That evening Leah spent time cleaning and doing laundry since she had been gone the entire weekend. On Monday her work schedule filled up dramatically, and she had little time that wasn't closely scheduled. The August weather had turned hot and dry, and by the time Labor Day came, Leah was ready for the long three-day weekend. She had several projects planned, including painting the rail fence in her backyard. It had been a shade of brown at one time, but most of the paint had weathered away. Two weeks ago she had managed to prime everything, and now she hoped to do the more laborious job of painting. Primer could be slapped on, but painting required more care. The phone rang just as she was opening the can of paint on the picnic table in the backyard.

"Hello. What? Right now? Well, yes, I guess I can be there in, say, half an hour. I'm wearing my old paint shorts and T-shirt, but I'll get there as quick as I can."

Gene had called to say that Janet's water had broken and that they were on the way to the hospital. He'd asked if she could come over to be with the girls. Leah decided to take an extra minute to change clothes, just in case they needed to go out in public. Then she jumped into her VW Bug and drove as fast as the speed limit allowed. Gene and Janet were already gone, and the girls were there by themselves, but it had only been for twenty minutes, and the oldest was eleven. Perhaps at the parents' request, the door was locked, and Leah had to ring the bell several times to get someone to answer.

"What were you doing? Didn't you hear the doorbell?" she asked Deanne.

"We weren't sure we should answer it. It could have been an escaped convict or something. Mom always said not to answer the door when we've here by ourselves."

"Okay, I understand. It's good to be cautious with strangers. Now, what do you want to do while we wait for news from your dad and mom? Have you had breakfast?" Leah asked.

"We had cereal. I don't know. What could we do? You wanna play a game or something?"

Leah wondered what a good activity would be to take their minds off the big event that was taking place only a few miles away. Then she had an idea. "How about doing some cooking and baking? I bet your mom would appreciate coming home to casseroles in the freezer and some cookies or brownies or whatever sweet treat she likes. You tell me what we should make, and then we'll run to the store to get the ingredients. Want to do that?"

"Yeah," the girls cried in unison.

Cara said, "Mom doesn't let us do much in the kitchen. She says we're too messy and it takes too long. You won't care, will you, if we make a mess?"

"Nope, I won't care an iota. Messes can be cleaned up. All right, let's make a list of what to cook and bake, and then we'll hit the store."

It took a good hour for the girls to decide what they wanted to make and then to look up the recipes and write down the ingredients they needed to buy. The three of them spent another hour at the store gathering everything, so by the time they returned home, it was lunchtime. "How about having pizza delivered? We ought to stick close to the phone because that baby could come anytime, and we want to be here when your dad or maybe both of them call." Pizza was voted as the lunch of choice. Leah called in an order, and they prepared soft drinks and some carrot sticks to accompany their meal.

At two o'clock they began cooking and baking up a storm and produced several casseroles, a batch of brownies, and two batches of cookies. Leah ended up finishing the cookies herself, as the girls had wearied of the whole process, but they did help with the cleanup later. Marcene's cooking-and-baking frenzy had come to Leah's mind as they'd prepared baked goods for the freezer. Leah hoped she wasn't becoming like her birth mother!

There had been no word all afternoon from the hospital, but at ten minutes before six, Gene called. "Leah, is everything okay there? Janet is concerned about the girls."

Leah assured him all was well, but said they were anxious for news of the new baby.

"Tell them they have a baby brother who weighs six pounds and ten ounces. He's so beautiful, Leah, not all red and wrinkly like you were and the rest of the kids too. I think we're going to call him Kerry, which is Janet's maiden name. Since she has no brothers to carry on the family name, this seems like a good thing to do. Her parents will be delighted. We haven't called them yet, but that's next on my list. I'll let Harmon, Russell, Charlene, and Stephen know too. I want to be here with Janet as long as possible. I guess I can even stay overnight. Her room has an extra bed for husband or parents or whomever, and the baby will be brought in as soon as they get him cleaned up, but I really think I should come home to the girls."

"Stay there, Gene. I can be here until tomorrow sometime, so stay with your wife and son. Enjoy those first hours of life with him. That's a gift that won't come again, unless, of course, you have more children."

"No more! We'll make sure of that. But this one is definitely a gift from God, and we're both so happy. I'd better go, but thanks for taking care of the girls. We owe you big time."

"You don't owe me anything. Call me on my cell before you leave so you'll know where we are. We may go to my house to spend the night. Greet Janet and tell her we're very proud of her. Bye."

Leah took Deanne and Cara home with her Saturday evening, and the next afternoon Gene came to pick up the girls so they could accompany him to the hospital to bring home Janet and the new baby. New mothers didn't get to spend very long in the hospital apparently. Janet's mother and father were on their way and would arrive sometime in the early evening, according to Gene. After they were gone Leah sighed. *"Too late to do any fence painting. It will have to wait another week."*

That evening in the quiet of her living room, Leah sat down to read a book, something she hadn't had time for in ages. She was on chapter 2 when the phone rang.

"Now what?" she said out loud. She answered the phone. "Hello, this is Leah."

"Hi, Leah, it's your brother Steve."

"Well, hi! It's good to hear from you. I sent you a couple of e-mails but didn't receive a reply. Have you been out of town?"

"Sort of. But first I want to thank you for your advice back in August after Charlene's wedding. I did what you said. The first time I showed up to see Connie, she slammed the door in my face, but I went back twice more, and the third time she let me in. And Leah, the minute I saw her, I knew I loved her. All those weeks I had been nursing my anger and disappointment, but when I saw her, I knew we could make things work if she was willing. She was so beautiful with her belly sticking out quite a ways, and I thought, hey, that's my child in there. I want to be part of his or her life. Maybe I had some guidance from somewhere ... above perhaps? I guess I said all the things I should have, and I meant every one of them. Connie cried, I cried, and then we fell into each other's arms. We were married five days ago and have been on a honeymoon from Thursday until today. We'll be moving into a condo near Loyola, and Connie hopes to get a job at the library there after the baby's born. We're having a girl, Leah. I'm thinking we ought to name her after you because we both agree we owe you for kicking some sense into me back in August. What do you think about that?"

"I'm so happy for you both. Congratulations and all the best wishes in the world. As for naming the baby Leah, I don't think that would be a good idea. She might turn out to be a loudmouth who can't help speaking her mind, which isn't all bad but isn't so good sometimes either. By the way, does your dad know?"

"No, I haven't called anyone but you. I'm a coward at heart. I told you that before, but I will let everyone know, and Dad and Janet will be first on the list. I hope you'll come to see us, maybe before the baby's born, but certainly afterward. You will, won't you?"

"I'll do my best. Maybe when Russ gets married, whenever that turns out to be. I tried to pin him down, but now they're thinking about next summer. He said there were too many McGregors getting married, so he didn't want to add to the confusion. Well, we'll wait and see. Keep in touch, Steve, and tell Connie I'm delighted to be an aunt. Did Gene call you about the birth of their little guy? They named him Kerry."

"Yes, I heard via e-mail, but I haven't responded yet. At least now I have something positive to tell him. I'd better stop so Connie and I can go out for ice cream before it gets dark. I'm glad you're my sister, Leah. Good-bye for now."

"Wow!" Leah exclaimed after hanging up. "Wow! I would not have predicted this outcome, but I'm surely glad it turned out this way."

The next day, Monday of Labor Day weekend, once more Leah hoped to get the fence painted. However, a midafternoon shower of rain chased her inside, where she cleaned her brush and put the paint away. Hopefully the following weekend would be nice, and she could finish the project. She had just changed out of her painting clothes when the doorbell rang. It was Harmon and Katy.

"I called you this afternoon but didn't get an answer. Then we stopped by Dad's to see if you were there, but he said he thought you were painting, so here we are. We wanted to give you our news face-to-face. We're moving to Minneapolis because I got a great offer for a job at Fairview that's too good to pass up, and Katy has been assured there will be a place for her there too. They can always use good nurses. The thing is, we're expecting a baby. Katy is only at six weeks, but we're so excited, and after we saw little half-brother Kerry, we're even more ready for this. I was able to hold him. Oh my, he's so little. I was astonished to see how Dad was acting. He's in seventh heaven with that new baby."

"That's a load of surprises. First of all congratulations on the baby. I'll be an aunt! And it's great news that you'll be moving up here." Leah hugged her brother and her sister-in-law, inviting them to share a little supper with her before they took off for Milwaukee. She didn't mention that she had just heard from Steve. It would be up to him to tell his siblings about his marriage and the coming baby.

"Wish we could, Sis, but I'm on call tonight, so I have to be there before eleven. It won't be long before we're here permanently and can see each other more often. The plan is to move before the end of the month. They'd like me to start tomorrow, but of course that isn't possible. We'd better head out. Traffic will be heavy, but we'll take our time, and don't worry: we'll drive carefully."

Leah waved to Harmon and Katy as they backed out of her driveway. She felt a tug of love for her brother, whom she had not even known existed just a short time ago. She watched their car until it disappeared around the corner two blocks away. This had certainly turned into a most exciting Labor Day weekend.

Leah decided to eat some suspect leftovers that ended up tasting fine once they were warmed up, and with a glass of milk and a couple of cookies for her dessert she was satisfied. She sat down to read the *St. Paul Pioneer Press* newspaper. The front-page news was nothing earthshaking, but a minor headline on page two caught her attention.

Chicago Woman Injured in Accident

Juneau Parkin of Evanston, Ill., was injured in a one-car accident on Interstate 90 on the south side of Minneapolis on Saturday morning. Parkin lost control of her car, and her vehicle left the road and overturned in the ditch. An eyewitness to the accident reported that Parkin passed him at a high rate of speed only seconds before. Highway Patrolman John Darnell, when interviewed, reported that Parkin sustained serious injuries, the extent of which are not known at this time. There were no other vehicles involved.

Leah wondered what Juneau had been doing in the area. Had she been on her way to see Alan? That certainly would not be something Alan needed. Even though they were no longer married, she was sure Alan would be notified and perhaps have to respond in some way. *Well, I can't worry about it,* Leah thought. *There's nothing I can do or should do.* The news about Juneau wasn't easy to put out of her mind, and to her credit, Leah said a silent prayer for Juneau's healing and recovery from whatever her injuries might be.

Chapter 33

Harmon and Katy moved to Minneapolis the third week of September, and Leah pitched in to help. The apartment they rented near the hospital where Harmon was now employed was very nice, with a bank of south-facing windows that promised wonderful winter sun. The day of the move they were surprised by the first light frost of the season. The report was for an early and long winter. Leah shuddered to think of it. Snow was fine, but the cold did not please her. Harmon turned on the furnace because it was so cold in the apartment.

September continued to be chilly, but October began to shows signs of a warming trend. On the first full weekend in October it was beautiful, and Leah decided to finish painting her backyard fence. She donned her painting clothes and began hauling out brushes, paint, and rags when the phone rang. Somehow this felt like another interruption of her plans, and she was right.

"Leah, it's your dad. We wondered if you would take care of Kerry for us today. It's so gorgeous out there, and this might be the last warm weekend, so we thought we'd take the girls to the amusement park. We'll be back before six—at least that's the plan. I'll probably be ready to leave long before that. Janet has everything you'll need for the baby, but please don't change any plans you had …" Gene trailed off.

"Bring little brother over. I'll be delighted to have him for the day. You did interrupt my plans to paint the fence, but quite frankly, I wasn't all that excited about painting. This will be more fun. When will you be here?"

"We'll aim for nine. I think the park opens at ten, so that should work out pretty well. Thanks for saying yes. Deanne and Cara are delighted. They've been wanting to go all summer, and we never got around to it. Janet wasn't sure about leaving Kerry. It's the first time for us to leave him for this long, but she trusts you and probably no one else. See you in a little while," he said and hung up.

There goes my painting again. But taking care of Kerry will be a delight, so I don't mind. Maybe I'll paint tomorrow, Leah thought as she put away the painting paraphernalia and changed into jeans and a T-shirt. Maybe she would have time to read a book while Kerry slept.

Janet and Gene and the girls trooped into the house carrying a load of equipment they thought Leah might need for the baby. There was a portable crib, a car seat, clothing, toys, food, bottles, diapers, and wipes. Everything was piled on the kitchen table, and Gene set up the crib in the sunroom. They finally left at twenty minutes to ten. The girls were clearly anxious to get going, but Gene and Janet obviously had a little anxiety over leaving Kerry all day for the first time. Leah had been to their house a few times to look after the baby and the girls so Gene and Janet could get out for a meal or just for a short break, but never for an entire day.

"Don't worry," Leah told them as they piled back in the car. "I'll take good care of my little brother." It was hard to believe that at her age she had a brand-new baby brother … half brother, of course … but brother nevertheless.

"*Well, here you are with a five-week-old baby. I hope you can do this, Leah,*" she said to herself as she sat down and held little Kerry. He had begun fussing, so she took a seat in the rocking chair, and in just a few minutes he was sound asleep. She carefully put him in his crib and then just watched him sleep. His long eyelashes so dark against his cheeks and his mop of dark hair curling slightly at his temples and neckline melted her heart. He had Janet's coloring. Gene was fair-haired, just as Leah was, but Janet had beautiful dark-brown eyes and almost jet-black hair. Deanne also had her mother's coloring, while Cara's hair was more of a soft brown, as her father's had been, or so Leah had been told.

She realized she would need to make lunch for herself while the baby slept, because once he was awake, she would be devoting her time and energy to caring for him. She pulled a container of chicken soup from the freezer and put it into the microwave to thaw and then made a couple of tuna-salad sandwiches. One would be for lunch and one for a snack later. She was just putting the sandwiches in the refrigerator when the doorbell rang. She hoped it wouldn't rouse Kerry from his nap.

The front door was open with only the screen separating inside from outside. The glare of the sun coming into the living room from behind the screen door revealed only a dark silhouette, but when she reached the door, she saw it was Alan. First a look of surprise and then a smile spread across her face.

"Hello, Leah. I was just in the neighborhood, so I thought I'd drop by." He was teasing her, repeating what she had said to him last April when she had stopped to see him on her way north and had never gotten any farther than his house.

"Alan Parkin. I can't believe it. Come in, please. I'm glad to see you. You're looking tanned and fit. Life at the lake obviously agrees with you. I see you've shaved your beard. I thought it looked good, but I think I like this look better." Leah stepped back and with her left hand held the door for Alan to enter.

"I had a little trouble finding you since I didn't know your address. You've moved since you wrote me that note. But my research skills as a former lawyer came through, and so here I am. You said I should come, so I took you at your word."

"I'm glad you're here," Leah said. Then she heard Kerry whimper, so she said, "Follow me; there's someone I want you to meet."

She led the way into the sunroom and stood beside the portable crib, smiling.

Alan looked shocked. "Oh Leah. Oh, were you pregnant when you came to visit me? Are you married?"

"Married? No. Oh, you think this little guy is mine? In a way he is. He's my brother."

"Your brother? How can that be?" Alan looked confused.

"Really, he's my brother. My biological dad married a much-younger woman about a year ago now, and so yes, this is my half brother, Kerry McGregor. I'm babysitting today while his parents and sisters are enjoying a trip to the amusement park. They'll be back by six to pick him up again."

"Oh, thank God. I thought … Well, I'm glad you're not married. Is it all right to say that? I don't care if it is or not."

Kerry now began to fuss big time, and Alan asked if it was all right to pick him up.

"Of course. Here's a diaper to put over your shoulder. I don't know if he spits up much or not, but just to be prepared …"

Alan leaned over and gently picked up the baby, cradling him first in his arms and then putting him against his shoulder. He walked back into the living room, speaking softly to the infant, with Leah following along behind. When Alan turned to look at her, his eyes were glistening. "This little guy reminds me of Colin with all that dark hair and those long eyelashes. He's beautiful. Absolutely beautiful!"

"Yes, he is, isn't he?" Leah said. "Come sit in the rocking chair. It may be time to feed him. I'll go look at the schedule."

Leah went into the kitchen to get the baby's bottle, which she warmed in a special plug-in warming cup that Janet had brought along, together with instructions on what temperature it should be. Alan had sat down with Kerry in the rocking chair and Leah handed him the bottle. There in front of her she saw a contented infant and a man with memories of his own son, finding joy. Leah's eyes were moist just watching the two of them. She was happy that perhaps Alan had been able to put away his anger and sorrow over the loss of his son. After all, here he was, enjoying another man's child. Maybe it was providential that Alan had come on this particular day when Kerry was in her care. A little miracle, Leah thought.

When Kerry fell asleep once again, Alan reluctantly laid him in his crib and joined Leah in the kitchen, where she had gone to warm up soup and take the tuna sandwiches out of the fridge. "We can hear him out here, can't we?" asked Alan as they sat down to have their lunch.

"Oh yes. The door to the sunroom is open, and I've heard him set up quite a fuss when he wakes up. Not to worry, we'll hear him."

"Okay, then there's something I need to tell you before he wakes up again. I was going to do this in a different way, but now I'm just going to say it. I bought a building on the north side of Saint Paul, and it's in the process of being rehabbed. It was in reasonably good shape, but the configuration didn't suit my purposes, so I hired a fellow to make the street level into what will be my law office. I'm going into practice on my own, and I'll be accepting pro bono cases as they come along. The upper level is in the process of being converted from three small apartments into one large one, where I plan to live. I'd love to take you there, but I guess that's not possible today, but maybe tomorrow if you say the word." Alan looked hopefully at Leah, who was speechless for a moment.

"You did it then! You changed your mind about law! Oh, Alan, I'm so pleased, so glad for your sake because you are a good … no, a *great* lawyer, and it's where you belong. I know it is. What made you have a change of heart?"

"You did! At least what you said to me finally soaked in. Others had said the same thing, but I kept hearing your voice in my head, telling me to go back into law. I also spent five months in psychiatric care. I saw a new doctor and got a new prosthesis, which is so much better. It's amazing how much better it is. I've just been pronounced cured by my psychiatrist. Well, that's not exactly what the doc said, but we won't be meeting regularly any longer, only when or if I feel the need. He suggested a whole list of things for me to do to help me back. That's the doc's word, *back*. Back to being who I am or at least who I want to be. I had changes to make, and I think I've been able to make them. Now I'm going to ask you, very sincerely this time, to forgive me. Will you forgive me, Leah, for neglecting to do and say what I should have almost two years ago? I let Uncle Horace run my life and let him influence me. I had to apologize to Juneau as well, for being unable to forgive her for what she did to me with her made-up story. I think you said I would have missed loving Colin if I hadn't married her, and that's true. I guess I hadn't thought of it before you said it. Maybe you hadn't heard, but Labor Day weekend Juneau sustained severe internal injuries and a broken left arm in a car accident. She was headed to the cabin to see me. Not a good idea. After her accident, they found my name and number in her purse. I understand that a concussion has slowed her down and she still has headaches, but I've not had contact with her. My doctor advised me not to try to save her. She was full of drugs and alcohol, and in some ways that was more damaging than the car wreck. I sent word that I would not be coming to see her." Alan paused and looked at Leah, perhaps to see how she was taking all this.

"I read about the accident in the paper. It said she had serious injuries and had been driving very fast at the time of the accident," Leah said.

"She's now in a rehab center in the Chicago area. She still has a friend or two there, but most of the people she hung out with have long since cut ties. My doctor says that sometimes it takes an accident with consequences to wake people up and push them toward recovery. I think Juneau could have benefited from psych care back in high school, but I doubt if Uncle Horace would have accepted the idea. He wasn't one who believed in mental illness. He thought if a person wanted to, they could by sheer force of will make themselves better. I'm free of Juneau now, and it feels good. I sincerely hope she can heal, both physically and mentally, but I can't fix her. I tried that a couple of times, and it didn't work. Now I just have to remember to keep myself healthy, mentally and physically. But enough about me. I really want to know about you, Leah. When you came north in April, you told me about finding your birth family, but you hinted that you were struggling with something then too. I was so full of my own pain that I didn't ask about your life from the time of your being fired until that day you showed up on my doorstep. Do you want to tell me anything at all about that time? I'd like to know, if you care to tell me."

Leah tried to decide if relating her own pain would only serve to open up more wounds for Alan. Maybe, she thought, she could be selective in what she said and still convey what life for her had been like. She was now able to look back and see that many of the so-called trials and tribulations weren't as bad as she had felt they were at the time. Good things had come because of some of them, and she had discovered she could survive loss, grief, pain, and disappointment. She had been blessed to have people help her do that, even though at the time she hadn't realized how therapeutic their words and actions had been for her.

"I suppose I should begin with my firing. I think you know about that. Your uncle was most unkind, but I think I said what I needed to say to him, although I thought of all sorts of things afterward that I might have said. I did experience some real pain with that job loss because I loved what I was doing. And I've already told you about going to meet my birth family and how difficult that was. My youngest brother, Russell, came to live with me, and I learned what having a sibling meant. Harmon also came into my life at an opportune time, and we became even closer than Russell and I had become, probably because Harm and I are so much alike. We think alike, and as many have said, we resemble each other physically. I've got a so-so relationship with Charlene, my sister, but we're working on it. I have a pretty good one now with my oldest brother, Stephen. Gene and I are making progress as father and daughter, but he'll never be my dad. He knows and accepts that, and frankly, I don't think he feels as though I'm really his daughter. I'm not like Charlene. I'm too much like Harmon, with whom he had a stormy relationship until just recently."

Leah stopped and got up to make tea. When the water was boiling, she filled the teapot and sat down once again. "Now we can have a little tea, and I'll hit the hard parts … the parts that involve how I felt about you, Alan. You know, for the first time in my life, I was in love, and I thought you felt the same way. I believed you loved me, but I began to believe that I wasn't as important to you as you were to me. At least that was my assessment after weeks of waiting to hear from you. I guess you were doped up some of that time, but I would have liked to have had a call from you after your marriage to Juneau—maybe not right away … but afterward … to tell me what happened. I began to wonder. Had I been negligent somehow? Had you been giving me a false impression of your relationship with Juneau right from the beginning? It occurred to me that maybe you did have something going on with her. After all, you were living in such close proximity, so it was possible. I was very conflicted, but finally I was able to put you into the back recesses of my mind, at least most of the time. I admit something would happen or someone would say something that reminded me of you, and then I'd have that whole argument with myself once again. Then I'd say to myself, 'Leah, stop it.'"

Leah paused to take a sip of her tea and to hopefully gain the courage to continue what almost felt like a confession. "I think love is hard to kill. It may die little deaths, but the killing blow has to be dramatic, and I never felt that killing blow. Maybe it would have been better if I had. I dated two or three different guys after your marriage but never went on more than one or two dates with any of them before I realized I could never be serious about them. So you see, you had a pretty tight hold on my heart. Getting into social work helped me the most. You can't be a good social worker if you don't develop empathy—not pity … but empathy. After my visit to your cabin, I felt empathy for you. It was so hard to just walk away, but I knew I had to. You know, Alan, I still have deep affection for you, but it's all mixed up with some other stronger feelings. Before I came up to see you, Jack Desmond told me he thought you needed someone to bring you out of your doldrums, or perhaps it was depression. I knew then I couldn't be the one. You had to do that yourself. Social work has taught me that much. But let's not end on a sad note. Here you are with a new life ahead of you, and I couldn't be happier for you."

Alan's head was bent low, and when he raised his eyes, Leah saw the pain she had observed all those months ago in the north woods. She wished now she hadn't said anything. What good was it to rehash the past? If she could have at that moment taken back her words, she would have.

"Oh God, Leah, I'm so sorry. When I said I was sorry a little while ago, it was nothing like the sorrow I feel right now for what I put you through, and yet you're telling me you still care about me and wish me success in my new venture. You ought to be mad as hell at me. I'm glad you're not."

Alan gazed out the kitchen window, silent for a few seconds, and then he returned to their conversation. "Now I have to tell you what else I was going to say, even though it will sound shallow and self-serving. I was actually going to ask you to come and work for me at my new law firm. I could see us doing great things together. I was going to say that maybe if the stars would align just right, we would end up finding we still loved each other. I was even going to tell you that I loved you and wanted to marry you, but I doubt that will fly now. I'm so sorry, so very sorry."

"Alan, don't say sorry anymore. In fact I think I need a hug from you. Remember when I left the cabin? I came back and hugged you. Maybe we both need that hug now, more than we did back then."

Leah rose from her chair and extended her hand to Alan, who hesitated only a moment before rising and embracing her. They stood there, arms around each other, and then Alan pulled away just slightly, looked directly at Leah, and kissed her.

Leah's knees went weak. Alan's arms around her felt so good, so natural, and the kiss was just as she remembered. She gently pulled away, a smile on her face as she said, "I guess we're still friends."

"Friends. Yes, we're friends, but how about exploring this friendship? What would you think about dating? We could go out for dinner on Wednesday maybe?" Alan said with a grin, undoubtedly remembering several Wednesday-night dinner dates in Chicago.

"I suppose it would be all right. We could have long conversations like we used to have and maybe explore Saint Paul. I still haven't done that. I came here and immediately started work, and now my free time is spent fixing up my house or babysitting my stepsisters and my half brother. Dating sounds like fun, so why not?"

Alan was still at Leah's house when Gene and Janet and the girls returned from the amusement park. Cara was full of excitement about the huge roller coaster they had ridden, more than three times apparently. Deanne was more excited about the two boys who had been attentive to her and had followed them around the park. At first Gene had been annoyed, but then he'd seen that it was twelve- and thirteen-year-olds flirting a little and just being twelve and thirteen.

Leah introduced Alan to her family, and because she had never told anyone but Harmon about Alan, they were curious about how they had met. It was easy to just say they had worked at the same law firm and now he was opening a practice in Saint Paul.

After Gene and his family had gone home, Alan asked Leah, "Would you have dinner with me tonight? Maybe afterward I could take you to see the new law office and the apartment. You might be able to give me some ideas about furnishings and even some of the finishing work that's still to be completed. I'd love to have you see the space and get your reaction."

"If I don't have to dress up too much, the answer is yes. I'd love to come, especially to see your new office and home. It must be exciting to be stepping out on your own, especially after being part of such a large firm. Or is it a little scary? I know I was anxious my first weeks at the agency, but that soon passed."

"You're right; I am a little anxious, but I think it will only make me try extra hard to do things right and make my dream come true. You know I wanted to do this way back when, but Uncle Horace influenced me to come work with him. That wasn't really where my heart was. Okay, let's go. You look fine as you are, but if you want to change, I'll wait right here."

In less than fifteen minutes Alan and Leah were on their way to a little restaurant Alan had heard about. It was quiet, and the decor was pleasing, but most importantly, the food was good. They lingered over coffee and tiny complimentary cookies with an anise flavor that they both thought tasted wonderful.

"Let's go inspect my soon-to-be office," Alan said. "It isn't far. Please be honest about what you see, and if there's something glaringly wrong, say so. It's not too late to change even some of the inside structural things like walls and counters." Alan was serious about his wish for feedback, so Leah promised she would do her best to be honest in her evaluation.

A new front door led into a hallway, and immediately to the left, another door opened into a large office space. Still another door in the hallway was the entrance to a stairwell that Alan said led to his apartment, but they inspected the office area first.

"Oh, Alan, it's so spacious, and I suspect quite bright and light with that bank of windows. I can picture chairs and a long coffee table perhaps, and of course over there is the area where the receptionist will have her desk. Am I right?" Leah asked.

"Exactly. My office is through that door. Come and take a look."

Alan's office appeared to be completely finished, with two walls of bookshelves and a window seat in front of a long, just-above-head-high window that let in lots of light but would keep those walking by from being able to see into the room. The ceiling was slanted upward to the windows and was lower where the bookshelves were. Leah thought it was a nice touch that worked well.

"I like the windows," she said, "because they make the room seem larger than it is." Alan pointed out where his desk would be and where clients would sit. Then he took her through an almost-invisible door. It led to a work area with built-in shelves and room for a good-size table.

"There's no furniture yet, but I have a line on some things from a defunct business. Some pieces they have will fit in here quite well, and I don't want to give an impression of opulence, so secondhand will work for me. Now I want you to see where I'll live."

Alan led the way up the stairs, which were wide and long. He said he planned to install a chair elevator and a dumbwaiter in an area next to the stairs. The floor of the first room they entered on the second floor was covered with tarps.

"What room is this? I can't quite see what you have in mind, but it looks like a tray ceiling being installed. I can imagine it will be beautiful when it's finished." Leah was studying the area with a critical eye.

"This is the formal dining room, and to the left is the kitchen. All the cabinetry is ordered and should be here next week. The dumbwaiter will lift groceries up to the kitchen. I didn't show you the back entrance. I'll save that for daylight. Through here is the living room. It goes most of the way across the back of the building and overlooks my garden."

"You have a garden? That sounds wonderful. I suppose it's too dark to see that tonight."

"Yes, it is, and you wouldn't see anything of it in the daylight either because right now it's a mass of weeds and junk. Someone is coming Monday to clear it out, and then it will be fenced and landscaped, but not until spring. It's quite a large area, which is one of the things that I liked about the property.

But there's more. That door leads to the bedroom wing. There's room for three or four bedrooms and for three full baths and lots of closets. The office space below isn't as large as the space up here. The apartment extends over a shop that houses a tax-and-bookkeeping firm. Now that I own the building, they will be paying rent to me. All the upstairs area can be devoted to my living space if I wish. I plan to leave part of it unfinished for now, except for walls and flooring and of course insulation. Time will tell what's to be done with it."

They walked into the area Alan had been describing, and Leah was blown away by the sheer size of it. Some walls had been knocked down already, and in one area, a new wall was taking shape. Chalk lines helped her visualize the room sizes.

"I believe you'll have more square footage here than most houses in Saint Paul. It isn't quite as big as your Uncle Horace's house, but it's close," Leah said.

"Oh, it's not close at all. You never did see the whole house. Maybe you should drive down with me next week when I have a meeting with the lawyers who are probating Uncle's will. He was richer than old Midas himself, so it's taking a long time to collect and catalog his assets. The lawyers will get a big chunk out of the estate for all their work, but it's worth it to me not to have to deal with it. I just sign the papers, of course reading them over before I do. There have been no buyers for the house so far. You can imagine why it's such a white elephant ... all that Victorian decor and the old-world-style rooms with their dark wood and mullioned windows. It's scary to go in there now. Juneau was living there before her accident, but she's been told she can't go back. Of course she'll be in rehab for a long time, but the main reason is that some work will have to be done before the house finally sells. How did this subject creep in? Tell me, Leah: What do you think about my new acquisition? Is it going to be a good place to live and work, or have I missed something?"

"It looks great, Alan. The space downstairs is especially nice, and it should be a good location. You're right in the middle of some already-thriving businesses. Upstairs is harder to visualize, but the size alone should give you more than enough space. I realize you've been used to having big rooms and lots of them, so I think this will suit you well. Yes, I think it will be just fine."

"But would it be a good place for a family and for children? What do you think?" Alan asked, looking out over the vast empty space and not at Leah.

"Oh, it should be a very good place for a family. I don't know where the schools are, but the neighborhood reminds me of where I grew up in Hyde Park. We lived right on the edge of a thriving business district, and I loved it, though I suppose it's not everyone's cup of tea." Leah could have said more but decided not to. Anyway, it was time to go home. It was almost midnight.

Alan took Leah home and walked her to her front door. Then, with his hand on her shoulder as she was inserting her key into the lock, he said, "I had a wonderful time today, and I'm looking forward to tomorrow. You mentioned going to church. I guess I'm ready for that, although I've only been twice since Easter. I suppose I'm still a little bit mad at God, but I'll be here to pick you up at nine thirty, and after church we'll have lunch and then look at my new building in the cold, hard light of day. I do want you to see the open space in the back that will become a garden and playground. Maybe you could give me some ideas about what could be done back there."

"Oh, Alan, I've never in my life had a garden. My mother and I tried to grow a few things on the windowsill, both inside and outside, but not with much success, so I'm not the one to ask. Maybe Gene could give you some pointers. You can ask him when you see him again."

"Does that mean we'll be seeing them soon? I don't think they realize our history. At least it didn't seem like they did. I'd very much like to get to know your father ... your birth father. I adore his baby son, Kerry, so yes, I hope you'll invite me to go with you to see them sometime soon. But now, good night, lovely Leah, until tomorrow." Alan leaned over and kissed Leah's forehead and then stepped off the porch and into his car parked in her driveway. There he turned and waved as he backed out and drove away.

Leah was having a difficult time believing the sort of day she had just experienced. Alan's sudden appearance was a wonderful surprise, but she was not ready to entertain thoughts that things might turn out better for them this time around.

Chapter 34

Sunday went as well as Saturday had; at least Leah thought so when the day was over and she was alone in her little house. She still found it hard to believe that Alan was back in her life. Their so-called engagement had been so long ago, and she had tried very hard to put him out of her mind. Now here he was, back in her life and hinting, hinting strongly, that they should rekindle what they'd once had. Would it work? She was hopeful yet not willing to be swayed by the wonderful two days they had spent together. Each day they had been in each other's company from morning until nearly midnight. Now Alan would be away until Friday, attending to Horace Marsden's affairs and trying to decide what esthetic changes he might make to the mansion that would appeal to potential buyers.

On Monday Leah drove to work and was soon fully engaged with several clients. Later in the day she made a call on a formerly homeless young mother and her baby for whom she had recently found housing.

That night Leah planned to go to bed early since she had been sleep deprived on the previous two nights. At nine o'clock she was already in her nightgown and was brushing her teeth when her phone rang.

"Hello. This is Leah."

"Hello, Leah. This is Alan. I miss you. I'm staying at the mansion tonight, and it's like a tomb. The caretaker and his wife live here, but they're downstairs and on the other side of the house, so I don't see or hear them. We made progress today, so maybe I'll get out of here on Wednesday or Thursday if things move along as well tomorrow. What was your day like?"

"Busy but satisfying," Leah said. Then she went on to give Alan a rundown of her activities. "I'm surprised you're at the mansion and not out with old friends. You haven't been gone for that long that they'll have forgotten you. I'll bet you could call any of them and have a nice chat and catch up with each other." Leah hadn't expected to hear from Alan, so she was almost tongue-tied, something unusual for her, but she was pleased that he had called.

Alan chuckled. "There isn't really anyone from the firm or any old friends whom I'd care to spend time with. As you know, I was a hermit for a long time, so being by myself isn't such a big deal, but I do miss you. I wish you were here. We could talk about the Northwestern game last Saturday. They won you know. It would be fun to go to a game together once again, maybe when they play Minnesota."

"Are you in your old rooms, or is there some sort of fancy guest room where you're staying while you're there?" Leah asked.

"I'm in my old room. I'm thinking about bringing my king bed back to Saint Paul with me. What do you think about crating up some of the lovely Victorian pieces for my living area? Would you like a chair or two?"

Leah could hear a muffled laugh. "That would be lovely, Alan ... just lovely," Leah answered with a hint of sarcasm.

"You have a sick sense of humor, Ms. Anderly. I'll never have anything Victorian. What about you? Is there anything I can bring you from Uncle Horace's house?" More chuckling.

"I think not, although there were some nice paintings in your old sitting room. They were more pastoral and not especially Victorian, but I seem to remember they too were rather dark, so no thanks. I'm happy with American secondhand, even from the 1950s. I've got a chrome stool right out of that era."

They talked for forty-five minutes, and finally Alan said he'd better let her get some sleep since she'd had two late nights over the weekend. "Good night, Leah, sleep well."

"Good night to you too, Alan. Maybe I'll see you on the weekend?"

"Or before. Count on it. Good night again."

Leah smiled, stretched, and climbed into bed. Her teeth had had only a quick brushing, but she'd make up for it in the morning.

Alan called again on Tuesday night, and their conversation extended to an hour. On Wednesday he reported that he would be flying back to the Cities late Thursday, so he wanted her to save Friday night for a "hot date." She questioned him about what a "hot date" involved, but he refused to answer, saying only that she should wait and see.

Friday's schedule for Leah began with a breakfast meeting and went from there to other meetings. It was peanut butter on crackers with a Coke at her desk for lunch, followed by a visit to the hospital to see a new mother and baby whose release was scheduled for three o'clock. That meant she would be delivering them to one of the five foster homes the agency now had. New mothers and their babies could spend up to three months in such a home. It was something new, and so far it seemed to be working well.

It was after five when she finally drove into her garage. She wondered if Alan had gotten back from Evanston as planned last evening, and if so, when she could expect to hear from him. As she got out of the car, Alan's Jeep pulled in right behind her. He jumped out and called to her, "Hey, you were working late. Sorry I didn't phone, but my cell went dead, and I have no phone service at the new office or apartment as yet, although that's on the agenda for next week. Are you ready for our hot date?" Alan smiled as he came into the garage and stood right in front of Leah, blocking the path to her door.

"I've been wondering all day what this so-called hot date could be. Can you enlighten me when we get inside?" Leah asked as she closed the car door. Alan was still standing right in front of her, grinning mischievously, which made her smile as well. "Well? Aren't you going to say anything?" she asked.

"Not at the moment. The hot date has to start with a hug, and we'll see where it goes from there." He pulled Leah into his arms, and they rocked back and forth, laughing as they almost lost their balance in the confined area of the garage. Alan held Leah at arm's length, looked into her eyes, and then kissed her. Her purse slid down her arm and fell to the floor of the garage.

"We'll get that in a minute. Now you can use both arms. I think I'd like that," Alan said.

"I should warn you, Alan, this is probably as hot as our date is going to get." Then she kissed him, and they shared another longish hug.

"Okay, okay. Let's go inside and talk about dinner. After that I want you to see my building again. A lot was done in my absence. It's amazing what five full days of work can do. I hope you'll like it. I'm excited about what's been accomplished. I thought we might have a little picnic, so I bought a card table and two chairs today, and we can pick up Chinese or something from the deli if you'd like. Are you okay with a picnic on the fifth of November?"

"It sounds great, but I need to change into tennies and jeans. Or is this hot date a formal affair?"

Alan said that it was definitely not formal and just to make a point he gestured to his own jeans, Northwestern sweatshirt, and tennies.

They decided to go with Chinese, as Alan said, in honor of the two times they had enjoyed that sort of meal when they'd worked late at the firm.

Leah preceded Alan into the dining room, where she saw a card table with a purple tablecloth and, in the center, a small bouquet of flowers. Also on the table were two place settings of some very elegant china, as well as knives, forks, and spoons that appeared to be sterling silver.

"This is lovely. But where did the dishes and silverware come from?" asked Leah, inspecting the blade of the knife and seeing that it was indeed sterling silver.

"I raided Uncle Horace's china cabinet. Actually, these were stored in boxes in the big pantry behind the kitchen. I think his first wife had these, and I suspect when he married Estelle she didn't want them around, so they were packed away. I made a note for the estate people, telling them I was taking a set of dishes and some silverware that had not been used in years. One of the lawyers who's working on the settling of the estate was there, and I showed him the boxes that contained the dishes and the silverware. They were all covered in dust, and I managed to put in some old cracked pieces the help used back in the day when there was a full staff. He looked inside and saw the cracked pieces on top and said I should take it since it wasn't worth anything anyway. So I did. I grabbed two of the nice plates and enough silverware for us and managed to put them in my suitcase. The rest will be shipped on Monday. So I will have fine china to dine upon ... enough to serve twenty-four people!"

"I suppose there's so much other china and silver that it wouldn't be missed, even if they had known of its existence, and why not have something of your aunt and uncle's? But twenty-four place settings? When will you ever entertain that many people?"

"I think you have at least that many relatives from what you've told me, so if I should ever want to invite them all, I'd have enough dishes to do it. Or the neighbors could be invited in for a housewarming. I suspect there could be multiple occasions for the use of these plates and spoons. Now let's eat before this gets cold."

After the meal Alan once again served as tour guide and proudly showed Leah some of the new additions, including the showers, tubs, and sinks that had been delivered earlier in the week for all the bathrooms. The kitchen had also taken shape to a degree. It was easier to see where the cupboards would be hung. The cabinets were out of their crates but not installed, but soon it would really look like a kitchen. The area seemed larger to Leah than it had on her first visit, but maybe it was the lighting that made the difference. All the overhead lights were in and, when turned on, lit up the large open area.

"Not much has been done in the bedrooms," Alan said as they walked into that wing, "but I decided since the king bed at the mansion was mine, bought and paid for, I would have it packed up and put on the truck with the dishes. All my law books were in boxes in one of the rooms back in Evanston, so they will be included, as well as some clothing and gear still in my old rooms. I'll have plenty of space here to store it until everything is finished."

"When do you think that will be?" Leah asked.

"Maybe February, but I'm not holding my breath. If it's done before spring, I'll be happy. So what do you think? Is it shaping up all right? Honest opinion, Leah."

"Absolutely. It's going to be grand. I wish it wasn't dark, so I could see the garden. Didn't you tell me they were going to clean everything out back there?"

"Yes, it's been done, but now it looks so bare. The fence can't go in until after any furniture is delivered, because the truck will need to drive into the alley and use the back stairs. Anyway, it'll soon be cold, and the ground will freeze, and they won't be able to do a good job of digging in the posts. It isn't critical to have a fence yet, as there are no little Parkins to keep fenced in, and the vegetable garden can't be started until May." Alan was grinning.

"You're really looking ahead, aren't you? And I don't mean to May for putting in the garden. Well, if we've seen everything, maybe we should clean up, and you can take me home. Oh, I guess we can't do dishes with no water. Or is there water somewhere?" Leah looked around, but of course the kitchen and the bathrooms were not yet hooked up to the water supply.

"I'll take them down to the office area tomorrow. The bathroom there is finished, and there's water. I'll take you home now, but would you give me a cup of tea before I head back to my lonely little efficiency?"

"I'll give you a cup of tea and chocolate brownies to go with it."

Over brownies and tea Alan said he really wanted to have a serious discussion but maybe it should be put off for another day. He looked at Leah for some guidance.

"If it's serious, maybe we should go ahead and talk about whatever it is. Tell me what's on your mind."

"I want to talk about us, Leah. The day I first came to your door I told you I had wanted to ask you to marry me, and I still want to do that. Is it too soon? Are you ready to commit to forever till death parts us? I am. In fact it's on my mind when I wake up in the morning and when I go to sleep at night. Can we talk about that? You know that I love you, but I guess I'm not sure you have the same feelings for me."

"I do love you, Alan. But … I don't know what it is … Something keeps me from saying what you want to hear. I really don't know what it is. I too think about spending my life with you. You know we made that commitment to each other once before, and maybe that's the reason I hesitate. Will something happen again to tear us apart? It's not you or anything from the past. I wish I could tell you what it is. Let me say that I'll think long and hard to try to reason out what is holding me back. This feeling isn't based on anything you've said or done, but it's there, and I'd better figure it out, because I want to say yes but I can't, not yet. Will you be patient with me until next weekend?"

Leah was so conflicted, which surprised her. Alan had never left her thoughts completely, even when things had looked bleak for their ever getting together again. Now that the obstacles had been cleared away, she was unsure. Something was stopping her, and she didn't know what it was.

"I'm not a patient person I'm afraid, but yes, I'll wait until you figure out what's stopping you from saying yes. I think I have an idea what's behind this, but until you can figure it out in your own mind and we can discuss it, I don't want to assume anything."

"I'll be in Rochester for three days for a seminar, but I probably won't call you. I'll have a tight schedule, and you'll be busy getting your practice off the ground. I'm so proud of you, Alan. I hope you know that."

"I do, and I appreciate it, but now I'd better go so you can start working on what's keeping you from saying yes to me. A hug and a kiss would be nice to send me on my way." Alan smiled and rose, put on his coat, and then put out a hand to Leah. She took it, and they stood there for almost a minute in a tight embrace. Then Alan put his hand under her chin and leaned down and kissed her. Leah felt her knees go weak again, which seemed to happen whenever Alan kissed her. She walked to the door with him and waved as he pulled out of the driveway and into the street.

What's the matter with you, Leah? She scolded herself. *Alan wants to marry you, and you have some sort of feeling that you can't identify, and so you don't say yes, even though you know very well you're dying to say yes. What* is *the matter with you?*

Leah prepared for bed and then gathered a change of clothing for her trip to Rochester. She was to pick up Louise Longmire at the agency in the morning to drive together to the three-day event. They would both be presenting papers. Before turning out the light, she ran over her notes to be sure she was ready.

The conference was filled with activities and lectures, and at noon on the third day they finished with a luncheon and a speaker who talked about how important a good donor base was to any agency. This was something Leah's boss had been struggling with. Finding donors who would contribute on a regular basis was an ongoing problem. Leah jotted down some of the presented ideas she thought they might try back in Saint Paul at the Interfaith Mission Agency. She arrived home a little before five, made a sandwich and some tea, and sat down to think about Alan. Then it was almost as though a lightbulb turned on in her head. She knew immediately what was bothering her.

She called him. "Hello, Alan. Are you busy right now, or can I ask you a couple of questions?"

"I'm not busy, but good news: I signed up my first client. He's gone now, and I'm about ready to go off to my lonely little efficiency, so ask away."

"I know you are a beneficiary of your uncle's estate, and I presume you received a substantial amount of money from him. I'm guessing you used some of that to buy the building and do the renovation. I guess my question is, if we were to be married, would we be living on Uncle Horace's largesse? Could we, between the two of us, make enough money to pay for the building and the upkeep and still have some left over for food and clothing and whatever else we might need or want, or will Uncle Horace be an ever-present specter in our lives? This probably sounds like a silly question, but I just wanted to know." Leah had no idea what kind of response she would receive. Alan might be offended that she had asked about money, but she needed an answer to her question.

"My dear Miss Anderly, you should never presume. Presuming gets you into a lot of trouble, and your presumptions might not even be anywhere near the truth. I did not use one cent of Uncle Horace's money. The only thing I have taken away from his estate are those stupid dishes we used the other evening, and right now I'm thinking about shipping them back when they arrive. I had a feeling you were perturbed about Uncle's money, but I thought you needed to figure this out for yourself. I do not intend to use my part of the inheritance for anything except philanthropy. I'll tell you later about what I have in mind, but first you need to know that the money I used came from my father's estate. It had been kept in a trust account that I was not able to access until I reached the age of thirty. I think my father was very wise, and I'm grateful now for his wisdom. If I had the use of that money when I was married to Juneau, she might well have depleted the amount by half, or I might have tried to buy her off with it. I'm glad I didn't have access to the money until now. Am I right? You're uncomfortable with Uncle's money playing a big role in my life and ultimately yours?"

"Yes, that's it! I figured it out this afternoon, so that's why I called you. Oh, I'm so glad to hear what you just told me. It makes a big difference. Maybe it shouldn't have, but I guess I'm still angry about being fired and being told I wasn't good enough for you. I ought to have gotten over that long ago, but sometimes it's hard to let go of anger when it impacts your life in so many ways. The other thing is, I still have some of Uncle Horace's money. I used a good chunk of it for tuition, food, and clothing and then for the down payment on my house. I didn't like doing it, but it wasn't given to me to make me comfortable or better off financially. It was what I called blood money, so I somehow thought it was different. Was it different, or am I guilty of doing what I thought you were doing?"

"Oh, Leah, it's not the same at all. You used that money well. The old scoundrel didn't hold it over your head like he did with me. He was always saying if I wasn't happy with my life in his house or if I didn't want to do my part in the firm, he would cut me off. I was foolish enough not to see through his threats. At last though, I saw him as he was and had always been. When Colin was taken away, I asked Uncle to help me get him back, and he flatly refused, telling me it was for the best. I think I alluded to that when we talked up at the cabin. I don't know if he could have done anything, but his refusal told me volumes about him. He was interested only in appearances and in his own self-image in the community, so to make public my fight for Colin, Juneau's colored child, wasn't something he was willing to do. That's when I decided I didn't want any of his money. It's different with you. You earned every penny he gave you. So now will you say yes to my proposal of marriage? You did the first time I asked, so I'm hoping you will once again be willing to cast your lot with me."

"I'll give you a firm answer on Friday night. Why don't you come over for dinner at six? We won't go out, but I'll fix Crock-Pot stew for you. We'll have entertainment of some sort and make an evening of it." Then Leah hung up. She smiled as she wondered what Alan would think about that.

It seemed to Leah that the rest of the week just dragged by. It was undoubtedly because Friday was when she would say yes or no to Alan. She already knew her answer, but she wanted to be sure she did it properly. Thursday night she prepared everything for their meal. She cut the meat and vegetables for the stew and stored them in the refrigerator. The Crock-Pot stood on the counter along with the spices that she planned to put into the stew. The sauce was in a container in the refrigerator, as well as what she needed to make a nice salad. The lemon-curd bars were cooling, and she had set out plates and silverware for their evening meal. Everything was ready. "But am I? Yes, I think so." She prepared for bed and crawled under the covers, snuggling down with a smile on her face. Sleep was not as elusive as some nights, and in a matter of minutes Leah was in dreamland.

Chapter 35

Leah was able to leave work a little earlier than usual on Friday, so she was home well before five o'clock. She set the table with the dishes she had taken out of the cupboard the previous evening. A small bowl of flowers from the grocery store deli section graced the table. She stood back and admired her work. *Not too much but just right,* she thought, including the aroma of the stew that permeated the whole house. She changed clothes and came downstairs just as the clock struck six. Alan was due any minute. She was ready.

The doorbell sounded, and Leah opened the door. Alan was smiling a huge smile and had a boatload of yellow roses in his arms. She almost melted on the spot. He still remembered they were her favorite flowers! "Come in," she said, stepping aside so he could enter, almost buried in roses.

"Ah, beef stew. There's nothing like that smell to tantalize the senses. Can I put these down somewhere so I can give you a hug?"

Leah took the flowers and found a very large container that would hold all of them, and she set them on the kitchen counter. She put her nose into the midst of them. They smelled wonderful!

"Alan, I want to ask you something. Did you leave one yellow rose in front of my door last New Year's Eve? There was no name on the card, but I couldn't imagine anyone else who could have done it. I was angry at first because it reminded me of what had not happened the previous New Year's Eve. But over time I saw it as maybe a symbol of your regret or even as a sort of apology." Leah wondered how Alan would respond.

"I suppose I shouldn't have done it, but I was leaving Chicago the next day, and somehow I wanted to … Oh, I don't know what I wanted to do. If you had been at home, well, maybe things might have turned out differently. I guess it was my way of bowing gracefully out of your life, or so I thought. I'm sorry if it made you angry. I suppose I didn't think about your reaction … typical Alan at that point. I was only thinking of myself. Can we forget that little episode? Please?"

"Absolutely. As I said, I got over it, so it's in the past." Leah touched Alan's cheek.

Alan put his arms around Leah and gave her a hug. Her face was buried in his neck, and like many times before, she could smell his aftershave and feel how smooth his cheek was. He had obviously shaved only minutes before coming over. She pulled back, looked at him, smiled, and kissed him. It was the first time in a very long while that she had been the initiator of a kiss.

"Well, that was a great welcome," he said. "I have a feeling this is going to be a special night. In fact, unless there's something burning in the oven, let's sit down on the sofa. I have something on my mind, and I think you know what it is."

Alan took Leah's hand and led her to the sofa, where they sat, very close to each other. He turned to her and said, "Leah, will you be my wife? Will you please say yes? It's something I want with all my heart."

"Alan, my answer is yes, and I too want it with all my heart. I was going to say a few other things, but what you said to me says it all, so I'm saying it right back to you."

"I have something I want to give you." Alan reached into his inside coat pocket and drew out a small box. It was covered in blue velvet, and Leah knew immediately that it must be a ring. She hadn't given a thought to a ring, but obviously Alan had. He opened the box and carefully took hold of the ring.

With his other hand he took hers, and then he placed the ring on her finger. It was a perfect fit.

"Oh, Alan, it's beautiful. I didn't think about a ring at all. I love it. You must have gotten busy this week, and I think it shows you were pretty sure of my answer. Oh, I love it. I love it!"

"No, Leah, I didn't get busy this week and pick out this ring. I've had this ring for a very long time. I bought it in Philadelphia the week after … after we decided to get married. When things didn't work out, I put it in a safe place and kept it all this time, so this ring has a history. It was in my dresser drawer up at the lake cabin the whole time you were there with me, and I've carried it around a few times when we went out together, thinking maybe the right time would present itself. I never felt the right time had come, but now this is definitely the right time."

Leah was blown away to think that Alan had had the ring all this while. If she had known about its existence, she would have assumed that he would have returned it when it had been apparent they wouldn't be married. She told Alan what she had just been thinking.

"But, Leah, I couldn't return it. There's an engraving inside. Take a look."

Leah slipped the ring off her finger and held it up to the light, and there she saw "LA&AP 4EVER."

"How do you like my clever way to get more for less on the engraving? You know, it meant something to me to have that ring. I would bring it out and look at it when I was down in the dumps, though somehow it didn't really make me feel a whole lot better. Yet the fact that I still had it made me think that maybe someday I would be able to do and say the right things and put this ring where it belonged. Now that time has come, and you've said yes. More than anything, I'd like to curl up with you right here on the couch and hold you tight, but I suppose the stew will dry up or something if we don't eat some of it. I am a little bit hungry, believe it or not."

Leah took Alan's hand and together they put the food on the table and enjoyed their meal, although afterward Leah couldn't remember the taste of anything she had consumed. As soon as they had cleaned up the dishes, Leah led Alan to the sunporch, turning on the stereo on the way. Dance music started to play. She put her hand on Alan's shoulder, and they began to dance. "I wanted to remind you of our dancing together the night you proposed to me. It just seemed like the thing to do tonight, to dance together."

"You're a romantic, Leah, and I look forward to many more dances with you, but now let's sit down on the couch and make plans for our wedding." As soon as they were seated, Alan said, "How about next weekend? Getting a license doesn't take long, and I think the waiting period is only a couple of days. I can check it out tomorrow. Remember we always said we wanted a small wedding with no fuss. We can do it, Leah ... next weekend."

"Whoa. I have a family that would probably disown me if I did what you're suggesting. I agree that simple is the way to go, but I'll have to invite Gene and Janet and the kids, plus Harm and Katy. And there's Charlene and Roger, Russ and Reba down in Chicago, and Steve and Connie. Don't you want to let your mother know? She should be invited to come, and what about your brothers? It's never too late to try to mend fences with a rather benign invitation to a wedding. What do you think?"

"You're not very realistic if you think my mother and brothers are going to fall into my arms after all this time. I don't think they'll come," Alan said, shaking his head.

"You could try. I have a great idea. Let's get married on December 31, just as we planned once before. It's not that far off, and we could have a small reception or a meal maybe. How's that big space in your apartment coming along? Could we do it there? You've got all those dishes you know." Leah had a wicked grin on her face.

Alan grabbed her and buried his face into her neck. "You're a planner and a schemer, aren't you? Well, maybe we could do

329

what you suggest, but I really don't want to wait that long. If we could get married tonight that would be my choice. You're so delectable I can't seem to think about anything except the two of us becoming one, but I suppose New Year's Eve makes sense. We'll make it work."

Leah couldn't stop smiling and snuggling in Alan's arms. She was truly happy, for the first time in so long. Or was this the joy her mother had talked about? Leah remembered one of the many John Denver songs her mother had loved and played over and over. It was called "Matthew," and one line said, "It was joy that he was raised on." Yes, she had been raised on joy, and here, with Alan, she had found another manifestation of joy.

Chapter 36

The wedding celebration had gone on longer than planned, and by the time the newlyweds left Saint Paul to drive north, the sun had dropped quickly into the western sky, leaving only a hint of light.

"I thought we'd never get out of there," Alan said. "You have too many relatives. To see them all together at one time is mind-boggling. I'm happy you have family, something I really don't have, and I'm sure I'll get to know and love them as you do, but I wanted to be on the way north an hour ago."

"I know you did. Sorry, but the McGregor clan is a gregarious bunch, and it's hard to get away from a gathering where they're all present. As for loving them all, I'm still working on that, so don't feel bad if that's a work in progress for you. I was really blown away when they all showed up, even two of Marcene's sisters. Sorry to say, there were a couple of cousins whose names I couldn't remember, having only met them briefly once before, that day after Thanksgiving when I showed up unexpectedly and Marcene threw a huge party to celebrate. I think one of them is the fellow who asked me if I remembered him, informing me that we had taken a bath together."

Alan laughed as he pictured Leah's surprise and then her embarrassment at the suggestion that the bath should have been a memorable moment for her.

"But, Alan, weren't you pleased that your mother and her husband came and your brother Ted? They seemed to be happy to see you, so I'd say that was a good thing."

"Yes, I guess so. But one day of being there doesn't make up for years of not being there. One thing I learned, though, is to never tell you something can't be done. I don't know what you said to my mother to get her to come to the wedding, but she was full of good things to say about you. Are you going to tell me, or is this really something you're going to go to the grave with, as you said? I'm glad they came, whether on false pretenses or not, so thank you, Leah."

"I didn't use false pretenses! What do you mean by that? I'd never say anything that wasn't God's truth. I just told them what a wonderful man you were and that you're one of the best lawyers in the state of Minnesota. I also told her that she could be sure of becoming a grandmother, probably before the end of this new year that we will celebrate tomorrow. She's not happy her sons haven't married and produced grandchildren."

"Well then, we'll have to work on making my mother happy, won't we?"

Chapter 37

The roads to Alan's cabin were clean and clear. They stopped half an hour into the trip to fill the Jeep with gas and to get soft drinks to take with them. Once they were back in the car, it seemed as though they had run out of conversation, and each of them sat quietly, enjoying the star-studded night and the newly fallen snow from the previous afternoon.

Alan broke the silence. "Leah, I haven't told you this before, but I've wanted to for some time now. I think until these last two months I was afraid something might happen to prevent our marriage, so I didn't want to tempt fate. Silly, isn't it?"

Leah turned in her seat to observe Alan's profile. He seemed to have on his serious face. She couldn't imagine what he was planning to say to her.

"You know, when you were on your way north and stopped in, I was so shocked to see you standing on my porch. I think I did say that to you at one point or another. Well, after you left, it took me most of the following week to realize that not only was your coming to see me a shock but also a wonderful surprise. Somehow I hadn't been able to articulate that. I had too much garbage in my life then, so I said nothing at all to you. I'm convinced that the snowstorm was a gift from God because we were able to talk as we had done so many times before, and for the first time I managed to share the whole story of Juneau, of Uncle, and of course Colin, as well as everything that went south for me and really for both of us."

Alan looked over at Leah as he finished his sentence and then continued, "When you got into your car to leave, I felt a sadness overtake me. But then you got out of the car and came to give me a hug, and for the first time in months a ray of hope surged inside me. Maybe I even felt a bit of that joy you talk about. You were not shutting the door on me! In fact you were keeping it open, telling me that I was still important to you. At that moment something jumped inside of me, which is the only way I can explain it. In the next couple of weeks I ran everything over in my mind that we had said and done over those few days, and after a particularly soul-searching night when I couldn't sleep, I decided I would start making my way back. And that's what I did. It took me a long while, longer than I thought it would. But thank you for coming to save me, Leah."

Leah put her hand on Alan's shoulder. She couldn't speak, because there was a lump in her throat and tears in her eyes.

The rest of the trip was spent reliving that little bit of time together but not dwelling on it. Instead they began to plan what they hoped their life would be like as husband and wife. Alan said, "I hope you might come to love my cabin as much I do. I'd like it to be our retreat from the world and the place where we will bring our children, who I hope would look forward to spending time there as I used to when my dad brought me up to this area. Is it a place you could learn to love as I do?"

"I love it already, Alan, but you do need to get that stairway to the loft built before any little Parkins come along."

Alan laughed and promised it would be on the to-do list, along with walls and a door for the bathroom and bedroom.

When they arrived at the cabin, someone had shoveled the driveway, and the steps to the house were also swept clean.

"Must have been Frank who came over to take of the snow," Alan said. "I was expecting that we might have to do a little shoveling, but it looks like we can go right in. Shall we grab as much of the luggage as we can carry, and then I'll come back out and bring in what's left?" Alan opened the back of the Jeep and lifted out several suitcases.

"What's in that big box? It must have already been in the Jeep because I don't remember seeing you load it when we were packing up," Leah said as she picked up several items to carry into the cabin. Alan unlocked the door and came back to pick up everything else, except the box, which was too large to hoist without freeing both hands.

"Just leave it," he said. "It's a surprise for later that I think you'll enjoy. Let's go in and see if Frank and Mary left us some sandwiches as they planned to do."

Alan cranked up the thermostat. He had installed a propane floor furnace sometime during the summer, and the cabin was no longer dependent upon heat from the fireplace and the small pellet stove in the kitchen area. It was soon warm inside, and they sat down to ham-and-Swiss sandwiches and a delicious gelatin salad that contained pineapple and cottage cheese. Leah remembered having something similar at the party Marcene had thrown for her. *Must be a Minnesota specialty,* she thought.

"Now, my beautiful bride, I'm going to call Frank to let him know we've arrived, and then I shall unveil the surprise. I'm going to need your help, but first the call."

"Hello, you old reprobate, we're home … Thanks, and thank you for the lovely repast that we just enjoyed and for cleaning the driveway. The timing should be about right to set the plan in motion, so if you can call a few people who can pass the word around, that would be great. It'll take us about thirty minutes to get started, so that gives you time … Right, Frank … Okay, sure. We'd love to. Until tomorrow."

"What was that all about? And what's happening tomorrow?"

"New Year's dinner with Frank and Mary. But right now we have work to do. Get your boots on and your coat and hat and whatever you need to keep warm. We're going out in the elements. It's not so cold, but we might be out there for almost an hour. Who knows?" Alan was being very mysterious and still hadn't revealed his surprise.

Leah was puzzled but finally said, "All right, I may as well do as you say. Is this already part of the love, honor, and obey that I agreed to?" Leah grinned mischievously but began pulling on her boots.

"You know very well that there was no obey in our vows, but I do need your help because, my dear wife, we are going to tell the world, or maybe only the people living along the lake, that something earthshaking is happening. It's not just the end of the old year and the beginning of a new one; it's our announcement that the two of us are beginning a new life together, right along with the New Year. There's a ton of fireworks in that box, so let's get out there and start lighting up the sky!"

Leah was speechless. Fireworks for her wedding! She would never have thought, even in her wildest dreams, that she would have fireworks to celebrate her marriage. But she loved it! Some of her fondest memories included trips to Navy Pier in Chicago to watch the Fourth of July display, and there had been fireworks on the two occasions when she had attended Chicago White Sox evening games. She had always loved fireworks, and now she would be able to help Alan set them off, and they could enjoy the show together.

They carried the box down to the lakeshore, and Alan took out huge rockets and set them up in the sand. There was almost no snow along the shore, so it made preparations relatively easy. After fussing with the rocket launcher, Alan assured Leah that everything was set, and he was ready to launch the first rocket. At a minute past midnight, a starburst rocket soared into the sky, exploding in a fiery red-white-and-blue spectacular blossom. Leah oohed and aahed, and Alan just grinned. One after another the fuses were lit. Alan encouraged Leah to light several of them but cautioned her to be careful. The last pyrotechnic displays were the best: a series of umbrella-like explosive blossoms, followed by three or four loud booms that echoed across the lake and then several more umbrella-like bursts that sent out brilliant white showers and sparks that continued to drop from each one for almost a full minute. Then it was dark. The show was over.

Leah almost knocked Alan over when she threw herself into his arms. "Oh, Alan, what a gift, what a fabulous, glorious, beautiful wedding gift! I love you!"

"And I love you. Remember that time, eons ago, when we had planned to be married, come hell or high water, a phrase I think I used more than once? Well, there was no high water, but we each went through our own hell. Yet we've managed to come through it, and as I said a little while ago, I've found that joy you talked about. You are my joy and my true better half. Now let's go get warm shall we? It's chilly out here, but I know a very warm place back at the cabin. Come on, wife. Let's begin our honeymoon!"

Epilogue

Carter Lake, Minnesota, Weekly Sentinel
Thursday, October 30

Mr. and Mrs. Alan Parkin are the parents of
twins, a boy and a girl, born October 20,
in Saint Paul, Minn. They have been named
Matthew John and Joy Elizabeth.

****

After the birth of the twins, Leah gave up her position at
the Interfaith Mission Agency and became a full-time mother,
and at Alan's encouragement, began working as a part-time
legal assistant for him. She still managed to use her skills as a
social worker when some of Alan's clients were in need of more
than just legal aid.

Printed in the United States
By Bookmasters